Health Czar

Health Czar

Glenn Haas

authorHOUSE®

AuthorHouse™ LLC
1663 Liberty Drive
Bloomington, IN 47403
www.authorhouse.com
Phone: 1-800-839-8640

This is a work of fiction. All of the characters, names, incidents,
organizations, and dialogue in this novel are either the products
of the author's imagination or are used fictitiously.

Published by AuthorHouse   12/12/2013

ISBN: 978-1-4918-4136-5 (sc)
ISBN: 978-1-4918-4135-8 (e)

Library of Congress Control Number: 2013922280

DEDICATION

This book is dedicated to my children, the
greatest gifts one could ever hope for:

Caroline, Kristina, Karl and Glenn, Jr.

AUTHOR'S NOTE

Although *Health Czar* is a work of fiction, I have used The Great War and several presidents' terms of office as firm timelines. I have conveniently ignored the 18th amendment to the U.S. Constitution (prohibition of alcohol) as a bad idea that never should have been. The Department of Health, Education and Welfare did not exist until created by President Eisenhower in 1953.

Mention is made of various government sponsored project. Several transpired after the time period of this novel but I took the liberty to reposition them into the 1920's in the hope that such action would benefit the manuscript. Likewise mention is made of medical therapy with specific activity against infectious diseases. Antibiotics as a class of drugs (e.g., sulfa drugs and penicillin) became commonplace several years after the timeline of *Health Czar*.

PROLOGUE

Simon Kraft sat in the backseat of the limousine with his wife Dorothy at his side. He stared out the window and studied the trees that lined the streets and dominated the walkways. It was early spring and one needed a keen eye to see the buds and young leaves on the trees as the limousine sped swiftly down the boulevard. The Capital of course was famous for the trees. The sky today was bright and the air was warm. He took Dorothy's hand in his and gently squeezed. "Nervous?" She smiled and looked down to where their hands were clasped together. She shifted her gaze up into his eyes and shook her head 'No.'

With his free hand he smoothed the front of his suit and tugged at his neck tie. He had given thought to wearing a tuxedo, possibly a morning suit of the kind a king might wear for his coronation, but thought better of it. He knew the good people in the audience today would enjoy their pomp and ceremony, but they would never relish or condone the ostentatious and the gaudy. The Good Lord could only guess how many might be in attendance. He envisioned the gathered throng staring up onto the platforms and the stages, craning their necks to catch a glimpse of history as it was being made. In his mind he repeated the words to his oath of office. It wasn't a long passage, only a few sentences really. Why shouldn't he know it by heart? He had stood in front of a mirror and repeated the oath almost daily for the past two months; pantomiming every so often when he would nod his head for emphasis, jutting out a firm jaw as a show of sincerity. Such gestures would play well before the huge crowds.

He was suddenly conscious that his mouth was dry. Not surprising. His mouth always became dry just before he had to speak in front of large crowds. Funny it should be that way, for when he did start to speak he was as glib and smooth as a snake oil salesman at a county fair. He had faced far more dangerous and difficult tasks than speaking in front of large crowds of people. With all the bullets and bombs that flew past him in the Great War, he never had a dry mouth. During the many hours and days spent in the operating rooms, he never had a dry mouth. Only now, while on the way to take his oath of office for the highest position he could ever imagine achieving in this nation, did he have a dry mouth.

He squeezed Dorothy's hand once again, looked to her and saw the face of the nineteen year old debutante whom he had courted so many years ago. "It's a long way from a share-cropper's shack in the back country."

Dorothy looked at him in poorly controlled amazement. She raised her free hand to her mouth to stifle a grin. In a soft, southern drawl she said, "Dr. Simon Kraft, you are indeed a scamp and a scallywag. You no more ever stepped foot inside a share-cropper's shack than did you ever walk on the moon. Your daddy was a rich banker and you went to college up north with the rest of those rich boys. After which you trotted back to the Commonwealth and stole my heart so that I might become a physician's wife." She moved her hand from her face and touched Simon on the nose. "But you did good for yourself, and for me, and I do love you for it."

Simon smiled back at her. Yes, he had accomplished a great deal, and this great position he would assume within the hour was a just reward for all the years and all the struggles. It was a new dawn for a new day in this country of his. At last, he would have the opportunity to implement and execute all the plans that had been so many years in the making. The nation was destined for greatness and it was meet and right that Simon Kraft should take command of the helm and help direct its course. He smiled and thought back to all he had done and all that had occurred. Today was a new day and it was a new beginning, and within the hour he would take the oath of office for the . . .

ONE

The sun shone through the expansive windows on the east wall of the operating room and provided most of the light that would be needed to perform the surgery, but the newly purchased floor lamps were a treasure. Rising eight feet off the floor, the yellow light from the electric lamps was glaring and hot but eliminated many of the shadows cast by the sunlight and made visible the organs that resided in the deepest corners of the patients' bodies. Simon Kraft, M.D., ignored the hissing sound that emanated from the lamps. Both of the operating rooms of Norwood General Hospital were now upgraded with heavy gauge electrical wiring necessary to power the floor lamps and Kraft took pleasure and pride, knowing he was the driving force that bullied the hospital administrators into making the changes that were necessary to modernize the county hospital.

The unmistakable aroma of ether fumes permeated the room and would become enmeshed in the fabric of the white surgical uniforms worn by the nurses and physicians. They wore caps, masks and gowns from head to toe and only their eyes remained unshielded. As Simon inserted his hands into the rubberized gloves the nurse held wide open for him, he stared at the mound that rested beneath piles of towels and drapes that balanced neatly on the operating table. He glanced overtop the mound to ensure the patient was lying face up, unconscious and on her back. He repositioned the beams cast by the lamps and focused the light on the one square foot patch of skin that wasn't covered by drapes and towels. The patient's navel rested in the top-center of the square.

He made a small skin incision beneath the navel, separated the flesh and muscle and picked at the tissue that lined the abdominal cavity. He nicked the peritoneum, opened the cavity and inserted the retracting instrument that would allow the cavity to remain open during the course of the procedure. Quickly he scanned and identified the organs. He used a large sponge to safely isolate and pack away the vital structures that would not be involved with the procedure. Effortlessly he grasped the fallopian tube from the right side with a clamp, lifted and suspended the tissue from deep in the pelvis. He transferred the clamp to his left hand. Without diverting his gaze he opened his right hand and the nurse assistant firmly laid the needle-driver clamp into his hand. At its tip the needle-driver held a curved needle threaded with silk suture. He lowered the tip of the needle driver into the pelvis and guided the needle through and around the tissue beneath the fallopian tube. With her free hand the nurse took hold of the clamp that held the fallopian tube. Kraft flicked the tip of the needle-driver clamp and the needle separated from the black silk thread. He laid aside the clamp and his fingers blurred as they tied and tightened down on the knot. The nurse took the long ends of the silk and incorporated them into her hand that now held the fallopian tube by both the clamp and the silk ligatures. Kraft took another needle driver-clamp from the nurse that held a second curved needle threaded with silk suture. He repeated placing and tying the ligature around the tube, one inch from where he placed the first ligature. He handed the long ends of the second silk suture to the nurse in exchange for scissors. Kraft cut through the tissue that was isolated by the two black silk sutures. Kraft curled the scissors into the palm of his hand and reached for a swab that had been soaked in carbolic acid. He dabbed at either cut end of the fallopian tube with the carbolic acid. He handed off the swab, uncurled the scissors from the palm of his hand and quickly cut the strands of the silk sutures one inch above the knots. He released the clamp that held the fallopian tube and the tissues dropped back into the depths of the pelvis. In a similar fashion he repeated the procedure on the left side.

For the first time Simon Kraft looked up from the open wound, toward the drapes that separated the patient's head and face from the operating field. He addressed the man at the head of the operating table behind the tented drapes, indifferent to who it was. "I'll be closing. Is everything fine?"

Hidden behind a mask and a cap was the anesthesiologist. For the past twenty minutes he had been dripping either onto a mesh mask that covered the woman's face. Relieved to know the case would soon be ending, he said in his soft down home accent, "Evra-thing's fine Doctah. Bring her home."

Nonchalantly Kraft removed the large sponge from the pelvic cavity and repaired the wound, running sutures through tissues that only a short time earlier he had opened and separated. "Is the next room ready?" he asked of no one in particular.

"Yes Doctor. They will be ready for you when you finish here."

Kraft tied the last stitch and said to the nurse, "Thank you very much. Apply the dressings and finish the chart." He removed his gloves and gown and allowed them to drop to the floor. He turned from the patient lying on the operating table and said to no one in particular, "Thank you all very much," as he exited the room

Once outside the room he asked, "Which way?"

A nurse directed him to his left. "Room Two."

At a sink outside the surgery room he scrubbed his hands with a foamy soap and a stiff brush for five minutes. As he entered the operating room a nurse handed him a towel which he used to dry his hands. He dropped the used towel onto the floor and kicked it to the far corner. Operating Room Two was similar in all respects to the previous room, with the bank of windows high up on the east wall and two eight foot floor lamps positioned at the far end of the operating table. The one stark difference in this room was the exposed genitals of the patient, isolated amongst the pile of drapes and towels. The patient's penis and scrotum appeared to sprout from the white mound like root vegetables from a garden floor. The anesthesiologist hovered over the face of the patient. The odor of ether was strong and penetrating.

"Are we ready?" Kraft asked as the nurse spread wide the gown and allowed Kraft to step into it. She helped him with his gloves as the anesthesiologist answered, "Ready when you are."

Kraft ran the scalpel blade across the top of the right side of the scrotal sac, separated the thin skin tissues and identified the spermatic chord that connected the testicle with the man's body. With a curved clamp he dug into the mass, teased away the extraneous tissues and isolated the chord and vessels within the sac. He closed the clamp onto the chord structure. As the clamp closed, it was firmly held in place by the interlocking ratchets. The closing action created a clicking sound that echoed off the walls and caused the anesthesiologist to wince involuntarily.

Kraft opened his right hand and the nurse placed a straight clamp into it. Kraft applied the clamp to the chord structures one inch below the first clamp, incorporating once again vessels, tubes, ducts and nerves. Again the reverberating clicks.

He opened his right hand and the nurse gave him scissors which he used to cut the tissues between the two clamps. He freed the testicle from the scrotal sac and the patient. Kraft handed off the specimen, still held in the straight clamp, in exchange for a needle-driver that held a curved needle threaded with black silk. He passed the ligature through and twice around the stump of tissue still held in the curved clamp, tying off and knotting the silk thread effortlessly. As he released the clamp he stared intently at the tissue and searched for the slightest hint of leakage or seeping blood. Seeing none, he stitched together the skin of the scrotum and repeated the procedure on the opposite side.

Once again he looked to the head of the table, stared at the drapes that separated him from the anesthesiologist and announced, "I'm closing. Is everything fine?"

A faceless voice answered from beneath a mask and cap, "Everything is fine, Doctor."

"Is the next room ready?" he asked of no one in particular.

"Yes Doctor. They will be ready for you in Room One when you finish here."

Kraft finished cutting the strands of the last stitch and said to the nurse, "Thank you very much. Apply the dressings and finish the chart." He removed his gloves and gown and allowed them to drop to the floor. He turned from the patient lying on the operating table and said to no one in particular, "Thank you all very much," as he exited the room

Once outside the room he asked, "Which way?" A nurse directed him to his right.

* * *

The day had been a long one and Simon looked forward to going home. He had performed seven surgeries and the fatigue he experienced was both pleasurable and exhilarating. Spending time in the operating room was one of the perquisites of his job that he was loath to relinquish. It was time spent away from the office: away from the meetings, away from the mountainous stacks of health reports and away from the endless blabber of bureaucratic sycophants. The position and title of Director of Public Health for the Commonwealth was just as important as it sounded. He was one year shy of forty and some thought him a bit young to hold the position, but not 'Uncle Billy.' William H. Cheltenham was governor of the Commonwealth and the man who appointed Simon to the office. Cries of 'nepotism' and 'cronyism' echoed throughout the capital. True, Dr. Kraft was the husband of the Governor's niece, but Uncle Billy saw something in Simon that he knew the Commonwealth needed. Simon Kraft was fresh blood, a fresh mind and a man trained and grounded in the sciences. He was a man who knew what needed to be done and would not hesitate to do it. Of course he was a political neophyte, but that deficiency had its benefits and any shortfalls that might exist would easily be ameliorated and smoothed over by Uncle Billy.

The synergy of their professional relationship was exhibited when they proposed draining the swampy regions inland from the tidewater and the estuaries. Simon Kraft argued with the state's legislature that, "The elimination of the miasmal swamps of the low country will result in the eradication of the breeding grounds for mosquitoes. Eliminate the mosquitoes and you will eliminate malaria and yellow fever. Eliminate malaria and yellow fever and you will save thousands of lives every year. Eliminate the misery and suffering caused by the disease carrying insects and the Commonwealth will save millions of dollars." Governor Cheltenham championed the argument, greased the political wheels and the swamps were drained. Reported cases of malaria and yellow fever dropped precipitously. As the New Year bells tolled and welcomed 1914, Dr. Simon Kraft was hailed as "The Man Who Conquered Malaria."

Simon opened the front door of his home and he thought he might have walked into the main tent of the Barnum and Bailey

Circus. Two little dogs raced around the room, zooming under the chairs in the parlor and over pillows that served as hurdles. The black Scotty followed the white Scotty under and over and around and around as they scurried throughout the room, all to the delight of Dorothy Kraft who sat on the floor and peeled with laughter. She whirled her arms in the air and the dogs responded by running ever faster.

"Watch darling, watch!" she shouted as she brought her hands together to form a circle with her arms. "Through the hoop!" she commanded. Up jumped the white dog and the black one followed through her arms once and then twice.

Dorothy clapped her hands and the dogs veered sharply and ran to her. She embraced them and scratched their ears and rubbed their bellies. "My children, my children, you are an act fit for the crowned heads of Europe," she said in a voice that dripped of southern gentility.

Simon smiled, for it was a funny scene and his wife was enjoying herself. "So when do you take Romeo and Juliet on tour?"

"We shall first make private appearances by special arrangements," she announced as she sipped from the high ball glass that rested on the table, "and then move on to the general public."

Simon took the glass from her hand and took a deep swallow. "Dorothy Kraft and the daredevil duo of drag-racing dogs and death defying dangers! You shall be a smashing hit, entertaining dog lovers the world over, and I shall follow at your heels like the faithful puppy that I am." He took both her hands and helped to lift her off the floor. He kissed her lightly and said, "Do you spend all your day training your troupe?"

"Hahrd-ly," she drawled theatrically. "The elephants in the back yard require much more of my time."

"Just shoveling after them should keep you very busy."

Dorothy tapped him on the tip of his nose for the barb, took the high ball glass from him and drained it. "Romeo and Juliet are our children and we must make the best for them and for our future 'grand-dogs.' They deserve the very finest that we can provide for them."

Simon nodded, acknowledging the Kraft's commitment to their legacy. "Are we still on for the theater this evening?"

"Yes we are. The Collingsworth's and the Bronson's and a few others will be there. We'll gather for drinks after the show and it will give me the opportunity to chat them up about the Christmas bazaar for the hospital. We need a few more *new* ideas and Samantha Bronson is always chock full of new ideas."

"Samantha Bronson's concept of a *new idea* invariably has the sobriquet 'Mister' for a title."

"Simon dahr-ling," Dorothy drawled, "a man in your position should not talk of such indiscretions in public company. Walter Bronson spoke with you confidentially and it would be bad manners to break such a confidence."

"It wasn't from Walter that I became aware of Samantha's dalliances."

"Shame on you Dr. Kraft. I trust it is not from firsthand knowledge that you speak," Dorothy challenged.

"As you said, I am at my honor to maintain my informant's confidentiality."

"Go, shower and make yourself presentable for the evening crowd. Althea left a plate of food for you in the kitchen. I gave her the night off. Perhaps later, after the show, we may have our own dalliance."

"Why wait until later?" Simon piped in.

"Be gone, knight errant, I am saving myself for my prince."

Simon stood sideways to the mirror. He examined the image he saw as he toweled himself dry. His steel gray eyes were round and full and helped to accent his square jaw and handsome face. Each day he thought he saw another gray fleck emerge in his thick shock of dusty brown hair. Playfully he pounded his stomach and was proud that it was still flat. He still retained much of the strength and tone in the heavy muscles of his shoulders that had made him such a strong swimmer. He continued to swim for exercise even though he was no longer as swift as when he swam in the Athens Olympics in 1896. The peace and the quiet and the steady repetition of stroke after stroke was a pleasant escape, while at the same time the activity melted away the aftereffects of heavy dinners and the wine and drink of political banquets.

During his college years he swam competitively, was very successful and the Athens' games were such a challenging novelty. His classmates urged him on, until finally he decided to test his talents against the world's best. Part way through his first year of medical school he took leave and sailed across the ocean to Athens. On board the ocean liner one late night party followed another, and whatever training routine he established evaporated before he passed the Straits of Gibraltar. Making matters worse, the races were not swum in swimming pools or on guarded lakes, but were contested in the Bay of Zea off the coast of Piraeus. The temperature of the water in the early spring was bone chilling. He finished the race well behind the leaders and was glad he didn't freeze to death. He was certain the winner of the event was either an Eskimo or a penguin.

Tonight's event was a mid-week affair and formal attire was not necessary, so a woolen suit would suffice. As he finished knotting his tie he cast a glance at his wife. She was still as gorgeous as when she was the season's top debutante fourteen years ago. He remembered attending her coming out ball as if it were yesterday. At the time he was merely a friend of the family and not involved with Miss Dorothy Lucille Cheltenham. Even then she was stunning and beguiling and had the other young men bewitched as only a Southern Belle could do so. Years later, when she asked why he was not one of her early suitors, he chided her. He explained, "I was allowing you time to season, like a rare and vintage wine. You forget, I was six years your senior and the risk of wagging tongues was not worth the effort." During the year of his internship at Norwood County Hospital he made his intentions known and Miss Dorothy became his bride.

She took a sip from the high ball glass that had been refreshed. Her evening dress was dark green in color and contrasted nicely with her light blond hair and the necklace that sparkled and lay across her chest just north of her modest cleavage. She sipped again and stared at her drink.

"Penny for your thoughts," Simon offered.

"Do you miss not having children?"

Simon heard the question, one that he had heard before, but as usual he did not respond. It was a question usually prompted by a modicum of alcohol or an unusually difficult day spent doing good deeds for the city's unfortunates.

"Really Simon. Children might have been such a gift and I find it hard not to think how different matters might have been."

Simon knew that continued silence would not suffice and a response was mandatory. "We can't miss what we never had."

"If we had been able to have children instead of Scottish terriers, how much better would that have been for us?"

The question was not so much a riddle as it was a portal to a cavern of dark memories from seven years ago. It was Simon's belief that the pain and agony of the memories were best left unresurrected, remaining buried deep beneath the surface of their everyday thoughts and musing. At that time Dorothy had been pregnant but complications developed. She started passing blood clots and within a few hours the hemorrhaging was torrential. It was lethal for the infant and life threatening to her. Only an emergency hysterectomy and three weeks of intensive medical treatment in the hospital saved her.

"Our life is fine now, Dorothy," Simon parried. "Some things are meant to be and others shall never come to pass. Is that not the preaching that I hear from the good Reverend Brewster?"

"If only we had been able . . ." She turned away from him, walked to the bedroom window and stared out at the setting sun.

Adoption during the intervening years would not be an option. It was a topic that Dorothy was unable to embrace without equivocation and second guessing. "People like us simply do not adopt," was her standard mantra. "We do not, as a rule, take on someone else's problems or castoffs." Simon usually chose not to offer argument and veered off the subject of children, adopted or otherwise, because no solution to their situation appeared likely to materialize.

"My dearest Mrs. Kraft, we have a pleasant evening on tap and a dalliance scheduled for later this evening. You shall remain a sparkle on my arm and I want nothing to cloud your thoughts or demeanor. If you wish, we may return to the subject at a different time." *But not ten minutes before we are to meet with a gaggle of friends and acquaintances and not after one too many high balls.*

Dorothy lifted her head, smiled and saw the wisdom of his suggestion. "Another time, yes. Now take me out to meet the finest of Norwood County."

TWO

Simon Kraft sat behind a large desk reading medical records. He sipped at a cup of very hot tea as he read. Although the desk was large, very little was on the desk: an inkwell, ink blotter and pen set, one folder with several typed pages and handwritten notes within, and the saucer for the teacup. A side table against the wall opposite to a large bookcase held stacks and piles of papers, documents and folders that were interspersed with medical texts and reviews of legal proceedings. The busy nature of the side table was justifiable, all but laudable in the mind of Dr. Kraft. He was a busy man and he wanted all who entered his office to have no doubt the Director of Public Health for the Commonwealth was a busy man.

The largest stack of papers on the side table referred to the bill that would be presented to the Commonwealth's legislators to facilitate the passage of a new law. Kraft was a familiar character in the Capital Building. Since he had taken office he introduced and facilitated passage of five new laws. Simon referred to them as 'Health Laws.' The five new health laws were enacted to improve the health of the general public and make the Commonwealth a safer place to live. Slowly and steadily other states in the union were adopting similar health laws in piecemeal fashion, but none so rapidly and thoroughly as Simon Kraft's Commonwealth.

Simon's secretary opened the door to the office and announced, "Mr. Preller to see you Doctor."

"Thank you Mrs. Magee. Show him in."

Edward Preller, as Assistant Director of Public Health for the Commonwealth, was perfectly suited for his position. He was a childhood friend of Simon's and tireless in his commitment to the job. His memory was extraordinary and his attention to detail was relentless. While in college he earned a business degree and a law degree from the Commonwealth's university and had done well in positions he held prior to the start of his work with Kraft. Essentially a droll and humorless man, Ed was a perfectionist. He did not tolerate fools very well and would not accept excuses for slipshod performance. The one chink in his otherwise shining armor was his phobic hatred for appearing in front of crowds and audiences. He was painfully aware he was not a handsome man. In contrast to Kraft's broad-shouldered athletic frame, Ed was thin and lean and there wasn't a suit made that seemed to fit him well. He wore half glasses that rested on the bridge of a boney nose and his thinning gray hair with a balding pate made him look closer to fifty years old than forty. His hands were thin, with long boney fingers and large knobby knuckles which could easily be confused for walnuts. Narrow slits that were his eyes were set deep in his thin face and during their teen years Simon often teased him that his cadaveric features were best suited to a career as a mortician or a gravedigger.

Consequently Ed Preller was most content to shun the limelight. He gravitated to positions where he could work behind the scenes and readily allowed others to accept the glory and bask in the acclaim for a job well done. He was the perfect assistant for someone in the political arena. Simon accepted all that Ed had to offer—lock, stock and barrel—and was rewarded with a fiercely loyal lieutenant.

"Good morning Ted my boy, how goes the crusade?" Kraft said as Preller entered the room carrying a briefcase in his left hand, typical of the variety carried by lawyers: fine leather with a thick strap that closed and locked with a key. Simon enjoyed taking a good natured jab at Ed by calling him 'Ted my boy.' It was a vestigial nickname from a time when they both wore short pants, and sailed into the face of the fact that Ed was three months older than Simon.

Ed nodded and took the seat opposite him across his desk. One of Ed's duties was to oversee the Division of Communicable Diseases. The titular director of the division, Dr. Matthew Rassmussen, was a physician but he rarely left his laboratory. When Dr. Rassmussen did emerge, he restricted his interests to the review of statistics and reports from the county health departments: grids and tables, charts and diagrams. It was Ed Preller who developed and monitored the budget, coordinated the hiring and firing of personnel and interacted with the other departmental divisions. The list of disease entities under surveillance by the Department was growing rapidly and ranged from typhus, malaria and yellow fever to tuberculosis, tetanus and strange tropical fevers. Venereal disease, the social disease, was now a hot topic and the subject of their meeting this morning.

"From the reports that I reviewed from last month," Kraft said as Mrs. Magee, in her grandmotherly way, set a saucer and cup filled with tea on a table next to Ed's chair, "there is an upward trending for reportable incidences of venereal disease in the past six months."

Ed smiled his thanks to Mrs. Magee who was unfazed by the topic of conversation. "Yes and no, Simon," Ed replied in his slow, melodic manner that still retained its soft drawl. "The trend is up in our big cities, up in the mining counties and down in the farm country. The numbers are increased in the mining towns because the unmarried young men spend their weekends in brothels and share their female partners with each other. The numbers are increased in the large cities because rubbish gravitates to the large cities. Among other issues, immigrants from abroad continue to funnel through the big cities and bring with them, besides their tired and their poor, their gonococcus and syphilis bacteria."

"What does Matt Rassmussen say about these numbers?" Kraft asked.

"Rassmussen hasn't had a novel thought in years. 'Some people who are naughty share their naughtiness. Men who are indiscreet develop the gleet,'" Ed mimicked, poorly suppressing a smile.

"Will that be the slogan for the Department to adopt?" Kraft asked with a wry smile. He pushed on and asked, "The case investigators, how successful are they with contact interviews?"

"As much as a Paddy or a Stanley would gladly boast with the boys of his Saturday night conquest, as they sit eating out of their lunch pails," Ed replied, "they clam up like a stone when the case agents visit with them to identify all their partners, both before and after the time of contact when they most likely contracted and/or spread their disease."

"Case agent investigations and interviews continue slowly?"

"Who wants to rat out their date from last week," Ed opined in a supplicating fashion, "despite the fact she most recently gave him a dose of the clap?"

"Is our Commonwealth so overrun with desperate individuals who are blindly in love?"

"Our Commonwealth is no different from any other state. Many of our people desperately seek sex, which occasionally impersonates as love, and are willing to expose themselves to the complications of sexual misadventures."

Kraft pressed on. "What is the opinion of Dr. Rassmussen?"

In a pedantic tone Ed replied, "He thinks VD is contagious and should be reported early and treated aggressively." Kraft's stare bore a hole into Ed. "Hey, don't blame me. Rassmussen's appointment was not made on my watch."

"Nor on mine." Kraft rose from his desk and walked to the window that overlooked Main Street. "He's a leftover from the previous administration and now he is a burr beneath my saddle. He's fine with a microscope and reading an X-ray but lacks passion and zeal. We now have the means to treat the disease. The antibiotics now available to us are wonder drugs and will successfully eradicate the disease once treatment is begun. We have to move quickly and steadily to get ahead of this curse. Citizens are becoming infected at epidemic proportions. The reporting of contacts and the treatment of all contacts is the only means we have to eliminate the disease. Men are loathe to use protection and women are too naïve to demand protection."

"I know, you've been saying it for years," Ed added. "'Venereal disease is like any disease; Prevention is cheaper than treatment.' That idea gets thrown out the window as soon as the people drop their pants. The blood drains out of their brains into selected organs."

Kraft said nothing, for he had another ace up his sleeve. Ed sipped at his tea, remained silent and listened as Kraft said, "What we've been doing is not working. How we've been doing it is not working. We have to become more aggressive. I've come up with a two-fisted approach that I plan to implement within the month."

"Pray tell, Doctor, what have you been cooking up in your laboratory?" Ed queried.

Kraft's eyes lit up as he spoke. "We are going public with venereal disease. We are going to bring VD out of the closet. I'm going to hire a public relations company and mount a campaign that will help us."

"Great! You'll get more hollering and screaming from the church groups than you will be able to handle."

"But people who go to church still contract VD. To compound matters, they are too shamed and embarrassed to seek treatment because they fear they'll be damned. You're correct. It's a touchy area but I can stand the heat. We'll get a top notch public relations firm from New York who can make Eskimo's want to buy ice boxes and pay double the asking price."

Ed added, "And for your follow up punch?"

"Exactly, more punch for your case investigators."

"Go on," Ed said patiently.

"When your case investigators meet with the patients who contract the disease, they have to be more thorough with follow up of all sexual contacts. Their interviews have to be more extensive and in greater depth."

"My agents can only get the information that the patients are willing to offer," Ed replied.

"That, Ted my boy, is no longer good enough. All involved are going to cooperate with our department and give us the names of their contacts, or else."

"Or else what, Simon?" Ed replied. "Our agents can't hold a gun to the head of every guy who has the drip. Our agents have no power."

"No longer. I will be meeting with Uncle Billy today and we'll discuss new legislation." Kraft pointed to the table against the wall that held various stacks of papers. "We have the statistics and we have more than enough reports. I want to introduce legislation that will empower the case workers. Within the month it will be as if they were carrying Colt .45 revolvers on their hips. The new law will make it a crime for infected patients to refuse to cooperate with the agents. If they refuse to give us names, if they refuse to cooperate, off to jail they will go. Believe me; no one wants to sit in a jail cell because he has VD. Venereal disease is a rotting, festering plague that rips at the underbelly of our nation. It strikes when least suspected with devastating sequelae. Insidious, morally debasing, relentless. One of our tasks in this department is to protect the general population from itself. Nowhere is this quest more pertinent than in the fight to eradicate this plague we know as venereal disease. No one person in this department, perhaps in this state, has a more important task than you, Edward Leroy Preller. But I know you are capable and I know you are up to it, or else I would not have assigned you to this, this . . . crusade."

Ed's lips thinned as he suppressed a smile. As his cold, hard eyes met those of Kraft, he said. "There is no Holy Grail out there Simon, but we'll keep plugging away anyhow."

Mrs. Magee poked her head through the door into the office. "You haven't forgotten lunch with the Governor today?" she asked.

"No, Mrs. Magee. We're finished here. I shall look forward to breaking bread with Hizonor."

* * *

The portrait in the lobby of the State House was large and very flattering to the governor. Some jokingly said it was like the governor himself, 'larger than life.' There was no mistaking that the State House was his building, and the legislature was his legislature and the Commonwealth was his Commonwealth. Such was the breadth and the depth and legacy of William H. Cheltenham, now serving in his third consecutive term as governor of the Commonwealth.

Simon Kraft was ushered directly into the private dining room of the Governor. Often he had been a guest in the governor's office and marveled at the fine woodwork, sculpted European marble and the plush carpeting. The office paled in regard to the grandeur of the dining room. The room was of modest size and eight chairs surrounded the table, which was dark in color and adorn with light colored fruitwood inlays of various geometric shapes and patterns. The upholstery on the chairs cast a sheen and Kraft was certain the fabric was silk. Sculpted wooden reliefs covered the walls and depicted woodland scenes of the orient and other far off lands. Two place settings were arranged on the table, complete with an abundant supply of side plates, bowls and no less than twelve knives, forks and spoons. The china was so delicately painted and designed that Kraft feared to touch it. The silver cutlery and covers for the serving plates sparkled and were near blinding in their radiance. Kraft sensed the room had a power of its own. He remained standing, unsure of the protocol involved while waiting for royalty to appear.

A door opened and the governor entered the room. He was of indeterminate age with silver hair combed straight back on his head and a pencil thin mustache that ran across his upper lip. He was of average size and build but when they shook hands, Simon was consumed as the Governor's gaze melted him into submission. "My God, Simon, it is good to see you again," Cheltenham gushed. "How is Dorothy, that lovely wife of yours? I guess I haven't been with her since Aunt Marion's birthday party last month. And you, you're looking fine as always."

"Dorothy is doing fine, Governor, and I feel great," was Kraft's reply.

Waving a deflective hand Cheltenham said, "No one is within listening range. Please, make it Uncle Billy and I shall be a happier man for it." Kraft smiled as he nodded acquiescence. "Please, have a seat."

Cheltenham sat at the head of the table and Kraft took the seat to his right. "Most days I munch a sandwich in the office when I am not among our citizens being courted and cajoled. This dining room offers a pleasant change and allows me to meet with people whom I truly like; plus, I may be able to conduct some business at the same time."

A man in a business suit entered the dining room from a door on the far side. He carried a tray with several bowls and a pitcher of a light colored liquid. "As I recall, Simon, turtle soup is among your favorites." Steam wafted from the bowls that the server placed in front of Cheltenham and Kraft. "A nice French white burgundy would be nice but since the taxpayers of the Commonwealth are paying for our lunch, lemonade is more defensible." The server dropped two ice cubes into their drinking glasses and poured from the pitcher.

"Propriety, appearances and be cautious of the paper trail that you leave behind, three credos by which politicians need to live," Cheltenham said with a smile. "As you continue in the public spotlight, amid their gaze and scrutiny, remember the three credos."

"Yes sir; thoughts worth remembering." Kraft sipped at the soup and thought it presumptuous to ask for sherry.

They exchanged small talk and as Cheltenham finished with the last of his soup he said, "Now, share with me this bill you think needs to be presented to the legislature."

"It is a public health bill off course, but it relates to a testy issue," Kraft replied.

"Go on."

"The bill will relate to venereal disease," Kraft said.

"Is the legislature to vote for venereal disease or against venereal disease?" Cheltenham asked with a straight face. "Until now I thought the more prudent stance would be to oppose venereal disease for the sake of the general public."

Kraft smiled and said, "From a public health standpoint we are losing the battle against VD. The good news is that medical treatment currently exists. The treatment is so effective that not only will it combat the disease, it will eliminate the disease. The problem is that not enough people are being treated. We must get the treatment out to the people who need it; into the streets and into the factories."

Cheltenham nodded approvingly as the server exchanged their empty soup bowls for a platter filled with food. "I recall you to be an avid quail hunter and I assume you, on occasion, sample your quarry." Simon saw a well-proportioned roasted quail on his platter. It was surrounded by roasted carrots, potatoes and a medley of green beans, corn and snap peas. "Everything before you was either grown or raised in our Commonwealth." The server lifted a silver cover to display a loaf of cut bread on a plate, adjacent to several pads of butter.

Between bites Kraft said, "The state employs case agents who interview patients who have contracted venereal disease. It is imperative that all personal contacts with the infected individuals be identified, interviewed and then treated."

"By contacts you mean sexual partners?" Cheltenham inferred and Kraft nodded. "And with people being polite and well meaning, they are hesitant to name too many names."

"Correct," Kraft answered. "They clam up when interviewed by our case agents and our agents have little recourse."

"This new bill of yours, I assume, will help your agents and force the interviewees to cooperate with the agents and answer their questions," Cheltenham surmised correctly.

"We need to empower the case agents to the extent that failure of the interviewees to cooperate is sufficient grounds for incarceration," Simon continued, explaining the essence of his new bill.

As they finished their meals the server removed the plates and served coffee. "This is your sixth bill since you have been Director, am I correct?" Cheltenham said as he added cream and sugar to his coffee and stirred.

"The five public health bills passed in the last few years have done wonders," Kraft replied. "Not only is our Commonwealth better for the laws, but we have become the model by which many of the other states are patterning and changing their own public health laws."

"What's your goal, Simon? What will be the objective to this exercise?

"There are several pieces to the puzzle," Kraft explained, "but a few remain blatantly clear. Prevention and treatment are two. To prevent a disease, any disease, from occurring not only save lives, but saves the money that would have been necessary to treat the disease. You saw that with the draining of the low country and our successes with malaria and yellow fever. The positive impact on the economy is significant; men do not lose time from work. Factories and shops do not need to shut down. The world does not have to come to a screeching halt.

"Treatment. We must aggressively treat as many people as possible who contract chronic and recurring type illnesses. Tuberculosis, for example, is a major killer; we must address head-on those with the disease and treat them very aggressively. Unfortunately the cure for TB is not within our grasp. On the contrary we are able to treat VD successfully."

"And in your opinion," Uncle Billy interjected, "venereal disease is another example of an illness that requires aggressive treatment." Simon nodded with a faint smile. Cheltenham reached into the inside pocket of his suit and removed a pack of cigarettes. He shook out a few and offered one to Simon. Simon shook his head 'no.' "Still swimming?" Cheltenham asked as he struck a match and lit his cigarette.

"Every few weekends we get out to father's house in the country. It has good size lake and stays warm from May through the early autumn. Swimming helps me burn off a few of the potato and dumpling dinners, but it also gives me some time to myself, when I can focus and plan and think about the future."

Cheltenham inhaled deeply and slowly blew out the cigarette smoke. "Whose future? Your future? Yours and Dorothy's future? Yours and the Commonwealth's future?" He took another draw on the cigarette and said as he exhaled the smoke, "Yours and America's future?"

"The state of the world is primed for America to emerge with its unbridled potential," Simon replied. "It is very important that we make the American people stronger and healthier. It will not be easy. America as a race, as a nation, must remain pure. Currently American bloodlines are being polluted."

Simon paused as he gathered his thoughts. "For one, marriage between the races weakens our stock, poisons our society and must continue to be forbidden."

"I agree," Uncle Billy said as he knocked the ash off the tip of his cigarette, "as do most of the states in the Union."

"We are being polluted by the continued influx of immigrants from middle Europe and the far off orient," Simon offered.

"Our immigration laws are some of the most strict laws in the world," Cheltenham replied. "I agree. Quotas need to remain low."

"We are being polluted by the weak, by degenerates, by the unfit," Simon said as he sat forward ever so slightly in his chair. "A vast number of individuals carry bad seeds for bad traits and these seeds need to be eliminated from society. These bad traits must be eliminated from the biological pool so to speak. It's the Darwin thing, Uncle Billy. It has to do with heredity and evolution and science. By surgically sterilizing the undesirables, we continue to remove the defective and unwanted characteristics from our general population. We have addressed these issues in the Commonwealth and have become the nation's standard bearer. America has taken notice of what we have been doing and what we have accomplished."

"Not so much we, but you," Cheltenham corrected him. "*You've* addressed these issues Simon, and the Commonwealth has followed your lead. You've become the standard bearer for our state and you have dragged us along with you. At your insistence we have passed the necessary laws that allow for the sterilization of the individuals with these bad traits that you describe. You operate several times each month to eliminate these problems and surgeons in eight of our Commonwealth's hospitals do likewise. Similar surgeries are being performed in several other states. They have listened to what you have said and done and like-minded men in those other states are following your lead."

Cheltenham drew from his cigarette and then crushed it in the ashtray. "You are different from most men, Simon. You're wired together differently. You are driven like no man I know. Okay. So you think America has a pollution problem and you now want to clean it up. How?"

"As Americans we must do on a national scale what we have been doing here in the Commonwealth," Simon explained. "We must continue to weed out the undesirables. We must do what is necessary to preserve and protect our American race. We have to stop these undesirables from poisoning, from tainting our American race."

"As you would call it, *prevention,*" Uncle Billy interjected.

"In a way, yes," Simon replied. "On a grander scale, only by excluding and eliminating the weak and the unfit can America grow stronger and more powerful."

"You truly believe you can reproduce nationally what you've implemented here in the Commonwealth," Cheltenham asked.

"With all my heart," Simon replied. "My goal is to allow for a better breed of Americans to emerge and to develop."

"And you suggest that modern science will allow us to make these improvements to our society," Cheltenham offered.

"Like no other time before us in the history of mankind," Simon replied.

"How far are you willing to pursue this crusade? How much are you willing to invest of yourself in this quest?" Cheltenham asked.

"I'm willing to do whatever is necessary and follow this all the way to the top, Uncle Billy," Simon replied in a manner that left little room for doubt.

"The top being the presidency of the United States?" Uncle Billy queried.

"If need be," Simon replied.

"The Commonwealth has sent more men to the Oval Office on 1600 Pennsylvania Avenue than any other state in the union. Our nation could do worse than to have you lead us on." The server laid before each man a slice of apple pie as Cheltenham said, "You are growing, Simon, and it has been my pleasure to watch and observe the process. You are growing in prominence and experience and in other ways. You have become a wise leader who knows when to rush in and when to be patient. Perhaps one day you will achieve your goal, and if you don't, it will not be for lack of trying."

Uncle Billy swallowed a mouthful of the pie and washed it down with a sip off coffee. "But remember, nothing happens in a vacuum. Consider the first bill of yours that required testing for syphilis when couples apply for a marriage license. I turned that into law and it cost the taxpayers new roads in Green County. Your second bill that allowed for the sterilization of the insane and the feebleminded; I turned that into law and it cost the taxpayers renovations at the State Hospital in Howard County. Your third bill about castrating rapists and sex offenders, well, you get the picture. Nothing happens in a vacuum. The legislators don't really care a fig about the why's and wherefores of your Public Health Laws. They listen to what I tell them and care only about how much pork they can gather at the feeding trough.

"What you say has appeal to many," the governor added, "not only in our Commonwealth, but in the other states. Whether the nation is ready for all these health laws and the accompanying changes, well, I don't know. I do know that many improvements are being made in the factories and in the cities: work safety laws and hygiene laws. But you are correct; America is head and shoulders above most of the other countries and is strong enough to stand on her own two feet. Well, by God, America may need only tread water while the rest of Europe drowns in the Atlantic. If what I hear is near to the truth, Europe is preparing to self-immolate. Passions run high, anger and hatred grow and there is mistrust among all the nations like no other time since the days of Napoleon Bonaparte. More than a dozen languages can be heard on the streets of Vienna. Paris and Berlin are at each other's throat. America must remain disentangled from Europe's mess. Fortunately President Wilson agrees and has promised to keep us safe from their collective insanity."

Uncle Billy finished his coffee and pushed his chair away from the table. As he stood he extended his right hand to Simon and said, "Yes Simon. The Commonwealth will adopt this sixth public health law of yours and become a better place for it. We will wait and watch and hope that America joins with us. If not, I will unleash you upon them."

THREE

"Mr. Pratt to see you," Mrs. Magee said as Simon waved a hand at her. Kraft's secretary disappeared and Nedley Pratt entered the office. More than ten years older than Simon, Pratt was shorter in stature and broader around the waist than The Director. His hair was jet black and Kraft suspected he used a touch of shoe polish to brighten the color. Pratt wore wire rimmed spectacles that wrapped around his ears and sported a thin and neatly trimmed mustache that started and stopped at the corners of his mouth. His $300 hand tailored suit, with creases on the trousers sharp enough to cut a beef-steak, confirmed he was a contracted consultant and not a state employee.

"How did it go at the hospital the other day?" Pratt said as he extended his right hand to Kraft. Kraft replaced his teacup on its saucer and stood to return Pratt's greeting.

"The operating room is the one safe haven that I can publicly enjoy without getting into hot water with some councilman or muckraker. It is almost like a day off, getting away from all of . . ." Kraft theatrically spread his hands and pointed to the side table on the opposite side of the room, ". . . all of this."

"Seven surgical procedures would never be my idea of a day off," Pratt replied.

"Oh contraire counselor, 'tis the grandest of all places to toil. The operating room staff are dutiful servants of the county and the Commonwealth, solely dependent upon the taxpayers for their salaries and subservient to my every whim and desire. The patients are fully anesthetized and offer neither a complaint nor remonstration. Remuneration for my services is the same, whether here or there, and on most days I'd sooner be there than anywhere."

"You are like an old war horse, Simon," Pratt added, "straining to get back into his armor, ears perking to the sound of the cannon and gunfire."

"Just doing the work of God, or is that the work of the Governor?" Kraft jibed.

"Is there a difference?" Pratt replied and smiled at Kraft's mock irreverence. "Two cases yesterday of castration?"

"One man convicted of rape," Kraft explained, "and one man convicted of child molestation. Men sentenced to prison and condemned by our Commonwealth for surgical castration. There was hardly a dry eye in the house."

"And the others?"

"All sterilizations. A mélange of unfortunates who carried traits and defects in need of obliteration. Unfortunately modern medicine cannot cure or resolve their problems but by sterilizing them, at least we can prevent their tainting future generations and prevent their passing on their afflictions to innocent children.

Pratt asked, "I assume all tolerated their surgeries." Kraft nodded as he sipped at the last of his tea. "The hearings for today will be more of the same. The cases will be presented by me and lawyers from my staff."

"Which keeps you in expensive suits, fast cars and faster women," Kraft said as he now smiled at Pratt.

"As you say, Simon, we serve our governor and our Commonwealth," Pratt replied.

"Who are the medical consultants you'll be using?" Kraft asked matter of factly.

"Castor and Comly."

"I assume Mr. Langfield will make an appearance," Simon offered and Pratt nodded with a wide smile. Kraft lifted the lone file that rested on his desk. "I've been reviewing the Boucher case; a bad lot."

Pratt nodded his head. "Three generations of criminals."

"As Manager John McGraw says in New York," Kraft said as he lifted and extended his right thumb, "three strikes and yer out. Three generations of criminals, three generations of medical undesirables, three generations of feebleminded—enough is enough." Kraft looked pensively at the top of his desk and said, "Most would agree that three generations is far too much."

"The laws are what the laws are, Simon," Pratt raised his hands in surrender and pleaded.

Yes, I know, Simon thought. *I wrote them.* "You'll have more than enough work to keep your staff busy for years. I'll poke my head in on the cases but my day is filled with appointments."

"As usual?" Pratt said rhetorically.

"As usual," Kraft said resignedly. He stood and offered his right hand. "Your staff will do fine. I'll see you when I see you." and ushered him out of the office.

*   *   *

"Would you please state your name for the court records?" Andrew Lewis asked. Lewis had what most people would describe as a baby face. Perhaps he shaved once a week whether he needed to do so or not. His eyes were bright and his hair was combed straight back. The suit he wore, although modestly priced, was of the current style common to the vast numbers of young professionals, like so many on the staff of Nedley Pratt's law firm.

"Francoise Boucher." Boucher, on the other hand, was dark and swarthy and the suit he wore was ill fitted and wrinkled and no doubt someone's cast off.

"And what is your age?" Lewis continued.

"I am thirty-two years old," Boucher answered.

"Mr. Boucher, where do you now reside?"

"In the state penitentiary here in the county," was Boucher's reply.

"Why are you in the state penitentiary?" Lewis implored. Quietly Simon Kraft entered the hearing room and took a seat near the door.

Boucher looked from the judge to his own lawyer. Boucher thought it foolish to answer questions to which everyone already knew the answers, including the judge in front of whom he was appearing. "I was arrested for armed robbery."

"Were you convicted for this crime?" Lewis asked. Boucher's face readily showed his annoyance with the continued rhetorical questioning. "For the record, Mr. Boucher," Lewis insisted, "were you convicted of this crime?"

"Yeah."

"Was anyone injured or harmed during the act of this crime?"

Boucher stared hard at Lewis and remained silent. Lewis waited for the response which did not come. Lewis allowed the silence to persist just long enough for a hint of the judge's annoyance to show before he repeated, "Mr. Boucher, was anyone injured during the course of the crime for which you were convicted?" At last Boucher nodded his head in the affirmative.

"Allow the court records to confirm that both the shopkeeper and a customer who was in the jewelry store at the time of the crime were injured by Mr. Boucher. Now Mr. Boucher, what was your sentence?"

Again Boucher was slow to answer. When Lewis turned to the judge, feigning exacerbation with the continued delays in the responses of Francoise Boucher, Boucher blurted out "Seventeen years."

Lewis continued in an even tone. "And you have been incarcerated at the state prison, here in Norwood County, for the last sixteen and one half years?"

"Yeah. Sixteen years, eight months and seventeen days."

"And you will be scheduled for release within the next few months?" Lewis continued.

"Yeah," Boucher said and for the first time the glimmer of a smile crossed his face.

"Now tell us, Mr. Boucher, tell us about your mother." Boucher looked confused; unsure what the lawyer wanted him to say.

"Your mother, Mr. Boucher," Lewis continued. "Tell us about the circumstances of your mother at the time of your birth." Boucher started to talk and then stammered. *Good Lord*, Andrew Lewis thought to himself. *Any more cases like this and I shall be here all day.*

"Mr. Boucher, isn't it true that your mother, Madeline Boucher, was an inmate at Jefferson County Penitentiary at the time of your birth?" Lewis waited and there was no response from Boucher. "Isn't it true that on your birth certificate there is no entry to identify who your father was?" Again there was no response from the defendant.

"Isn't it true," Lewis continued, "that at the time of your birth you were removed from your mother and sent to the orphanage in

Jefferson County where you resided until you ran away at the age of twelve? Three years later, after being arrested several times for multiple offenses, isn't it true you committed the armed robbery for which you were convicted and for which you have been incarcerated these past sixteen years and eight months and seventeen days?" Boucher nodded his head indifferently.

"Now, Mr. Boucher, would you please tell the court why your mother was in prison." Boucher looked from Lewis to the judge and shrugged his shoulders as he looked down at his shoes. He started to speak and then declined. Lewis handed another packet of papers to the judge and said, "Allow the records to show that Madeline Boucher was convicted for attempted murder by poisoning and served nine years in Jefferson County State Penitentiary until her death in 1891.

"Mr. Boucher," Lewis said, now a bit more softly and with an entreating manner, "tell us what you know of your mother's father. From time to time you visited with your mother while she served her time in prison. What did she tell you of her father, your maternal grandfather?"

Boucher complied with the question, speaking from long past memories. "His name was Merced Boucher."

"What were the circumstances surrounding the time when your mother last saw him?" Lewis continued.

"It was in Romania."

"Yes," Lewis replied. "Bucharest. And what, exactly, were the circumstances?"

Boucher paused but Lewis added quickly, "Was not Merced Boucher a convicted felon, doomed to hang from the gallows for a capital offense? Did not Madeline Boucher last see her father on the day he was executed, in 1881, in his prison cell? And did not Madeline Boucher, in short order, emigrate to the United States and start her own life of crime on our shores?"

Andrew Lewis approached the judge and gave to him more packets of papers and documents. "Your Honor. Here are the records necessary to substantiate my statements, despite the reluctance of the witness. Nothing more, your Honor." Andrew Lewis took his seat next to his assistant behind a table with its stacks and piles of papers and books.

"Counselor Worley?" the judge nodded to the lawyer who sat at the table opposite to Lewis. Raymond Worley was the court appointed lawyer assigned to the case hearing of Francoise Boucher. He was young, with a bland and unremarkable face. He wore his hair long and straight with a well-defined part that ran down the middle of his head. His suit was neatly pressed and not unlike the many that were mailed directly from the woolen mills courtesy of the Sears, Roebuck and Co., mail order catalog service. "Have you anything to ask of Mr. Boucher?"

However short on experience Raymond Worley, Esq., may have been, he was neither foolish nor fool-hearty. There was nothing Boucher might offer that would have an impact on the soon to be delivered verdict. The laws of the Commonwealth were reasonably clear, straightforward and inflexible. "No, your Honor."

"Very well," the judge replied. "Mr. Boucher, you may step down." He did and walked back to the table were Raymond Worley sat and took his seat. "Mr. Lewis, your next witness?"

"Mr. Langfield, please."

A tall, gangly man who walked with a visible limp was led into the court room. He carried under his arm a bundle of poster boards, which he set on the floor beside the witness chair. He carried in his other hand an easel, which he set up next to the chair and took his seat. "Could you please state your name for the court record?" Andrew Lewis asked.

"Harry Langfield," he replied.

"Mr. Langfield, where do you work?" Lewis asked.

"I am the Assistant Director for the Eugenics Research Institute, located in the District of Columbia," the man replied with a decidedly New England accent.

"Could you, for the record, explain one of the services you provide on behalf of the Institute?" Lewis asked of the witness.

"We research and study human hereditary. We collect information on families, their good qualities and their bad, and analyze the information."

"Specifically," Lewis continued, "what is it that you and your team of researchers look for?"

"Traits."

"Traits?" Lewis repeated.

"Yes, traits," Langfield replied. "We have an extensive set of qualities and conditions that are evaluated. The qualities refer to anatomic characteristics like hair color, eye color, stature, bone structure, the size of the ears and the shape of the nose. Hundreds and hundreds of anatomic findings make up each individual person. We identify and catalog these hundreds of characteristics."

"How is this of hereditary significance?" Lewis.

"We have been able to identify various trends and patterns within family groups. From generation to generation there are consistencies," Langfield replied.

"Consistencies like what, for example?" Lewis asked.

"In some families, children commonly have six fingers on each hand. Another trait is hair color. In a family where everyone has black hair, it is almost a certainty future children will have black hair. This fact in part explains traits common to the different races. As a rule, Asians have black hair. Such a trait is passed down from generation to generation. We can predict that each succeeding generation will have black hair. The Negro races have woolly hair. That trait is also passed down through the generations. Study of past generations allows for an accurate prediction for future generations."

"Mr. Langfield, what of the propensity for medical issues?" Lewis asked.

"There are quite of few medical conditions that are very common within family groups," Langfield replied. "It is important to evaluate all of the individuals who contract or exhibit the diseases so they may be evaluated from a hereditary standpoint."

"What are a few of these diseases?"

"There are quite a few: epilepsy, diabetes, nervous disorders, insanity, feeblemindedness, syphilis, tuberculosis, cancer. Of course there are hundreds of illnesses that we study that have no hereditary significance: smallpox and typhoid fever for a few."

"You mentioned character traits. "What character traits have you identified that are linked to hereditary?" Lewis continued.

"Courage, an industrious nature, criminal behavior, alcoholism, pauperism, sexual promiscuity, shiftlessness, just to name a few."

"You mentioned criminal behavior, did you not?" Lewis asked.

"Yes sir," Langfield replied.

"Is your research based on any scientific principles?" Lewis asked.

"Gregor Mendel and Charles Darwin, each in his own way, have shown that every living organism is the sum of the parts passed on to him by his parents. Each parent is a contributor. When we perform our research, we investigate unit characters; characteristics that are basic, indivisible and passed down through the generations as discrete hereditary units. We can now state unequivocally that each of these hereditary traits, as exhibited by an individual, is the result of information passed down to him from each of his parents. Each parent contributes, in equal parts, discrete hereditary units to the offspring."

"Is there a way that you can better demonstrate this set of scientific facts to the court?" Lewis asked, full well knowing what would soon transpire.

Langfield reached for the bundle of poster boards and lifted them onto the easel. Multiple boxes were drawn on the first poster he displayed. Inside each box was a name. The boxes were aligned in rows and connected by straight lines that ran in several directions. "These are what are known as genealogy charts. We use genealogy charts to help us construct pedigree charts to interpret the results.

"The first chart is a representation of Queen Victoria and Prince Albert's family tree." The British royal family was the world's most famous family. Among the nine children and forty grandchildren, eight sat upon thrones in seven European countries. Two boxes were located near the top of the poster with 'Queen Victoria' written inside the box on the right and 'Prince Albert' written inside the box on the left. "Below the boxes for the grandmother-queen and her husband, you will see nine boxes, each representing their nine children. From left to right the boxes read Frederick, Alfred, Beatrice and so on." Lines connected the boxes of the children to the line that connected the boxes of the parents.

Langfield placed another poster onto the easel. It was much more complicated with dozens of boxes, many lines and much small writing. "As you see, the chart becomes far more busy when the names of the husbands and wives of the Queen's children are added, including the names of the forty grandchildren. What is important to remember is the framework of the charts and that careful inspection will reveal the appropriate genealogical information for each of the family units."

Langfield shuffled the posters again and displayed another that demonstrated three boxes, one stacked atop the other. The name inside the top box read 'Merced Boucher.' A horizontal line was drawn to a question mark. The name inside the middle box was 'Madeline Boucher.' Another horizontal line was drawn to another question mark. The name inside the bottom box was 'Francoise Boucher.' A third horizontal line was drawn to a third question mark.

"This chart represents the Boucher Family Pedigree Chart. As we follow the trait for criminal behavior we first note the maternal grandfather, Merced Boucher, was a convicted criminal. Mr. Boucher's mother, Madeline Boucher, is represented in the middle box, also a convicted criminal. What is of grave significance is that regardless of whom either Merced or Madeline copulated with to create a child, the trait for criminality remained dominant and persisted. As one reviews the evidence displayed on this pedigree chart, it becomes clear that regardless of whomever Mr. Boucher would take as a wife, all their children will grow to be criminals."

Simon Kraft smiled at the show Harry Langfield was performing for the court. It was the same testimony and most of the same posters he used for every one of his performances. He varied his last few posters to adapt to the defendant on trial and his or her deficiency. *Well done, Mr. Langfield.*

"Do you have any questions for the witness, Mr. Worley?" the judge asked.

"No, your Honor." Worley replied, for who was there to refute what so few people understood?

"Your next witness, please, Mr. Lewis."

Lewis nodded and announced "Dr. Charles Comly."

Comly rose from his chair and took a seat next to the judge.

"For the court records, please state your name."

"Charles Thompson Comly."

Lewis continued, "What is your profession?"

Comly replied, "I am an attending physician at Norwood County Hospital and assistant professor of medicine at the Commonwealth University."

"Dr. Comly," Lewis turned to look at the judge while he spoke, "in what capacity do you appear today at this hearing?"

"I have been asked to serve as an expert consultant for the benefit of the Commonwealth," Comly replied.

"As a consultant, Doctor, have you become familiar with the case of Francoise Boucher and his pending release from the Norwood State Penitentiary?"

"Yes."

"As his case relates to the public safety of the Commonwealth, could you please review his situation for the court," Lewis requested.

"Mr. Boucher was convicted of a major crime. His mother was convicted of a major crime. His grandfather, as direct bloodline ancestor, was convicted of a major crime. Mr. Boucher currently is serving the last year of his sentence and will be a candidate for parole and release shortly."

"Thank you Dr. Comly," Lewis replied. As scripted Lewis said, "Could you please relate for the court the terms for his release and the basis for said terms?"

Kraft watched from the back of the room as Comly tugged at the vest of his suit as if to straighten a wayward wrinkle. "Mr. Boucher is the third in his family bloodline to be convicted of a major crime. Because of recent advances in the natural sciences and medical experimentation, especially as they concern evolution and human biology, we know for a well confirmed fact there is a hereditary predisposition to the development of a criminal mind. One who possesses a criminal mind cannot help but to commit crimes and felonies. Individuals such as Mr. Boucher, because of their bloodlines, are doomed at an early age to become criminals.

"Mr. Boucher has undergone counseling and behavioral therapy for the past sixteen years," Comly continued. "Such therapy and counseling was provided to improve the possibility that he would not return to a life of crime subsequent to his release from the penitentiary; for the benefit and safety of the general public."

"Mr. Boucher now approaches the date for his release from the penitentiary, isn't that so Dr. Comly?" Lewis asked. "How goes his counseling and behavioral therapy?"

"As well as can be expected," was Comly's reply.

"You do not sound optimistic, Dr. Comly."

"I certainly do not."

"Please explain for the court," Lewis questioned on cue.

"Because of his hereditary predisposition, Mr. Boucher is destined to a life of crime. Try as we might," Comly explained, "with our counseling and medication and therapy, the rate of recidivism is exceptionally high. Routinely our attempts to redevelop and rescue such individuals are for naught."

"But we, as a society," Lewis continued to help support his consultant, "valiantly try despite the slim odds." Comly nodded. "How significant is this recidivism, this rate of failure that you describe?"

Dr. Comly looked to the judge when he said, "More than ninety percent of individuals convicted of major crimes will be convicted a second and third time of committing a major crime. Individuals such as Mr. Boucher cannot change destiny. His legacy is imprinted into his bloodlines and for him there is little chance for salvation."

"Dr. Comly, we, as a society, know this how?" Lewis continued.

"Heredity and breeding," Comly replied firmly. "Recent advances in science now allow us to understand what farmers and cattle breeders and horse traders have empirically known for centuries. Good qualities and traits are handed down from one generation to the next. The same is true for bad qualities and character deficiencies. The character trait for a criminal mind and criminal personality, which invariably will eventuate in criminal activity, is handed down from father to son and from mother to daughter."

"Or in the instance of Mr. Boucher," Lewis amended, "from father to daughter and from mother to son. Dr. Lewis, for the good and safety of the public, how do we address a situation of the like of Francoise Boucher?"

"God is merciful and grants forgiveness," Comly replied, "so we must follow in his fashion. Mr. Boucher, however, carries within him a bad seed.

"The mark of Cain?" Comly nodded. "And what of the legacy of Francoise Boucher?" Lewis questioned.

"Mr. Boucher should have no future legacy; in legal terms he should not be permitted to create issue. For the safety of the general public Francoise Boucher must not be allowed to propagate. The criminal trait that he carries, that is carried in his bloodline, must be eliminated."

Andrew Lewis looked to the judge whose expression did not change. "Go on, Doctor."

"The flaw that Mr. Boucher carries in his bloodlines is a contaminant to our society. The prospects of washing such traits clean are unlikely. In medicine, prevention is overwhelmingly more successful than futile attempts at correction. Unwanted and undesirable traits carried by individuals like Mr. Boucher must be eliminated; they must be prevented from re-entering our general population. During his incarceration for the past sixteen and one half years, his undesirable social traits were not allowed to enter into and circulate among the general population. Moving forward, following his release from the penitentiary, these same undesirable traits must not be allowed to enter the general population."

"Are there financial issues associated with this course of action?" Lewis asked.

"Absolutely," Dr. Comly replied. "The Commonwealth will save thousands of dollars. As we assume correctly that Mr. Boucher's children will be criminals and commit crimes, there are costs associated with the judicial system to bring the children to trial. Once a guilty verdict is handed down, there will be costs associated with their continued and prolonged confinement. The money required to address these issues is derived from the taxes paid by the citizens of the Commonwealth. The Commonwealth has only so much money. By preventing individuals like Francois Boucher from procreating, the Commonwealth will be able to avoid raising taxes and otherwise spend that same money building roads and building schools."

Perfectamente, Kraft mused from the back of the room. *Exactly as I scripted, exactly as I planned; every chapter, every line, every verse. Hard science is impossible to refute and futile even to try.*

"So, Dr. Comly," Lewis tread ever closer toward his denouement, "in the interest of the general health of the public, what is to become of Mr. Boucher?"

"As per the laws of our Commonwealth, in order to be released from the penitentiary, Francoise Boucher must agree to sterilization," Dr. Comly explained. "He must undergo a vasectomy."

"Absent his compliance with such a decree?" Lewis queried.

"There will be no release from the penitentiary for Mr. Boucher," Comly answered.

"Thank you Dr. Comly. I have no further questions." Andrew Lewis returned to his seat.

The judge asked, "Mr. Worley, do have any questions for Dr. Comly?"

What Raymond Worley knew of the law, of life in general, was how to recognize a predetermined, pre-judged presentation when he saw one. At every judicial level of the Commonwealth, through appeal and re-appeal, few laws were ever so soundly, thoroughly and unanimously accepted and enforced as the current flock of laws relating to the scientific and hereditary improvement of society. On this particular morning, relating to the case of Francois Boucher, nothing he might say or present could stem the tide or abort what was soon to transpire. Cases like Francois Boucher's were the prototypical examples around which the health laws were constructed. Although this morning's hearing was a necessity mandated by the Laws, the outcome of this morning's hearing was inevitable. "No questions, your Honor."

As Worley turned to his forlorn client to offer condolences, Simon Kraft slipped out of the room. Boucher returned a sneer of insolence to his lawyer, disgusted as he was with the current judicial process, and resigned himself to the fact that a minor surgical procedure was a small price to pay for being able to walk away from the penitentiary.

* * *

"Would you please state your name for the court records?" Nedley Pratt implored of the young woman who sat in the chair next to the judge in the courtroom.

"Julia Ann," was her reply

"Do you have a last name, Julia Ann?"

"I don't know," was her reply as Kraft entered the hearing room and took a seat in the back of the room.

"What is your age?"

"I'm not sure but I had a birthday last week," she answered as her face lit up with a smile. She spoke slowly and the words tended to stick together as if the tongue in her mouth were a bit too thick.

"Miss Julia Ann," Pratt continued, "where do you now live?"

"With Barbara," she replied, pointing to a woman who was seated behind the table where George Duncan, her court appointed attorney sat. Mr. Duncan looked no different in general appearance than Raymond Worley. He was young and clean cut and wore suits off the rack or from mail order companies. Barbara was dressed in the attire of a nurse.

"Do you work or do you have a job, Julia Ann?" Pratt asked and Julie Ann shook her head 'no.'

"Can you read or write?" he continued and Julia Ann again shook her head 'no.'

"Julia Ann, do you attend school?"

"Yeah," she answered.

"What do you do, what do you learn at school?" Pratt continued.

"We color in books and play with blocks and teacher reads stories to us."

Pratt nodded. "Thank you."

Pratt returned to his seat and the judge motioned to the table where the defense attorney sat. "Mr. Duncan, do you have any questions for the defendant?"

"No, your honor." What was he to say? Julia Ann Landis did not have the intellect of a six year old.

The judge said, "That will be all, Julia Ann. Thank you very much."

The bailiff walked to the side of Julia Ann and escorted her from the chair beside the judge to the chair behind the table where George Duncan sat. The judge said, "Next witness, Mr. Pratt."

Pratt nodded to the woman who was dressed in the nurse's uniform. She rose from her chair, walked to the front of the room and sat in the chair next to the Judge.

"For the court records, what is your name?"

"Barbara Luddington," the woman replied.

"Where do you work, Miss Luddington?" Pratt asked.

"I work at the Norwood County Home for the Mentally Infirm."

"What is your occupation and what are your duties at the Home, Miss Ludington?"

"I am a nurse supervisor in the building that houses the mentally retarded patients."

"Is Julia Ann Landis one of you patients?"

"Yes she is," Barbara Luddington replied.

"How old is Miss Landis?" Pratt continued.

"She is seventeen years old."

Pratt nodded, paused, and asked, "Julia Ann became pregnant during the past year, did she not?"

"Yes."

"At what point in her pregnancy did your staff become aware she was pregnant?"

"In her fourth month," Luddington replied.

"How so, Miss Luddington? Why the delay?"

Barbara Luddington looked to the judge and then to Pratt before she answered. "Patients such as Julia Ann frequently have irregular and erratic menstrual cycles. Younger women not infrequently have irregular menstrual cycles. None of the staff had any reason to suspect she might be pregnant."

"Miss Luddington," Pratt interrupted, "this hearing is not an indictment against the competency or powers of observation of your staff or institution. We merely wish to gather information relative to the events that involve Miss Landis. Now please, what led you or your staff to suspect Miss Landis was pregnant."

"While she was bathing the staff noted that her abdomen was swollen. She was examined by the medical staff and tests confirmed she was pregnant."

Pratt walked to the table where his papers were neatly stacked, lifted one, and referred to it. "Was Miss Landis aware that she might have been pregnant, or possibly how she became pregnant?"

"No," Barbara Luddington replied. "She had no recall for any events relative to her becoming pregnant."

Pratt continued, "Does anyone on your staff have an idea on how she became pregnant?"

Luddington paused, sensitive to the volatility of the question before her. "There is speculation and suspicion, but no clear evidence or answer."

"Please explain."

She took a deep breath before she said, "During much of the day, the men and adolescent boys are separated from the women and adolescent girls. For several hours in the morning and at meal times all of the residents mingle. We keep them separated to help with control and we allow them to congregate, together, for a sense of community. Orderlies and matrons are always in attendance to . . . to . . ."

"Provide protection for the residents," Pratt finished her thought. "So, we do not know who Miss Landis's partner, or partners, were. For that matter, we cannot be sure that one of the orderlies wasn't responsible for impregnating Miss Landis."

Carol Luddington offered no response.

"What was the result of Miss Landis's pregnancy?" Pratt pressed on.

"She delivered a baby girl," was the reply.

"Healthy?" Luddington nodded and smiled. "Does Miss Landis care for the child?"

"No."

"Where is the child now?" Pratt asked.

"The child was admitted to the county orphanage."

"Thank you Miss Luddington," Nedley Pratt said as he handed a sheaf of papers to the judge.

"Anything Mr. Duncan?" the judge asked and once again George Duncan shook his head 'no.'

As Barbara Luddington returned to her seat the judge asked of Mr. Pratt, "Next witness, please."

Pratt nodded to the man who sat behind his table. The man rose, walked to the front of the room and took the seat next to the judge. "For the record please state your name."

"Dr. David Castor."

Pratt continued, "What is your occupation?"

Castor replied, "I am the chairman of the department of Pediatrics at the Norwood County Hospital."

"In your role as chairman, have you become familiar with the case of Julia Ann Landis and her residence at the Norwood County Home for the Mentally Infirm?"

"Yes."

"As this case relates to the public welfare of the Commonwealth, could you please review her situation for the court," Pratt requested.

"Miss Landis is a ward of the Commonwealth," Dr. Castor answered. "She receives all care, education and all the comforts of daily life at the county home. While a resident at the home she became pregnant and delivered a baby girl. Due to her mentally retarded state, she is not able to care for the child."

"How long will baby-girl Landis remain at the orphanage?" Pratt asked.

"That is difficult to predict," Castor replied. "She might be adopted at any time. If for some reason no family wishes to adopt her, she will remain a ward of the Commonwealth until her eighteenth birthday. During that time all expenses for her education, medical care, room and board and all other services necessary for normal life will be the responsibility of the Commonwealth."

"What if . . ." Pratt asked and then paused for a moment. "What if baby-girl Landis were retarded like her biological mother? What if it were not possible for her to leave the orphanage?"

"Most likely she would be remanded to the Norwood County Home for the Mentally Infirm."

"Where she would remain a ward of the Commonwealth," Nedley Pratt completed the answer, "and receive all care, education and all the comforts of daily life at the expense of the taxpayers of the Commonwealth for the remainder of her life." Dr. Castor nodded in the affirmative.

"What shall be the disposition for Miss Landis?" Pratt asked.

"Miss Landis," Castor replied, "most likely will remain a resident at the County home for the remainder of her life. To date, no interested family has made arrangements to assume her care."

"As we have just heard, while a resident at the County home, Miss Landis will continue to congregate and . . . and *mingle*," Lewis emphasized, "with residents of the opposite gender. Is it possible, or should I say, is it likely that such mingling was a factor in how and why Miss Landis became pregnant this past year?"

"Most definitely," was Castor's reply.

"In consideration of Miss Landis' current state and condition," Pratt continued, "how likely is it that she will become pregnant again?"

"There is nothing to suggest she will not become pregnant again," Castor replied.

"Which, in all probability, will produce another child who will become a resident of the orphanage and a ward of the Commonwealth and the financial responsibility of the Commonwealth," Pratt proposed.

"Yes."

Pratt paused and gazed at the judge. "How, Dr. Castor, do we resolve such a dilemma, or rather, interrupt such a vicious and improper cycle?"

Without pausing Castor answered, "For residents of the Commonwealth's county homes who are determined to be mentally deficient and become pregnant, sterilization becomes necessary. As per testimony, residents such as Miss Landis are unable to take responsibility for their sexual conduct and are unable to care for the products of their pregnancies. If a child results from the pregnancy, the Commonwealth must assume the costs and responsibility for raising the child. There also is the possibility of legal repercussions. In so far as the Commonwealth assumes the responsibility for the care and protection of the County Homes' residents, lawsuits have arisen from the families of the female residents who became pregnant. To date all have settled out of court, but there is a potential legal burden attached to the female resident who becomes pregnant."

Excellent, Castor old boy, Kraft mused as he left the court room. *Score one more for the Commonwealth.* Pratt, Lewis, Castor, Comly, Langfield. The lawyers and consultants were interchangeable and their performances and testimonies never wavered or varied.

"No more questions, your Honor," Pratt said.

The judge spoke to Mr. Duncan, "Any questions, counselor?"

Again George Duncan shook his head 'No.'

* * *

Simon walked outside the court house to return to his office. The afternoon remained clear and bright and a bit too warm for some of the people who worked in the city today. It was summer and it was August and there was no reason to believe that a hot day in August of 1914 would be different from any other August day in any other year in the Commonwealth. Who knew how an assassination in the Bosnian city of Sarajevo would change the world forever?

FOUR

Simon Kraft remained standing for he did not want to wrinkle the pants of his army dress uniform. Not today, not here in the Oval Office of the White House. With the palm of his hand he patted at his thinning hair, now more gray than brown, ensuring that each strand was in its proper place. Delicately he picked a piece of lint off his right sleeve and brushed at either cuff. He flicked at the multicolored patch on his shoulder that showed the world he was a member of the famous "Rainbow Division." He straightened the front of his jacket for the umpteenth time, ensured that his ribbons were still in line and patted gently at the medals that hung beneath them. He stood immobile on the same spot where he had been standing for the past twenty minutes. He was hesitant to walk around the room, fearful he would leave an impression in the deep blue carpeting, or tread too close to the Great Seal of the United States that was woven into the carpet and dominated the center of the room. The table tops glistened, the sofas and chairs looked as if they had never been used and the desk near the window looked more like a shrine than a work site. He looked around the room at the pictures on the walls and at the high ceilings. A man in a business suit silently stood by the door. Through the windows, outside the room, he could see marine guards standing at attention.

An opening in the wall materialized and his wife, Dorothy, and another woman were escorted into the Oval Office by the same attendant who had deposited him into the room. Dorothy was radiant. Her all too beautiful face sparkled with a teenager's giddiness, in wonder at how she had come to be in the same room with the President's wife. The other woman extended her right hand and Simon took it. "Good morning, Major. I am Edith Wilson."

It was a firm voice with a soft drawl and Simon nodded his head politely when he replied, "Good morning, Mrs. Wilson."

"The President and I are so glad that you and Dorothy were able to join us today."

Simon smiled at the inference he would ever decline an opportunity to meet the most famous person in the world, refuse an order from his Commander in Chief, or, most importantly, deny Dorothy the opportunity to be part of everything that was to happen today.

The attendant looked to Mrs. Wilson as if to gain her attention. As she looked to him he said to Simon, "We will be going into the Rose Garden shortly. The ceremony will take place there. There will be reporters and cameras. There will be a great deal of people, many of whom you may not know. The President will appear and the presentation will be made."

A marine guard opened the French doors that connected the Oval Office with the garden area. He nodded and the attendant said, "If you please, Major."

Simon paused, as if to allow the women to exit first, but the attendant stepped to Simon and steered him through the doors into the Rose Garden. Once through the doors cameras whirled and the flash of magnesium powder wafted into the air. There was a podium in the center of the gathering area and off to the side he saw Uncle Billy, along with a few men in military dress who were in his company. William Cheltenham was now Senator Cheltenham and he beamed as he was allowed to take a position next to his niece and the First Lady. Simon was guided to the side of the podium and glanced from his wife to the crowd and then back to his wife. All heads turned to the right as a man in a business suit approached the podium. He looked every bit the university professor he previously was, stately and relaxed and ever so confident in himself. Recently returned from France and the pre-eminent nominee for the Nobel Peace Prize, Woodrow Wilson was the most recognized man on the globe.

"Congratulations Major," he said in a voice Simon remembered from 25 years ago when they were both at Princeton University. "You have done a great service to your nation and today we wish to honor you."

The attendant handed a folder to the President, who took a position behind the podium but kept Simon close at his left elbow. He said "By act of Congress, the Medal of Honor today is bestowed upon Major Simon Kraft of the 42nd Infantry Division, United Sates Army. The award reads:

> During the Meuse-Argonne offensive of October 6-8, 1918, Major Simon Kraft established a dressing station behind the line of fighting of his company. As casualties mounted he converted the dressing station to a field hospital. His company was overrun and retreated. Major Kraft and his staff were unable to evacuate the wounded and volunteered to remain with them. The territory on which the field hospital was located changed hands four times during the three days of combat. The field hospital continued to receive fire throughout the battle. Despite receiving several wounds himself, he continued to care for the wounded of the allied forces and the wounded of the enemy. By exposing himself to the deadly fire of combat, Major Kraft risked his life, rallied his staff and provided life-saving medical treatment."

President Wilson placed the folder on the podium, took the ribbon with the white stars on the light blue field and placed it around Simon's neck. Simon looked down at the gold star that was surrounded by a wreath. He saw an eagle and the word "Valor" inscribed on the medal. Gentle applause followed. The President extended his hand in congratulations as did Edith Wilson and Uncle Billy. Dorothy stepped forward and kissed him on the cheek. The men in army uniforms gathered around him, shaking his hand and patting him on his back.

"Perhaps we could spend a few minutes inside," Wilson suggested, "after the press is finished with us." President Wilson and Simon posed for the cameramen and Simon gave short answers to their rapid fire questions. He would meet with the press for interviews sometime later in the morning.

When Simon and the President entered the Oval Office, Mrs. Wilson and Dorothy were seated together on a couch. Servants had brought in silver trays of coffee, tea and sandwiches cut into small portions. President Wilson took notice of the dark green ribbon with the thin red stripes on Simon's uniform. "I see our French brothers have honored you in a similar fashion."

Simon cast a glance at the Croix de Guerre and said, "Our unit received the award for manning the field hospital, several posthumously." Wilson nodded solemnly. "Our unit also received a letter of commendation from the German Director of Hospitals. We treated more than forty of their wounded and evacuated as many as we could. In a strange twist they provided us with medical supplies during the time when they controlled the area. After the fighting we agreed to a four hour truce and allowed the Heinies . . . the enemy, to take their wounded back across the lines. They were very thankful for what we did for their men."

"It's comforting to know," Wilson added in a tone that still retained the faint hint of a genteel inflection, delicately drawing out his words in a soft and feathery manner, "that even during periods of inhumanity, tenderness and mercy often emerge. Major Kraft, what plans do you have following your discharge from the army?"

"I shall return to the Commonwealth, Mr. President. Although a different man now sits in the governor's chair, Senator Cheltenham assured me I could return to my previous job."

"That being the Director of Public Health?" Wilson replied and Kraft nodded. "Excellent. I am most familiar with the successes you people have enjoyed by way of reducing the numbers afflicted by summer fever and malaria. We duplicated your efforts here in the Capital. It was a major undertaking but the results have been life-saving."

"Thank you, Sir. I have taken to heart the speech that you gave to the students, about Princeton University's service to our nation."

"That is very kind, Major. Did our paths cross while you were at Princeton?" Wilson asked.

"I was never in any of your classes," Simon replied, "but I was in attendance often when you spoke. After I graduated, I returned to attend a football game in October of 1896. I was fortunate to be present during your commemoration speech."

"Yes, that was a special day for me also," Wilson said as he thought back to the many years he spent at the university, as a professor and later as the school's president.

Simon lifted his gaze to the far wall and recited from memory. "The duty of an institution of learning is not merely to implant a sense of duty, but to illuminate duty by every lesson that can be drawn out of the past."

Wilson smiled. "I was fortunate to strike upon a quotable phrase. I have used those words several times since then."

"Mr. President," Kraft said, "with the war now over, it is imperative that we follow your lead and make it our duty to make America a stronger nation and the world a better place to live. It should be the duty of every one of us in political office or governmental service to make the lives of Americans healthier and safer. We must strive to protect our women and children, and somehow make their lives better."

"Such a thought has merit, Major Kraft," the President said with the trace of a smile on his face.

"Sir, currently all the world looks up to us as the savior of the war," Kraft offered. "We now have the opportunity to assume the mantle of the world's leader in medical care. As we move into the future, we must establish standards for everyone else to follow."

Wilson nodded as he poured tea into a cup. He spooned in sugar and stirred. He brought the cup to his mouth as he said, "How would you suggest that we address such an issue?"

"A healthier nation will become a stronger nation," Simon offered. "Administratively our government may not be in the best . . ." Kraft caught himself and paused. He looked to Dorothy and then to Mrs. Wilson. "Sir, permission to speak freely?" Wilson nodded.

"Consider only the public health issues. Presently one agency looks to the welfare of the children. Another unrelated group looks to the safety of food and the medicines people use. There is no *one* entity responsible for these related issues. The same is true relative to disease control, injuries in the workplace, which person may or may not receive vaccinations . . . Sir, the system is hodge-podge. The best solution is to place the many related agencies and departments under one roof."

"Woodrow," the First Lady asked, "does your cabinet have a position for a Secretary of Health?"

"We have a Public Health Department," Wilson answered, "that concerns itself with providing care to retired merchant marines, Indians on their reservations and immigrants at Ellis Island. The Food and Drug administration has their responsibilities and The Child's Bureau has theirs. The Department of Labor addresses work related injuries. Each is housed in a different department. For example, the Public Health Service is part of the Treasury Department." A whimsical smile spread on Wilson's face as he thought of the absurdity of the department's lineage. "No, Edith, everything is not under one roof and there is no cabinet position for the director."

"Major Kraft," the First Lady asked, "what suggestions would you offer?"

Simon Kraft looked to the President, then back to the First Lady. "All of the agencies that relate to the public and general health of the people of this nation must be centralized under one directorship. There must be one department and one voice speaking for the benefit of the people and the nation.

"I believe we can duplicate on a national level what I, what we accomplished in the Commonwealth. Consider the advancements that have been made in science and medicine; by enacting legislation, the basic tenets and rudiments will flow to the people. There is much more to the issue than merely attention to public health. Without waving the flag too boldly, my goal is to help make America a better place to live and to make Americans a better race of people."

President Wilson reached for one of the sandwich portions, took a few bites and swallowed. At first Kraft was unsure if he had said something to upset his commander. He didn't think so. Woodrow Wilson was a man who understood breeding and the purity of the races. He was the man most responsible for making the nation's capital a segregated city and a man who would defend to the death the ban on inter-racial marriages. He also was the leader of the nation that most recently had saved the world from self-destruction and was committed to the concept that America was singularly and inarguably the superior nation on earth. Kraft was certain he had the full measure of his man.

When he looked to the First Lady and saw her sitting on the edge of her seat, eyes twinkling, anxiously waiting for his next suggestion, he knew he had her won over. He knew her to be a strong opponent of the factors that rendered young women and troubled families vulnerable to the ravages of vice and the social evils of prostitution. He knew her to be a woman who was quite outspoken concerning the depraved miscreants who did nothing to improve their squalid living conditions. He knew her to be a leader of the National Society for the Promotion of Practical Eugenics.

Kraft continued looking at Mrs. Wilson when he said, "Mr. President, within the span of one generation, by maintaining the integrity of our native stock, by eliminating our undesirable traits and by enriching the greatness that is already in place, we Americans could assume the center stage of the world and never relinquish it."

Wilson's mind shifted to the images of the people who most recently were laid low by the influenza epidemic and the wounded soldiers who continued to arrive on ships from Europe. *These are the people who need our help.* In a different and darker vein he thought of the undesirables; the people who stir the political unrest, who fill the nation's prisons, who instigate the union strikes, who instigated this past summer's race riots that tore apart Washington and two dozen other cities across the country. These were people America did not need. Yes, there was merit in the elimination of such 'bad character defects' that polluted the nation and soiled the purity of America.

Wilson gathered his thoughts before he summarized, "If I am hearing you correctly, Major, I believe you are suggesting that in order for America to lead the world, America itself must be led by the best of its people with the best of character traits. The malignant and inferior pieces must be removed and not be allowed to diminish our greatness or limit our successes."

"Exactly, Sir."

"Wouldn't it be a good idea . . . ," Edith Wilson started but held her tongue.

Wilson theatrically looked at the sandwich he held in his hand and said, "Food for thought." All smiled politely. The President stood and said, "Once again, congratulations on your medal and thank you for the service you provided to your men and our nation. Good luck as you return to your *new-old* position. Mrs. Wilson and I have our work cut out for us. We start a tour of the country next week to petition for congressional approval of the peace points agreed upon during the meetings in Versailles. America's participation in the League of Nations will be paramount to continued peace in Europe. I must work hard to convince Congress to approve our acceptance of the League's charter. There will be several busy weeks ahead of us."

*　*　*

The air in Norwood County was brisk and clear now that autumn had chased out the last vestiges of summer's sweltering heat. Simon Kraft sat in *his* chair at *his* desk in *his* office and it was as if he had never left. Books, papers and documents were stacked in piles on the side table. One case report and one file neatly rested on his desk. Inkwell and pen were at the ready.

"I am happy to report that your thirty day probationary period is over," Ed Preller said as he stepped into Simon's office.

"I thought I had a secretary to keep out the likes of characters like you."

"Suh-h-h," he replied in a prolonged drawl as if he were addressing General Robert E. Lee himself, "it is the likes of minions like me who make the job for heroes like you that much easier."

"Are you kidding? Sifting through the backlog will take forever. Did you people do anything during the past two years?" Kraft needled away.

"Matthew Rassmussen was the happiest man in the world when he was told last month to clean out that desk you now sit behind and go back to his laboratory. When Uncle Billy first told him he would be the 'acting' Director until you returned, I thought we would have to use a crow bar to extricate him from the basement. The department would have done better to hire one of those mannequins from the department store. He didn't screw up too badly though. I wouldn't let him. I gave him papers to sign, made certain he got to his meetings on time and gave him his scripts to read when he met with the newspaper men. I tried to run this place as close as I could remember to how you ran things. I guess we did something right. The Commonwealth didn't come tumbling down around our ears."

"No it didn't, Ted my boy. Things could be worse. At least we're not speaking German."

Ed pantomimed a salute and said, "I have the reports from Green County that you asked for yesterday . . ."

"Don't worry about Green County," a voice from outside the office bellowed. "Leave it for Rassmussen," Uncle Billy ordered as he walked into Simon's office.

"So says the junior senator from The Commonwealth." Simon countered as they all shook hands and exchanged greetings.

"Don't let your bottom get too comfortable in that chair, Dr. Kraft," William Cheltenham said. "I come bearing orders from my boss, whoever he or she may be."

"Orders for whom, for what?" Kraft questioned.

"You've been promoted," Cheltenham said. "I would say that you were drafted, but that would be demeaning for the hero of the army."

Cheltenham handed Simon an envelope. He opened it and read the letter it contained.

"The White House was kind enough to allow me to deliver the good news," Cheltenham added.

"What good news?" Ed challenged.

"Go on, Simon, tell him," Cheltenham urged.

"The President has created a new department," Simon explained, "and a new cabinet position; the Department of Health and Welfare. He has appointed me the new Secretary of the Department of Health and Welfare." He handed the letter to Ed to read, "For the United States of America."

As Ed read the letter, eyes that were set so deeply in his head widened and a rare smile spread across his thin and skeletal face.

"How, why?" Simon asked again.

"Apparently," Cheltenham explained, "when you met with the President and his wife you made quite an impression. Whatever you shared with him was something that he took to heart. He called me into his office for a chat. I assured him you did not torture cats or rob banks and we left it at that. I didn't hear anything more."

"I wonder what caused him to change his mind," Simon mused.

"More accurately, *her* mind," Uncle Billy corrected him. Ed and Kraft lifted an eyebrow to Cheltenham, soliciting an explanation. "President Wilson has been ill and many believe the First Lady labors in his stead. The press reports he has influenza but no one has heard or seen him for more than a month. Congressional bills, treaties and documents go into his office and they come out with his signature on them, but we can only speculate as to how that process works. The consensus is, Edith Wilson is running the country."

"What about Thomas Marshall?" Ed asked.

"The Vice-President has been denied an audience with President Wilson," Cheltenham said. "Even Joe Tumulty, the President's Chief of Staff, has limited access. Apropos to you, Dr. Kraft, my guess is Edith Wilson liked what you had to say and decided you would make a good Secretary of Health."

Simon Kraft closed his eyes and took in a deep breath as he grappled with the news.

"Don't let it boggle your mind," Cheltenham offered. "The annals of history are sprinkled with stranger stories than this one. Congress still has to approve your appointment but that should be only a formality. Go home, tell your wife and pack your bags. Whoever comes back to fill your chair is the governor's problem."

Uncle Billy slowly wagged his finger at Simon. "Remember what I told you about the politician's credo: propriety, appearances and always be cautious about the paper trail that you leave behind. You may not think yourself a politician, but at the very least you are the appointment of a politician, and you sure as hell better exhibit expert political savvy if you wish to keep your job."

"Whoa, hold on there," Ed ordered. "If you are going to Washington, I'm going to Washington. This deaf ear of mine kept me out of the fight to kick out the Kaiser, but you cannot leave me here to chase after and clean up for Dr. Rassmussen again."

They shook hands again, Simon thanked Uncle Billy several times over for whatever help he may have offered and promised Ed Preller a position on his staff. After they left he sat in his chair and tried to gather his thoughts. Where would he live, what should they do with their house in Norwood County? How soon would he be expected in Washington?

* * *

The press conference in the lobby of the State House started promptly at 11 AM. With Dorothy at his side, the favorite son of Norwood County fielded questions with the skill and deft of a seasoned bureaucrat.

Q. Cleaning up the Commonwealth was one thing; straightening out the rest of the 47 states is another matter. How do you plan to do it?

A. I'll do the same job as I did here in the Commonwealth. We'll form a strong team, we'll work hard together and we'll eradicate as many diseases as possible.

Q. Politics in Washington can be a circus. How well do you think you'll do?

A. Politics in Norwood County wasn't a cakewalk. I was fortunate to work for the greatest governor in the nation. I sat at the knee of one of the finest men ever to enter public service. What I learned from Senator Cheltenham I shall take with me to Washington. If and when I have a question, I'll know where to find him.

Q. George Washington threw a coin across the Potomac River. Will you try to swim across the Potomac River?

A. That river is deep and wide and I'll be swimming in enough paperwork and red tape to keep me busy for years to come.

The questions were polite and allowed Kraft to shine. He belonged to Norwood County and they were proud and happy for him. As the session drew to a close, Simon fielded one last question.

Q. When your time is done in Washington, how do you want your legacy to read?

Without the slightest hint of hesitation he replied, "I want to be remembered as the man who made the Commonwealth a better place to live. I want to be remembered as the man who made America a better place to live. I want to be remembered as the man who made

Americans a healthier race of people; the greatest race of people on earth. I guess I have some work to do boys. See you later."

Cameras clicked as he put his arm around his wife. All in attendance cheered and even the hard boiled newspapermen applauded and wished him well.

The banners on the newspapers the next morning told the story. The lead for the Norwood Sentinel was "WAR HERO GOES TO WASHINGTON TO MAKE WAR ON DISEASE." The lead for the Daily News was "KRAFT—FIRST IN WAR, FIRST IN HEALTH." The lead article in the op-ed section of the Post-Dispatch was "OUT OF THE OPERATING ROOM AND INTO THE CAPITOL DOME." But none captured what was so dear to the thoughts of Dr. Simon Kraft as what he read in the headlines of the Norwood Bulletin:

KRAFT BECOMES AMERICA'S HEALTH CZAR.

FIVE

The young woman who sat in the law office of Loretta Frontenac was mildly attractive in a plain way. Her hair was combed straight back and the blouse and dress that she wore were neat and clean. She wore no make-up of course, for they were country people, she and the man and woman whom she sat between. Cosmetics and God's will did not go hand in hand.

"It's a personal matter," Miss Frontenac had been told. The family from the outskirts of Oxford Corners needed a legal opinion for a personal matter. Loretta Frontenac was 31 years old and it seemed to her that most of the clients in her small legal practice in Oxford Corners came to her to consult on 'personal matters.' Although a few families from this farming region in southern Norwood County consulted her on money matters and business matters and on occasion, death matters, personal matters was by far the most popular concern.

"So tell me, Miss Summerdale, how may I help you?" Miss Frontenac asked. She wielded a pencil in her right hand, poised above a fresh piece of paper. In contrast to the country mouse who sat across from her, Loretta Frontenac was strikingly attractive but had taken measures to suppress her beauty. Her radiant shoulder length red hair was combed straight and tied back in a neat bun. She wore only a hint of blush on her cheeks and the slightest amount of lip cover. Her dark eyes that sparkled and gleamed in such an intoxicating fashion hid behind tortoise-shell eye-glasses more common to male accountants and clerks. The cotton jacket that she wore was dull gray-brown in color and modestly tailored so as not to accentuate in an unseemly fashion any of her body parts. The white blouse she wore had a few ruffles at the throat and was politely understated. As the only female lawyer in Norwood County, she was more intent on growing a practice and earning the respect of county's judges and other lawyers than the leering stares and indecent glances of the locals. She asked again, "Miss Summerdale, why is it you are here?"

The young woman picked at her fingernails and looked from the older woman to the older man. "Well," she started haltingly, "I had this operation." She squinted her eyes as if she were looking through the fog, trying to see more clearly an object in the distance. "I ain't so sure the operation were right."

Loretta Frontenac continued to stare at the young woman. The room remained so quiet that Loretta heard her pulse pounding in her ears. She waited, allowing the young woman to expound on her response. At last she asked, "You had an operation?" The young woman nodded tentatively. "Miss Summerdale, what type of operation did you undergo?" The young woman shifted her gaze, away from Loretta and away from the two people who sat at her side.

At last the man on Miss Summerdale's left said, "She got spayed. The doctors spayed Alma."

Loretta continued to stare at Alma Summerdale as the room remained silent. "Are you folks Alma's parents?" They nodded 'yes.' She took a less formal tack and softened her voice. "Alma, how old are you?"

"Nineteen gone on twenty."

"When did this operation occur?"

"In 1916."

"Three years ago?" Alma nodded. "Where was the operation performed?"

"In Norwood Hospital," the father answered. The mother buried her hands into her dress as she balled them together, straining hard to maintain her composure.

"And you believe the operation involved your female organs?" Loretta asked Alma.

"Tha's what Miss Clary at the store tol' us," Alma replied. "Miss Clary runs the store in the center of our town."

"How is it that Miss Clary became involved in your personal matter?" Loretta asked.

"Miss Clary is Wilfred's aunt," Alma replied.

"And who is Wilfred," Loretta asked.

"Wilfred Algon. Wilfred Algon's the boy what asked me to marry him," Alma said as she frowned.

Loretta wrote down the names of the players and tried to connect a few with lines and arrows. "How old is Wilfred?"

"Twenty-two," Alma replied. "He's back from the war and he asked me to be his wife. But now he's changed his mind."

"Wilfred Algon asked you to marry him," Miss Frontenac said as she rubbed at her temples and tried to clarify what she was hearing, "and now has changed his mind because his Aunt Clary told him you had an operation on your female organs?" All three Summerdale's nodded their assent.

"Again, how did Aunt Clary get involved in your marital plans?"

Alma's face reddened and tears formed at the corners of her eyes. Loretta waited for nearly 30 seconds before Mr. Summerdale said, "Alma and Wilfred got familiar; probably too familiar. No doubt it was some of that behavior what was acceptable in France during the war, but . . . Anyways, Alma's got a scar from her operation and Wilfred seen the scar. Wilfred took to asking questions. When Alma said she never had no 'pendicitis or sicknesses, he got more inquisitive."

"Why did he get so inquisitive?" Loretta asked.

Mr. Summerdale cleared his voice and said, "I suspect they was too familiar for six months or more; since Wilfred come home. Wilfred couldn't understand why she hadn't gotten pregnant with a baby. I guess he thought that was part and parcel to the bargain. He asks her to marry, they have relations and then she has his baby. I guess then they would finally get 'round to getting married. It's not the order I would have chosed and not the order God has written down for us, but . . . By jingo, he ought to marry her for just being too familiar with her."

Mrs. Summerdale started to sob and Alma bit nervously at her lip. Loretta stared at her notes and struggled to identify the legal problem. Alma was no child and the sexual relations were consensual. Breach of promise over a marriage proposal was a tacky argument that would prove to be sordid in the extreme as matters became public record. Alma wasn't pregnant so there was no offspring in question. Miss Clary. Aunt Clary. Concerned that a witch's tongue was wagging in the wind, Loretta asked, "How or why did Aunt Clary suggest you had an operation on your female organs?"

"She read the hospital records," Mr. Summerdale replied. "Alma and me went to the hospital and got the hospital records. In order to give satisfaction to Wilfred, in order to give him an answer, we went to the hospital and got her records."

The hospital records. "Do you have the hospital records?" Loretta asked. Mrs. Summerdale nodded. "With you now?" She nodded again.

"May I see them?" Mrs. Summerdale reached into the bag she carried and produced a folder with several type-written pages. Loretta took the folder and placed it on her desk.

"When again did you have the operation?" Loretta asked Alma.

"1916."

"That makes you sixteen years old at the time." Alma nodded. "You were not old enough to give permission for the operation. Who agreed to the operation?"

"Nobody said nothing and nobody signed nothing," Mr. Summerdale answered. "The judge ordered it."

Loretta Frontenac drummed her fingernails on her desk and tapped out a simple tattoo as each nail clicked on the wood and echoed off the walls. "From what you remember Alma, from your understanding, why did you undergo the operation?"

"For my convulsion fits."

"Do you mean epilepsy type convulsions?"

Alma nodded. "But Doctor Edmunds says I ain't really got no epilepsy."

"Did you ever have a seizure?" Loretta asked.

"Had three of them." Mrs. Summerdale spoke for the first time.

"You have had three seizures?" Alma nodded 'yes.' "Do you remember when you had them?"

"She had her first fit when she was little," Mrs. Summerdale replied in a soft but steady voice. "She was maybe two years old, had a terrible high fever, so's we put her in a tub of water. Bathed her down. Then she started to shivering and the fever came back. Before we could put her back into the tub she started to twitching her arms and her legs. Her eyes went crazy and she starting sniffling and snorting. After a few minutes it passed. She got better and we didn't think no more about it.

"When she was about twelve she fell off the back of a chair. She bumped her head and started to twitching again. Wet herself. Luckily she was home. We cleaned her up, she had a headache for a month, but then it passed. When she turned fifteen she started to take spells. Dr. Edmunds says she was having sugar diabetes spells. Light in the head and dizzy. Then she had a fit but we stopped it by giving her a sugar cube. Doc Edmunds said to keep sugar cubes 'round the house. So's we do. Sugar cube brings her to. Alma normally stays away from the sugar and the sweets, except when she gets light headed; then we give her the cubes."

Loretta was writing on her fourth sheet of paper with arrows that went in six different directions. She looked to the folder that contained the hospital records. "Excuse me for just a moment." She opened the folder and scanned the physician's admission note. She glanced at the surgeon's report. She fingered a paper that had the seal of the Commonwealth embossed on it. It was a court order. She shuffled the papers again and her eyes fixed on a few statements and passages.

"Mrs. Summerdale, do you have a history of epilepsy or fits and seizures?" Mr. Summerdale shook her head no. "And you, Mr. Summerdale?"

"No ma'am," he replied.

"Did either of your parents have seizures?" Both parents shook their heads no.

"Did either of you, did any of you read the hospital record?" All three Summerdale's shook their heads 'no.' "How many people in your town can read, besides Miss Clary?"

"A handful," Mr. Summerdale replied.

"Do you remember going to a courthouse, for a trial or for a hearing?" Again all three shook their heads no.

"We had a county solicitor come to our house to ask a few questions," Mr. Summerdale answered. "We thought he was a census taker at first. He asked a few questions; we gave him a cup of coffee. He said he was there to take care of Alma's convulsions. Next month an ambulance came to our house and took Alma away to fix her convulsions. We didn't know she was to have an operation, but thank the Lord she didn't have no problems with it. We visited her in the hospital and at the time everything went fine. Now we're not so sure."

Loretta fingered the file of hospital records and looked into the face of the young woman who sat before her. "Alma, I will take your case," she said. "I still have quite a few questions and I do not have many answers for you at this time. There are more records that I must obtain." Loretta was unsure how much to tell them and how much to withhold until the issues made sense. She looked at the papers again and suspected it would never make sense. "I must have these records reviewed by a physician and I must get records that concern the solicitor's visit to your house. The secretary outside will ask you to sign a few papers. I will send word to you as to when we can meet again."

Loretta offered her hand to Mr. Summerdale and reluctantly he shook it. After they left the office she opened the folder again and reread the court order. It stated that Alma Summerdale had been ordered to undergo sterilization because she was the third generation of the Summerdale line to be afflicted with epilepsy. Because of

> "the clear and indisputable familial tendency and genetic predisposition of the disease, the only recourse available to eliminate the disease within the Summerdale family is to eliminate the possibility that Alma Summerdale might conceive and bear children."

How did Alma quote her physician, Dr. Edmunds; 'she ain't really got no epilepsy.' Loretta read the surgical record for a third time that described Alma's procedure as "division and ligation of fallopian tubes, bilaterally." The record was signed by Simon Kraft, M.D. Loretta looked up from the report and stared out the window as she whistled through her teeth. *That Simon Kraft.*

SIX

The Christmas season in the nation's capital was a season for entertainment and socializing. Simon and Dorothy Kraft were committed almost every night to a party or a gathering at the home of one dignitary or another. The timing of Simon's appointment during the holiday socializing season had its benefits. The couple was afforded the opportunity to socialize with a large number of people whom Simon might not have been able to meet for several months. Their whirlwind schedule did, however, prove to be a nightly challenge. Following introductions and while drinking a high ball with one hand and balancing hors d'oeuvres with the other, he had to remember their names, titles and the states that sent them to the Capital.

On the plus side, Simon had the opportunity to gather with the various congressmen who were assigned to the committee that helped to develop the Health Department. Admittedly it was a 'work in progress,' but all were enthusiastic. One of the committee members was a congressman from Louisiana, and before too long conversations shifted to the merits of building dikes in the bayou region in order to eliminate malaria infested swampland. The congressman offered, "My aide will call upon you within the month, Mr. Secretary, so that you two may exchange ideas and address the details."

Simon shared a ribald story about two bulls on a hill with the committee member from Georgia. Their conversation soon shifted to the concept that one separate division within the department should be responsible for the tracking and investigation of infectious diseases. As the congressman warmed to the idea, Simon suggested that a designated facility to oversee the matter, perhaps in one of the states in the deep south, would be an excellent recommendation. The congressman promised to remember the story of the two bulls and retell it often. He also suggested that "My aide will call upon you within the month, Mr. Secretary, so that you two may exchange ideas and address the details."

Dorothy introduced Simon to the wife of a congressman from western Pennsylvania. Conversation touched upon the mining industry. Simon posited the idea of opening an office of industrial hygiene that would benefit the entire nation. He suggested the office would best be located nearby the new office of Bureau of Mines—which happened to be located not far from Pittsburg. Before he could refill his drink, the congressman appeared and suggested his aide would call upon Simon within the month to exchange ideas and address the details.

Simon thought back to Uncle Billy's comments about the politicians' needs to gather as much pork as possible from the government's feeding trough for their constituents. He was becoming a first-hand witness to the phenomenon. He also was concerned that the successful operation of his fledgling department would be directly related to how well he doled out the pork in the New Year.

Dorothy was in her glory. "My Lord," she beamed, "I was bred for this." She was indeed, for not only was the job of the Secretary's wife to be a socializer, she also needed to be a social planner. Her calendar for the upcoming months soon filled with visits to hospitals for military veterans, visits to hospitals to meet with sick children and visits to hospitals to spend time talking with mothers in the maternity wards. She visited soup kitchens for the poor and orphanages throughout the region. Winter cotillions, spring fetes, receptions for visiting ambassadors and luncheons with New York socialites—she attended them all with boundless energy and a soft southern gentility that was priceless. Where Simon was at times stiff or formal, she was gay and charming. When on occasion Simon was too business-like, she offered a casual and light view on the matter. They were an excellent team and readily welcomed to the nation's capital.

* * *

"Walk me through this again Dad," Loretta Frontenac said as she dabbed at the corner of her mouth with a napkin.

"Many people who have epilepsy have seizures, but not all people who have seizures have epilepsy," Dr. Guy Frontenac explained in his plain and simple fashion that he used to explain similar quandaries to the patients in his medical practice.

"All collies are dogs but not all dogs are collies?" Loretta recited, as if the line would clarify a fuzzy topic. "How many different types of convulsions or seizures are there?

"Several. Some seizures involve only one side of the body," he replied. "Sometimes the patients blank out and stare absent-mindedly for a few minutes. Then of course there is the grand mal seizure, when the patients fall to the ground and their bodies convulse in general. There are several causes for generalized seizures besides epilepsy. A big tumor in the brain may act as a trigger to create mayhem and cause the body to seize. Free blood should not be in contact with the brain tissues. When blood comes in contact with the brain, say from a blood clot or a hemorrhage, the blood acts as an irritant and causes the patient to seize."

"Clear as mud, Dad," Loretta replied and looked to her mother, Emma, who could offer no relief.

"For one hundred people who have epilepsy," her father said, "the cause of the epilepsy remains unknown for more than 90 of them. We do not know what is responsible for causing the patients' brains to act abnormally. And yes, the most common manifestation of the condition is the grand mal seizure that we call a convulsion. But from what you have told me of your client's history, your client does not have epilepsy."

"So says Alma's own doctor." Loretta squinted, then frowned and then pursed her lips as she had done so many times before when her father struggled to explain something to her, be it algebra or history or the translation of Dumas into English. "Then what problem does my client have?"

"Your client indeed has *had* convulsions," Guy Frontenac explained, "but they appear to be secondary to three different medical problems." He lifted his plate with the remnants of his Sunday dinner on it and set it aside. He picked up the salt and pepper shakers and positioned them in front of him. He separated the two shakers and placed the sugar bowl between them.

"Oh Dad," Loretta exclaimed as she looked to her mother who shuffled plates from the dining room back into the kitchen. "You're not going to try to explain football to us again, are you?"

"Your fault," Loretta's mother chided. "You asked the question and now you get the lecture, complete with drawings and diagrams."

"Three different episodes of seizures, each with its own explanation," her father the professor continued, inured to the slings and arrows of familial abuse.

"A febrile fit," he said as he lifted the salt shaker, "occurred when she was two years old. Very common. Common with infected mastoids and infected ears, common with the measles.

"You see," the man with thinning gray hair and wire rimmed spectacles said as he pointed the salt shaker at his daughter for emphasis, "the brain is a bundle of electrical activity. The coordinated firing of electrical currents allow us to speak and talk and scratch our noses. For some reason a high fever will scramble the electrical currents and cause an electrical storm. As a result, the body will convulse. Febrile convulsions are common in little children until they reach five or six years of age. Strangely the children almost always outgrow the seizure problem. When the kids grow into adults, most never have a convulsion again."

"You said that children will outgrow the convulsions caused by fever," Loretta said and her father nodded. "Why?" she asked.

"Don't know. Some of the universities have galvanometer machines and are testing adults, but children are harder to test. With wires and coils and batteries within boxes, galvanometers look like something devised by Lucifer himself. Obviously they scare the wits out of little children, so it is very hard to test them without anesthesia. What sane person would ever don a helmet with so many crazy attachments? By the way, two or three of the children you went to school with had fits when they were little."

"Who?" Loretta asked.

"None of your business," Guy replied. "I was called to their homes, tended to them, they grew up and never had a seizure again. Now," he said as he fingered the pepper shaker, "when your client fell off her chair and bumped her head, she jumbled some more of those electrical currents. Brain injury, whether a concussion caused by a knock on the head or a fractured skull, may leave a bruise on the brain. Such an injury will disrupt and confuse the electrical firings in the brain and may also result in some type of clonic seizure. We've seen a great number of seizure problems with the men returning from the war."

Loretta blinked involuntarily as images of exploding bombs and whizzing bullets flashed through her mind. "You're suggesting that the seizure she had when she was two years old and the seizure she had when she was twelve years old are not connected."

"As you lawyers are want to say, 'With 100% certainty and in my professional opinion, they were unrelated.' Almost always, the convulsion experienced during a childhood fever and the convulsion that results from a new or fresh injury to the head ten years later are not related."

Guy picked up the sugar bowl and cradled it with both hands. "Your client has diabetes. Not only does the sugar content in her bloodstream tend to rise very high, such patients are prone to very *low* levels of sugar in their bloodstreams. Remember, the brain needs sugar to function. When the sugar level drops in the bloodstream, the sugar level drops in the brain. Functionally the brain stops working and the electrical firings become jumbled, disorganized, and manifest in a grand mal seizure." Gently he replaced the sugar bowl on the table. "Your client has diabetes, not epilepsy," he explained.

"What is this nonsense," Emma Frontenac asked as she placed a cut piece of pie in front of the other two at the table, "about the parent's being afflicted with epilepsy?"

"Just that," Loretta answered as she poured coffee from the pot. "Nonsense. There is neither documentation nor evidence in hand to suggest that anyone else in the family has or had epilepsy. None of her family members have been confined in an institution anywhere for epilepsy, nor for any other nervous disorder. All the grandparents have died and she has three brothers who are otherwise healthy."

"So why did they do that terrible operation on that young girl?" Emma asked.

"There is a law on the books that allows the Commonwealth to sterilize people who have hereditary illnesses," Loretta answered. "Most often the patients who have the operations are confined to state institutions and are wards of the Commonwealth."

"It's a bad law," Guy growled between bites of his pie. He swallowed, took a sip of his coffee and explained, "Ostensibly the law is meant to save money. Many of the insane and people with uncontrollable epilepsy are confined in state institutions. The patients are there because we are unable to help or cure them. We have neither the operations nor medicines to make them better. In most instances their families can no longer care for them. Left with no alternative, they become the problem of the state. Treating and caring for them costs money; for room and board, for personnel to tend to them, for medication. It is supplied at a cost to the state. The state argues that if a person with epilepsy wishes to marry, he or she may be precluded from obtaining a marriage license for fear the children will be born with epilepsy. The laws apply similarly for other diseases thought to be hereditary like insanity and idiocy, but it is all rubbish. There is no rock solid evidence that such illnesses are inherited. Millions of healthy children are born to parents who have epilepsy and other nervous disorders. Millions of healthy parents bear children who develop epilepsy. Nothing is absolute and there are no guarantees one way or the other. Tendencies exist, but there are too many damn factors that influence the appearance or manifestation of such diseases. The idiots are the men who passed such laws."

"Why does the law exist?" Emma asked again.

"Like Dad said," Loretta explained, "it is cheaper to prevent a problem from happening than to pay for the consequences and long term issues of the disease."

With his hackles raised, Guy challenged, "What's to say the state will not extend the law to include people with color-blindness? What about people with freckles or big noses. It's a bad law based on quack science formulated by crackpots with an agenda."

"Quack science?" Emma queried.

"Yes," Guy Frontenac answered, "parents with blond hair are likely to produce children with blond hair, but red headed and brown headed babies get born to them every day. Same with married couples with blue eyes or big ears. Sure there are tendencies, but breeding in people is not absolute. Consider when a colored person and a white person marry; the offspring are neither white nor black but a blend. Not all characteristics penetrate 100% of the time. There is nothing to confirm that a pure line will develop. Only tendencies.

"The quackery appears," Guy continued, "when the pseudo-scientists suggest that talents and skills and personal preferences are passed from one generation to the next, like playing the piano or being an artist or," Guy picked up the salt shaker and smiled when he said, "or like being a standout football player. We know that various physical qualities are controlled by heredity, like size; but two tall parents may certainly produce a small child, and two midget parents may produce a normal size child.

"Many of these people have taken what Mendel and Darwin have written and twisted it around. Darwin suggested that Nature allows the strongest to survive and the weakest to be eliminated. Twist it and you allow for the rich getting richer and the poor to be ground into the dust—quite possibly to extinction. Follow this to its illogical conclusion," he said in a calmer voice. "Those in power should be allowed to grow stronger and the rest of us should be forced to admit that such a circumstance is Nature's way. With these Health Laws in effect, the state government is acting as Nature's proxy. By legally forcing sterilizations, society has taken on the responsibility to eliminate the weak and the incurables. Unfortunately, the law is being applied with such a broad brush that many of the innocent are being caught up by it inappropriately."

Emma offered, "It is work best left to the good Lord."

"And the Commonwealth has no business," Guy Frontenac added, "trying to play God, or trying to outsmart God by preventing him from making a mistake."

* * *

"Yes, Mademoiselle Frontenac, you have a very good case, but first you must decide which course of action to take and how to proceed."

He spoke in a soft voice, somewhat throaty and with less timbre than the deep baritone that she remembered from when Maxwell Higbee Lawrence was the Dean of the Commonwealth University School of Law. But each word rang true and echoed exactly the same question that had been nagging at her for the past few weeks. Loretta didn't have a quick and ready answer to this haunting question, so she traveled to visit the now retired dean to solicit his thoughts and guidance.

"Your client has been injured, willfully and wantonly," said the man who was in his mid-seventies. He sat in a wheelchair in the parlor of his apartment. His frail hands cradled a cup of tea from which he periodically took a sip. Loretta noted he wore a suit and tie, complete with a handkerchief in his front coat pocket and a boutonniere on his lapel. She remembered he was always a natty dresser, with a full mane of silver-gray hair that was combed straight back with a flair for the extravagant. But it wasn't for being a clothes horse that he made his reputation. He was a fierce prosecutor for the District Attorney's office in Norwood County and served for nine years as the Commonwealth's Attorney General. He was a jurist whose opinions helped to make case law and whose counsel was universally sought. "How do you wish to proceed with the case?"

Physically Lawrence was a shell of his former self, injured when the railroad car on which he was traveling ran off the tracks five years ago. He survived, but the crash played havoc with his spinal cord and rendered both legs useless. Fortunately his wit remained sharp and nothing could cloud the keen memory that rested behind his bushy eyebrows that bounced and danced when he spoke.

"At the very least, Professor Lawrence, medical malpractice has been committed." Loretta was in heady territory, for the man who was her teacher and proctor for several years was now being approached as a colleague. *Present your issues,* she said to herself, *substantiate your train of thought, don't get tangled in minutiae and move on.* "An incorrect diagnosis was made by someone."

"How did such a misdiagnosis come about?" Lawrence asked in a leading fashion.

"By way of an egregious review of scattered and diverse medical records," Loretta replied. "Prior to the legal disposition by the Commonwealth, no physician examined Alma Summerdale for the express purpose of a court hearing. The diagnosis of epilepsy was made by inference; incorrectly made by inference."

"Granted," he said in his soft voice. "But suppose the diagnosis had been correct."

"The Commonwealth Health Laws are clear that prior to any definitive medical treatment, the defendants in question are due a hearing. At such a hearing their cases are presented by a lawyer for the Commonwealth, defended by their own counsel and heard before a judge."

"Did such a hearing occur?" Lawrence asked.

"I can find no record that such a hearing occurred," Loretta replied. "I have the written disposition of the court and the mandated order to perform the surgical procedure on Commonwealth stationary. But no, I can find no record that a hearing occurred."

"So the Commonwealth has a procedure to address such issues and apparently has not followed its own policy," Lawrence summarized. "How or where did the Commonwealth uncover the family history of epilepsy?"

"From thin air," Loretta answered with a mild hint of disgust. "The mother and father can offer nothing to suggest that anyone in their family suffers from epilepsy or any other nervous disorder. Some other family members may have sugar diabetes, but nothing to suggest epilepsy."

"In the wake of a medical misdiagnosis," Lawrence continued, "and in direct violation of policy and procedure as dictated by the statutes of the Commonwealth, your client underwent a surgical procedure. What can one make of it? Has a crime been committed?"

"Do you mean assault and battery?"

"You have prima facie evidence that will be difficult to ignore or dispel."

"You're talking about criminal charges," Loretta said somewhat tentatively. "You're talking about bringing criminal charges against Simon Kraft, the Secretary for the Department of Health and Welfare, the Health Czar. Do you really believe we could send to prison the most prominent physician in the nation?"

"You do realize," Lawrence said with a faint smile, "that I have brought criminal charges against people in the past." He sipped from his teacup and waved a hand. "I am more concerned with your client's constitutional issues, but that is grist to mill on another day. It is unlikely this case will ever see the light of day. Serious mistakes have been made and this case will serve as a wake-up call to the bureaucrats in office. They simply cannot ride roughshod over the residents of our Commonwealth."

Maxwell Lawrence paused as his wife entered the parlor and refilled their cups of tea. "I am sensitive to the outrage that you feel and the angst that seethes within you concerning your client and her liberties that have been violated. You may not be able to make this right for your client," Lawrence paused as he took in a breath, "but you will be able to make this better for her and others like her who most likely have received similar treatment."

Loretta picked up her head slightly at this last comment. Lawrence narrowed his eyes and offered in a soft and leading voice, "I am certain you suspect she is not the only person who may have been violated."

Loretta nodded. "Yes, I believe there might be more than this one case lurking in the darkest of dark hollows within our Commonwealth. But I can't lose focus. Right now I must do the right thing for my client and avoid the distraction of other issues."

Lawrence nodded in agreement with his former student. "You are absolutely correct, Mademoiselle Frontenac, but I remain concerned there is a much bigger picture for us to examine. There is a force that is growing that threatens the rights of many of our citizens. There is a groundswell of public opinion, a hard and callous opinion, which takes umbrage with the existence of those of us who are less than perfect. It will take courage to stand before this avalanche that is rushing down the mountain at us.

Us. Loretta's eyes brightened at the suggestion that Dean Lawrence was taking more than a passing interest in her case.

"You have always been a remarkable young lady, most likely from the days before you became the only female student at our law school. I have followed your progress and take vicarious delight that you have established yourself worthy of the trust of your clients. More importantly for your client from Oxford Corners," Lawrence continued as he took in a breath, "you should first take civil action by way of a suit and try to recover as much in damages as may benefit this young lady. Rattle a saber ever so softly in the direction of a criminal case. In addition to the individuals' names at the bottom of the documents that you hold in your hand, the Commonwealth is very much at fault. Win your case and then I'll help you take your next step. We have a great deal of work ahead of us."

SEVEN

The whirl of activity in the Capital was dizzying and the pace was frantic. Work schedules soon became overfilled and a scheduled appointment, either given or made, soon became a prized achievement. Bills were discussed, proposals were offered, trade-offs were negotiated, amalgamations were suggested and deals were brokered. Simon was amazed how often a proposed bill to improve sanitation conditions in South Carolina was linked to farming subsidies in Nebraska or logging rights in Montana. "Benjamin Franklin was right," Simon said late one evening to Ed Preller after they finished dinner in a Georgetown restaurant. "Making laws is just as messy as making sausage. No one should have to watch too closely to see how either is made."

Since their arrival in Washington, Simon had worked hard to develop relationships and earn the respect of both the appointed and elected officials, but it was Ed Preller who summarized best the political landscape that stood before them and how best to navigate through it. "We have work to do." Simon looked to him curiously, fairly certain the frenetic 100 hour work weeks for the past six months qualified as 'working hard.'

"If you wish to accomplish what you think this nation needs, we have a great deal of work left for us to do," Ed replied. Drawing out his words for effect in a soft, down home drawl, he continued, "Listen here my friend. As I fathom the situation there are two distinct groups of people in Washington. One group, which I call the 'Ins,' includes the office holders and the people who are hired by the office holders; like you and me. In almost every instance they want to remain in office or continue working for the office holder. Again, like you and me. The other group is those who are out of office and want to get back into the show. The 'Outs.'"

"The true ins and outs of working in the Capital," Simon reiterated with a smile.

"Yes. Quite naturally," Ed continued, "the lobbyists, the power brokers, the men on the selection committees and those with services to offer all look to the roster of those who currently are on the in. They give only a passing glance to those who are not. They have learned over the years that more doors will be opened by the people on the in and greater profits will be made by working with the people on the in. Such is the way of Washington, D.C. and the workings of the U.S. Government.

"You do realize that your appointment was made by a lame duck president; a lame duck president who for all practical purposes has been an absentee president. A reclusive man with a stroke is not a strong and visible leader. The Democratic Party is in shambles. The democratic nominee, whoever he might be, has little chance of winning the November election. When the republicans come back into power, we will be out of office on our collective ears." Ed swallowed the last of his coffee and said, "And all your plans go out the window with you."

Simon nodded in agreement, considering for the first time his political mortality.

"Face it Simon, you do not believe for one second that whoever moves into the White House will keep us around because of the good work we've been doing?"

Simon's eyes narrowed as he looked down into the empty teacup he held in his hands. Ed added, "Take heart, there is a glimmer of hope. Even in the face of such a severely competitive environment, we both have seen that groups which seem to be so naturally pitted against each other will often make alliances that are mutually beneficial."

"Are you suggesting we consider switching party affiliations?" Simon questioned.

"We are democrats by convenience," Ed explained. "We could just as easily be republicans if it were convenient. In order for us to remain working here, you must remain in office. Switching parties is a minor and inconsequential price to pay. Switching parties is the least of our challenges."

"So what are you saying?" Simon asked.

"I'm saying that we need to look around for a new boss. We have to figure a way to align ourselves with the next man who will move into the White House, the man who will be glad to keep you as the Health Czar of the United States.

*   *   *

Simon Kraft looked down on Michigan Avenue as he waited for Harry Daugherty to arrive. The room in the Blackstone Hotel was large enough to have a dining table, on which sat a tray of drinks and sandwiches. The window was cracked open on this 10th day of June and Simon grew increasingly anxious as he paced the floor, glancing from his watch to the door to the window and then back to his watch. Ostensively he was in Chicago to meet with executives at the meat packing facilities and was registered at the Drake Hotel. His registration at the Blackstone Hotel was under a fictitious name, for the Blackstone housed the people who orchestrated the presidential nominating convention for the Republican Party.

The meeting with Daugherty was scheduled for 10 AM, but when the knock sounded on the door, Simon's pocket watch read 10:45. He opened the door and saw two men. The first man wore a vested business suit and looked every bit the professional he was purported to be. He was of average build in his mid-fifties. He extended his right hand and said, "Harry Daugherty, nice to meet you." A second man followed Daugherty into the room. He was larger than Daugherty and also dressed in a business suit, but his mopish appearance was comical. His hair was unkempt and food stains were sprinkled across his shirt and tie. He wore strange looking black frame glasses that comedian Harold Lloyd made popular and sported a brush broom mustache. "My associate, Jesse Smith." Smith nodded and walked directly to the dining table.

"Bourbon good for you, Harry?" Smith asked as he picked at a sandwich.

"Not yet, Jesse; perhaps later," Daugherty replied. "Mister Secretary, what brings you to the fair city of Chicago?"

"I'm visiting with the Armour factory and the Swift factory," Simon answered. "We have no scheduled inspections of the slaughterhouses, mind you. This is just a quick visit to let them know we are thinking of them."

"Nothing official, just as you suggest, off the record," Daugherty said as he waved at the furniture in the room and the food and drink on the table. Kraft nodded. "Just like the meeting we are not having now. Is there something we might be able to do for you, Mr. Secretary?"

Simon had rehearsed this conversation dozens of times with Ed Preller and a dozen more times on the train ride between Washington and Chicago. Each time he started it differently and each time he ended it differently. "Emphasize your agenda," Ed encouraged him as he listened to each version. "Explain how the agenda is so important for the country."

"Mr. Daugherty," Simon began, "as you know, my appointment as Secretary came at a point when there was not much time left in the term of office for . . . for the current administration. Although we have made great strides, there remains a great deal left on our agenda that we need to implement; not only for the benefit of the current administration, but moving forward for the benefit of the nation."

"Sounds noble, Mr. Secretary. What's that mean to me?" Daugherty replied.

"Although the nomination process has proven to be testy, I believe your candidate stands the best chance to secure the nomination. Once past the nomination process, the November election will be a breeze. I want to finish what I have started. I have implemented a number of reforms that have received luke-warm acceptance by the Democratic Party. There are quite a few more changes that have to be made. As we know, as the country knows, the Republican Party is known as the reform party.

"Our programs," Kraft continued, "have benefited the downtrodden. We have implemented changes for a safer workplace environment. Our office is as progressive as any man in your party. Your candidate, following his election, no doubt will continue along these same platform lines."

"So you think my Mr. Harding will get the nomination?" Daugherty questioned rhetorically.

My Mr. Harding. Simon Kraft looked hard into the small eyes of Harry Daugherty and replied, "I do with every fiber of my body."

"I would have thought you a Leonard Wood man," Daugherty replied. "General Wood also was awarded the Medal of Honor, aren't I correct?"

"I have yet to meet with General Wood and certainly have not benefited from his counsel," Simon replied non-committedly.

"Wood still has a large chunk of the delegates, but he can be a condescending son of a bitch. He thinks he invented the army and the army is there to serve him. Okay, you want to keep your job, who doesn't?" Daugherty looked to Jesse Smith and pointed to the liquor bottles. Smith put down the sandwich he was chewing and poured a drink from the bourbon bottle. Daugherty took the drink and swallowed half of it. "So what is it that you have to offer me that will change the mind of the delegates?"

"I have been working hard with the Veteran's Bureau to improve the delivery of medical care for the war veterans. Currently we want the Public Health Service to provide the care. General Wood disagrees and wants the care to be provided only by military physicians. He refuses to accept the fact that the army ranks are being reduced and army posts are to be closed. The Great War is won and is over. The nation is demobilizing and returning to a peace-time status. General Wood agrees with none of the changes that will be implemented and has made several unfortunate statements and created a flock of enemies. The army ranks soon will be thinned and there will not be enough physicians to provide the care. He is fighting the change just for the sport of the fight. If he were to prevail, many of the veterans will go without treatment.

"What is General Wood's beef?" Daugherty asked.

"During the war, General Pershing got the command that General Wood coveted. General Wood was passed over for several postings because he and President Wilson could never agree on anything. If Wilson said white, Wood would say black." Simon handed Daugherty copies of two letters Ed Preller had prepared for him. The letter Simon Kraft had written explained the proposed suggestions. The other was a letter written by Wood, arguing against the change. "It is a politically damning letter, especially coming from a military man. He places his wants and needs ahead of the veteran soldiers who need the medical treatment."

Daugherty read one letter, then the other, and then reread the first letter. "Pompous son of a bitch." He folded the letters and placed them in the left inside pocket of his coat. From his right inside coat pocket he removed a cigar. He took a seat at the table, struck a match and lit the cigar. Blue smoke circled above his head. As if acting on cue, Jesse Smith lit a cigar of his own. Within a minute the room was filled with cigar smoke.

"This," Daugherty said as he patted his coat where the letters rested, "is not a knock-out punch, but it will help start a new conversation. I'll have to sweeten his deal with a plum assignment comparable to his governorship of Cuba, but I am certain we will be able to agree upon something. Preferably an assignment far away.

"Mr. Secretary," Daugherty continued, "I would suggest that you keep doing your job and we will continue to do ours. At the appropriate time Mr. Smith will call upon you. Assuming you are correct, and my Mr. Harding prevails with the nomination of his party and the general election in November, we will have another conversation. At that time we will enter into various agreements. As you well understand, the men who will make up the new cabinet will serve at the pleasure of The President."

Smith refilled the glasses and poured one for Simon as the three men toasted one another. "To a better America. To a prosperous America."

EIGHT

"We *must* award grants for research," Simon Kraft implored as he stood behind the podium on the floor of Congress. There was only a scattering of men in the room who sat at their desks and most of the seats were occupied by aides or someone other than state representatives. "We *must* make appropriations for scientific investigative studies to produce medical breakthroughs. The U.S. Government *must* take on the responsibility to provide the means and the incentives for bold men to experiment, to create and to invent. Advancements made by Americans will make America a healthier nation and demonstrate to the world who rightly deserves to be known as the greatest of all nations on the globe. Advancements made by Americans will make the world a better place, a safer place to live and to travel."

The awarding of grant money for institutional and individual research was a new concept for the congressmen to accept. Heretofore most of the money that had been doled out by the Department of Health and Welfare was given by way of matching funds. At the urging of Simon Kraft, states created projects like the opening of maternity centers for the indigent, smallpox vaccination centers for the general public and food centers for the downtrodden. The projects were meant to benefit large segments of the states' populations who otherwise could not afford the services or who could not gain access to the services.

Once the project plans, including the budgets, were submitted to the Department, Simon Kraft worked his magic with Congress and found money that would be applied to the projects. Although it was not always a dollar-for-dollar matching, the money given to the states for large projects was thousands of dollars. It was a winning proposition for all involved. The matching-funds system was well trumpeted to the general public and demonstrated the beneficence of the federal government. The projects brought money into the states and created jobs. The elected officials who petitioned for the projects looked like heroes to their constituencies. The system also provided Simon with the opportunity to disperse the pork and develop a cadre of elected politicians with a sense of obligation and fealty. Ed Preller jibed at Simon that "*Fealty* in Washington, D.C. is quite the oxymoron, with congressmen and senators no more loyal than a pack of wolves or a school of sharks."

Simon replied, "Right you are Ted my boy, but wolves and sharks need to eat in order to maintain their jobs and return to Washington every year in order to serve their constituents. They also serve a purpose by giving us what we need. We'll keep shoveling out the pork and make sure the boys have a place at the feeding trough. Political favors are the coin of the realm, and the coins must continue to flow to allow the political system to operate. Matching funds allow us to transform favors into obligations."

But now it was Simon Kraft who was the obligated party. During the days following the November election, Simon received his favor. He was retained as the Secretary of the Department. The notification was unceremoniously delivered in person by Harry Daugherty's flunky, Jesse Smith. The message was clear, unambiguous and there was a price attached to it. "You serve at the pleasure of the President. Take note, Dr. Kraft: what pleases Harry Daugherty pleases Warren G. Harding."

As Smith explained matters ever so clearly, Simon Kraft would continue as Departmental Secretary only as long as he continued to provide hard cash to various slush funds that Daugherty established. Simon now faced an intriguing conundrum: he wanted to remain in office, but he was at a loss as to how he would meet Harry Daugherty's cash demands. He did not have sufficient personal wealth to pass money into the greasy fingers of Jesse Smith. He was not an elected politician and could not produce handfuls of money by dipping into a huge war chest made up of political contributions. He could never run to Senator William H. Cheltenham for a handout that would be used for graft and bribery. How would that paper trail smack of impropriety?

Simon met with the President-elect and there was nothing about the man he liked. As far as politicians were concerned, he lacked the gentility and grace of President Wilson and the warmth and sincerity of Uncle Billy. Harding exuded the aura of "What have you done for me lately and what can you do for me tomorrow?" For Simon's purposes, Harding was a means to an end, a necessary evil that would be tolerated in order for Simon to accomplish his mission. One immutable fact remained; Harding was his boss. To serve at the pleasure of his boss meant that Simon needed to please Harry Daugherty. Simon was forced to accept the reality that there was a price attached to his appointment and it was a bitter pill to swallow. Such was the way of Washington. The *modus operandi* for the current administration was clearly understood; only the jingling of coins would satisfy the obligation to Daugherty and feed the machine that the boys from Ohio had created. Now that the season of the inaugurations and oath swearing had passed, the bill was due and payable to the Republicans in power.

Simon and Ed took all this into consideration. Their solution to the problem was to create a process whereby money would leave the coffers of the U.S. Government and move to the institutions and individuals who performed research and medical investigations. As the money flowed along its path, bits and pieces would drain off for various 'ancillary' services. Such a system would allow them to siphon off enough cash to satisfy obligations thrust upon them by Harry Daugherty and remain employed by the Department of Health and Welfare.

Research grants were different from matching funds or outright appropriations for public service projects. Each grant application was submitted on a singular basis and the merit of each study was evaluated on an individual basis. The approval or denial of each application was made on a confidential basis and the final word on who might receive the grants was made solely by the Secretary of the Department of Health and Welfare. Most importantly, the budget for each grant application would be subject to 'adjustments.' Such adjustments would include funds dedicated for 'ancillary' services.

"Smith may not be the sharpest knife in the kitchen," Simon explained to Ed Preller, "but he and Daugherty are not men to be trifled with. With that in mind, here's how we'll work the deal. Each application for a grant requires a suggested budget by the research team. We write into each budget an expense for a tangible necessity. 'Consulting services' would raise a red flag. I'm thinking of routine services that every project will need: stationery, glassware for the laboratories and new typewriters and desks for their offices. Each grant will be awarded with the caveat that such 'discount' services are required to be performed by a 'government approved company' for a sense of," and Simon smiled as he thought back to the words spoken so often by Uncle Billy. "A sense of propriety. We'll establish a paper trail and for appearance purposes, everything will look fine."

"I presume the discounted services will be anything but discounted," Ed surmised.

"Exactly," Simon replied. "Excelsior Business and Research Services, for want of a better name. The company must be thoroughly detached from us but under the watchful eye of one Jesse Smith. You must never meet with or be in contact with Jesse Smith. The process will be blind to both you and him." Ed nodded his agreement. "Unfortunately I must come in contact with that lizard, but will do so infrequently as possible. The services *will* be provided, so all will pass scrutiny, but at an exorbitant profit margin. Remember, the system for awarding the grants is not immune to congressional oversight. Any suggestion of an indiscretion will not be tolerated, but there is sufficient fluff in the files to withstand budgetary manipulation and oversight review. At a base level, this is government money that will be channeled back into the current administration so the government will continue to run smoothly."

"A bit counter intuitive and self-serving if I might say," Ed offered.

Simon Kraft smirked and agreed. "You have work to do, Ted my boy. Set up the company and distance us as far away from it as possible. With that keen business mind of yours, I expect only the very best. I'll rework the budgets for the research teams and start to announce the awards. I plan on staying in Washington for a long time and this is a good start to work along with the Harding people."

*   *   *

"How does this sound for our releases for the public relations department? 'Medical research will be the foundation for medical discoveries that will bear fruit in the form of medical breakthroughs and improved health for mankind.'"

"That is quite a mouthful, Dr. Kraft," Ed Preller said with a wry smile.

"'Tis the dawn of a new age for the Department of Health and Welfare. You should feel humbled to be a part of its genesis, Ted my boy," Simon responded, allowing a touch of theatrical license to create a magnanimous perspective. A smile slowly came to his face as he agreed with his friend. "Yes Ed, the caption sounds quite lofty, doesn't it, but if we find a cure for something more serious than a hangnail or sleepwalking, we'll be doing something good. Don't forget, by awarding grants we keep the money flowing to Daugherty and his friends."

The two men sat in Simon's office in the McMurray Building on K Street, which was not unlike the office he inhabited when he worked for the Commonwealth. A large desk was positioned in the center of the room with only writing tools set off to the right. A side table stood against the wall and was piled high with stacks of books, files, records and reports. Two winged-back chairs were positioned in front of the desk for those fortunate to gain an audience with the Secretary.

"Ten men will interview with us this afternoon," Ed said. "These are the finalists and they get fifteen minutes each. I'm not the expert, but I think we'll identify a few who should prove worthy."

"Are their budgets sufficiently flexible and subject to alterations?" Kraft asked.

Ed Preller nodded in the affirmative and then ushered Professor Zondek into the office. Zondek was from the University in Cincinnati.

"Our research will focus on perfecting tests to confirm or deny early pregnancy in women. Currently testing is performed utilizing mice in the laboratory," he said for the benefit of Ed Preller. The man was in his mid-forties and spoke in a quick, machine-gun manner. "Currently a sample of the woman's urine is injected into an immature female mouse. After five days the mouse is sacrificed and her ovaries are examined. When ovulation in the mouse is detected, the woman's pregnancy is confirmed. Our project will follow similar techniques with rabbits. Some refinements will be necessary but we believe that accuracy will be much improved, as well as shortening the incubation period to 48 hours."

"If successful," Simon offered, "your 'Rabbit Tests' will be repeated thousands of times each day."

"We can only hope so," Henley replied.

The wheels in Simon's head started to whirl. *Laboratories crammed with beakers and glassware, rooms well stocked with the finest and newest equipment—all supplied by Excelsior Research. A pleasant sight*, Simon mused. "When copyrights and patents emerge, you will be open to share the wealth, the, the acclaim with those who support you?"

Again the man smiled as he nodded and replied, "Absolutely."

Hah, thought Simon Kraft, *like asking a drowning man whether he would thank a sailor in a life boat for a life preserver.'*

"You will be made aware of our decision within the month," Ed Preller offered.

After the man left Simon pondered, "I believe a private investment may be more appropriate than government funds. A small fortune can be made in the private sector with this project and it would be a shame to miss out on such an opportunity. If only we weren't so cash poor, Ted my boy. I am reminded of the New York City health commissioner, Dr. Lederle. He found some early success with diphtheria antitoxin, left the employ of the city for Long Island and started his own laboratory."

"If we were to provide grant money for Zondek's research," Ed proposed, "Uncle Sam's name would be included on the patent and our department would receive the royalties."

"And we would receive the recognition. Always thinking Mr. Preller, always thinking."

The next interviewee introduced himself as Dr. John Charles. "I was a surgeon in the last war. I now work for the Public Health Service and am stationed on Staten Island."

"But your application notes that the research will be performed in Guatemala?" Ed replied.

"The Pan American Sanitation Bureau is as committed to the eradication of venereal disease as we are in this country," Charles said. "Joint funding from various groups will be necessary because the scope of the project may prove to be so large."

"Please explain," said Simon.

"The test subjects will be prisoners in the penitentiaries and patients in mental health facilities. We will have absolute control of the study because, essentially, we have a confined population that is restricted, and . . . well controlled."

"You suggest as many as two thousand subjects may be necessary."

"If the project proves successful in the early stages, two thousand may not be necessary," Charles replied. "But yes, it is a study that needs to be done on a wide scale."

"As per your application, Dr. Charles, you wish to prevent venereal disease." Simon looked up from reading his file and stared at John Charles. "Quite noble. Please explain."

"Almost always a man and a woman approach the sex act willfully and with forethought. All too often such forethought does not consider the possibility of contracting venereal disease. This was very much the case during the war when nearly 18,000 American soldiers were reporting for venereal disease treatment *daily.* It was a rate much higher than our French and British allies because their soldiers had been warned appropriately, and with greater frequency they took necessary precautions. Our doughboys were too naïve and the American general staff officers thought our boys would never do anything naughty enough to contract VD."

Simon and Ed smiled as they looked to each other, recalling the many conversations they had concerning this very same issue.

"Vaccines, as you know, are not very successful," Charles continued. "Antitoxins given after the fact are questionable. Arsphenamine and Neoarspenamine work well enough for syphilis once the subject contracts the disease. Our goal will be to try to prevent the disease from taking root. Instead of providing condoms to the men, various compounds and medications will be used. The medicinal compounds will be applied topically, by rubbing them into the affected parts. Several different compounds will be investigated."

"Affected parts?" Ed queried.

"Yes," Dr. Charles replied, "the genitalia. The genitalia are to be prepared prior to sexual relations."

"Excuse me; we *are* discussing incarcerated individuals in prisons and confined patients in hospitals, are we not?" Simon challenged.

"Individuals cut off from the public; cut off from the brothels and the streets."

"Guatemala allows for prostitutes to visit the inmates in prisons," Dr. Charles replied. "We will identify prostitutes with infections and encourage their 'enterprise' with as many different inmates as possible."

"What of the patients in the mental health facilities?" Simon asked.

"We will introduce the virulent organisms to them directly, either through injections or by abrading the skin and creating a skin affliction."

"For both gonorrhea and syphilis?" Simon asked.

"Yes."

"Which medicinal compounds will be tested?" Simon continued.

"For gonorrhea we will use mercurochrome. For syphilis we will use a cream made from both Arsphenamine and Neo-arsphenamine. We will also experiment with other mercury and arsenic compounds."

"Please tell me you will not use government funds to procure and reimburse the prostitutes," Ed pleaded.

"No sir. Such funds for those services will come from other sources."

"Thank you, Dr. Charles. You will be made aware of our decision within the month," Ed Preller offered. When the man left the room, Ed said to Simon, "Should we open a bordello in Guatemala and scoop the competition?"

Dr. Oliver Clark, another physician in the Public Health Service, discussed with them a project to "observe and monitor the untoward effects of untreated syphilis."

"Where are you stationed, Dr. Clark?"

"In Macon County, Alabama. We believe the disease affects the white race differently from the colored races. We believe the white race is more susceptible to neurological sequelae and the colored races are more prone to cardiovascular diseases. We will follow the natural progression of the disease. Macon County is rural; most of the people tend to be born, live and die in the same county."

"I assume your research will involve only colored subjects."

"Yes, Mr. Secretary."

"Do you have any plans to investigate the effects of the disease in white subjects?"

"Not at the present time, no."

"Review again for me how you will enroll the subjects," Ed asked.

"First we will affiliate with Tuskegee Institute. It's a local college for colored students in the area. Many of the people down there are sharecroppers or descended from sharecroppers' families. They have had 'bad blood' for years. Bad blood includes everything from anemia to high blood pressure to advanced syphilis. We'll guarantee them free treatment, free meals and free burial insurance. Before they're buried we'll perform autopsies to examine the extent of their disease."

"You say you will offer them treatment," Ed countered, "but if you plan to study the extent of the untreated disease, what form of treatment will you offer them?"

"Aspirin," Clark replied.

"What if the subjects go elsewhere for treatment?" Simon asked.

"A list of the names of the subjects in the study will be sent to all the local hospitals and physicians' offices, asking them not only to decline treating the subjects specific to syphilis, but to return them to our offices for continued study." Dr. Clark explained, "This will be a long-term study, over the course of several decades I hope. The results of the study will allow us to know what adverse effects are most likely to evolve on a racial basis. Consequently we will be able to treat the patients accordingly."

"But the patients will continue to believe they are receiving treatment, when in fact they will receive no treatment?" Ed asked for clarification.

"Placebo therapy is always one component of research, Mr. Preller," Dr. Clark replied. "Besides, the subject population is somewhat expendable." Neither Simon Kraft nor Ed Preller refuted the statement.

The procession of interviewees continued. Two surgeons, one from central New Jersey and one from West Virginia, suggested novel treatments for tuberculosis. Currently they offered the confined patients a chance to rest and recuperate at their facilities. It was believed that both the pine forests in central New Jersey and the sulphur springs in the West Virginia region were therapeutic. To further rest the diseased lungs, they suggested a study whereby the patients' affected lungs would be surgically collapsed and benefit from complete rest. The objective of the study was to determine the added effect of the surgical procedure to the aroma therapy of the pine sap and the sulphur vapors.

One applicant suggested experimental studies on animals that would simulate battlefield trauma. The consensus from the War Department was the surgeons who were called to duty during the last war were not well prepared for the grisly array of injuries encountered. Similarly, another applicant suggested similar studies to simulate automobile injures. With the growing popularity of the automobile, increased numbers of accidents and injuries were soon to follow. Simon Kraft thought such studies might be better placed within the purview of the War Department or the Department of Transportation.

"Mr. Secretary," Ed said as he ushered in a man with a full beard and a shock of unruly hair on his head, "this is Professor Korpinski from the Rockefeller Institute for Medical Research in New York."

Simon rose and extended his hand to Korpinski. "A pleasure Professor. I am familiar with your research on infantile paralysis and the work of the Institute."

"As I am an admirer of yours," Korpinski replied with the faint trace of an eastern European accent. He was approximately the same age as Simon Kraft and wore wire rimmed glasses with thick lenses that magnified the size of his eyes.

"How and why does the Rockefeller Institute want our money?" Simon asked.

"As we continue the great work of Dr. Fletcher and his staff, we may be six months away from testing our vaccine on patients, on children."

"Samuel Fletcher," Simon explained to Ed, "was able to transfer the polio virus from human patients to monkeys and monitor the progression of the disease."

"Because the polio virus is able to remain viable in monkeys, without killing the monkeys," Korpinski continued, "we have a ready source of the infecting agent that has allowed us to develop an early stage of a vaccination."

"Tell me of the plans for testing," Simon said.

"We will inactivate the virus, develop our vaccine and inject it into twenty to forty children," Korpinski explained. "We will then infect the children with the live polio virus. We will follow their clinical course and monitor the levels of antibodies that the patients produce."

Kraft nodded his understanding. Ed asked, "Where will you get your patient volunteers?"

"There are several institutions in New York City," Korpinski answered, "for children with epilepsy and intellectual deficiencies. There would be no shortage of test subjects."

"The Rockefeller Institute is a private, philanthropic center for research, funded by the profits of Mr. Rockefeller's oil fields," Ed said. "I'll repeat Dr. Kraft's question. Why does your center wish for assistance from the U. S. Department of Health and Welfare?"

"The Rockefeller Institute relies heavily upon the philanthropy of individuals *other than* Mr. Rockefeller," Korpinski answered. "In some instances we receive donations despite Mr. Rockefeller's association."

"So the approval of one or more of your research studies by the Department of Health is worth its weight in gold," Simon surmised.

"In a manner of speaking," Korpinski replied.

"Your project is most interesting," Simon explained, "and we'll be sure to get back to you within the next few weeks."

By mid-afternoon both Ed and Simon were worn down by the parade of men who offered solutions for the ailments of the world. "A fresh cup of tea, please," Simon begged of his secretary as they prepared to meet with the last interviewee of the day. His project perked Simon Kraft's attention like no pot of tea he ever sampled before.

"Artificial insemination of humans."

"Go on, Professor Van Kirk," Simon ordered.

"More than 30% of the married couples in America are barren," he replied.

Barren, Simon repeated in his mind. Such a harsh term; so cold, so desolate, so final.

"Quite possibly 30% of the worlds' married couples are barren also, so the number of people who might benefit from our research may prove to be . . . well, quite high."

Professor Ronald Van Kirk was older than Simon, with thinning gray hair and a no-nonsense manner to his appearance. Even at this late hour, after hours of waiting, he was clear-eyed and confident in his presentation. He sported a thin mustache above his upper lip and a neatly trimmed V-shaped beard that was common to the upper classes in Europe.

"I'm familiar with some of the work that has been carried out on farm animals," Simon suggested.

"Yes." Van Kirk replied. "Nearly every domestic animal proves amenable to the procedure. Rabbits, dogs, horses, even cattle. Of greatest significance, the procedure has been reported to have been performed in a married woman."

"You're kidding?" Ed said disbelievingly.

"It was performed in Philadelphia many years ago and only recently reported in the medical literature," Van Kirk explained in an even tone as he kept his hands folded on his lap. "A married couple for many years was unable to conceive. They consulted with Dr. Pancoast. Semen was collected from a medical student and introduced into the woman's uterus. She successfully became pregnant and gave birth to a healthy child."

"Do not tell me you were the student of Dr. Pancoast and the father of the child," Ed ordered.

"I was a student of Dr. Pancoast," Van Kirk replied matter of factly, "but not the donor of the semen."

"How difficult, how hard, what type of results have you experienced?" Simon peppered the man with questions.

"Not very difficult and reasonably successful with larger animals," Van Kirk answered. "I have worked for many years in Europe where the procedure was not uncommon before the war. Semen is collected, cooled and stored. When a fertile cow or mare reaches her most receptive time in her menstrual cycle, the semen is injected into her uterus. Depending on the animal species, success approaches 80%."

"Eighty percent," Ed said with widened eyes. "That is one impressive batting average."

"The results are even better with dogs and rabbits," Van Kirk replied. "Even on the most successful cattle ranches, it is rare that 65 to 75% of the cows will calve naturally. Artificial insemination allows for nearly 100% of the cows to produce calves."

"So, if I hear you correctly," Ed said, "the bull and the stallion are all but obsolete?"

"Not at all," Simon answered the question. "As semen donors they are without replacement. It is their stud services that may no longer be mandatory. Professor, using the techniques that have been developed and perfected for animals, I assume you will duplicate the technique for men and women." Again Van Kirk smiled as he nodded.

"There are certain caveats," Van Kirk explained. "The male donors must have viable sperm. The woman must be fertile and without anatomical defects of her reproductive organs."

That excludes Mrs. Simon Kraft, Simon mused. He paused as he folded his hands, intermittently making a steeple with his index fingers and tapping the tips of his thumbs together. "Who will be your donors?"

"There is no shortage of intelligent, healthy young men in our region, especially college students," Van Kirk said with a smile. "They will be screened for any medical problems and deformities. The young men chosen will be the type of young men any woman would be proud to bring home to meet her parents."

"I assume you will reimburse the young men . . ." Ed searched for the proper phrase, "for their services?"

"Reimbursement will be nominal," Van Kirk replied, "but to a struggling college student, it's easy money."

"Where will the test subjects, the women, come from?" Ed continued.

"We will send letters to the physicians within 100 miles of our laboratory," Van Kirk replied, "explaining our research. Every busy physician has a number of women in his practice who might benefit from our services. Test subjects will not be a problem."

"Professor Van Kirk," Simon offered as he rolled a pencil in his hands, "I assume that if a stallion were to win the Derby, he . . . or rather his semen, would be in great demand."

"And if you perfect your storage techniques," Ed added, "he could remain popular and significant for years after his death."

Van Kirk's eyes narrowed and a grandfatherly smile crossed his face. "The same is true for the bull that wins the State Fair's blue ribbon."

"Thank you Dr. Van Kirk. We will get back to you shortly." Ed escorted the professor from the room as Simon sipped at his tea and stared out the window of the now dark city.

"His work goes beyond helping childless families," Simon said, unable to clear the image of Dorothy from his mind. "His research could be put to use in many other ways. Much of the work we have been doing, both here and back at the Commonwealth, has been to eliminate and delete bad character traits and unmanageable conditions. What Professor Van Kirk offers is a way to accentuate the positive attributes of our society, to produce a better race of men and women if we were to take his technique to its philosophical end point."

"Be cautious that we continue to speak of Dr. Van Kirk and not Dr. Frankenstein," Ed offered."

"Do you think Congress would question financing a human stud farm," Simon countered. "Perhaps if only republicans were allowed to be bred . . ."

NINE

"Mr. Pratt, please," Simon Kraft said into the mouthpiece of the telephone and waited for the receptionist to transfer his call.

Although no more than twenty seconds passed, Simon seethed at the delay that seemed interminable. Anxiously he tapped his pencil onto a pad of paper, gouging and scratching the pad the longer he waited. A voice came onto the line. "Nedley Pratt."

"Mr. Pratt, this is Dr. Kraft," he said with the mock air of strained formality. "I suspect your morning has had a better start than mine."

"Good morning Simon," Pratt replied in his ultra-smooth voice that so annoyed non-lawyers. "It sounds like another wonderful day in the nation's capital

"Like hell. I had papers served on me this morning. I have been named in a law suit."

"How, why?" Pratt sputtered. "In reference to what?"

"It was a surgical case from before I went into the army," Kraft replied with a bitter edge to his voice. "The Commonwealth is being sued, I'm being sued and so are you. Don't you people read your mail or are process servers so common in your office, you give them free lunch and beer." Simon banged the pencil hard onto the pad of paper and broke the point.

"Slow down, Simon. I'll check with the people in the front."

"Is that office of yours so big . . . ?" Kraft seethed. "You better get your head and your ass wired together."

"Hold on," Pratt spouted into the mouthpiece as he called out, "Shirley, Shirley, come here please." Simon heard him mumble something to someone. As another thirty seconds elapsed Pratt said. "My people are checking it out now."

"Your people are who got me into this jam," Kraft said in his most accusing manner.

"Wait a minute, Simon, wait a minute," Pratt begged as he tried to smooth the ruffled manner of his long-time friend and provide a delaying tactic as the office staff frantically combed the baskets and files on their desks to find the notification. "Okay, Simon, I have the papers now. Give me a moment."

More waiting continued to broil Kraft's disposition. "Let me tell *you* what I read in this thirty seven page treatise on legal incompetence," Kraft snarled, "perpetrated by your people and the incompetent nitwits who work for the Commonwealth. This Summerdale girl had her constitutional rights trampled, was denied due process to a court hearing, had her medical condition misdiagnosed—all as a preliminary for me to attack her and bludgeon her and render her sterile. There may be some additional high crimes and misdemeanors that I overlooked, but I am certain your hotshot legal eagles will be able highlight them for me."

"Hold on, Simon, allow me to review this," Pratt parried. "There's no reason to panic and there's no reason to jump out of any windows. We'll look into this and handle it accordingly."

"*Accordingly* my ass," Kraft answered sourly.

"I've never heard of this Frontenac person," Pratt said. "She probably has an office in the back of some general store next to the hayseed bags and the outdoor privy."

"I'll tell you what she has; she has the Commonwealth by the balls."

"We have forty-seven lawyers here on staff. We'll come at her with everything we've got and blow her and this puny case out of the water," Pratt said.

"You're insane."

"Aside from any validity of the accusations or . . ." Pratt rattled on as he tried to derail Simon's fury.

"I'm going to say it more slowly and clearly. Mistakes were made. The big, bad state beat up on a 16 year old girl. Do you know who loves David and Goliath stories more than the newspapers? Nobody."

Simon's thoughts raced to the image of banner headlines, pillorying him for the entire nation to see.

HEALTH CZAR SLASHES LITTLE GIRL
KRAFT THE RIPPER
KRAFT'S SLAUGHTER OF THE INNOCENTS

Simon was embarrassed and concerned. His name would be front and center before the public. His name would be the only one people would recognize and remember. His name would be the only one sullied by this issue, regardless of the final legal disposition of the matter. Was there a concern for his job? What of his future? All the hard work, all the long hours, all the deals, all the compromises, all the maneuvering and all the . . .

There were other issues simmering beneath the surface that gnawed at Simon. Was this lawsuit a threat to the Health Laws? How would this lawsuit affect the status and reputation of the Health Laws? How would this lawsuit reflect on his goal to have the Health Laws accepted as an amendment to the constitution? The laws were sound and based on pure science and common sense. The greatest minds of the enlightened men in the country all agreed with him. Such laws were necessary for the future of the country. But now, with this mess of a lawsuit, would the common man look upon the laws in a different light?

There was no doubt in the mind of Simon Kraft, M.D. that the Health Laws were what America needed. What Simon did not need was a horseshit lawsuit filed by a bumpkin lawyer from some bump-in-the-road town to throw a wrench into his plans and his future. Everything had been moving ahead so smoothly. He had become a man whom people sought for guidance and counsel. He had become a man whose opinions mattered. He had become an integral component of the administration of two of the nation's Presidents. By God, if this lawsuit moved forward, America was in as much trouble as he. What America needed was for this lawsuit to disappear.

To Simon's wary eye, a blister had formed and was making itself into a nuisance. The blister's name was Loretta Frontenac. What he could not allow was for this blister to fester and become putrid and progress to gangrene. The idea that a country mouse could emerge to tweak the nose of the state and nip at the future of the entire nation could not be tolerated.

"Let me tell you what you're going to do," Kraft said in a manner that left little room for quibbling or retort. "You are going to bury this case so deep, it will never see the light of day. You are going to make this case go away. You are going to meet with this Frontenac person, sign whatever papers are necessary, agree to what she has to say and settle the issue. More importantly nothing, repeat nothing, will be shared with the newspapers or the public. This case must be settled and the judgment must be sealed."

Pratt listened silently and heard the tone and the emotion and the force and the fury. "I think I appreciate your position and what you're thinking."

"You have no idea what I'm thinking, other than to make this case go away," Simon replied. "By the way, you and your people should take a second look to see what might be hiding in the woodshed. Where there's one mistake, a second may be lurking."

*   *   *

Loretta Frontenac had no doubt there were problems in the Commonwealth's woodshed. Buoyed by her first case against the Commonwealth, she was determined to pry at the door of the woodshed as if it were the Commonwealth's Pandora Box. But first she needed to address the case at hand.

Summerdale vs. the Commonwealth, Nedley Pratt, Simon Kraft, et. al., never went farther than the conference room. The defendants' only plausible argument referred to the expiration of the statute of limitation. They argued that because the surgery was performed in 1916 and the lawsuit was filed 1920, the 2 year time limit expired in 1918. Loretta countered that the statute applied to the date when damages were identified or recognized, and subsequently when the suit could be filed. She explained before the judge that neither Alma Summerdale nor her parents could read and none of them understood the purpose or nature of the operation. Their clock functionally started ticking the day Miss Clary read to them the Norwood County Hospital record in 1919. Much to the chagrin of Nedley Pratt, she prevailed and the suit was allowed to proceed.

The jousting, parrying and positioning dragged on for months. Very little in the way of legal issues or constitutional improprieties were discussed. Most of the action was no more than the huffing and puffing of the Commonwealth's legal team. Nedley Pratt tap danced as best he could, more for the sake of appearances and to suggest that the state would not relinquish a king's ransom for some country girl's miseries. Loretta Frontenac held firm as she weathered one team of lawyers after another. Strengthened and fortified by Maxwell Lawrence's words of encouragement, she stood taller after each meeting. As her confidence grew during the latter stages of discussions, she looked forward to standing toe to toe with them; staring into their eyes and brushing aside their feeble attempts to intimidate her. Loretta Frontenac held their collective feet to the fire and secured one of the largest settlement awards ever given to an individual in a negligence lawsuit. Much to Nedley Pratt's chagrin, they did pay a king's ransom to the country girl from Oxford Corners for the state's blundering and the lawyers' indiscretions and Dr. Kraft's surgical misadventure.

As Loretta sat alone in the conference room, after the last of Pratt's staff left her behind, she stared at the slip of paper she held in her hand. The writing on the check blurred as tears welled in her eyes. Her heart was sorely vexed with mixed emotions. She had brought the Commonwealth to its knees and had bested the largest and most indomitable law firm in the county. She had watched herself grow from a simple country lawyer to a more mature and secure attorney without fear of failure or intimidation. She had followed her gut feelings about a case and through hard work she had won. But then there was Alma Summerdale. Alma would always remain precluded from having children and the state of her barrenness would unfairly haunt her as she entertained future suitors. The scar that she bore on her belly was deep and painful and permanent. Any recompense she might receive for all that was taken away from her was bittersweet. Fortunately, because of Loretta's best efforts, there was recompense.

The bank check for $87,000 was an unimaginable amount of money. The $29,000 Loretta would take as her fee was more than she had earned in the last three years. The $58,000 Alma Summerdale and her family would receive was more than they would earn in several lifetimes. To the Commonwealth, $87,000 was just the correct amount of money to make an annoying blister disappear.

The terms of the settlement were extensive, very clear and Loretta suffered a mild pang of remorse as she agreed to them. The Commonwealth would admit to no wrongdoing, nor would any of the other named defendants. All documents would be sealed and secreted away into the cryptic vault of the Commonwealth's archives, never to be seen or heard from again. Loretta and her clients would be forced to sign non-disclosure statements in order to settle the case. The restrictions agreed to in the non-disclosure statements were severe.

"You must never," Loretta said in a tone of voice she remembered her father using when she was a little girl, "all three of you must never discuss the issues of the case with anyone. Not with your brothers or sisters or with your cousins in West Virginia or Arkansas. Not with Aunt Clary in her general store and not with your ex-boyfriend, Wilfred Algon. You must not, you will not discuss any details surrounding this case with anyone.

"By taking the money from the Commonwealth, you," Loretta paused as she pondered the wording of the documents. *You aver, you avow*; what do words such as these mean to people who can barely read and write their own names?

"By taking the money from the Commonwealth, you admit that you understand what the non-disclosure statement means. You are telling the people who gave you this money that you will agree to abide by . . ." No, she shook her head. *Abide.* "You will agree to follow the order of the statement that says you will discuss the matter with no one but me, your lawyer." All three nodded their heads in agreement.

"If any of you violate this agreement, if any of you decide to talk with friends or strangers or someone who comes knocking on your door and says he works for the newspaper, you are in violation of the agreement. If you do so, and word gets back to the state, you will be in very, very big trouble. Any money from the settlement that remains will be taken from you." All three once again nodded.

"You will face serious fines. The fines will be so high, the state will seize your home and your farm and sell them at auction. Yes," she reassured them, "you will be thrown out into the street. You will be taken to court, face a trial and in all likelihood be sentenced to spend no less than ten years in prison." Once again the Summerdale's nodded their heads that they understood. Alma Summerdale was not the Commonwealth's finest hour and the Commonwealth was serious about limiting to a bare minimum the number of people who knew or were aware of the issues.

To Loretta, $58,000 was a great deal of money. For the Summerdale's, $58,000 was an unfathomable amount of money that somehow had to remain a secret known only to the Summerdale's. In their home town on the outskirts of Oxford Corners, with a population something less than 397 souls, any new pattern of spending or extravagant purchases by the Summerdale's would raise eyebrows and start tongues to wagging. Loretta had no confidence these God-fearing people could resist being helpful neighbors who would readily come to the aid of someone in the town who faced a financial crisis. She also was certain they would never be able to weather the requests of downtrodden family members from near and far who would note that the Summerdale's, through good times and bad, continued to live 'comfortably.' Temptations, with or without good intentions, would soon overwhelm these simple people, so Loretta took the necessary steps to protect them from themselves. She established a trust fund, named the three of them as beneficiaries and herself as the executor. Loretta would place them on an allowance sufficient to cover immediate and day to day needs, but below a level that otherwise would be seen as ostentatious to the 397 citizens who lived in Oxford Corners. Exceptions could be made, but they would be subtle, few and far between.

During the course of deliberating the Summerdale case, Loretta continued to explore the possibility that other citizens of Norwood County had been similarly wronged by the actions of the Commonwealth. Loretta encountered one roadblock after another. The task of obtaining records from the hospital of those patients who underwent surgical procedures as mandated by the Commonwealth was no easy matter. The hospital denied all requests pending written permission from the patients or their representatives. Unfortunately Loretta had no idea who the patients were. The courthouse did not keep separate records clearly identifying those individuals who were the subjects of such hearings, nor did they keep separate records for those who had such judgments rendered against them.

"It is difficult going on a fishing expedition when one is unfamiliar with the stream or the lake where one will be fishing," Maxwell Lawrence offered Loretta as a feeble attempt to improve her spirits. "I have a thought."

"Please," Loretta pleaded, "I am chasing too many dead ends and I feel as though I am stumbling in the dark. Anything is better than banging my head against the wall."

"Think like a law clerk and not like a lawyer," Lawrence offered. "One solution to our conundrum is to pore through the daily logs at the Norwood County Courthouse for age appropriate females. In most instances their cases will be public record. Request their hearing and trial files so the cases may be reviewed."

Loretta thought for a moment and agreed. "You are correct. It is tedious work and time consuming. Unfortunately I may not have sufficient time to invest in this project."

"And I am not up to the task either," Lawrence added, "but I have a suggestion. Phoebe Belden."

TEN

The invitation was decidedly understated, merely some printed words on a white stock card. Dorothy paid it little heed as she nonchalantly opened the envelope, glanced at the writing and tossed the invitation onto the pile of letters that arrived in the afternoon mail. After their evening dinner, as Simon lingered at the table finishing the last few ounces of wine from his glass, he sifted through the mail and noted the invitation.

You are cordially invited as a guest to the reception of
The Friends of the American Eugenics Society
Friday, March 31, 1922 8:00 PM
The Waldorf Astoria
301 Park Avenue
New York, New York

He was well aware of the Society and the names of many of its members. Most were men from the business world, successful men from the business world. They were not like the herd of back-slapping lobbyists and glad-handing shysters who worked in and around the Capital and fancied themselves 'connected to the right people.' More than a few of the people who were in the Eugenics Society *were* 'the right people;' the class and breed of elite individuals whom politicians approached when they sought favors. Simon also knew many of these men to hold strong opinions. Simon smiled as he considered the mix of strong opinions, money and political connections. All too often such a cocktail party resulted in the emergence of political action and the implementation of policy change.

Simon swallowed the last of his wine as he fingered the invitation. He was both proud and flattered that he had done something creditable to warrant their attention. There was no doubting they were a group that shared his thoughts on how to make a better society. It was now the second year of the Harding administration and Simon Kraft held tight to the political capital that he continued to cultivate and accrue by way of doling out favors and dispersing federal funds for various state projects. The most recent task that captured his interest was to modify and fortify the Health Laws from the Commonwealth and work them into a bill that would be presented to Congress. The major components of the new bill would be similar to the Commonwealth's Health Laws, but he planned to introduce new language that would prohibit marriage on a national level between couples when either party was determined to be insane, feebleminded or afflicted with epilepsy. The bill also contained wording on a federal ban of inter-racial marriages, in addition to reduced immigration quotas with stricter health restrictions for émigrés from Asia and Eastern Europe. When passed, the bill would become the National Health Laws Act that would guarantee "to preserve and protect the integrity, health and future of citizens who live in the United States of America."

Yes! He would accept the invitation. There was much to be gained by attending their reception. Their thoughts and comments would be invaluable and a worthy reflection of how the nation would embrace the issues addressed by the new health laws. These were powerful people who might prove to be politically invaluable. *How better*, he mused, than to further his own agenda by rubbing elbows with people who didn't have to grovel for votes or appointments in order to achieve success. *How better*, he thought, than to preach to the choir and garner their support and enthusiasm for a new set of laws destined to make the nation a better place to live. Once passed by Congress, perhaps the new bill would become better known as the Kraft Health Care Act that eventually would evolve into an amendment to the U. S. constitution. Perhaps.

The meeting room at the Waldorf-Astoria resembled a private ballroom in a European castle. The incandescence from the crystal in the chandeliers shone like the noonday sun. The room was plush and rich and extravagant: from the army of waiters in their fine tuxedos to the thick carpeting that covered the floors. As he guided Dorothy across the room, they were treated to the sound of classical music offered by a trio of musicians who casually played their instruments and ignored the dozens of guests in the room. Near the middle of the room they were met by a man with a thin white mustache and a neatly cropped beard that ended in a sharp point. "Dr. Kraft, how wonderful to see you. I'm Irving Fisher."

Simon knew the name; who didn't? He was the most famous economist in the country who had become enormously rich when he invented a card index filing system that rolled and rotated over itself. He was also a professor at Yale who wrote a book on healthy living that was in its tenth reprinting. "Good evening, Professor," Simon said as he extended his right hand to Fisher. "This is my wife, Dorothy."

"Very delighted, Mrs. Kraft," Fisher said as he nodded. "I hope you're enjoying New York." Before Dorothy had a chance to reply, Fisher said to Simon, "There are a few people whom I would like you to meet." Fisher took Dorothy's arm and with Simon in tow he maneuvered the couple around roadblocks of chatting people who had taken up station in the room. Wheeling left and right, Fisher touched one person after another and introduced them to Simon and Dorothy.

"John, come meet Dr. Kraft and his wife. John Rockefeller, Dr. Kraft."

"Jack, Jack my man. Dr. Kraft, please meet Jack London."

"Come, Dr. Kraft, meet an old friend of mine. Tom, Tom, say hello to Dr. Kraft. Dr. Kraft, this is Tom Edison."

And so it went for the next hour. There was big money in the room; Simon could see it and feel it. He met Mark Holyoke from the Carnegie Foundation and shared a drink with Warren Eden from the Ford Foundation. Anthony Convent, John Paul Morgan's assistant director of operations for US Steel, shared one story after another with Dorothy. It was a veritable Who's Who of the men who made America great. Each was pleasant to meet, each had his own thoughts on how to make society better and none were too shy to share their opinions.

"Philanthropists are the bane of our society," Fisher shot a barb at John Rockefeller. "They shower their beneficence on the delinquent, the defective and the dependent classes and force the government to do likewise. They ignore the fact that the unfit are a drag on our civilization and a social menace." The man who single handedly reinvented the study of economics by making it dependent on mathematical formulas sipped from his martini glass and added, "There are nearly 100,000 people in prisons and asylums who individually cost the taxpayers $200 every year. There are 3 million more with inferior blood who also require separation from society; who should be separated from society so they can interbreed. That's 3 million times two hundred dollars."

"You have that in your piggy bank, don't you John," Jack London chided John Rockefeller.

"And by separation you mean either selective sterilization or institutionalization?" Warren Eden interjected.

"Yes. The implementation of Dr. Kraft's marriage laws will also create restrictions to prohibit the unfit from obtaining marriage licenses," Fisher replied. "I calculate that nearly 10% of our total population are carriers of these hereditary maladies. If the government continues to operate as they have in the past, taxes will need to increase constantly to address these costs."

"Fortunately we all agree that the actions taken for the sake of eugenics are the highest forms of patriotism and humanitarianism," John Rockefeller replied.

"Here, here!" Jack London offered. "We must not forget that survival of the fittest is not possible if a society artificially preserves its feeblest members. The quality of such a society is lowered if those who are least able to care for themselves are sustained and supported artificially."

All seemed to buy into the Society's party-line. Simon meandered into the company of two other physicians. He knew William Welch who was the Dean of the School of Medicine at Johns Hopkins. He also was the president of the American Medical Association. The other man was younger and introduced himself as "John Kellogg, from Battle Creek, Michigan. I admire your work and your efforts Dr. Kraft, and am proud to say that we are kindred spirits."

"Thank you for your kind words," Simon replied.

"I do not believe the blessings of liberty and full domestic tranquility can be enjoyed if persons civilly unfit are permitted to procreate their species and scatter their kind among normal citizens," Kellogg added. "It is important to remove from the stream of life the poisonous elements of physical and psychological decay."

"Reproduction of the unfit is not only a crime against their offspring, but a crime against the state," a man offered as he joined the group. "Wendell DeJoseph," he said as he introduced himself. "I am the superintendent of prisons in North Carolina and I know something about crime."

"Sterilization is now proven to be the most prudent solution for women who have gravitated to the world of prostitution," Dr. Welch added.

"I agree," Kellogg said. "One constant that persists is that children begotten in lust are destined for abnormality."

"Very true, doctor," DeJoseph replied. "Likes beget likes. Defectives produce defectives and the insane beget insane."

"The hereditary propensity to bad behavior, like prostitution, is embedded in the plasm of the women," Kellogg said. "A national eugenic program will prevent the transmission of this terrible trait, in addition to having a positive effect on the goals of social hygiene."

"We have seen time and again," Wendell DeJoseph added with a rumbling air of self-certainty, "once these women undergo sterilization surgery, they are cured of the wants and desires to return to the squalid life of prostitution. The surgery not only is cheap, but it benefits both the moral and mental condition of the women."

Simon nodded and smiled his agreement. Simon felt as though he had been whisked away to Versailles in the Hall of Mirrors. Everywhere he turned and everyone whom he spoke with recited and reflected the mantra he was preaching. Sometimes it was said with more resonance and sometimes they offered a different verse, but they were of one mind and one will and were singing from the same hymnal. Although not everyone was certain that sterilization was the best way to *cure* the problem, all agreed that isolation of the unfit individuals was the best way to *prevent* the problem.

As Dorothy stood across the room chatting up Mrs. DuPont and Mary Harriman, the widow of the railroad magnate, Simon sought a brief respite at a table where a man sat nursing a drink in a tall high-ball glass. "May I?" Simon asked.

"Sure, take a load off," the man replied in a soft, southern accent Simon was prone to appreciate. "Quite the mix. Scientists and scientist-wannabes. Rich people and folks who want to be rich. Egg-heads and ne'er do wells."

Simon drained his glass and asked, "May I buy you one?" The man nodded. "I'm guessing bourbon." The man nodded again.

When Simon returned from the bar he handed the man his drink and extended his right hand. "Simon Kraft."

The man nodded and stood up. "Lamar Schreyer."

Simon nodded. In his best down home manner he asked, "You wouldn't be of a relation to the Lynchburg Schreyer's?"

The man smiled and replied, "And the Lexington Schreyer's and the Calumet Schreyer's and probably a few more who escaped the hangman's noose."

"I am not, personally, a fan of horse racing," Simon replied, "but I do have a passing interest and I do appreciate a good product when I see one."

"Thank you, sir. I appreciate your *interest.*"

"I would venture to say," Simon said, "that you have extensive knowledge and a handsome background in breeding and bloodlines yourself. What else brings you to the Society's meetings?"

"The quality of a thoroughbred is improved by careful and controlled breeding," Schreyer said as he sipped at his bourbon. "Bone structure, durability, character. I am concerned that when it comes to our own race, by jingo, we think that any sort of seed is good enough to plant with."

"I assume you, like many others," Simon offered to the man, "believe that what is learned and practiced in animal breeding and animal husbandry programs should be transferable to the human laboratory?"

"A wise man once offered that being a good animal is the first requisite to success in life," Schreyer explained. "More importantly, being a nation of good animals is the first condition of national prosperity."

Simon smiled as he nodded at the homespun country wisdom of the man whose horse racing stables were the gold standard of the industry. He drained the last of his drink and was certain Lamar Schreyer's thoughts were one and the same as the thoughts of men in black robes in ivy covered institutions and men in blue collar shirts who worked on rural farms and in urban factories alike.

"Simon, Simon," Irving Fisher approached and took Simon by the arm and led him back to a group that had formed near the center of the room. "Before the night is over, please share with us a few thoughts from the Capital, on your efforts and our interests."

Simon looked about his audience and saw nothing but approving faces. These were the people who would spread the gospel. These were the people with enough *power and puissance* to make the Kraft Health Care Act a reality. "The road this nation takes to normalcy," Simon offered, "demands that we must always think and say: 'America First.' We, all of us, must seize the opportunity to allow America to remain the greatest nation on earth, both genetically and fundamentally.

"We, in the government, are striving to create an environment to accentuate our better characteristics and allow them to blossom. The goal will be to allow for a better breed of Americans to emerge and prosper. Prevention and isolation and selective sterilization go hand and hand. Modern science will provide the torchlight for America to prosper."

As he spoke to the group and heard what he was saying, he came to the realization that it would be his task to make these words the creed of the American people.

*　*　*

He took long strokes and cut smoothly through the water leaving little or no wake. Effortlessly, quietly, he glided across the pool's surface like a skiff skimming across the waters of a still pond. The YMCA in Georgetown installed an indoor swimming pool last year, one of the nation's first, and Simon had become a frequent figure at the pool. The enclosed room did have a few drawbacks. The odor of chlorine dominated the room; time was indeterminable because the walls lacked windows; visibility was poor because the overhead lighting was dim and yellow, but Simon would be the last man to complain. Up and back he would swim for thirty minutes, twice each week, enough exercise to limber his joints and keep his waistline at thirty-four inches. Like always he was alone in the pool at this early hour of the morning, but the time he spent in peaceful solitude allowed his thoughts to take form and organize and prepare him for the rest of the day. As he lifted his head for a gulp of air he saw a man in an overcoat walk through the door. When he reached the wall at the near end of the pool he stopped swimming to identify him.

"Do you bribe the janitor to open this place so early in the morning?" Uncle Billy's voice boomed and echoed off the walls of the pool room. "Or perhaps you don't have any friends who want to play with you."

Simon lifted himself out of the pool, reached for his towel and dried himself. "Good morning to you, too. And yes, the janitor is kind enough to open the building and allow me to swim this early so I can get in my fun before I go to work." Simon rubbed hard at his head to dry his hair. "What brings you here before sunrise?"

"I wanted to be the first to tell you, to warn you," Senator Cheltenham replied. "This isn't the year."

Simon gave him a quizzical look as he explained, "The Senate is not ready to consider your Health Act. It will have to wait until next year."

Simon stopped drying himself. "What happened?"

The Senator shrugged his shoulders and said, "Now is not the time. When I talked up the highlights of the bill I could appreciate no consensus. Those who were in favor of the marriage laws did not agree with sterilization. Those who were in favor of sterilizing hereditary criminals were not in favor of castrating sex offenders and rapists. Two of the senators are Roman Catholic and they would not agree to any of it. Don't get me wrong. Perhaps one third of the aides and senators whom I spoke with agree with all facets of the bill, but one third of ninety-six will not be sufficient to pass a bill. As of today, too much work would be required to fight for additional votes. Remember, despite the gray hairs that populate the top of my head, I am still a junior senator and do not have enough clout to turn water into wine."

Simon was crestfallen and his face was unable to hide his disappointment. "Another option exists," Uncle Billy offered. "We could break down the Health Laws Bill into components parts and try to attach the component parts to unrelated bills as riders. We could adjust the wording, bury them deep inside a farm subsidy or military appropriation bill . . ."

"No, Uncle Billy," Simon replied grudgingly. "The components of the bill must be judged and approved on their own merits. These issues are too important to be labeled 'afterthoughts' and be sneaked into law on the coattails of some bill to honor hog farming or the fertilizer industry. The senators must embrace the idea that passage of the health laws *en toto* is what is necessary for the American people and the American race. We must approach this issue head-on and with a firm heart, not by means of subterfuge or by smuggling the bill in through the side door."

"Take heart, Simon," Uncle Billy said. "You did strike a popular chord with many. A few of your proposals are in line with many in the Capital and will be implemented. We will see a drastic reduction of immigration quotas. Immigration applicants with criminal records will continue to be denied citizenship status. Almost as important, 30 states now have anti-miscegenation laws which ban marriages between white and coloreds and between the whites and Asians. All thirty states will reaffirm their stance on the law and will stiffened their penalties for violators."

"Thank God. There still are a few clear minds working in Congress."

"Politics is a strange game, Simon," Uncle Billy said. "You are receiving a great deal of credit for a bill that will not be acted upon. It's time will come, Simon. Be patient, it's time will come."

ELEVEN

Loretta Frontenac warily examined the young lady who sat across from her. She glanced again at the sheet of paper resting on her desk that described the young lady's past work experience. Loretta needed someone to help her. She needed someone with a modicum of experience working in and around a courthouse, but was this young lady, this Phoebe Belden, that person? The meeting this morning was half interview—half favor to Maxwell Lawrence. Phoebe Belden was his granddaughter whom he described in his understated fashion as 'interesting.' He also suggested she may prove to be helpful.

Phoebe Belden was strikingly attractive. Her hair was platinum in color and bobbed. She wore rouge on her cheeks and a pink gloss on her thin lips. Hoop earrings dangled on either side of her head and the bracelets she wore on her wrists jingled softly when she motioned with her arms. Her fingernails were polished and painted Chinese red. She wore a dress that was made of silky material and clung tightly to her lithe body. There was hardly a natural curve to her figure and Loretta was certain she couldn't fit into Phoebe's dress with a crowbar. The dress shimmered, even with the mellow overhead lighting in the room. Scattered in the dress' fabric were sequins and tiny bobbles that caught the light and reflected light pink and yellow flashes. As she sat, the hem of her dress rose high on her legs to reveal both her knees. Her eyes were radiant. They were round and full and lined in a way that captured one's gaze and held it. Her small nose was all but non-existent and her lips hardly moved when she spoke. Loretta found she was somewhat embarrassed, as an unmarried woman, to think Phoebe beautiful. Sitting in a law office in a quiet corner of Norwood County, Phoebe Belden was by all standards quite the anomaly. As best Loretta could determine, she was what the people in New York City called 'a flapper.'

"You attended law school for one year or two?" Loretta asked as she read from the sheet of paper the young lady had given her.

"Actually a year and a half; at Columbia." Her voice was smooth and confident and had a pleasant tone to it.

"One and one half years," Loretta said and the young lady nodded. "You left after 18 months?" Again she nodded.

After a pause Phoebe said, "I had a baby and the baby needed a mother. Law school could wait but the baby couldn't."

Loretta smiled and nodded. Anxiously she scanned the paper in her hand but could not find what she was looking for. "You're married?"

"No." There was a pause. "I was married," Phoebe replied. "My husband was a captain in the merchant marine. During the war his ship was sunk by a U-boat, somewhere in the Atlantic."

Loretta bowed her head slightly and said, "I'm sorry."

"Little Eddie was born that same year," Phoebe continued. "I was by myself in New York City. My mother still lives here in Norwood so I came home."

"Why did you enroll in law school?" Loretta asked.

"When my husband was away at sea he would travel for months at a time. I was working at the time but I needed something more to do, to keep myself busy. So I enrolled in law school."

Loretta attended law school to become a lawyer. She could think of a few less rigorous ways to kill time, but . . . "It says here Mrs. Belden," Loretta referred once again to the paper that was on her desk, "that you presently work part-time doing office work."

She nodded. "Eddie starts school in the autumn. I'll have more time then, when he goes to school."

"Did you work before you had your baby?" Loretta asked.

"Yes. I was a dancer."

Loretta looked at the paper again. There was no mention of her being a dancer. "Where were you a . . . a dancer?"

"On Broadway. I was a dancer in Ziegfeld's Follies."

Burlesque. "You were a showgirl?" Loretta asked.

"Yes. I needed money to pay for law school. When I left Norwood for New York City, I studied and trained in formal dancing and acting. I got pretty good at it. I auditioned, performed well enough and made the grade."

"You were a dancer for Flo Ziegfeld performing at nights and went to law school during the day," Loretta said as if to clarify matters in her mind.

"As I said, I had time to kill while my husband was at sea," Phoebe Belden answered to explain her life choices.

Loretta examined the young lady with her stylish clothes and New York hairstyle and painfully good looks. "Do you miss New York?"

"It's hard to find a cheese blintz in Norwood County," Phoebe replied in her most diplomatic fashion.

Maxwell Lawrence was correct. Phoebe Belden was interesting.

* * *

Getting into and out of costumes had become second nature to Phoebe during the time she worked on stage in New York City, but her wearing a nurse's uniform presented a new experience for her. Seldom in her past acting career had she intentionally tried to look so frumpy and unattractive. She suspected there were a number of reasons, both practical and philosophical, for the unflattering garb, but such discussions were not pertinent to her present task. Her challenge was to get into Norwood County Hospital and retrieve the information that Loretta needed.

The clerk at the uniform store was helpful when Phoebe explained she was a recent nursing school graduate who would soon start a job at the hospital. She needed a new uniform because her old uniforms were lost when her suitcase was stolen.

"Darn shame, miss," he replied in his slow talking manner. He eyed Phoebe and offered, "Dress size six?" Phoebe nodded in response.

"Shoe size seven?"

"Seven and a half," she replied.

"Good thing to have the shoe size correct, what with you nurses being on your feet for so many hours," he said. "That's what all the girls complain about, how sore their feet get."

Talk about sore feet, try dancing on stage for ten shows each week, she wanted to say but continued with her part. Phoebe looked at an advertising poster of an attractive woman in a nursing uniform who looked pleased to be doing whatever she was doing. Mentally she checked off what she needed: white dress, white stockings, white blouse, heavy clunky shoes. Cap. "I need a cap also," she said.

"You got a cap when you finished nursing school, didn't you?" he asked.

Phoebe presumed she'd better say, "Why yes, of course."

"Where'd you graduate from?" he asked.

Where? Where? "Ziegfeld School of Nursing," she replied.

"Must be from out of town," he replied. "Well, you'll have to write them and ask for a new one. Better make that two or three; since you lost your cap, you better ask for a few extra. Most schools have their own style and colors. You know that. They all look funny to me, but I guess they run out of ideas for attractive ones so's they just keep making silly ones so's they look different from each other. The caps don't hold back the hair very well, so most of the girls buy one that works.

"Here," he said as he took a plain white cap from off a shelf and handed it to her. "Put this on that pretty head of yours until you get your new cap from that Ziegman school for nurses."

The nursing uniform was a necessity for her to get past the receptionist who sat behind a desk and monitored who could and who would not pass from the lobby of the hospital into its hallways. A tall man dressed in a faux policeman's uniform stood by the desk and loomed ominously as the receptionist's protector. Last week Phoebe spent time sitting in the lobby of the hospital, away from the direct view of the receptionist, and watched the coming and going of the traffic. Those who were dressed in normal street clothing were stopped at the receptionist's desk and Phoebe presumed they were in the hospital to visit an ill friend or family member. They were checked in, their names were taken and subsequently they were led away by a female guide to the appropriate room. Men dressed in business attire, invariably carrying a briefcase or a valise similar to the ones carried by the door-to-door salesmen she had seen in New York City, also had to sign in with the receptionist. In turn, they would be directed to one of the many hallways beyond the desk of the receptionist. Several other men offered friendly greetings to the receptionist who recognized each of them. They were allowed to pass unhindered and Phoebe presumed these men were either physicians or men who worked with the hospital administrators. Most importantly Phoebe noted that all the women dressed as nurses walked freely past the receptionist; young, old, tall and short.

Phoebe removed the polish from her fingernails, ensured all remnants of her make-up had been cleaned away, combed out her hair and pinned it tightly to her head. No earrings, no jewelry, no bangles or beads. The awkwardly designed white uniform hung on her body as if she were a coat hanger. The blouse had long sleeves that puffed at the cuffs. The collar was stiff with too much starch and the lapels were long and pointed. The dress was heavy with multiple pleats and the hem dragged on the floor. She pulled up the apron front and struggled as she crossed the straps behind her back to ensure they were neither twisted nor crumpled. The bib in her front was awkwardly oversized and Phoebe presumed Florence Nightingale, or whoever designed this uniform, envisioned all nurses to be heavily endowed with ample bosoms. Phoebe ensured all her buttons were fastened and aligned correctly. No angel of mercy but close enough.

In the early morning Phoebe lingered outside the hospital doors. A clutch of four nurses, chatting idly, opened the doors of the hospital and walked into the lobby. Phoebe followed in their wake and merged with them. She smiled politely at their comments, nodded her head every so often and walked along with them as they ambled past the receptionist. "Hello's" and "Good mornings" were exchanged. Once past the receptionist she stood in what appeared to her to be a main hallway. She scanned the walls for directional signs and spied what she needed: "Cafeteria."

Phoebe followed the signs to a large room where people gathered at tables and chatted quietly as they drank from cups and picked at food in front of them. Several of the men sat smoking cigarettes. Off to one side were several men who wore tunic style long-sleeve shirts that wrapped around their upper bodies. Phoebe was certain the men were surgeons. At the opposite end of the room were similarly dressed women gathered around a table sipping from their cups. Phoebe walked to them.

"Morning folks," Phoebe said with a down home accent. "Y'all are from the operating rooms, aren't you?" she said by way of greeting.

Indifferently one of the women nodded and said "Yes."

"Mr. Clark from administration asked me to confirm," Phoebe rambled, "if there had been any change to the scheduling when the court mandated patients arrive to have their operations. He wants to ensure that we have enough beds to accommodate them."

"Tell Mr. Clark it's still once a month," the short nurse replied. "Same as always. First Wednesday of the month."

"First Wednesday; next week, next Wednesday," Phoebe replied for confirmation and then added, "like always."

"Like always, like clockwork," the taller one replied. "Roll them in and roll them out. Most of those poor people don't know what hits them," she said to the short nurse, essentially ignoring Phoebe. She tapped at her forehead with her index finger and said, "Some ain't so swift in the head and the other half have lost their marbles. The ones from the prisons are mean and surly. Before they know it, they're back in their rooms waiting to go home to whatever cell they came from."

"Does Dr. Stewart still do most of the surgery or is it Dr. Thompson?" Phoebe asked.

"Don't know Thompson, but Dr. Priddey has been doing the cases for the past few years," the short one answered.

"Dr. Priddey from in town?" Phoebe asked and the tall one apathetically nodded her head. "Thank you. Have a nice day," Phoebe offered as she left them. *Tough group.*

*   *   *

They met in the apartment of Maxwell Lawrence as a convenience for him because of his mobility difficulties. "Dr. Priddey and Nedley Pratt are both members of the same country club," Phoebe explained what she had discovered. "Pratt's law firm, as you know, prosecutes the cases referable to the Health Laws for the Commonwealth. Both the surgeon and the lawyers are paid by the Commonwealth for the work that they do."

"Nothing illegal about any of that," Lawrence said.

"No," Loretta said, "just a little too chummy."

"Don't fool yourself," Lawrence said. "More deals have been made and more laws have been created on the golf course or at a poker table than one can imagine."

"What is problematic is that all court records remain out of my grasp," Phoebe said. "I have spent hours digging into the daily logs and continue to hit a brick wall; one dead end after another. Despite all the cross referencing I have done for the past month, I have nothing to show for my efforts."

"That is because the records have been sealed," Maxwell Lawrence said. Both Phoebe and Loretta cast disbelieving glances at him. "Sealed. Undiscoverable and unreadable. No longer for public consumption," he said with haute eloquence.

"How do you know this?" Loretta challenged.

"I still have a few friends at the court house," he replied. "More than a few, thank you very much. I spoke with Judge Spencer. He does not hear any of the Health Law cases but he told me that for confidentiality purposes, all files related to the cases are sealed once they emerge from the typewriters. The ink is hardly dry before the cases disappear to the archives of the Commonwealth."

"So that is the reason we have had so much difficulty . . ." Loretta mused. "For how long has this policy been in effect?"

Lawrence smiled his grandfatherly smile as he said, "Since shortly after the check from the Commonwealth for the Summerdale case was placed in your pretty little hand."

"How, why?" Loretta challenged.

"You wounded them sorely, Mademoiselle Frontenac." Lawrence explained. "The Commonwealth is not in the habit of making large payments to correct a mistake that was better left buried in its own sea of paperwork. Elbridge Passmore is the current Attorney General for the Commonwealth. I have been told that he vowed never to allow another such case to see the light of day. Although the malfeasance did not occur on his watch, he was irate. Given the opportunity he would have wrung the necks of Nedley Pratt and the previous Attorney General, for he certainly had motive. Only the people named in the cases may have access to their own files."

"Or the patients' lawyers," Phoebe offered and Lawrence confirmed.

"So to preclude any future investigative nightmares," Loretta offered, "the hearings are closed and the verdicts are sealed."

"Essentially, yes," Lawrence replied. "Unless we can show just cause that such hearings require either public notice or oversight, or that the constitutional rights of the individuals are being infringed upon, there is nothing we can do to make the hearings public."

"More importantly," Phoebe offered, "there is nothing we can do to make the judgments or verdicts public. If some of these people are being railroaded, no one is the wiser."

"Everything happens in the dark behind curtains," Loretta lamented. "The patients go from the judge's bench to the operating table then back to where ever they came from and no one is the wiser. Patients slide into and out of the hospitals and their records become entombed." Loretta slowly shook her head. "This is becoming an epidemic."

"Make note, Mademoiselle Frontenac," Maxwell Lawrence offered with a stern and downcast frown, "of what you see here in Norwood County, with our court house and our hospital. The Norwood County story is only the tip of the iceberg. There are nine other asylums scattered throughout the Commonwealth for the insane and feebleminded. They also serve as hospitals and each one performs court mandated surgeries in a fashion to what occurs here."

"You're right," she replied. "And don't forget all the state penitentiaries throughout the Commonwealth."

"The challenge will be what it has always been: to identify the aggrieved individual," Lawrence summarized.

"I should have something on that tomorrow," Phoebe said.

*   *   *

Once again Phoebe Belden donned her nurse's garb and entered Norwood General Hospital. She studied the directional signs on the walls, passed through and along several hallways, and made her way to the corner of the hospital that housed the operating rooms. A set of large double doors stood at the end of the hallway. She moved to the side of the hallway, sidled up against the wall and watched as patients on litters were wheeled through the doors and into what appeared to be a waiting area adjacent to the operating rooms. As the double doors opened and closed, the sweet smell of ether wafted into the hallway where she stood. Although most of the nurses wore white uniforms, many of the men wore the tunic style long sleeve shirts Phoebe had seen last week in the cafeteria. Through the open double doors Phoebe could see people moving constantly. They shuffled and shuttled patients on gurneys from one room to another. Many of the nurses carried trays and bundles that were wrapped in towels and shrouds.

Outside in the hallway a door to the right of the double doors opened and closed constantly as men and women alike entered what appeared to be an office. Phoebe suspected that somewhere behind the door was the entrance to the operating rooms. Phoebe followed a nurse as she walked through the door into the office. All of the men and women wore tight fitting caps on their heads. Many of the people who scurried from room to room wore surgical masks that left only their eyes visible. There was a continuous hum of noise as people spoke softly to one another. No one shouted and no one's voice dominated. Everywhere she looked there were white towels, white sheets, white gowns and white bundles. Phoebe found herself in a large open area with a waist high wall on the right. People who appeared to be clerks sat behind the half wall busily scribbling and writing onto charts and into ledgers. The half wall separated the office region from the busy traffic of the area's holding region. Phoebe turned to look down the hallway and saw the scrub sinks outside the operating rooms. She stood up on her toes and with trepidation tried to steal a glance inside one of the operating rooms, unsure what she might see and unsure how she might react.

"You're getting in the way, ma'am," a voice behind her said. "You need something?" the voice asked.

Phoebe turned to the sound of the voice and saw one of the women whom she thought to be a clerk. Phoebe glanced at the counter top that sat above the half wall and saw clipboards lined up in a neat row and stacks of papers positioned at the far end. She scanned the area. There were too many prying eyes; there was no way she could examine a chart or a clipboard without drawing undo attention. She had something else in mind, something that was neither a secret document nor off limits. It was something that actually was well distributed throughout the hospital on a daily basis.

"May I have a copy of today's surgery schedule?" Phoebe asked. "Mr. Clark misplaced his copy and the administration office would like one."

"Sure, take one," the voice replied.

Phoebe took a carbon copy sheet from one of the stacks, scanned it and noted Dr. Priddey's name. Bingo. "Thank you," she said as she folded it and put it in her pocket. She turned from the counter and once again tried to glance in the direction of the operating suites. She saw people at the sinks washing their hands, she saw people hustling into and out of windowless rooms, she saw patients lying on the litters that had been left in the hallways outside the operating suites.

"Anything else, ma'am?" the voice said.

"No. Thank you," and Phoebe left the office.

* * *

"Six patients on the surgery schedule are listed with Dr. Donald Priddey as their attending surgeon," Loretta said as she reviewed the sheet of paper Phoebe obtained from the hospital.

"Hernia repair is not what we're looking for, right?" Phoebe offered.

"Right," Loretta replied.

"Scratch one. Same with a tonsil . . . tonsil . . . tonsillectomy?" Phoebe sputtered.

"Scratch two," Loretta said.

"That leaves two female patients for Fallopian Tube ligation, one male for castration, and one male for vasectomy," Phoebe said.

"We have to talk to these people," Loretta said. "We have to find them and talk with them. These four are only a start, but they're a start in the right direction. There are hundreds of people out there like these four patients."

"You are correct when you say we are facing an epidemic, but it is something more, something worse," Maxwell Lawrence said. "This is a purging, a cleansing on a scale that begs the imagination."

"And next month," Phoebe added, "next first Wednesday of the month, we'll get a new list and a batch of new names."

TWELVE

"What do you know of oilfields in Wyoming and California?" Ed Preller asked Simon Kraft in late autumn of 1922. He had in his hands the morning newspaper. On the front page of the *Washington Post*, below the fold, was a two column article about disgruntled people in the oil drilling industry and a congressional investigation into alleged 'improprieties.'

"Not a thing," Simon replied.

"It seems as though some people in the Department of the Interior got rich overnight by leasing government owned oilfields to Sinclair Oil," Ed said. "A place called Teapot Dome."

"The Interior is Albert Fall's department." Simon took the newspaper and quickly read the story. His gaze drifted to the ceiling as he wondered how soon the walls would start to crash down on his head like what was happening with so much of the administration. First it was Thomas Miller with the Office of Alien Property. During the War more than 30,000 companies with whole or partial German ownership were seized. The companies produced everything from explosives to medicines and included a great number of breweries. The total value of all the companies approached one billion dollars. The companies were allowed to operate only after management was found to be, without question, loyal to America. In many instances new management was brought in to run the companies. The seizures had two objectives: to deny Germany the use of the goods that were being produced and to stem the flow of money that might be channeled back to Europe. After the war many of the companies were sold off to American investors at auction. It was rumored that significant information was withheld from most of the prospective buyers and provided to a select few who were willing to pay for such information. In many instances companies were being sold off for ten cents on the dollar. Thomas Miller now faced charges for taking bribes and granting favors.

The Veteran's Bureau was a disaster. Charles Forbes, head of the Veteran's Bureau, had been charged with embezzlement and graft to the tune of 250 million dollars. Government lands were being sold off indiscriminately, cost overruns for the construction of veteran's hospitals were the norm and the charges for equipping the hospitals with supplies were exorbitant. Veterans who required services frequently complained that their requests for treatment went unanswered unless accompanied by a "processing fee."

The names of Harry Daugherty and Jesse Smith repeatedly were associated with both Miller and Forbes. Smith also faced heat from a different direction. Somehow he insinuated himself into the process by which licenses were granted for the transportation of liquor across state lines. Such licenses were issued upon special request and all requests had to pass through the office, and sticky fingers, of Jesse Smith in the Attorney General department. Accusations also were surfacing that Smith was orchestrating liquor smuggling operations of gargantuan proportions.

Double, double toil and trouble, Simon mused. *Fire burn, and cauldron bubble.* The naughty the boys from Ohio who gathered at the little green house down the lane on K Street continued to dig themselves into ever deepening graves. What additional mischief did they continue to brew? What other disasters lurked in the shadows to be trumpeted by an unsatisfied accomplice who thought he had not gotten his fair share of the spoils? What other deals or fixes had been made and now waited to be exposed by a nosey journalist or a righteous do-gooder? Most importantly, who else knew about the genesis of Excelsior Business and Research Services and how were the company's profits being distributed?

Simon picked up the telephone and said, "Connect me to the office of the Attorney General. Yes. The office of Mr. Daugherty. Yes. Mr. Daugherty himself."

Simon drummed his fingers on his desk as he waited. "You've never met Jesse Smith, have you?"

"Thankfully no," Ed replied. "Only spoke to him on the phone once or twice when he crawled out from beneath his rock, and that was a few years ago."

"Good morning Mr. Secretary," the voice on the other end of the line greeted the not so jolly Simon Kraft. "How is the good doctor this morning?"

"Apparently I am doing better than Secretary Fall with the Department of the Interior. Off the record, what is going on with Mr. Harding's administration?"

"For the record, Mr. Secretary," Daugherty replied, "Albert Fall is a *prima fascia* jackass. To lease the oilfields is legal, as far as I understand, but I know nothing of how the leases were awarded. Secretary Fall claims to be a lawyer, did not want the opinion of the Attorney General's office, and no doubt he wanted as few people to know about the operations as necessary. Some small time oilmen lost out, cried foul and raised a stink. That's all I know. All the rest of the people in the administration are working hard, yourself included."

Simon suspected that Harry Daugherty's disapproval of the actions of Albert Fall had more to do with the likelihood that Daugherty had not been cut into Fall's schemes and had not benefited from the proceeds of the deals. "And how is Mr. Smith fairing these days?" Simon added.

"Busy as ever."

"You do remember," Simon added, "that Excelsior Business and Research Services provided much of the equipment that went to the veteran's hospitals that are now under scrutiny with Colonel Forbes?"

"Such was purely a business arrangement," Daugherty replied, "complete with contracts, notices for delivery and payment invoices."

And Jesse Smith negotiated every contract; complete with 2000% profits and invoices for goods that were sold three different times to three different facilities. Simon took a deep breath and was thankful he was not party to how and where the monies were distributed. "Nice talking with you, Harry."

"Nice talking with you, Doctor."

*   *   *

Winter became spring and difficulties within President Harding's cabinet not only tortured the administration but were grist for the mill of the newspapers throughout the country. Charles Forbes, head of the Veteran's Bureau, fled to Europe. His legal assistant and bagman, Charles Cramer, ended his own problems by firing a .45 caliber bullet through his head. Rarely did a day go by that Jesse Smith's name wasn't mentioned in conjunction with one shady deal or another. Most recently, newspapers were reporting on his entanglement with a lawyer who represented a six million dollar company that was seized by the Office of Alien Property. The lawyer claimed that the company was in fact owned by Swiss businessmen, not Germans, and they were seeking reimbursement. The lawyer also claimed that Jesse Smith demanded payment of $250,000 "to expedite the claim through his acquaintances in Washington." One of the 'acquaintances' happened to be Malcolm Daugherty, the banker-brother of the Attorney General.

For the three years that Simon Kraft had known him, Jesse Smith always seemed to be in the middle of some deal or scheme. He was an accountant by training and although there was never a suggestion he was the originator of the schemes, he performed well in his role as the middleman of the schemes. Although he frequently seemed to be enshrouded by a dense aura of befuddlement, emerging every so often to stuff money into a billfold or suitcase, Simon had thoughts to the contrary. He suspected that Smith's presentation as the muddled and mentally dim gofer for Harry Daugherty was a canard and Simon grew to appreciate how well Smith's perceived lack of ingenuity served so well to cloak the sly and crafty fox

Rumors freely circulated throughout Washington that the Daugherty-Smith enterprise was a conglomerate of diverse and unrelated projects that focused on one objective: the generation of vast amounts of money. Although both Daugherty and Smith repeatedly swore that the money generated by Excelsior was earmarked for the operations of the Republican Party, Simon suspected the cash seldom moved any farther than the Daugherty-Smith treasure chest. As they continued to turn up the heat on Jesse Smith, Simon Kraft did not wish to go up in flames along with him. Simon was equally concerned that Smith might be smart enough to wiggle out of the problems that were threatening him, become a witness for the investigators and leave behind a trail of broken men with ruined careers and tarnished reputations.

Simon traveled to the Wardman-Park Hotel in the northwest section of the Capital to meet with Jesse Smith where he shared an apartment with Harry Daugherty. Simon knocked on the door and stood in the hallway for nearly a minute before a big gawky man opened the door. He held a tumbler glass in his hand and said by way of greeting, "Well, well, well; Dr. Kraft. What brings you to this section of town?" He did not offer his hand to Simon.

Simon stared at the man, inspecting him as he entered the room. Smith had lost a good bit of weight since Simon had seen him last. His normally doughy and frumpy appearance looked haggard and tired. Simon replied, "I was visiting the zoo, was in the neighborhood, and thought I'd stop by to say 'hello.'"

Smith cocked his head to the right at the unlikely story. He walked to the bar that sat beneath a bookcase. "Bourbon?"

"Bourbon's fine."

Smith half-filled a glass and handed it to Simon who swirled it and took a sip. Smith motioned to the chairs in the living room as they both sat and looked across from each other in awkward silence. "Keeping busy, Jess?" Simon asked innocently.

"You know how it is, no rest for the weary," Smith replied.

Smith was worn down. His jowly face sagged and the pleading eyes that hid behind his round glasses darted about the room nervously as they sat. Simon offered, "Nice place you and Harry have here." It was a lavish apartment, with artwork on the walls from the orient and carpets on the floor from the middle-east. The furniture was heavily embroidered and all the lamps in the room were painted in a wild array of colors and patterns. Simon noted that Smith's hands nervously tapped on the arm of his chair and his head bobbed ever so slightly. Still in a business suit, he absent-mindedly patted at his tie and pressed down on the front of his jacket.

"How are you holding up," Simon said to break the silence, "with all this muck-raking hoopla circling about." Simon swirled his glass in the air and motioned toward the ceiling.

"Dr. Kraft," Smith replied, "we aren't what most people would call friends. I suspect at some level you don't even like me. So why now, why your concern for my well-being?"

Simon nodded, acknowledging the veracity of his statement, and said, "Let's say we've been business associates in the past and it is in my best interest to see how well you are holding up . . . how you're weathering the storm."

"A storm you say," Smith replied with throaty 'humph' and a sideways stare. "As long as the police aren't knocking down my door or shadowing me when I go to work, it's not so bad. All the talk that's out there is newspaper rumors and gossip. It's politicians spouting off, hoping to get more votes."

Smith took a long swallow from the glass he held in his hand, stood and walked to the bar to refill the glass. Very little bourbon was left in the bottle and Simon suspected he had drained the bottle well past its shoulders much earlier in the day. "Everything we did, every project we started, was perfectly legal." He remained standing as he answered the question that had not been asked. "There were always open bids for the contracts. The companies we established were always done legally. The donations from the companies back to the Party were always documented. Yeah," he sneered, "even your Excelsior company."

"When last I heard, I don't own the company and I never shared in the profits," Simon Kraft countered. "It isn't exactly my company."

Smith took a swallow from his glass and then refilled it. "Yeah, but Excelsior kept you in office, along with a great number of other people."

"Have you ever been to the circus Jess," Simon asked, "under the tent with the peanuts and popcorn?" Smith nodded plaintively. "I'm reminded of the juggler who kept the balls floating in the air. He would start with three balls, usually different in color, and they would float up and down and it was as if the juggler hardly touched them. Sure enough, when one ball came down, almost immediately it would float up again. Before long he would add another ball, and then another. Quicker than you can say Jack Robinson there might be five or six balls, all different colors, being juggled in the air."

Smith sat in his chair, cast a wary glance at Simon and pursed his lips as if to ask, 'So what?'

"I always admired that juggler," Simon continued, "for the balls never fell back to hit him on the head and he always finished his act. Safe, unhurt, ready to perform again. The audience would applaud

121

and cheer and beg for more. Once I even saw him perform his act while walking on a tight-rope. He did his juggling while walking on the wire, but he was no fool. There was a safety net below him. I never did see him fall, but the net was there below him never the less. Juggling and walking and safe from any fall while he was doing his act."

Jesse took another swallow from his glass. "The audience isn't cheering anymore," Simon said and then added, "and many have become concerned for the juggler."

"So you're wondering what some others might be wondering," Smith replied in a voice that was thicker and heavier than when Simon first arrived. "What safety net has poor ol' Jess set up so's he won't fall flat on his face? What plan has he been brewing so's he won't end up in jail if this shit really does hit the fan?"

Left unsaid was the question of how many men Jesse Smith would throw under the bus to save his own skin. "Not to worry, Dr. Kraft. You're safe in my book."

Yeah, Simon thought, *as safe as all the rest of the men whom you've tied up in your schemes over the last three years.*

"Harry was concerned for me, just like you," Smith said as he removed a revolver from his jacket pocket. It was a small handgun, not unlike what a woman might carry in her purse. He put the gun on the coffee table in front of him and said, "Harry thought some others out there might not be so patient and understanding as you. He thought there might be some who thought I would turn into a canary if things got tight."

"First off," Simon replied as he cast a glance at the gun, "who's to say you've actually done anything wrong. Who's to say what information the authorities have? Nobody is saying anything about who might be dragged into your situation."

"Right you are. Just like I said, Dr. Kraft," Smith finished his drink and said, "A lot of rumor and gossip and hot air."

Smith rose from his chair and walked to the bar to pour another drink. When he sat he took another swallow and said, "I guess you're really not a bad egg, Doc. You're stiff around the edges and cold as an ice cube, but you're okay in my book. Okay in my book." He cast a sideways glance once again into the dining area. A ledger book rested on the dining table. Just as quickly he looked back at Simon.

A quick chill seared down the spine of Simon Kraft, for the worst of his suspicions was now confirmed. *Smith's book.* He wondered how many times his name appeared in Smith's book. How many other names appeared in Smith's book? Involuntarily he shuddered as he realized he no longer was the Secretary of the Department of Health and Welfare. He no longer was a physician or a war hero or the man who conquered malaria. He was a bargaining chip in Jesse Smith's quest to escape the full might and fury of the federal judicial system. No longer was he the Health Czar, but rather one of hundreds of alleged 'contributors' and 'working associates' that was logged into the ledger. Although Excelsior Research was as legally remote from him and Ed Preller as possible, the implications and insinuations would be more than problematic; they would be lethal.

Smith emptied his glass and jiggled it, as if to ask Simon if he wanted a refill of his drink. "No thanks Jess," Kraft replied. "I have to be going. I still have some work to finish in the office. Like you said, no rest for the weary."

Each of the men stood and Simon extended his right hand. "Good luck and keep your head down low." Smith took his hand and nodded.

Simon left the apartment and walked down the hallway toward the elevator. A man dressed in denim coveralls walked past him carrying a tool chest. They nodded politely at each other. The man stopped at the door of Jesse Smith's apartment. Simon heard him say, "Hotel plumber, Mr. Smith," in a thick southern drawl as the elevator doors separated. Smith's door to his apartment opened as Simon entered the elevator and descended to the lobby.

The plumber explained to Jesse Smith, "The apartment below y'all reported a water stain in their ceiling. Gotta take a quick look-see in your kitchen."

Smith replied, "Fine. Go ahead." He sat back in his chair, lifted his glass and drained it.

The plumber placed his tool chest on the floor of the kitchen, turned on the faucets and allowed the water to run forcefully and freely into the sink. "Gotta check the bathroom too," he announced. The noise of the running water was the only sound in the otherwise quiet apartment. Through groggy eyes Jesse Smith watched the water pour out of the faucet as the plumber walked out of the kitchen and behind the chair in which Smith was sitting. Quick as a flash the plumber picked up a pillow from the adjacent chair and covered Smith's face with it. He interlocked his long boney and knobby fingers and held the pillow with both hands over the mouth and nose of Jesse Smith. The plumber leaned back as Smith frantically flailed at the man's face, scratching and clawing at the man's arms and hands. Smith was never able to clutch more than the denim fabric of the coveralls or the fringe of the pillow. The plumber held firm. Desperately Smith stretched out his arms and with his fingers fully spread he futilely clawed in the air. The plumber tightened his hold and leaned back with dogged tenacity. Smith kicked and wriggled but to no avail. Thirty seconds and Smith weakened; sixty seconds and Smith was still. The plumber waited another thirty seconds and there was no hint of movement from Jesse Smith.

The plumber saw the revolver sitting on the coffee table. He picked up the revolver with his right hand and thumbed back the hammer. With his left hand he held the pillow against the side of Smith's head. He pushed the muzzle of the gun tight against the pillow and pulled the trigger. The sound of the gun's report was a muffled 'pop,' but the force of the blow was enough to throw Smith's head across the back of the chair. Blood and brain matter flew against the upholstery of the chair and splattered the adjacent lampshade. The plumber inspected the small hole above Smith's ear and saw two small, gray feathers. He picked the feathers away from the wound and put them in his pocket. He laid the revolver on the table and felt for a pulse at Smith's wrist. Nothing. He picked up the revolver again, allowed it to hover above the right hand of Smith and dropped it to the floor.

The apartment room was quiet once again, except for the water running from the faucet in the kitchen. The plumber turned off the water and the room was still. He spied the ledger book in the dining room. He opened the book and scanned a few pages. He opened his tool chest and put the book into it and snapped the lid shut. He unbuttoned his coveralls to the waist and tucked the pillow inside them. He re-buttoned the coveralls, patted at his now larger belly, and made sure the pillow was fixed in place. He spied the near empty bottle of liquor on the bar, lifted it and took a long drink. He opened the door of the apartment, glanced into the hallway and saw no one. With tool chest in hand he walked down the hallway to the elevator.

He rode the elevator down to the basement of the hotel, passed the garage doors by the loading docks and walked onto Connecticut Avenue. He spied the automobile where another man waited in the driver's seat. He walked to the vehicle, opened the lid to the trunk of the car and placed his tool chest inside. He closed the trunk, opened the door on the passenger side and got into the automobile as the driver put the car into gear and drove away.

THIRTEEN

The reported news from the west coast was both confusing and tragic. Last month the President was recovering from influenza. Through this week he still had symptoms of ptomaine poisoning. One of his attending physicians was treating him for an enlarged heart. Although speculation and rumor were associated with his continuing health status, the most recent report was incongruous, bizarre and laced with inconsistencies. The president was dead. Sometime last evening he died alone and unattended in his bedroom. Within hours he was embalmed, his coffin was placed on a train leaving San Francisco for Ohio and Calvin Coolidge was the new president of the nation. In the early morning hours, in a country store in rural New Hampshire, Coolidge was sworn into office as President of the United States by his father, a retired notary public.

Simon Kraft had not known Harding well, even while attending cabinet meetings with the man on a regular basis for two and one half years. Harding never seemed to be involved with the operations of the government and didn't seem to know many of the men who worked in the administration, which of course was the appropriate and accurate criticism thrown at him by the newspapermen and his detractors. Harry Daugherty had done most of the hiring and firing, which was a process based more on repaying political favors than on the merit of the appointee. Harding was content to delegate authority and allow the country to run itself. Such a policy was fine with Simon, for it allowed him free reign to implement a program without someone looking over his shoulder.

Simon now was forced to ask what would be the policies of this new president and how would he fit into Coolidge's new administration? Over the last few years Simon had met with Mr. Coolidge on several occasions while he served in his capacity as Vice President. He thought the man an interesting contrast to his former boss. He was private and taciturn and not inclined to idle chatter. He was a family man who respected his marriage vows. In marked contrast to his predecessor, he readily acknowledged that the nation and its people should be the beneficiaries of his service in public office, not his friends and cronies. Most significantly, he decided to allow all of Harding's cabinet secretaries to finish their terms in office.

The one appointment President Coolidge did make threatened to muddy the political future of Dr. Simon Kraft. He named C. Bascom Sloane, the seven term congressman from the Commonwealth, to be his official Secretary. Mr. Sloane's selection was noteworthy on a few accounts. He was a career politician, the only elected congressman from the predominantly democratic Commonwealth who was a republican. For the past two elections he worked for the Republican National Committee. Simon had known the congressman during his years working in the Commonwealth's capital before the Great War. Although they would never be considered friends, theirs was a first name relationship that had never been strained or tainted.

During the first six months of 1924 Bascom Sloane was the busiest man in the Capital. One of his tasks was to oversee the hiring and firing of the president's staff workers. He retained those whom he thought he could work with and dismissed those who were entrenched with how the former administration functioned. One by one he met with all the department secretaries and the chairmen of the various management bureaus. Said meetings were a cross between an employment interview and an inquisition, for Sloane labored to ferret out those who were deeply mired into the muck of the Ohio Gang. The ever growing list of names implicated in the various schemes and get-rich-quick scandals of the last administration threatened everyone's sense of 'permanency.' Speculation mounted in regard to the existence of Jesse Smith's infamous ledger book. Who had possession of it? Whose name might or might not appear in it? When would it surface?

As the time drew near for when the delegates would meet in Cleveland at the Republican National Convention to select the man who would run for president, Secretary Kraft preempted Secretary Sloane and scheduled a meeting of his own over lunch at the Willard Hotel in early May. "I trust you find the working accommodations at the White House every bit as comfortable as the working conditions in the Commonwealth," Simon said to the elderly man from his home state.

"I do, Doctor, I do," he replied in his syrupy down-home manner. "I have known Mr. Coolidge for many years and this appointment will allow me to serve this great nation of ours once again."

Ed Preller had information to the contrary which he shared with Simon prior to this luncheon. "Coolidge and Sloane don't know each other very well. Sloane is a life or death Republican with the national connections and exposure that Coolidge lacks. He was hired to ensure Coolidge wins the primary elections hands down and the national election in November."

"I regret," Sloane added, "that I am no longer in the company of our dear senator from the Commonwealth as often as I would like, but I shall ask you to pass on my warmest remembrances."

Simon smiled. Governor Cheltenham and Congressman Sloane routinely were polar opposites on their views and opinions, but they were always professional and congenial when in common company. Simon assured the President's chief administrator, "I shall, I shall. When your name was mentioned as a probable candidate for the President's secretary, Senator Cheltenham took great pride in the fact that a man from the Commonwealth would be working so closely with the new president and would be such a valued addition to his administration. When I told him of our scheduled meeting for today, he asked that he might be remembered to you and your wife."

"Thank you Simon, and do thank the Senator. So, what brings us to this hotel besides the turtle soup?"

"I am working on some bills and health care measures," Simon lied politely through his teeth. "We are in the early stages mind you, and I wanted your opinion."

"Go on, Doctor, go on."

"The health care measures will address issues related to coal mining." Simon let the thought linger while he drank from his cup of tea. "I have been in conversation with the people at the Department of Labor and the Department of the Interior and all seem to be on board with the basic ideas and tenets of my plan. I wanted your input and your thoughts." Ed Preller's research also noted that the Sloane family had amassed a fortune in the southwest section of the state in the coal mining and timber industries.

Sloane drank from his cup and narrowed his gaze at Simon. "Go on, please."

"As we all know, explosions in the mining industry account for 85% of the accidents and injuries. Miners are subject to any number of hazards, but explosions . . ." Simon paused, deciding on which words not to use. *Explosions allow for the least chance of survival. Explosions kill the most men. Explosions create the most widows and orphans.* "Explosions create the most sudden type of accident."

"Accidents in the mines are a constant threat as you say," Sloane replied, "and the loss of lives is most regrettable. Often the greatest precautions are taken and the strike of a match or the arcing of a lamp results in catastrophe."

"All the engineering consultants agree," Simon offered, "that ventilation of the mineshafts will reduce explosions and fires more successfully than any other improvement. The best estimates approach a 90% reduction in accidents."

Sloane nodded and when he started to speak Simon politely interjected, "They also suggest that the money invested to ventilate the shafts would be returned within the year with a decrease in time lost because of workers' illnesses and reduced time lost for repairs of structural problems."

Men who made their fortunes off the backs of the men who risked their lives deep in the mines were in no hurry to take away from their profits to improve the safety of the workers. The workers were expendable and easily replaced. Profits were not. As with most enterprises, money was the most critical issue. The mine owners were most concerned with only two questions. How can profits be maximized and how can expenses and lost time be reduced?

Very gently and delicately Simon cast out the line. "Before talks of legislation move forward, we are looking to initiate a pilot study to confirm what we suspect. We are looking for a few mine owners who would consider accepting money from the government, for investigation purposes mind you, to install ventilation shafts into their deep mining operations. Once installed, people from one Department or another would monitor the results."

"You're considering giving mine owners money?" Sloane asked. "My Lord, I work for the government, why don't I know about this?" he lamented with a grandfatherly smile.

Patiently Simon allowed the lure to drift with the current. No one knew about the pilot study because in large part it was a product of Simon's imagination. Last week he first raised the idea with the undersecretaries of the Departments of Labor and the Interior. Between sips of coffee the topic had been raised with neither follow up or deeper explanation.

"It is unclear whether it would be provided by way of matching funds, an outright grant or through tax credits. Any actions that would be taken as a result of this pilot study would be landmark. The mining firms involved would attain pre-eminent status within the industry."

"What would you like from me, Dr. Simon Kraft?" Sloane replied.

With deft and skill he neatly set the hook. "Within the next few weeks some information will be offered to a few newspapermen who in turn will want to follow up the story in a timely fashion. I want to be able to state that President Coolidge is most interested in the safety of the miners and is aware of the studies I will reference. The President will be able to state that he would love to see the elimination of all mining accidents for the benefit of the mine owners, the men who work in the mines and the families of the miners. The President will welcome the best efforts of the various department secretaries to address the issue. Simultaneously I will rely upon your best judgment to identify an ambitious congressman to champion such measures. I am certain there is a republican congressman in one of the mining districts who could benefit by such a windfall of opportunity."

Sloane stared up at the ceiling and thought for a moment. "What sort of timeline do you foresee to accomplish such a feat?"

Ever so slowly Simon reeled in the catch. "I plan to roll up my sleeves and invest a great deal of time in this project sometime into the next election cycle," Simon replied and took another sip of his tea. The pause allowed time for the statement to sink in and allowed time for Mr. Sloane to do the arithmetic. *Sometime in 1925—after President Coolidge is re-elected.* "As I appreciate your input and support, I will not take any further steps until I hear from you," he lied as he knew he had meetings to schedule with the appropriate department secretaries.

C. Bascom Sloane chuckled. He was a stately man and not one prone to frivolous mirth or winsome merriment. "So the man who is said to have conquered malaria sets his sights on the prevention of mining accidents. I am proud of you, Simon Kraft. I am proud the Health Czar hails from the Commonwealth. I am pleased that we are on the same side."

FOURTEEN

—— ❧ ——

"Thank you Miss Beck for seeing us today," Loretta Frontenac said as she and Phoebe Belden sat at the table across from a woman dressed in a heavy coarse cotton sack dress. It was dull grey in color, without a collar and buttoned in the back. Her court records stated she was only 28 years old, but the deep creases in her leathered face and at the corners of her eyes suggested otherwise. Her hair was dull brown in color and tied back away from her face. She had scattered pock marks on her cheeks amid the reddened heaps of acne scars. She slouched indifferently in her chair, hands folded atop the table, and made no movement when Loretta and Phoebe entered the room. Her sleepy eyes shifted ever so slowly as she watched them take their seats. Brown nicotine stains discolored her fingers and her dark fingernails were thick with deep lines and grooves. Her eyelids rose slightly as Loretta placed two packs of cigarettes on the table in front of her. Dorrie Beck's hand reached out and the cigarettes disappeared. Loretta introduced herself and Phoebe as she removed a tablet of paper and a pencil from her briefcase. "We understand you recently had a surgical operation and hope that you are on the mend and doing well."

"Gets me outta doin' work," Dorrie replied apathetically.

Loretta nodded and politely smiled, acknowledging the subtle perquisites attached to the Commonwealth's sterility program. "Although I have your records and have reviewed them," Loretta half lied, "we would like to ask you a few questions. We promise not to take up much of your time."

"Shee-it lady, time is all I got here," she chuckled. A humorless smile exposed a mouth full of brown and broken teeth. Her voice was hoarse and phlegm rattled deep in her throat.

"Miss Beck, you have been here at this institution for three years; am I correct?"

"Dorrie," she answered.

"Beg your pardon?" Loretta replied.

"You can call me Dorrie."

Loretta smiled and nodded. "Dorrie, you have been here at Norwood for three years; am I correct?" Dorrie nodded. "Do you understand why you are here, at Norwood?"

"Why?"

"Yes, do you know why you are here at Norwood?" Loretta continued.

"Why?"

Loretta pursed her lips, unsure how long this ordeal might last, unsure how long her patience could weather the give and take of interviews with patients who were court-committed to the Norwood County Home for the Mentally Infirm. What made matters worse, Dorrie Beck's diagnosis was 'Feebleminded,' which portended to make the interview that much more challenging.

"Well, I was trying to gauge your understanding . . ."

"No, no. I was askin' why you was here, askin' me questions in the fust place," Dorrie challenged. "You a lawyer, right?"

Loretta answered "Yes."

"I ain't done nuffin' wrong. Been here t'ree years like you say and I'll be leaving in t'ree months. I ain't done nuffin' to cause no police or lawyers to come nockin' at me."

"We represent other women," Loretta stretched the truth again, "in situations similar to yours. We have reason to believe they were not treated appropriately. We have spent time in court to see that such women are now being treated fairly. We thought, we believe, that what you have to tell us, what answers you may be able to give us will help other women who are our clients."

"You mean like some other women here at Norwood?" she asked.

"Yes, Dorrie," Loretta answered, "like some other women here at Norwood and some women in the other hospitals throughout the state."

Dorrie glared at the two women who sat across from her. "What do I care about them other women?"

Phoebe opened her purse, removed an open pack of cigarettes and shook the pack. Several cigarettes half fell out. She offered one to Dorrie who took it. Phoebe replaced the pack in her purse, removed a box of kitchen matches and struck one. The matchstick flamed. She waited for the sulphur to burn off and held the light to Dorrie's face. Dorrie put the cigarette into her mouth, moved Phoebe's hand with the burning match and lit her cigarette. Dorrie continued to hold Phoebe's hand as the match burned down. As the flame approached her fingers, Phoebe gently blew it out but allowed Dorrie to continue holding her hand. They stared at each other for another five seconds before Dorrie released the hand.

"I'm here because it's easier than bein' in prison."

"Easier?" Loretta said.

"Hell yeah. It looks a lot like a prison and acts a whole lot like a prison," she said in her slow and lazy manner, "but believe you me, sweetheart, this ain't nuffin like being in a women's prison. I get used to the loonies here. I ain't never got used to the dykes and the bitches in prison bustin' at my ass."

Loretta did have access to Dorrie's criminal file. Dorrie was arrested, convicted and sentenced for prostitution three times and illegal drugs twice. "You did time on several different occasions."

"Most were 30 day stretches but it weren't no picnic. Tha's just in the Commonwealth. Got busted wonst for hookin' in Maryland. Because I was so young, them records don't show up."

"Your last arrest was for possession of a great deal heroin," Loretta said. Dorrie Beck made no reply.

Prostitution and drugs. Vices and crimes. How and why was she here in the asylum? "Do you have any children?"

"No. I did. A girl. They took her from me." Dorrie turned her face away from Loretta and her half open eyes looked somewhere far off into the distance.

"Do you know where she is now?"

"Was livin' in an orphanage. She died with le grippe."

"I'm sorry," Loretta said. She waited a moment before she asked, "Dorrie, have you ever been to school?"

Dorrie drew hard on her cigarette and held the smoke inside her chest as she knocked off the ash into the metal tray that sat on the table. She exhaled the smoke and nodded her head.

"Can you read or write?" With sleepy, lazy eyes she nodded her head once again. "I assume you know your numbers." Dorrie's expression did not change as she drew on her cigarette again.

Loretta scratched 'insolent and cagey' in her notes. She wrote 'DIM BUT NOT DUMB' in capitals and circled the phrase. Between 'hosp' and 'prison' she drew an arrow.

"Dorrie," Phoebe spoke for the first time, "you said something about preferring to be here instead of prison. How is it, how did it come to pass that you had a choice of where the state would send you?" She studied Dorrie's face and saw something more than the 'awe shucks' dolt she was trying to portray. "Whose idea was it for you to come here rather than go to prison?"

Dorrie raised her right eyebrow and shifted her gazed from Phoebe to Loretta. "I had a smart lawyer," she replied. "He schooled me. He tol' me not to put on any airs about bein' any smarter than a bag of rocks. 'Play the fool, drool if necessary' he squawked at me and I played dumb jus' like he say."

"Were you examined by physicians?" Loretta asked.

"Yeah," Dorrie replied. "They asked a passel of questions; din't answer none right. They spoke about some bible verses and asked if I knew their meanings. Said I din't. Play actin' came easy that way; easier than tryin' to act half way smart."

"But you are not quite so dumb as you let on?" Loretta offered. Again Dorrie lifted an eyebrow and smiled wanly.

"The operation you had last month," Loretta said as she tread into unknown territory, "it was an operation to prevent you from becoming pregnant. Am I correct?" Dorrie slowly nodded her head. "The operation you had, the operation you underwent is called a sterilization procedure. Do you remember anyone using that word: *sterilization*?" Again Dorrie slowly nodded her head.

Each shot into the dark found its mark. Loretta stared at the notes she had written on her tablet and closed her eyes for a few seconds. When she opened them she looked into Dorrie's eyes. "There is no mention in your file about a scheduled release date. You weren't sentenced to Norwood for a specific number of years for drug possession. You were sent to Norwood because the doctors determined you were too feebleminded to understand that you were committing crimes. You were sent here for being feebleminded; potentially, for the rest of your life."

Dorrie's face remained still but her gaze shifted from Loretta to Phoebe. "Now those same people," Loretta continued, "offered you a chance to leave this asylum, to leave and be on your own again, but there was a string attached."

Dorrie brought her first two fingers to her mouth and pantomimed smoking a cigarette. Phoebe reached into her purse and removed the pack of cigarettes. She put them on the table, along with the box of matches. Dorrie removed a cigarette and lit it. She inhaled deeply and then exhaled the blue-gray smoke toward the ceiling.

Loretta continued. "The operation wasn't your idea, was it?" Dorrie offered no reply. Her eyes narrowed slightly and her head lifted just a bit. Loretta continued, "You didn't ask to have the operation did you?"

"The doctor here said if I had the operation I could leave Norwood a free woman," Dorrie explained. "They took me to court for some type of hearing. Lawyers in suits and all. They did some talkin', asked some questions. At the end of the hearing my lawyer tol' me the judge said if I had the operation I could leave Norwood."

None of it made sense to Loretta. How could sterilization be a requirement for parole from an insane asylum? She scratched a few notes onto her pad, after which she drew a line through each note. Phoebe broke the silence when she asked, "Your lawyer, do you know who he is?"

Dorrie pursed her lips and smirked at the foolish nature of the question. Phoebe continued, "Had you met him prior to the day of the hearing?" Dorrie shook her head 'no.'

Dorrie inhaled again and blew out a series of smoke rings. "Look, I have no reason to birth no more babies," she said slowly, "so's I din't have no call to fight it. The way my luck's been goin', I might be in an' outta jails for the rest of my life. I din't see no reason to go through getting' pregnant again, just to have 'em take my baby away from me. Ain't no babies here at Norwood. Any baby born to a woman in this place goes to the orphanage. Ain't right having a baby that's goin' to be taken away from its mother without her ever seein' or holdin' it."

Again Dorrie stared off vacantly into her distant memories. "Besides, I grew up separated from my mother and it weren't no good. Ma was what she was, but she was good to us when we was with her."

"You were taken away from you mother?" Loretta asked.

"Yeah, when I was a kid," Dorrie answered. "Don't know how old, 'xactly.

"Where did you live, who raised you?" Phoebe asked.

"Got passed around to some aunts and uncles," Dorrie answered. "Some of the uncles got too familiar, so's that's when we lit out. Me and Carrie had to run away."

"You and Carrie?" Loretta asked.

"My sister. Carrie's a year younger than me. They was gettin' familiar with her too and finally made her pregnant. We ran away wonst and got caught. Ran away again but Carrie cried all the time and was gettin' her morning sickness. She went back but I kept running; went to Maryland for a few years.

"When Carrie got back with Aunt Nettie, Aunt Nettie din't want nuffin' to do with her. She was suspicious of Uncle Frank laying with Carrie, but accused Carrie of hookin' and being stupid and wouldn't take her back in.

"Is your sister Carrie Beck?" Loretta asked as she wrote the name in her notes. Dorrie nodded.

Phoebe asked, "Was she a patient here at Norwood?"

"Yeah," Dorrie answered. "She had her baby while she was here and they sent the baby to an orphanage."

"Have you seen her recently?" Phoebe asked. Dorrie nodded. "When?'

"Off and on for the last t'ree years," Dorrie replied. "Carrie lives in Riverton and works on a chicken farm."

"Near the Packs River?" Loretta asked.

"Yeah, Carrie's there. You can talk with her too, but you can't talk too fast. Carrie really is a little slow up here," Dorrie said as she tapped her head with her fingers. As she did she wiggled them at Phoebe, begging another cigarette. Phoebe slid the pack to her, along with the matches. For the first time Dorrie smiled a hearty jack-o-lantern smile. "Carrie's the reason they come at me to take me to court. Tain't really fair to blame her personally, but she's why I had to go to the hospital and have the operation."

Both Loretta and Phoebe looked to Dorrie in amazement. "Carrie got spayed several years back, before I got here. They said she was feebleminded, which is sorta true, but they also said her baby was feebleminded. When she turned twenty-one they gave her a deal. If she had the operation she could go free. She had the operation and left."

Dorrie inhaled from the cigarette and brushed the ashes along the sides of the ashtray. "They said because Carrie had a baby what was feebleminded, any babies I might have would be feebleminded. With me being listed on their records as feebleminded, well, I couldn't argue all that much. They gave me a chance to leave this place, but I had to agree to the operation. If I din't care to leave here, I din't need to have the operation. Seemed clear and fair enough to me. Like I said, I din't care all that much for having more babies so's I din't put up a fight."

Loretta looked to Phoebe and closed her eyes as she struggled through what was happening to this family. "Dorrie, you do realize the Health Laws state there must be proof that three successive generations in the family must be confirmed as being afflicted, regardless of the disease. Epilepsy, mental illness, feebleminded even. Three direct, different generations; not sisters and brothers, or aunts and uncles.

"Yeah, well, they got their t'ree generations," Dorrie countered.

"How so?" Phoebe challenged.

"Ma," Dorrie said. "Ma is tetched mightily in the head. Some days she's here and some day's she's walking with the man on the moon."

"How do they know?" Phoebe persisted. "What proof do they have?"

"See for yourself," Dorrie told her as she pocketed the open pack of cigarettes. "She's here at Norwood. Her room's on the fourth floor."

The point of Loretta's pencil broke as she stared vacantly at Dorrie, who in turn smiled eerily at Loretta's muddled state. "Ma had problems with her nerves," Dorrie said. "Bad nerves the people tol' us. Plus she was awful forgetful. She would forget where she put things, forget about pots on the stove, get lost coming home from the store. Tha's why we was taken from her, me and Carrie. They said she was feebleminded and brought her here. Like I said, we was little, but when we was livin' together she always treated us good. They said she was a danger; danger to us, danger to herself, danger to others."

"What of your father?" Phoebe asked.

"Ma never married," Dorrie replied. "People in town looked at Carrie and me like we was dirt, but I don't guess none of their family trees was ever so sparklin' clean. Anyhow, Ma had man-friends from time to time. I don't recall any, but there was a few. Then she took sick in her head with nerves and we was taken away for good. We got to see her from time to time. Usually she was happy to see us, but sometimes . . . Well, sometimes she couldn't always control herself and sometimes her nerves got the better of her. After a while we din't come no more."

Dorrie struck a match and lit another cigarette. "Got word that Carrie got sent here several years back, so's when I came for a visit, was like a damn family reunion," she said as she made a throaty chuckle. She coughed a few times as she tried to dislodge the phlegm that rattled in her lungs. "Ma don't always recognize me when we're together. Don't matter much one way or the other cause she don't make much sense on a good day when we talk together. But they take care of her here, good care, and I guess tha's important."

"Perhaps," Loretta said to both Phoebe and Dorrie, "we'll come back to visit with your mother on another day." They said their good-byes as Loretta and Phoebe left the asylum.

"This case is like a rotten, stinking onion," Phoebe said. "Each layer we peel back becomes more offensive."

*   *   *

The Packs River ran through the southwest corner of Norwood County and emptied into the Chesapeake Bay. Currents were swift and ever changing, so that over the years sandbars came and went with natural impunity. The resultant channels were tricky to navigate but promised ready access to the deep water traffic lanes. River Town grew up as a city of moderate import, two miles upstream from the confluence of the two bodies of water. The early settlers in the region were tobacco farmers and noted that the currents were more placid upstream from the bay, but still deep enough to accommodate deep hulled ships approaching 20 to 40 tons. Tobacco was the prime money crop and River Town became a port that sent and received more than one hundred ships every year.

The Civil War disrupted the tobacco trade, but the quiet and shallower waters upstream on the Packs River became a popular collecting area for the fast moving cutters of the Confederacy, intent on evading the Union blockade. Riverton served as a supply center for both the military and the civilian population. After the war the roads were improved, railroad lines were rebuilt and Riverton continued as a supplier of tobacco, produce and poultry products.

With the turn of the century big companies emerged nationally as factories and processing centers became common appearances. Riverton was not immune to this evolution. Small, family owned poultry farms were joined together and morphed into assembly-line processing centers. Chickens and turkeys by the thousands were raised, slaughtered, plucked, butchered, packed and transported from Riverton up and down the Atlantic Coast and inland as far west as Chicago and St. Louis.

Despite advancements made during the industrial revolution and America's large scale mechanization that was so well displayed during the Great War, much of the processing of poultry was still performed by hand. Over the years engineers developed multiple varieties of processing machinery, but the machines jammed, broke down with confounding frequency and were prone to maim those who tended to the equipment. People who slaughtered and plucked chickens didn't jam and if any broke down, there was a ready supply of replacements waiting to step into the line.

On the line in a chicken slaughterhouse is where Loretta Frontenac and Phoebe Belden found Carrie Beck. 'Workin' the line' was piece-work and Carrie was paid three cents for each bird she plucked and cleaned. They arranged to meet with Carrie after her shift finished so as not to interfere with her work. They also promised to drive her home to her boarding house because their meeting would interfere with her riding the bus home from the plant.

Loretta and Phoebe waited outside the plant, standing by Loretta's Ford automobile, and were conspicuously out of place. Most of the workers who entered or exited the plant were colored and most were men. They carried lunch pails, small buckets, baskets and the occasional milk bottle, empty or filled with something other than milk. As the workers walked past them, in almost every instance, the men lifted their hats and the women smiled politely as they passed on a greeting to Loretta and Phoebe. Two white women, younger in age than most of the workers, were laughing and talking when they walked to the curb where the car was parked.

"Ya'all must be the lawyers," the one in the gingham dress said.

"Yes, I'm Loretta Frontenac. This is my assistant, Phoebe Belden."

Loretta extended her hand and the woman accepted it. "I'm Carrie. Carrie Beck. This here's," Carrie said as she turned to the other woman, "Laura." Laura indifferently nodded her head. "Laura and I share a room." All nodded a greeting.

"Is there someplace we may go," Loretta asked, "somewhere perhaps for a cup of coffee and a sandwich, where we may talk?"

"Red's Café sounds good, don't it Laura?" Carrie offered.

"Yes," Loretta said. "I saw it on the ride here."

Laura nodded. "You'll make sure you get her home all right?"

"Yes Laura," Loretta replied. "I promise."

"It's all right, g'wan," Carrie said to her friend. Laura nodded and walked to where people waited for the bus. "Laura's a good roommate. She's smart and everything."

Phoebe opened the passenger side door to allow Carrie to enter. "This your very own car?" Carrie asked.

"Yes it is," Loretta replied.

"Shee-it lady. Youse livin' large. Can I ride in the front?"

Phoebe smiled, stepped into the back of the car and took a seat.

"Bet you thought I'd come out covered in blood and chicken guts and feathers?" Carrie said with a chuckle to Loretta. "We wear heavy aprons and they let us clean up in a washroom. They're nice that way."

The gingham dress was clean, although a bit frayed at the hem. Her hair was stringy and hung down on her shoulders. She was much heavier than Dorrie and also shorter. One needed to strain to appreciate any family likeness. Her almond shaped eyes were set wide across a nose that had a prominent bump on the bridge. Her complexion was light and fair and tainted with several blotches, but it lacked the heavy creases and wrinkles that plagued Dorrie. Her mouth was much wider than Dorrie's, with thicker lips and a stronger chin.

"Do you get to ride in many automobiles?" Loretta asked.

"A few," she replied. "Jes' not many driven by women."

Red's Café was adjacent to Red's General Store and Red's Feed and Seed.

"Red ain't been around for a while," Carrie said as she exited the car. "As the story goes, Red was a pirate or sumpthin'. He stole a whole bunch of stuff and sold slaves and finally got hung. I guess people thought the name was catchy."

The three women sat at a booth in the diner. As they ordered coffee, Loretta removed a tablet and a pencil from her briefcase. "We have been meeting with a number of young women who have undergone operations that were ordered by the Commonwealth. We understand you had a surgery performed that was ordered by the Commonwealth."

"Yeah. Tha's right. On my belly," Carrie replied.

"Do you understand why you had the surgery?" Loretta asked.

"Yeah. So I wouldn't have no more babies."

Loretta nodded and continued. "Yes, but do you know why the court decided you should have no more babies?"

The coffee came and Carrie poured a generous portion of sugar from the container into her cup. "The judge and the lawyers said I wasn't none too smart. Said Ma wasn't none too smart. They said my baby, Vivien, wasn't none too smart." Carrie used her spoon to swirl the coffee as she stared into the cup. She ladled a spoonful of coffee into her mouth and then poured more sugar into the cup. She used her spoon to swirl the coffee more and then tasted the coffee once again.

"You delivered your baby Vivien while you were living with your Aunt Josephine?" Loretta asked.

"That's right," Carrie replied. "Nursed her for a bit but within the first month I was sent to Norwood asylum and Vivien was sent to the orphanage.

"Did you get to visit with her?" Phoebe asked.

"From time to time," Carrie answered. "They was nice that way."

Loretta nodded. "How old was Vivien when you had your court hearing?"

"Wasn't a year," she replied. "I don't remember much 'bout the hearin' but that a bunch of strange people what came in and talked. Doctors, nurses. In the end they came to me and said I could leave the home if I agreed not to have no more babies. I said, 'How can I guarantee that?' They said if I have an operation that will make it impossible to have babies, I can leave the hospital."

"And you agreed to have the operation," Loretta offered.

"Yeah. Most anything was better than living in the home," Carrie answered. "After I had the operation one of the people at the hospital found me a job down here in Riverton, so's I came down here."

"But you were not allowed to take Vivien with you?" Phoebe added.

Carrie shook her head 'No.' "Vivien got adopted. Even after all the lies they said about Vivien being slow, a nice family took her and made her happy. A good family. She gets to wear clean clothes and they take care of her real good. She even goes to school."

"You know the family?" Loretta queried and Carrie nodded her head. "It is very uncommon for the natural mother and the adopting family to know each other, to be in contact with each."

"May be," Carrie replied, "But with the hearin' and all, Vivien had to be examined and the new family got involved. See, they adopted Vivien while the hearin' was taking place. They was heartsick. They was afraid the judge was goin' to take Vivien away from them. Then, when the judge said that Vivien wasn't none too smart, I was afraid the new family wouldn't want Vivien no more. But they a good family and kept her anyway. I know they love her and I have to believe they'll be better for her than I would be. Shee-it, I can hardly take care of myself, so's I guess . . ." Carrie trailed off.

"Have you seen or been with Vivien since you left the home?" Loretta asked.

Carrie paused and shook her. "No. The new family thought it best that Vivien only have one mother. They din't want to confuse her. Tha's okay, I guess. She doin' good and she's healthy and she's real smart too. Not like the judge said and not like what them other men said."

Loretta narrowed her eyes and studied Carrie. "What do you mean she's smart?"

Carrie reached into the pocket of her dress and removed an envelope. She removed a folded card and a photograph. "Here; I carry this wid me all the time. It's Vivien."

Loretta viewed the photograph of a little girl in a dress. She was standing outside of a church and held in her hands a clutch of flowers. "The flowers are violets," Carrie explained. "Violet flowers are here favorites."

Loretta smiled and took the card. It was a report card from Madison Elementary School for Vivien. Loretta read the report front and back. "Carrie, did you read this?"

"No. I don't read any good but Laura read it to me. She says the report says Vivien is smart. Ain't that so?"

"Yes Carrie," Loretta answered her. "The report card says that Vivien does excellent work."

FIFTEEN

"'Tis a grand day for a select group of the people of America," Ed Preller spouted in his feaux Irish Brogue. "The right and honorable director of our namesake department will be dispersing Uncle Sam's money like he was printing notes in the basement."

"For a noble cause Ted my boy," Simon Kraft replied, "for a noble cause. There is no limit to what I would spend of our treasury's money to advance our Republic and improve our nation."

"Well, good doctor, you do have a limit, as imposed by Congress and regulated by our department's oversight committee."

"Spoilsport," Simon said with a theatrical grimace. Today's schedule included interviews with several individuals who submitted applications for federal grants for their studies, in addition to the approval of continued funding for previous recipients. "One item we will not be troubled with is the inclusion of Excelsior Research into the budgets and the funneling of money to the Ohio Gang."

"No more Harry Daugherty and no more Jesse Smith," Ed said.

"Yeah; one tied up in the courts and one buried in the ground," Kraft replied with a wry smile.

"And their absence makes America a better place," Ed added.

"Let the games begin."

"Mrs. Stringer is here to see you," Ed said and Simon nodded.

An attractive woman in her mid-forties entered the office. Simon rose to greet her. Her dark hair was stylishly close cropped and covered by a small hat that fit neatly atop her head. She was clear eyed with a tastefully modest amount of make-up on her lips and cheeks. She walked into the office with an air of confidence and purpose.

"I'm very glad to meet you, Mrs. Stringer," Simon offered, "or should I refer to you as Mrs. Stevens."

"Mr. Stevens wouldn't argue with you," she replied, "but James and I both agreed before we married last spring that for professional purposes, I am more recognizable by my former name."

Simon gestured for her to take a seat. "I have followed your work with the American Birth Control League for years. In many respects I believe we are kindred spirits." Simon knew Margaret Stringer to be a fierce warrior for her cause. "I became familiar with the early issues of *The Woman Rebel* before the war, during a time when I took a very aggressive stance on venereal disease. We in the Commonwealth were afflicted like every other state in the union and struggled on how to make our problems more public. Your articles in *The Woman Rebel* were bold and audacious. I was inspired to go into the public light with our quest to combat the disease."

"I thank you for your comments," she replied. "We have faced many struggles but fortunately we have made some progress." She smiled a beguiling smile and added, "Which is what brings us together this morning."

"Yes," Simon replied. "Tell me about your clinic in New York City."

"It is in Harlem, actually, and we named it the Clinical Research Agency," Stringer explained. "We are staffed by physicians, all women by the way, because only physicians are able to order and distribute birth control devices in New York State. We educate the men and women in our community about the science of parenthood and the science of breeding. A clinic like ours is imperative for it is the only way to breed out of this race of people the scourges of transmissible disease, mental defect, poverty, lawlessness and crime. The people in Harlem are breeding like weeds and something must be done to slow their growth." Both Simon and Ed nodded their understanding.

"Nothing happens in Harlem if you do not solicit the ministers from the churches to become involved in your projects," Margaret Stringer continued. "Without their approval and support, well, you have no project. Consequently we have invited ministers and many of the local civic leaders from the community to serve on our board of directors."

"Wise decisions," Ed added.

"Necessary decisions," Stringer corrected him. "I've been struggling in New York City for more than ten years. As you well know, we face a crisis in our nation with an ever increasing amount of human waste being born each year. Consider that problem magnified by an order of ten for the people in Harlem."

"We here in this office are most interested in any progress and success you might enjoy with your clinic," Simon said. "One goal, obviously, would be to duplicate your efforts and successes on a grander scale."

"Thank you, Mr. Secretary," Margaret Stringer replied. "I applaud the efforts and accomplishments you have made in regard to limiting the birth rates of those who obviously should not be procreating within the states' institutions. I believe our nation is ready to take the next step and extend the concepts of your health laws *beyond* the state institutions. One of our nation's greatest problems is the over-fertility of the inferior classes."

Inferior classes. "What in your mind constitutes the inferior groups?"

"Immigrants for one," she replied quickly. "I know you spoke before Congress prior to the passage of the Immigration Act and our nation applauded you."

"And the colored races?"

"Those who are impoverished are a menace to the American race," Margaret Stringer said with an even tone. "The impoverished breed like rodents without regard to how the children will be taken care of. Consequently they become dependent upon the normal and the fit and the upper classes of society for their support. Procreation of this group, along with the others, must be limited.

"I have traveled extensively in the Orient, Mr. Secretary. Do you know how the Chinese practice family planning? Female infanticide. Obviously there is a better solution and it remains for the U.S. government to set a sensible example to the world. I propose that the government offer a bonus or yearly pension to all unfit parents who allow themselves to be sterilized by harmless and scientific means. In this way the morons and the diseased would have no posterity to inherit their unhappy condition."

"A bonus?" Ed asked with a quizzical look on his face.

"Yes, a bonus," she replied. "It would be wise and profitable and the salvation of American civilization. Such a plan would reduce the birthrate among the diseased, the sickly, the poverty stricken and anti-social classes; elements who are unable to provide for themselves. Such a plan would also reduce the burden that society is forced to carry."

"We, the government, thank you for your comments and suggestions," Simon replied.

"Mrs. Stringer," Ed added, "you will hear from us within the month."

All rose and when Margaret Stringer left the room a glow remained on Simon's face. Ed broke the silence when he said, "You realize Margaret Stringer has remarried and currently has a husband.

Simon waved a hand at Ed feigning disinterest. "G'wan, I have paperwork to do. Van Kirk isn't due for another hour."

Simon reviewed applications for continued funding of previously approved projects. The work with the syphilitic patients at Tuskegee Institute would be a long-term study, perhaps continuing for another 30 or 40 years. Simon was pleased to note that nearly 200 men had been enrolled in the study. The costs to the Department were low, mostly for administrative services, and Simon readily approved the continuation of the study. He smiled to himself, mindful that the costs for medication were always a significant factor in any clinical trial. Well, not for the Tuskegee group. Another applicant wanted grant money to investigate whether the extracted insulin from hogs would be more effective and less allergic than insulin extracted from beef cattle. He smiled when he read that the study would be performed at the University of Cincinnati in the 'Queen City'—hog capital of the nation.

Dr. Charles was making progress with his venereal disease study in Guatemala and Professor Korpinski was making great strides with his polio vaccination experiments at the Rockefeller Institute. The last piece of paperwork for review was Professor Van Kirk's work with the artificial insemination project. As Simon picked up the forms to scan Ed knocked on the open door. "Professor Van Kirk is here."

Simon rose from his chair to meet the nattily dressed professor with his pointed beard and wire rimmed glasses. "So good to see you again, Professor Van Kirk." To Ed Preller he said, "I'll meet with Professor Van Kirk today, Ed; no need to tie you up," and closed his office door.

"Mr. Secretary," Van Kirk replied.

They exchanged pleasantries for a few minutes before Simon asked, "So what is the current tally of babies produced by your good efforts?"

"One hundred and seven babies, Mr. Secretary. One hundred and seven. And, if I might say, *our* good efforts. If it were not for you and your department, none of this would have happened. None of the early success that we now enjoy would be possible without you."

"Well, as George M. Cohan might say, 'I thank you, my department thanks you and a great nation thanks you.'"

"Not only have we made 107 married couples happy with new babies, another 37 couples will be expecting new arrivals over the winter."

Barren couples barren no more, Simon thought. "Marvelous. Now, tell me, what difficulties are you experiencing?"

"Not many, really" Professor Van Kirk replied. "Unfortunately not every procedure proves to be successful. A few women, after four or five attempts, fail to conceive. For those couples we have to refer them to adoption centers. But we do continue to make refinements. Preservation techniques for the transport of the semen continue to improve. By mixing various concoctions and preservatives with the semen, we are able to extend the life span and expand the volume of the donations. We have found that the same semen donation may be used for multiple women."

"It sounds like you have developed quite an assembly line at your facility, something that might make Henry Ford jealous," Simon offered.

"Yes, we have. Perhaps you would like to visit us. Why don't you join me on a day when I have a few procedures scheduled?"

"Yes. I would like that," Simon replied. In a lower tone he asked, "And the courier service continues to work well?"

"Yes sir, like clockwork."

Simon stared out the window for a moment, as if to allow for his thoughts to form. "Professor, do you receive many requests from unmarried women?"

"A few. Yes, more than a few," he replied.

"Under the scope of the current study, we've limited ourselves only to married women, correct?" Van Kirk nodded. "What if the program were to expand to include unmarried women? Unmarried for any number of reasons; widows, divorcees, women who might be interested in raising a child but have decided not to take on the . . ." Simon pursed his lips as he searched for the correct phrase. "I might say *pleasures* of a husband but let's use the term *burden* of taking on a husband?"

"Dr. Simon," Van Kirk replied, "Great Britain lost the better part of an entire generation of men during the last war and Germany fared no better. Situations do present themselves."

"Yes, yes, situations do arise," Simon countered, "but in a generic sense, consider the unmarried woman who wants a child."

"Societal issues, mores and condemnation aside?" Van Kirk asked.

"Correct."

"There would be no new or different issues of concern; neither operational or biological," Van Kirk answered.

"What if we . . . , er, what if you, Professor, what if you were to work on a model whereby exceptional young women with various healthy and outstanding traits were entered into the program?"

"If you like," Van Kirk offered, "we could expand the program with little difficulty."

"If we were to implement this new program," Simon suggested, "we could modify the process whereby we might unite the best of selected women and best of selected sperm donors. It would simulate what one might call in the husbandry industry, a selective breeding program."

"The goal being to join together the best of the best; to create 'super' offspring?"

"Exactly," Simon replied.

"There would be little difficulty in that respect, Mr. Secretary. The only challenge would be the procedure by which the parents would be chosen," Van Kirk said.

"That process will take care of itself," Simon said with a nonchalant waving of his hand. "Generate a work plan, Professor. Send me your plans and we'll see what we can do to jumpstart the program," Kraft ordered.

He reached into his desk and removed an envelope stamped PERSONAL TO THE SECRETARY. "Send the plan directly to me.

*   *   *

As he drove his automobile across the 14th Street Bridge toward Arlington, Simon gazed down at the Potomac River, noting the quiet ripples that danced across the top of the water. He enjoyed the time away from his office; away from the noisome appointments and meetings and favor-seekers. It was his quiet time. It was now late autumn in Virginia and the wind blew fallen leaves across the road. Most of the leaves that remained on the trees were brown or dark shades of red and orange. He thought back to his youth and to so many days like today, for autumn days were days for hunting with his father. He remembered when they would walk across open fields and follow dirt roads alongside each other. In his mind's eye he watched each of them carrying a shotgun over their shoulders, anxiously waiting for the next rabbit to scurry across their path, or for the next quail or pheasant to take flight in front of them. Although Simon had been that young boy, he would never be that man alongside his son. Unknowingly he grimaced and pursed his lips. A cold shiver worked its way up his spine. *It will soon be cold* he thought. Perhaps this weekend he should trek down to the basement to get the winter clothing out of moth balls and . . .

The brick building that housed Tomorrow's Children looked better suited to house business offices than a medical research facility. It stood three stories high and was short on windows. The parking lot for the automobiles was unremarkable and the sign on the wall of the building revealed only a street address: '2462 Lafayette Street.'

The receptionist recognized him and allowed him entrance to Professor Van Kirk's private office. It was more a cave than an office. Little light shined through the window and the bulb in the desk lamp was more orange than yellow. Stacks of journals and books rose from the floor and were piled high on tables. Frames that contained various diplomas and certificates covered the walls in no discernible pattern. Simon forgave the man his eccentricities.

"Good morning, Mr. Secretary," Van Kirk announced as he walked into his office. He extended his hand in greeting as he said, "I see that you have escaped the craziness of the Capital for the peace and quiet of our laboratories." He wore a long, white laboratory coat over his white surgical garb.

"Always a pleasure, Professor."

"I have two cases scheduled for today," he said in his matter-of-fact manner. "Their stories are similar. They've been married four and six years respectively and have been unsuccessful trying to conceive children. The women have normal pelvic organs. One husband had mumps when he was a child and produces no sperm. The other husband has few viable sperm as seen under the microscope. Both couples are excellent candidates for the procedures."

"I enjoy returning here to watch your work," Simon said.

"You miss the operating room, don't you?"

"I do," Simon replied reluctantly. "I'm sorry to say I really do miss the operating room. I've been away from surgery so long, I am reluctant to use anything sharper than a butter knife."

Van Kirk flashed a rare smile, guided Simon out of the office and said, "That shan't be a problem today. The changing room is there," pointing to his left, "and the wash room is here," pointing to the right. "Your being here today eliminates the need for the courier service."

After he donned his white surgical uniform Simon joined Van Kirk in what served as a procedure room. The patient lay on a table beneath a mountain of drapes and towels. A nurse sat at one end of the table where the patient's head was positioned. Simon sniffed and his mind raced back in time to identify the faint, sweet aroma of nitrous oxide in the room. Laughing gas. He cast a glance toward the nurse and noted that she held an anesthesia mask over the face of the patient. She politely nodded her head toward Simon.

At the opposite end of the table the patient's knees were drawn up so that her lower legs were parallel to the ground and her toes were pointed toward the ceiling. "We use light sedation with nitrous oxide for the procedure," Van Kirk said, "to ease the cramping women occasionally experience when we manipulate the uterus." His hands moved quickly with no wasted motion. He used an instrument to lay open the birth canal. An assistant repositioned the floor lamp so the light beam shined where Van Kirk would be working.

"We apply an instrument to the cervix of the uterus for control." He turned from the patient to a table where multiple instruments were spread out. "We keep the semen specimens in cold storage, diluted in an organic saline solution, until the day of the procedure. Once warmed to room temperature the specimen is maintained in a sterile vial. Fresh specimens require no treatment other than placement into a vial to avoid infection."

Van Kirk picked up a syringe partially filled with a clear solution. A wide bore metal needle was attached to the end of the syringe. He pierced the rubber stopper of the vial with the needle and withdrew the semen specimen. He replaced the metal needle with a curved plastic tube that was no less than 8 inches in length. He turned once again to the patient, used his left hand to steady the instrument that held the uterine cervix, and inserted the long plastic tube through the opening of the cervix into the cavity of the uterus. Slowly he emptied the syringe into the uterus. He withdrew the plastic tube, removed all instruments and backed away from the patient. "Not quite how nature drew it up, but there you have it."

The assistant turned off the floor lamp and then repositioned the patient's legs onto the table. The drapes and towels were removed, a blanket was placed onto the patient and within a minute she was awake and removed from the treatment room. Hardly fifteen minutes from start to finish.

"The patient will lay flat for the next hour." Professor Van Kirk picked up the patient's chart and took Simon by the arm. "One more patient and then you can take me to lunch."

SIXTEEN

Mrs. Lawrence carried a tray into the parlor of their apartment and said with a broad smile, "Lemon, sugar and cream are setting on the side table so you may fix your own tea. Only the professor will be served."

"Well, aren't we special," Loretta teased.

"You spoil him, Grandma," Phoebe added.

"People as old and withered as Maxwell deserve to be spoiled," Mrs. Lawrence replied as she patted the top of his head.

"Rank, age and infirmity have their privileges," Lawrence added as he sat in his wheelchair and theatrically straightened his tie and smoothed the imaginary creases of his suit coat.

"Just tell them we are like an old wines, Professor," Dr. Guy Frontenac said. "We continue to improve with age and deserve as much special treatment as possible." Loretta had asked her father to join them because of the complexity of the medical issues that continued to arise."

"So where are we," Lawrence asked, "with your research and fact finding endeavors?"

"Within Norwood County," Phoebe read from her notes, "despite the sealing of so many records, we have documented more than 200 cases of sterilization. This number is only within the county, mind you. There are nine other asylums scattered throughout the Commonwealth. The final numbers may prove to be staggering."

"Quite the crusade," Lawrence offered.

"Like similar Health Laws in other states," Loretta added, "our Commonwealth's laws provide a veil of protection to the states' prosecutors and physicians who are involved with the sterilization campaign. Essentially they are immune to any adverse criticism, jeopardy or repercussions As they continue with unbridled furor, one can only speculate on the current number of surgical procedures that are being performed nationwide."

Lawrence waived a hand dismissively and replied, "This project is large enough. Do not presuppose we can take on the injustices perpetrated throughout the entire nation. Allow us to restrict our endeavors to some portion of these 200 cases within our own county. Then we can address the rest of our state. Perhaps if we create a significant groundswell, others will join us as attention shifts to issues nationwide."

"Of these cases Grandpa," Phoebe said as she stirred her tea, "most followed the standard protocols as established by the law. The patients had legal representation, hearings took place and the defendants were assigned a guardian to facilitate the right to appeal. The letter of the law was followed, judgments were handed down and the surgeries were performed."

"The process appears to be consistent and appropriate only when the cases are viewed from a distance," Loretta said. "Upon closer inspection flaws emerge. For one, there has never been a successful appeal. Only a few guardians or patients have completed the appeal process but no judge has reversed the initial judgment."

"Is there any suggestion as to why there has never been a reversal of a court decision?" Lawrence asked.

"Nothing," Phoebe answered. "As we said, the defense lawyers for the patients in almost every instance were appointed by the court. Another interesting finding: the court appointed lawyers have never won a case. Invariably the decisions of the hearings result in a court order for sterilization."

"A monumental display of futility," Lawrence offered. "One must also question whether there was due process and execution of the *intent* of the laws, if not the *letter* of the laws.

"Incompetence and malpractice are more like it," Guy Frontenac suggested.

"I believe misfeasance may be an issue, but not incompetence," Phoebe countered. "The laws are being misused and misapplied to achieve what they consider to be a 'greater good.' When I reviewed the court documents of the few cases I was able to obtain, I came across a mountain of stationary from Pratt's law firm. I discovered that the names of the public defenders who represented the patients, with disturbing frequency, found their way onto the letterhead of the stationery for Pratt's law firm at some later point in time. Within three years of first appearing in the court records, more than half of the court appointed defense lawyers landed a job working for Pratt's law firm."

"A peculiar coincidence indeed," Maxwell Lawrence said as he sipped at his tea.

"Isn't that collusion?" Guy Frontenac asked.

"No." Lawrence replied. "Such an environment has always been a proving ground for young lawyers hoping to impress the decision makers with the high profile law firms. Whether one works as a public defender or as an assistant prosecutor with the county or the state, young lawyers are able to hone their skills and gain valuable experience slugging their way through cases, representing the down-trodden and those tortured by misfortune."

Lawrence raised his teacup to catch the eye of his wife and silently begged for a refill. "But you are correct to remain suspicious. How does losing a case impress a future employer and why would an employer reward such ineptitude? Unless, of course, if some group or entity were intent on steamrolling through this problem with a minimal amount of difficulties or opposition. What better way would there be than to prop up silhouette teams of court appointed public defenders who would roll over and play dead? The very thought of such a scenario is disturbing."

"Another interesting finding," Phoebe offered. "Only two physicians have served as the medical experts for nearly all the cases: a Dr. Castor and a Dr. Comly.

"Interesting and disturbing," Lawrence replied, "but not illegal. Improper, possibly. Grounds for an appeal, no."

Loretta added, "The operations that were performed routinely were vasectomies on men and the division and ligation of the fallopian tubes on women. In many instances, for either criminals approaching the time for their parole or for those determined to be feebleminded, a carrot was dangled on the end of a stick. Undergo the operation and we will discharge you from our institution."

"Which enters into the discussion a good many questions," Lawrence added. "We note the high number of court cases whereby a judgment was handed down that demanded sterilization. How many individuals were *coerced*? How many poor souls went to the operating rooms kicking and screaming and how many saw the operation as a means to escape confinement? Was the sterilization operation an enticement, or was it blackmail, or was it a deal with the devil?"

Loretta explained to her father, "The key wording in the law states the Commonwealth may perform the operations to 'promote the welfare of the patients.' One is meant to accept the supposition that female patients, when discharged from the institutions, will not be capable of safeguarding themselves from pregnancy. In regard to the male patients who are discharged, society will be protected from those who are unable to take the necessary precautions to avoid impregnating their partners."

"As the issue of discharge is presented to the patients," Dr. Frontenac summarized, "it would appear that the law empowers the state to render the targeted patients sterile."

Loretta nodded and answered, "Yes, in many instances. There is no option for those convicted of rape and sexual molestation when castration is mandated at the time of their sentencing. For the severely mentally retarded, this group remains confined to the institutions following their operations. On the contrary, the epileptics and feebleminded become eligible for discharge following their sterilization procedures."

"*Confined in a state supported institution* is the operative term associated with the court decisions," Lawrence whispered. "'Confinement to an institution that is maintained and paid for by the state' was the original pretext championed in the Health Laws when they first came into existence. So long as the patients remained wards of the Commonwealth, the Commonwealth was free to make decisions and take actions to safeguard these patients and make decisions that were fiscally responsible. As we have crept along through the years, the Health Laws have been extended to people, in institutions, who would soon be released into the general population.

"As we have seen with the Summerdale case, we are but one step removed from having the Health Laws applied to the general citizenry. If certain individuals have their way, the good people of

America in the general population will be scrutinized, evaluated and placed under a microscope. Those with defects, or purported defects, will be sterilized in an effort to sanitize the population. This 'extrapolation' of the Health Laws is inconsistent with the original intent and spirit of the laws. This extension of the laws will affect individuals who are no longer wards of the state. This unnatural progression of the laws will leave no home safe from a possible invasion of self proclaimed 'do-gooders.' This cleansing of the unfit has one very clear purpose: to create a race of *better people.*"

"The welfare of the patient is no longer at issue," Guy Frontenac said, "and is superseded by the welfare of the state."

A pall settled on the room and no one spoke as they looked at one another and drained their teacups. The silence was broken by Maxwell Lawrence when he uttered, "A thoroughly gruesome and daunting eventuality."

"There is another issue to consider," Dr. Frontenac offered. "The likelihood of complications following the surgical procedures." All three heads turned to him. "No surgeon or group of surgeons can perform hundreds, even thousands of operations and not have some number of complications. Infection, heart problems, even death. No one can guarantee perfection 100% of the time."

"How would the Commonwealth be impacted by an untoward outcome of an operation?" Phoebe asked.

"The Health Laws include wording that protects the Commonwealth and the surgeons. They are held harmless from complications of the surgeries and the wrong doings enacted upon the patients outside the courtroom," Lawrence answered. "However, if some issues were to arise with how the judgment was made, or if there were any procedural improprieties, then it would prove more difficult for the Commonwealth to separate itself from the problem.

"You mean," Dr. Frontenac asked, "if the Commonwealth made a mistake during the hearing and the patient died from the court ordered surgery, the Commonwealth might be implicated or held liable?"

"It is possible." Maxwell Lawrence sipped his tea. "I repeat that we have before us a task of gargantuan proportions. Miss Frontenac, you have had some modicum of success picking apart past judgments for violations of protocol. I have no doubt that if you were to sift through even a portion of the more than 200 cases to which Phoebe referred, you would stir up enough dust to benefit both your clients and yourself. Such efforts," he intoned, "might prove to be financially quite rewarding."

Loretta pursed her lips and thought back to the day she received the check for $87,000 on behalf of the Summerdale family. She wondered how many other large dollar awards might be lurking among Phoebe's cases.

"There is another path to pursue that may not be mutually exclusive," Lawrence offered. "Yes, continue to investigate 'Phoebe's unfortunates,'" he said with a flourish, "but think down-stream. Think of how these people may have had their constitutional rights violated or abridged. Our Commonwealth's Declaration of Rights and our nation's Declaration of Independence both refer to a citizen's inalienable right to 'the pursuit of happiness.' Is the choice, is the option to procreate and raise a family an inalienable right of every American citizen? If so, does having an infirmity like epilepsy, or does being feebleminded void this right, and preclude someone from the option to raise a family? Even given the possibility that one or more of the offspring might continue with the disease and/or pass on the condition to his or her offspring, is sterilization a just solution?"

"Isn't sterilization a punishment?" Dr. Frontenac asked his daughter. "Is it the appropriate punishment for being a dimwit? If so, there are quite a few politicians walking about who certainly should be candidates."

All smiled but Maxwell Lawrence added, "Cruel and unusual punishment is argued as a matter of degree. Torture is not allowed but death by execution is. Remember, the health laws are not meant to punish the institutionalized for the conditions that landed then in the prisons and asylums. The laws are meant to apply only to the hereditary nature of the defect that landed them in the institutions."

"Does that mean," Loretta challenged, "that we, as a nation, should tolerate and condone assault by surgery as recompense for the government's eliminating an affliction that is totally beyond an individual's control?"

"The state will argue," Lawrence replied, "that because one cannot control the hereditary and genetic destiny of one's affliction, they, the government, must step in and do so. The intended benefit of the Health Laws is that society will be improved. It will be argued, and you will hear this argument time and again, the unfit must make sacrifices for the public good."

"Ergo," Phoebe said with theatrical flourish, "the issue at hand is whether sterilization violates or is in compliance with the eighth amendment to the constitution. Is court mandated sterilization a punishment, a cruel and unusual act, or is it the savior of mankind?"

"Your argument is absolutely correct, young lady," Lawrence intoned. "Allow me to offer a second issue. Are the patients in the asylums being treated, or subjugated if you will, differently from people with similar afflictions who reside outside the institutions in the general population? Is the young man sitting on Main Street in Anytown, USA subject to the same threat of sterilization as a different young man who resides in the Norwood County Home for the Mentally Infirm? If they are being treated differently, they are no longer being equally protected by the laws of the land. As such, the health laws would be in violation of the 14th amendment to the Constitution.

Lawrence turned and spoke to Guy Frontenac. "Tell us about your meeting with Carrie Beck's mother."

"We met last week," Dr. Frontenac replied. "Her name is Annabelle Beck and the woman has her share of problems. She suffers from schizophrenia. When I talked with her she bounced from one idea to another and most ideas are totally unrelated. Consequently her ability to stay focused on one issue or topic is a challenge she cannot handle. When lucid she is able to carry on a conversation, but her mind soon wanders." Guy Frontenac fluttered his hands to simulate a bird in flight.

"The testing performed by the Commonwealth demonstrated she is no more advanced than a ten year old. She is able to perform basic arithmetic and work her way through easy bible parables like the Good Samaritan or the golden rule. Unfortunately her low levels of mentation and understanding make dealing with her mental health issues problematic."

"So, let us chart a plan," Lawrence said. "Phoebe and Loretta shall continue as the ombudsmen for the offended. They will continue to work on the cases they have in hand and identify as many flaws as possible. Ever ready and eminently able shall be the good doctor to assist you where and when he can. I shall enmesh myself in the Carrie Beck appeal."

"Because Carrie has become a vicarious part of her daughter's life," Loretta offered, "we know where Vivien goes to school and we should be able to obtain a court order that will allow for an examination of the child."

"Excellent. We'll attack their experts with the newly discovered information. We'll invalidated their premises and render their conclusions illogical. We'll expose their flaws and gut them like a trout. How I look forward to crossing swords once again with the Commonwealth's Supreme Court. Oh but a grand and glorious band are we."

SEVENTEEN

※

Loretta and Phoebe shuffled papers and realigned index cards as they struggled to make sense of the inexplicable. They sat at the table in their office on a Saturday morning in dresses better suited for housecleaning or gardening. They agreed to dress casually because they wouldn't be seeing any clients and they had no public obligations. They thought that spending a few hours during a time when they were least likely to be interrupted would allow them the opportunity to plow through the mountains of information that were accumulating so rapidly. Phoebe's hair was now cut short and she wore it curled and frizzy, wrapped in a yellow bandana. Despite her wearing neither make-up nor jewelry, Loretta still thought her too chic and too 'New York fashionable' for the homespuns who walked down the main street of their sleepy little town of Oxford Corners. Loretta wore a cotton blouse and dress and her thick auburn hair was tied back in a plain fashion, secured with a bow of heavy red yarn.

Phoebe's digging and ferreting uncovered nearly four dozen new cases, several of which were identified in the adjoining Jefferson County. A review of the court documents clearly suggested that judgments were being handed down in bulk fashion. Batches of people with similar plights and infirmities were being addressed and processed in a collective fashion. The system was growing more slick and efficient. The names of the patients were not easily discovered and only dogged determination resulted in her identifying them. Several continued to live in the Commonwealth's institutions but more than half had been released and were living with families.

'Patients' and 'the confined' and 'the institutionalized' no longer were apt terms and Loretta now referred to them all as 'victims.'

Loretta struggled to maintain an emotional distance from the victims, but the task was proving to be increasingly more difficult. As a group, the victims were vulnerable and at risk to whatever the system might do to them. Their natural powers of reasoning were limited and their innate sense of self-preservation was compromised. The institutions that at first were their protectors were evolving into their prosecutors. As she dug deeper into their files, it became increasingly more apparent that the victims' access to appropriate legal representation was a sham. Their legal defenses were rote, unimaginative and universally futile.

As the number of cases continued to multiply, the work required on the cases increased exponentially. Loretta was at a crossroads. She was concerned she wasn't investing enough time to address all the victims' issues. She still had an obligation to the other clients in her practice, those clients who were not impacted by the Health Laws—the paying clients who made it possible for her to pay her bills.

"Good Lord," she would whisper to herself when she felt most tired and frustrated, "it's only the three of us." A crippled old man, a washed out legal student and a country lawyer tap dancing from case to case. But then her thoughts would fly back to the victims. Early in their investigation the names were just that; names. But Loretta and Phoebe collectively underwent changes of gut wrenching proportions after they spent so many hours in meetings and interviews with the offended victims. A face was put to a name and each victim's case evolved into each victim's own story. The more she reviewed and studied the facts and the issues of the victims' cases, the firmer she became attached to their plights and their miseries.

"What do we have on Carrie Beck's mother, specifically?" Loretta asked.

"I visited with Annabelle again last week and her story changes with regularity, depending on how I ask the question." Phoebe held a sheet of paper in each of her hands and referred to both as she read. "Even the court documents are fuzzy. She had no children with her first husband, Frank Beck; that's for certain. While they were married she would go off on what she called 'adventures' with other men for several days at a time. After several years she separated from Frank without divorcing him and gave birth to Dorrie and Carrie. Each apparently had different fathers. Frank Beck caught wind of the girls' births and realized he might be responsible for child support for kids who were not his. He divorced her for infidelity when the girls were infants.

"On several occasions she was arrested for prostitution. Still unmarried, she gave birth to a third child, a baby boy. After her last arrest she underwent a medical examination and was determined to be feebleminded. Instead of prison she was committed to the County Home. Carrie and Dorrie were moved from one foster home to another; sometimes living with strangers and sometimes living with aunts, uncles and cousins. Finally Annabelle's sister agreed to take in the girls, which as we now know, proved to be an unfortunate circumstance for both the girls. The little boy was placed in the orphanage and subsequently adopted by a family in Jefferson County.

"Annabelle certainly has some demons floating in her head. She's not bright but she isn't stupid either. Like your father said, her major problem is her nerves and consequently she is not always very lucid. In her past, her major flaw was her promiscuity. Her infidelity, diagnosis and treatment for syphilis and arrests for prostitution were the major determinants when they categorized her as feebleminded. Now that she's in the County Home, she is out of circulation and the attendants keep her on a short leash. At the time of Carrie's hearing, Annabelle's infidelity and promiscuity were emphasized."

"Only a feebleminded woman would consider infidelity," Loretta parodied to emphasize the idiocy of the court's opinion. "A clear thinking, intelligent women would never contemplate an *illicit* affair."

"Believe me," Phoebe said as she narrowed her eyes and smiled coyly, "I danced in the chorus line on Broadway with some girls who were smart enough to kiss and *not* tell. They had a different man waiting for them by the stage door almost every night. Some of the men were married and some weren't, but nobody talked and nobody bothered to whisper because it was so common. Most of the girls were young and were interested in a good time; others did it for their own reasons. They were a lot of things, but feebleminded was not one of them."

"So in many respects Carrie paid for the sins of the mother," Loretta said and Phoebe agreed. "So what prompted anyone to investigate young Vivien?" Loretta asked.

"Annabelle's sister, Josephine Barrow, was the aunt who took in Carrie and Dorrie." Phoebe now referred to another batch of notes. "Remember, the girls ran away but only Carrie returned. By now Carrie is pregnant. I suspect at some time Josephine Barrow does the arithmetic and suspects Mr. Barrow may have played a role in Carrie's motherhood. After Carrie gives birth to Vivien, the less loving and more vengeful Aunt Josephine petitions the courts to take Carrie away from her home. She argues that Carrie is promiscuous like her mother, the proof of which is that she ran away and got herself pregnant. She also argues that the Barrow family cannot be responsible for Carrie's future actions. We know that Carrie confided in her sister Dorrie the story of the incest, but by now Dorrie is long gone. Carrie, young and alone with baby Vivien, is now accused by Aunt Josephine of promiscuity and as being incorrigible. The Commonwealth obliges and makes the determination that Carrie is feebleminded."

"That promiscuity thing again," Loretta interjects.

"Yeah, that, and the fact that Carrie really is a little slow; but as we saw, she isn't the town idiot. Carrie, essentially, was evicted from the Barrow home. Carrie kept her story of shame to herself and buried it, never to reveal it, even at her hearing. At the time of Carrie's hearing, Josephine decided she could no longer have the incestuous love child of her husband living in her home. I am unsure whether it was scorn or embarrassment or revenge, but Aunt Josephine has her way when the Commonwealth takes baby Vivien away from her feebleminded, incorrigible mother. The baby was placed in the orphanage and Carrie was sent to the County Home."

"And the Commonwealth hires a quack physician," Loretta offers, "who cobbles together a report that describes the infant as being unintelligent to justify the sterilization."

"No. Not even close," Phoebe replied. "Aunt Josephine sticks her nose into matters again and reports to the orphanage that baby Vivien is 'slow.' A nurse is dispatched to the orphanage to examine the baby. The nurse determines the baby is 'backward,' and it was her opinion alone that sealed the deal. The nurse's opinion is entered into the court records without any firm evidence or documentation or physician's input. The phrasing they continue to use is 'backward.'

Can you believe it? Backward. You saw Vivien's report card from her school. Backward children do not get good report cards."

"Great. No physician, just the documentation of a nurse and asylum administrators." Loretta tapped the notepaper with her pencil again. "Carrie gets caught in a deal with the devil. Undergo the sterilization and you may leave the home for the insane. You were feebleminded before but after your surgery you will be cured. Go and sin no more."

"Carrie gets a raw deal all the way around," Phoebe summarized. "Granted, Annabelle was never a candidate for 'mother of the year,' but that is not Carrie's fault. Carrie was raised in a home without a father and later abused by Uncle Frank. Aunt Josephine abandons her. She's tortured further when Vivien is taken from her and victimized again by the Commonwealth's surgeons. All against her will. There is no way in hell a self-respecting lawyer would have allowed this charade to transpire."

"I don't know, Phoebe," Loretta replied. "These Health Laws are strong and firm and unforgiving. The deck is stacked, which makes our task all the more difficult."

The door to the waiting room opened and a little boy poked his head into the office. "Mom, I need something to eat."

"Be right with you Billy," Phoebe responded. He was six years old and had the full, round face and clear features of his mother. "I have sandwiches in the basket."

Billy held several crayons in his hand. "Whatcha drawing Billy?" Loretta asked.

"Animals," he replied and held up several pieces of paper with animal forms in various sizes and colors.

"We visited the zoo in Washington last weekend," Phoebe explained, "so now we're starting an art gallery."

"Which animal is your favorite?" Loretta asked.

"Giraffes," Billy replied as he shuffled through his drawings and displayed the mild likeness of a gangly yellow animal with large brown spots."

"Looks great," she said as Phoebe ushered him back to the waiting room, cleared the table on which he was drawing and placed a sandwich on a napkin on the table.

When Phoebe returned to Loretta's office, Loretta said, "He's a great kid."

"He's the best thing that ever happened to me," Phoebe said.

Loretta nodded and smiled. Indifferently she stared at the desktop and remained silent for 15 seconds before she said, "Marie would have been a few years older than Billy. I suspect she would have liked animals too."

Phoebe looked to Loretta and asked, "Marie?"

"My daughter." Loretta continued staring at the desktop as she said, "Yes, I was married once also. To Ronald. Ronald and I met while we were both in law school. His family was from up north, Pennsylvania. He didn't finish law school, didn't like studying the law and if the truth be told, didn't like too many lawyers."

Loretta smiled and looked up at Phoebe as she said, "Always showed good taste, Ron did. No, he became a teacher. He taught history and algebra at high school and loved every minute of it. When Marie came along he turned into America's father-of-the-year. He loved to cook and doted on Marie. He made life splendid for both of us. In many respects he was both father and mother to Marie as he took up the chores most mothers might do. He gave me time to work long hours here and continue in my own law practice. Life wasn't perfect but it was awfully damn good.

"I lost them in the influenza epidemic. We all had it. Marie died fast from the fever but Ron developed pneumonia and suffered for a week. I was a wreck for a month or two but my parents were great. Somehow I got back on my feet, buried myself in my work and, well . . . Work seemed to make the days go quicker and the nights shorter."

"It's been six or seven years, Loretta," Phoebe offered. "Any thoughts of marrying again?"

"I date now and then but nothing serious. If the right guy comes along I might get interested," Loretta replied with a faint smile, "but until then I'll troll the waters and avoid getting snagged."

Both Loretta and Phoebe sat in silence for a short while, lost in distant thoughts and memories of husbands loved and lost. Their reverie was broken by a knock on the outside door. They looked at each other, surprised that anyone knew they were in the office. Phoebe rose, walked through the waiting room and opened the door.

She saw a woman wearing the gray-green sack dress so common to the patients in the Norwood County Home for the Mentally Infirm. Her dark hair was a tangled mess and her face was smudged and dirty. Her shoes were muddied and the stocking on her right leg had fallen to the ankle. Her wide eyes shifted nervously side to side. She looked through Phoebe into the waiting room as if danger lurked behind the door or beside a chair.

"Can I help you?" Phoebe asked.

"Dorrie Beck said you could help me," she replied.

"Move your stuff, Billy," Phoebe said as they sat the woman down on a chair in the office waiting room and raised her dirty and bedraggled legs onto the table.

Tentatively the woman allowed Phoebe and Loretta to attend her, still wide eyed and nervous. "Looks like you've been traveling some," Loretta commented by way of a greeting.

In a tired voice she asked, "May I have something to drink. Water will be fine." Phoebe nodded, took a coffee cup in hand and walked into the hallway where the wash rooms were located. "I haven't had anything to eat or drink since yesterday morning," the woman in the gray-green sack dress added.

Phoebe returned with the cup of water and gave it to the woman. She took it with slightly tremulous hands and gulped it down in three quick swallows. "Thank you," she replied.

Loretta studied this woman who appeared to be in her mid-twenties. "You said that Dorrie Beck sent you. What's your name?"

"Eloise Foulkrod," she answered in a voice that was soft and southern, less raspy now that she had her drink of water. "Yes, I live at the County Home; I guess you can tell. I left yesterday morning."

"Do they know that you're gone?" Phoebe asked.

"I think they know by now I'm not there, but I don't think they know where I went." She looked down at her shoes that were dirty and spackled with mud. She pulled on the stocking that had fallen to her ankle and tried to straighten it. "I must really look like something."

"Miss Foulkrod," Loretta said, "why are you here? Why did you leave the County Home?"

"I left yesterday after breakfast. Just oatmeal and coffee. Left when the cleaning people made us leave our rooms. I walked out the door and jes kept walking. I had your address in my pocket; Dorrie gave it to me. I hid in the woods until sundown and walked all night to get here."

"That's nearly fifteen miles, Miss Foulkrod," Phoebe said. Eloise Foulkrod made no response.

"So Dorrie sent you. Why?" Loretta pressed.

"They want to cut me," she answered.

"Who wants to cut you? Where, how?" Loretta continued.

"The people at the hospital want to spay me like a bitch hound. Judge tol' me so."

Phoebe and Loretta looked at each other. "Billy," Phoebe said to her son who was now sitting in another chair in the office, mesmerized by the strange woman. "Get us another cup of water please." Billy took the cup and left the waiting room.

"Miss Foulkrod, did you have to attend a hearing with a judge and some lawyers present?" Loretta asked and Eloise nodded. "And the outcome of the hearing was that you would have to undergo a surgical operation to prevent you from having any children, any more children?" Again she nodded.

"Miss Foulkrod, have you had the operation yet?" Loretta continued. To the relief of both Phoebe and Loretta she shook her head 'No.' At first blush Eloise Foulkrod did not appear to Loretta to be either feebleminded or totally deranged. In fact, despite her wearied state she appeared to be logical and well in control of her faculties. "You said you came from the County Home. Why are you a patient there?"

Matter of factly she replied, "I have melancholy. I've been at the County Home for three years now. Actually I've been in and out of there for three years. See, the melancholy comes and goes; sometimes it's worse than other times, sometimes it's not so bad."

"You said that you are in and out of the home; with whom do you live when you are not . . . not a patient in the home?" Loretta asked.

"I live with my mother and my sisters, here, in Oxford Corners."

"How is it, why is it necessary for you to be in the County Home?" Loretta continued.

Eloise Foulkrod unfolded her arms and opened her hands to reveal multiple scars across her forearms and across the insides of her wrists. "How many times?" Loretta asked.

"Three times. Twice on my birthday and wonst at Christmas."

"I suppose that may have been a little too much for your mother to handle?" Loretta offered and Eloise nodded.

"Eloise," Phoebe said in a softer tone, "how long ago was your court hearing?"

"Last month," she replied.

Phoebe continued, "And the result of the hearing was for you to undergo a surgical procedure for sterilization purposes?" Eloise nodded. "Did your lawyer file an appeal?"

"Last week," was the answer. "We got turned down."

"What condition or medical problem do you have," Loretta asked, "that makes you a candidate to undergo the surgical operation?"

"My melancholy," Eloise replied. "They say that as dangerous as I am to myself, I might kill any babies I birth. Tha's a terrible thing to say, ain't it?"

*   *   *

"I understand you will be appearing before the Appellate Court in three weeks?" Loretta asked as she sat with Professor Maxwell Lawrence in the parlor of his apartment.

"Yes," he replied in a strong voice that belied his frail and fragile state. "Phoebe has me as well prepared on the social and clinical facts of Carrie Beck as possible. I have spent so many hours at the law library at the University I have nearly taken root, but I am as well prepared as possible concerning the legal issues. Now it is just a matter of collating and boiling down all the information into a thirty minute presentation before the court of judges. I know a few of them by reputation and one or two personally. Several of the new men, well, we'll have to take our chances."

"And our chances are?" Loretta asked nervously.

Lawrence shrugged his shoulders and extended his hands in a supplicating fashion. "As we discussed, I will argue the case on constitutional grounds, contending that the Health Laws are in violation of the eighth and fourteenth amendments. I suspect the Commonwealth's Appellate court will not wish to confront the issues head on. Some of the new lions on the bench may have had a hand in the passage of the laws over the past decade and I suspect a few might defer."

"Defer?"

"Defer, not uphold, almost the same thing. Essentially they will state there is no new evidence in hand. The will state there is no information that is present now that wasn't known at the time of the hearing. Ultimately they will decide there is insufficient evidence to overturn a previous ruling. When the laws initially made their way into existence, the Commonwealth contended that since the inpatients at the state's institutions were the Commonwealth's responsibility, the Commonwealth could attend to them however they wished; both medically and financially. If it were proven to be safer and less expensive to sterilize X number of them, so be it. The Appellate Court in all likelihood will support the previous determination."

"Which means . . . ?" Loretta said, leading on her professor to the decision both knew would be unavoidable.

"Yes," Lawrence replied. "I will have the opportunity to make an appearance before the brethren on the Supreme Court."

"So you're preparing for the big boys as a rehearsal to take on the bigger boys," Loretta said.

Maxwell Lawrence smiled, folded his hands piously and closed his eyes as he spoke. "There may not be a great deal that we can do for Carrie, but there are a great many other Carrie's throughout the country for whom we are fighting." He opened his eyes and wagged an ancient and arthritic finger at Loretta. "It is for their plight and for their future that we continue with our struggle. It is for the unborn children of these Carrie Beck's about whom we will shout the loudest. If the Supreme Court does not hear our voices and recognize our pleading and begging, well then, you shall have to think of something else to do and possibly pray for divine intervention."

Mrs. Lawrence entered the parlor carrying a tray with a teapot and several cups. "Good afternoon, Loretta. How goes the work for the weary?" She poured his tea and handed it to him. Loretta knew the routine and fixed her cup herself.

"I'm doing fine, Mrs. Lawrence."

"I'm unsure whether to thank you or chide you for what you have done to Maxwell," Mrs. Lawrence said. "He's busier than I've seen him in years."

"That's a good thing, isn't it?" Loretta asked.

"Easy for you to say," Mrs. Lawrence replied. "Who do you think has to cart him to the law library? Who do you think has to fetch him his books? Who do you think has to listen to his ramblings as he spouts off against this judge or that judge?"

Loretta looked to Maxwell Lawrence who sheepishly rolled his eyes. "And for that I thank you," Mrs. Lawrence said as she winked her eye and left the room.

Lawrence gave a deep harrumph as he cleared his throat and repositioned himself in his wheelchair. "So tell me of this prodigal patient who happened upon your doorsteps."

"Eloise Foulkrod is the living, breathing and walking evidence that truth is stranger than fiction," Loretta replied.

"Where is she now?" he asked.

"She is in her home living with her mother. Her admission to the asylum was voluntary, so although she technically could not come and go as she might please, we filed a petition to allow her to remain home for 'safety reasons.'

"The same reasons which resulted in her initial and repeated confinements; lack of safety to herself and others," Lawrence surmised.

"In my opinion she is in far greater danger as a patient in the asylum than walking the streets of Oxford Corners. My father admitted her to his hospital from my office for observation because she was dehydrated from her overnight journey," Loretta said. "Her blood sugar readings were quite abnormal. Apparently she has undiagnosed diabetes. My father was able to bring her blood sugar levels under control and many of her symptoms of melancholia resolved. She improved and was discharged without any problems."

"Does your father believe the diabetes was a trigger for her melancholia?"

"Yes, in part," Loretta replied.

"What do you plan to do for this young lady?"

"We will argue for an immediate injunction to prevent the sterilization because due process was not followed during her hearings," Loretta replied. "That should buy us time. More important is whether the Commonwealth pursues her and fights to carry out the judgment while she remains outside the County Home. The greatest danger to society, relative to the Health Laws, is that the Laws may be perceived as having no limits. There may be no safe haven where one might retreat to escape their wrath. If certain ruling parties have their way, the Health Laws will follow us into our homes and touch anyone, anywhere.

"The second and more grave issue," she continued, "is just how far our elected officials are willing to push the envelope and extend the Health Laws to address a lengthy list of health issues. How many diseases are they going to blame on heredity and how many diseases are going to end up on that blasted list?"

"Such issues must be terribly disturbing to your father and his colleagues," Maxwell Lawrence intoned.

"Yes, and many of his colleagues are concerned and at wits end with the issues," she replied. "The American Medical Association as a body has remained silent, but several of their officers are affiliated with the eugenics movement. The consensus of many of the physicians is their understanding of genetics is very limited. Almost no one can say unequivocally that the offspring of two parents with a clinical problem will have that same problem *all the time*. There are tendencies but no absolutes."

"Why are we being told to accept the concept that because certain individuals are cursed and plagued with the hereditary transmission of diseases," Lawrence murmured out loud, "annihilation of those affected is the only solution? We are treating these poor individuals as if they were a herd of cattle with hoof and mouth disease. Bang, bang, bang, one after the other. It sounds like a wretchedly devised scheme, based on the convoluted principles of Darwin and Mendel, concocted by a Jules Verne on some far off planet and then implemented by Machiavelli, Herod or Attila the Hun."

EIGHTEEN

"Your 10:00 appointment is here," the secretary said as she opened the door to Simon Kraft's office.

Without looking up from the report he was reading he said, "Show her in."

As Loretta Frontenac walked into Simon Kraft's office she took a deep breath to steady her nerves. Was she truly daft? That was how Maxwell Lawrence described her idea to schedule a meeting with the Secretary of the Department of Health and Welfare so she could discuss various aspects of the Health Laws as they pertained to Eloise Foulkrod. Daft. Maybe so, but she reasoned they couldn't hang a girl for trying.

She knew she would be granted only a short time with the Secretary so she decided to limit herself to only a few salient discussion points. If she could coyly pry from him a kernel of useful information she might do her client a great service. If she were too clever or too forceful, she might alienate the good doctor and do no one any good. If she were to annoy the Health Czar and tweak his nose impolitely, she might be thrown out of his office on her ear.

She cleared her voice as she approached his desk and said, "Good morning Mr. Secretary. Thank you for meeting with me today."

Simon looked up and over the reading glasses that were perched near the end of his nose as he heard the unfamiliar voice. He saw a strikingly attractive woman dressed professionally in a dark skirt and waistcoat. Her blouse was light gray in color with a few ruffles in the front and at her cuffs. She carried a small briefcase in her left hand. He rose as he said, "Well, yes, welcome Miss . . . Miss." He glanced at his appointment book, used his index finger as a guide and theatrically ran it down the page a few inches before he said, "Miss Frontenac." Nonchalantly he removed his reading glasses, held them in his right hand that he extended toward a chair that was positioned in front of his desk and offered indifferently, "Please have a seat."

Sly old polecat she thought to herself as she recalled Maxwell Lawrence's advice. 'He wants to meet you about as much as he wants a boil on his neck. Be direct and firm and do not lose the initiative.' Loretta sat in the chair, set the briefcase on the floor by her left leg, folded her hands together to steady herself and said, "Mr. Secretary, you and I share something in common and I wanted very much to meet with you so that we might discuss a few issues."

"You're not a newspaper reporter or a writer for a magazine, are you?" Kraft asked.

Sly old polecat. "No, Mr. Secretary. I'm a lawyer."

Kraft nodded and said, "And what is it that we have in common, Miss Frontenac?"

"We each have a burning interest in the Health Laws." Again Kraft nodded. "More specifically, I represent a client who has a vested interest in the Health Laws. A first hand, intimate, interest in the laws."

"How so, Miss Frontenac?"

"My client was subjected to a hearing while receiving treatment in a State Hospital," Loretta answered. "The outcome of the hearing was a court order for her to undergo a surgical operation; a sterilization procedure."

Kraft's face showed no change in emotion. "The law is the law. I am certain the hearing was executed in a thorough and lawful fashion."

"There is indeed some question of that matter," Loretta replied. "More importantly I believe the law, or rather, the laws which you helped to formulate have transformed into something unforeseen and unintended."

"How so, Miss Frontenac?" Simon asked with ill-concealed innocence.

Loretta paused for a moment, took a breath and said, "My client was not a permanent resident in the asylum. As a matter of fact she committed herself to the institution. She suffered from melancholia which in large part was caused by or made worse by her diabetes. Now that her diabetes is under control, her melancholia has disappeared."

"I am very happy for your client, Miss Frontenac," Simon Kraft offered.

"Dr. Kraft," Loretta asked, "is diabetes a serious threat to mankind?" Simon narrowed his eyes as if he did not understand the question. "Does the existence of sugar diabetes threaten the human race with annihilation?"

"I wouldn't think so, Miss Frontenac," Kraft replied.

"Is diabetes treatable?"

"Yes. There are ways to manage the disease but the disease is not curable," he answered.

"Does the United States government provide money, grant money, for research for the development, manufacture and purification of insulin, which is the one medication most successful in the treatment of sugar diabetes?"

"Where are we going with this conversation Miss Frontenac?" Kraft asked.

"I will take that as a 'Yes.' If you will agree that diabetes is treatable, treatable with a medicine whose manufacture and production is being underwritten with the help of American taxpayer dollars, why is having a complication of diabetes a trigger to undergo surgical sterilization in the Commonwealth; our very own state?"

"Say again, Miss Frontenac."

Loretta narrowed her eyes and said with firm conviction, "Dr. Kraft, the list of clinical conditions that warrant surgical sterilization in the Commonwealth for patients who reside at the State Hospitals is growing and no one is certain where the list will end. The situation which you helped to create is spiraling out of control."

"Miss Frontenac, I would beg to differ with you."

"Off the record, Dr. Kraft, do you agree that the symptoms of an illness are sufficient grounds to proceed with sterilization?" Loretta pushed. "Even though the cause of the symptoms is due to a treatable disease.

Coyly Kraft replied, "*For the record*, the law is the law."

"But Doctor, you just told me diabetes is treatable. Not only do you agree with that statement but the government of the United

States agrees. One might even suggest that in the not so distant future diabetes will be curable. If such were the case, why is having the disease an indication for surgical sterilization?"

"Is this a cross examination, Miss Frontenac?" Kraft asked as he pushed at his desk and rolled his chair away from it.

Chalk up one tweaked nose Loretta silently bemoaned. Half expecting to be ushered away by armed soldiers, she offered, "I'm sorry, sir, I didn't mean to accuse . . ."

Simon waved away her apology. "I know practically everything that pertains to the Health Laws; in the various states, across Europe and even so far away as *our* Commonwealth across the river. I will say again, the law is the law."

"Dr. Kraft, do you not believe that the laws should be made by the people and for the people in order to benefit the people?"

"Miss Frontenac," Kraft replied, "There is a considerable body of scientific evidence that is the basis for the Health Laws. It is, and will be, the American people who will benefit from the scientific advancements that have become the Health Laws." Kraft paused and leered at Loretta sitting in her chair. "Notwithstanding the opinions and the best efforts of you and your associate, Maxwell Lawrence."

Loretta's eyes widened as she looked to Simon Kraft with a startled expression. "I told you before," Simon continued, "I know practically everything that pertains to the Health Laws. I know that Lawrence appeared before the Appellate Court of the Commonwealth and they sent him packing." He raised the packet of papers he was reading when she entered his office. "I have here the proceedings of the appeal and the opinions of the appellate judges. Professor Lawrence presented a coherent and relevant argument but the outcome was never in doubt. Nevertheless I commend him for his efforts.

"As for you, Miss Frontenac, near the top of her graduating class of 1913 at the Commonwealth University's law school, I rarely forget someone who has named me in a law suit."

A thin, embarrassed smile crossed the face of Loretta. She recovered and said, "Then I shall be able to provide you with another treat. I plan to call on you as a witness *for* my patient with diabetes induced melancholia who was an infrequent resident at our state's institution and narrowly escaped sterilization. I am comforted that your medical opinions are consistent with the opinions of physicians worldwide; but that creates quite the oxymoron. We, as a nation of citizens and lawmakers, sit upon two horns of a dilemma. The government cannot give hope to the people by funding research for medication that will treat or cure a disease, and in the next breath punish the people and condemn them to sterility for having the disease."

Kraft nodded. "What we do, and what has been done, is designed specifically to aid and benefit the American people. We must keep in mind what our objectives are; we must not lose sight of what the final goal is. We must take what steps are necessary and execute them in the most professional manner possible." He folded his hands and placed them on his lap. As he steepled his index fingers and gently pointed them in Loretta's direction he continued. "Just as we labor for the good of all the people, I am certain you will do what is best and most appropriate for your client."

Loretta knew her allotted time was short and basically she had accomplished what she had come for, but Kraft's chummy affect and solicitous manner grated on her. She decided to cast one more shot across his bow before she was tossed out of his office into the hallway. "You realize Professor Lawrence will appeal the Beck case to the Supreme Court." Kraft's expression did not change. "The Commonwealth's appellate judges did not disagree with him. They neither told him he was wrong nor did they refute his arguments. They deferred. They couldn't even mount a logical, cogent argument to shout him down. He's going to the Supreme Court and he is going to win. He will win one case at a time and then one dozen at a time and before too long that old man in a wheelchair will unravel the mess that the Health Laws have become."

"Not in his lifetime and not in your lifetime," Simon Kraft replied. "The Health Laws are bigger than you or Maxwell Lawrence or any of your feeble attempts to interfere with what is most important. They have been developed and are in place to make our nation great, well into the next millennium and the millennium after that. The principles and doctrines and benefits of the Health Laws are greater and more important than all of us. *Bon chance, Mademoiselle Frontenac,* until we meet again."

*   *   *

"So how much did you enjoy meeting with the lady who named you in a law suit?" Ed Preller teased Simon as he ran the glass of brandy beneath his nose and sniffed at it while they sat in the bar of the Willard Hotel. "Here tell she's a real looker."

A wry smile crossed Simon's face as he stared into the cadaveric appearance of his long-time friend. "Yes, she was indeed easy on the eyes, but if I were you, I wouldn't stay awake nights waiting for her to telephone you. Whatever league she may be in, it's about three levels up from where you're playing."

With a self-effacing smile Ed added, "Smart too. I like them smart."

"I've seen and been with the women you date. Your only requirement is that they have a pulse. But right you are; she is smart and determined and will not be scared off so easily."

"What's the next move?" Ed asked.

"The old man has a date with the Supreme Court. One option is to wait for his appeal to the old wise men and wait for what they say," Simon answered. He lifted his glass and swirled the brandy in it. He looked at it from several different angles. "She was right. He made an excellent argument and damn near made me want to agree with him."

"That good?" Ed asked.

"His argument was brilliant and his logic was irrefutable." He swallowed a portion of the brandy. "I read the proceedings three times. He overwhelmed the appellate judges and he intimidated them. They were reeling on their heels and were up against the ropes. They had no alternative but to defer. Many of them had approved portions of the Health Laws in the past and to reverse themselves, well, that wasn't going to happen."

Simon swallowed the last of his brandy. "He will be brilliant before the Supreme Court and those judges will not be able to defer." He paused and gazed at his empty glass before he said, "It's late and tomorrow is a new day."

*   *   *

"I sent your suit downstairs to be pressed, Maxwell," Mrs. Lawrence said from the bedroom of their hotel suite as she finished unpacking the last of his clothes. "You must look your best for tomorrow."

"Grand. Grand. We have a dinner engagement with Loretta in the hotel dining room later this evening," Maxwell replied. "She's very excited to sit at my side before the Supreme Court at such a young age. Yes. Very Excited." Lawrence himself was also excited, even at his advanced station in life. He also was confident. His presentation to the Appellate Court of the Commonwealth had gone well and he was buoyed by their response to his argument. No, his appeal was not upheld, but his arguments were sound. Tomorrow would be different. He would be appearing before the Supreme Court and only a fool would not be excited to some degree.

"This will be my third time before them, Henrietta. Won one and lost one. Fifty-fifty. This case will break the tie. Tie. Tie. Henrietta, I need a new tie for tomorrow; a new tie for a bit of luck."

Henrietta emerged from the bedroom to hear him better. He continued, "There is a men's shop in the hotel lobby downstairs. Please buy me a plain, dark tie to match my suit. It must be neither flashy nor roguish nor should it distract the judges."

"That's not your style, Maxwell," Henrietta replied as she pulled on a sweater.

"Charge it to the room, take your time and buy yourself a cup of coffee or a dish of ice cream," Lawrence ordered in mock pomposity. "This afternoon is for relaxing. We've worked hard preparing and now the hard work is behind us."

"Be back in a while. Why don't you lie down and take a nap," Henrietta said as she opened the door and left the suite.

Lawrence turned the wheels of his wheelchair so the chair rotated. His frail arms pushed on the wheels as he moved closer to the window and stared into the park below. *Yes*, he mused. He was as prepared as well as possible. It was a long road and he was a bit tired, but it was the welcomed fatigue of doing a job well. He thought of Loretta and the hard work she invested into the case, preparing the presentations and sitting through all the interviews. And Phoebe. He was proud of the work Phoebe had done. Perhaps if they continued to achieve bits and pieces of success she might save some money and go back to law school and graduate. It would be hard, hard on her and hard on Billy, but she would be much better off with her degree and . . .

Lawrence heard three quick knocks on the door. "Plumber. Room above you has a leak."

"Plumber?" Lawrence repeated as he mumbled to himself. Instinctively he looked to the ceiling and saw nothing. No. The leak would be in the bathroom. "Come in," he said. "The door is open."

A man in denim coveralls walked into the room carrying a box of tools. "Sorry to bother you, suh," the man said with a thick drawl. "Can I go into your bathroom?"

"Certainly," Lawrence replied. The plumber walked past Lawrence in his wheelchair into the bathroom. Lawrence's gaze returned to the park across the street. "I hope there is no damage to the . . ."

Lawrence never finished the thought or the sentence. A pillow came down over his face with a rush and a force that was too much for him to overcome. His frail arms swatted at the pillow and the thin, boney, knobby hands that held it so tightly to his face. It was to no avail. Within thirty or forty seconds his arms no longer had the strength to move and he soon went limp in the chair. The plumber kept the pillow over Maxwell Lawrence's face for another full minute before he removed it. He pulled at Lawrence's eyelid and saw the fully dilated pupil. There was no pulse at the base of his neck. The man smoothed the pillow and replaced it on the bed. He waited another minute, stared intently at the slumped figure in the wheelchair and saw no movement. He picked up his box of tools, opened the door and left the hotel suite.

NINETEEN

The Supreme Court granted Loretta a continuance, sent their condolences and rescheduled her appearance for the following month. The coroner determined Maxwell Higbee Lawrence's death to be caused by a heart attack. There was no autopsy. He was 78 years old and had a laundry list of medical ailments. He was buried in the cemetery behind the Norwood Presbyterian Church. Henrietta requested a private burial, which was logical and wise given the vast horde of people who attended his viewing during the previous afternoon. The flags at the University were flown at half mast, as well as the flags at the State House and the Court House in Norwood.

Loretta gathered all the notes and rough drafts that Maxwell Lawrence used to construct his appeals. She tried to rewrite several paragraphs to better suit her speaking style, but with chagrin she realized she did not have his flair and command of the English language. Few did, but she struggled on and when April 22 arrived she was ready for her presentation.

The court room was far different from what she imagined. The ceiling was high and burgundy drapes with gold trim hung over the windows. It was nearly ten o'clock and she could feel her heart beating in her throat. She looked across the aisle at Elbridge Passmore, the Attorney General for the Commonwealth. She wondered if he were as nervous as she. She swiveled around in her seat, saw several people sitting in the gallery and didn't recognize any of them. She held the four pages of her brief in her left hand and picked up a pencil with her right. She tapped her notepad with her pencil and waited.

"Take a deep breath," Phoebe offered.

"I shouldn't be doing this," Loretta said. "Maxwell should be doing this."

"Well, Grandpa isn't here and you'll do fine," Phoebe replied. "He prepared you for this, so don't let him down."

"All rise," someone bellowed and jolted Loretta from her edgy state. The door on the far right wall opened. Nine men in black robes entered the room, stepped up and onto a riser and walked to their chairs behind the long bench that separated them from the rest of the room. A hushed quiet dominated the room and Loretta felt as if she were in church sometime before the start of the sermon.

The justices were still standing when the voice bellowed "The Honorable Chief Justice and the Associate Chief Justices of the Supreme Court of the United States. Oyez! Oyez! Oyez! All persons having business before the Honorable Supreme Court of the United States are admonished to draw near and give their attention, for the Court is now sitting. God save the United States and this Honorable Court."

Loretta started to resume her seat but thought it best for the judges to sit down first. To her surprise the judges mingled together, shaking hands as if they were at a banquet. When they finished they sat and the rest of the people in attendance followed suit. She looked up at the men behind their benches. In front of each of them was a tall white quill. In the center of where the judges sat was a huge man. Loretta was certain it was Justice Taft, the former president. To his left was a wizened old crone. Justice Holmes. The faces of the other men were less distinct but a name plate rested in front of each of them, identifying who the other men were.

The marshal of the court spoke again. "Beck versus The Commonwealth will be the first case heard today. Miss Frontenac, please."

Phoebe squeezed Loretta's hand as she rose. She had read and recited her brief dozens of times. She would be given thirty minutes to present her case, so she trimmed her brief several different ways so it would fit into the time allotment. She carried her brief in one hand and her pencil in the other to the podium. She took a quick breath, "Good morning. The original *Beck vs. The Commonwealth* decision was a miscarriage of justice when viewed from every angle. As a legal issue it is an affront to and inconsistent with the Constitution of these United States of America. As a law based on science, it has no greater foundation than Tarot cards, a Ouija board or the roll of the dice. As a solution for social issues, it is akin to demolishing a home in lieu of repainting a room or replacing a broken window. As an economic issue, it is consistent with purposely starving a family to reduce the bill at the food market."

Phoebe silently mouthed the words along with Loretta. She had practiced and rehearsed with Loretta so many times she knew the brief by heart.

"The Health Laws have established two distinct and very different classes: one class for those who reside in state maintained institutions and one class for those who live outside the institutions. As written, the laws address only residents with various medical diseases and clinical conditions who are confined to state institutions. The laws remain silent on those people with similar conditions who reside outside state institutions; as such they are not subject to the laws. Carrie Beck, because she was described as being feebleminded and was confined to a state maintained institution, was subjected to the Health Laws. Another woman, of the same age and with the same diagnosis of feeblemindedness who lives outside a state maintained institution, would not be subject to the laws. In fact, she would be fully protected from the laws. Clearly and incontrovertibly Carrie Beck was not afforded equal protection in the courts as guaranteed by the fourteenth amendment to our Constitution. The force of the Health Laws currently applies to one class only. Carrie Beck has been relegated to a class that is singularly very narrow and vulnerable.

"An unspeakable and most frightening extrapolation of the Health Laws would be the application of the tenets of the laws to afflicted individuals throughout the entire United States who reside outside of state maintained institutions. Such an extrapolation would be consistent with the fourteenth amendment, thereby allowing all citizens to be equally impacted or protected by the same laws. Such a holocaust of events would never occur. The even-handed application of the laws to those citizens living in their private and public communities is not only reprehensible, but would be unacceptable to and by the populace, primarily because of the abhorrent nature of the law itself.

"By no means would the people of the United States tolerate such a law that might invade their very hearth and home and brutalize beloved family members. By no means would they take to heart the cruel enemies of human freedom who seek to enshrine eugenics in American law and utilize police power to enact such legislation. If the laws cannot be applied equally to all citizens, the laws should be applied to none of the citizens.

"Our founding fathers did not construct edicts and documents to *guarantee* us wealth or success or happiness. What is guaranteed is the *opportunity* to seek employment in order to acquire wealth and achieve success; the opportunity to pursue ventures and follow pathways that might result in our happiness. Neither did the founding fathers construct an itemized list of conditions that might preclude innocent, law abiding citizens from the pursuit of such endeavors. Why then does the Commonwealth presume to confound and void Carrie Buck's inalienable right to go through life with full body integrity? Why then does the Commonwealth assume the right to deny various classes of individuals, such as Carrie Beck, the opportunity to raise a family and enjoy the happiness of motherhood? Such a denial is a punishment. Carrie Beck committed no crime yet punishment was meted out to her. The Commonwealth interfered with Carrie Buck's sacred and natural right to the possession and control of her own person. The court mandated sterilization of Carrie Beck was a condemnation, condemning her to a life of no maternal reward or happiness. By its very nature, such a condemnation is a punishment enacted upon a vulnerable class of people: a punishment for being an epileptic, a punishment for being less than brilliant, a punishment for having a mental or nervous disorder. Such a punishment is cruel and unusual and in direct violation of the eighth amendment to our Constitution."

"It is an abomination to create a set of laws predicated upon the indiscriminate mixing and matching of Gregor Mendel's yellow peas and green beans. Why have we been subjected to the vagaries of vegetables, cultured and grown in a laboratory, to dictate the fate of our citizens? The Commonwealth would have us believe that the offspring of Carrie Beck would have had a twenty-five to fifty percent chance of exhibiting signs of imbecility. What they did not say is that Carrie might have had a seventy-five percent chance of producing a child of normal intelligence. What I can now tell you is that Carrie Beck's daughter is absolutely normal. Vivien is a child who now sparkles as a student in her classroom. One hundred percent of Carrie Beck's offspring are normal, a surprising and embarrassing rebuttal for the Health Laws of The Commonwealth.

"The Commonwealth purports to use the laws as a means to improve society. More accurately the Commonwealth raises the specter of mass sterilization as if it were wielding a weapon of cultural elimination. It is not enough that we hide away our deformed and our unfit in state institutions. Now we must eliminate them from our thoughts and our consciences and bar their future existence. Must we now abandon our progressive natures and dispose of every ounce of our humanity as the Commonwealth decides to obliterate the poor and the weak and evaporate the afflicted and the infirm. Sterilization for eugenic purposes is specious in theory and brutalizing in practice. When applied too conservatively it will be short of its mark. When applied too liberally, a pogrom ensues.

"The Commonwealth would have us believe that the laws were in part implemented for economic reasons. The Commonwealth argues that the deranged and the unfit will produce offspring destined most assuredly for subsequent confinement which would require additional state dollars. The Commonwealth has determined that it is far more prudent to spend a small amount of money on a court hearing and a surgical operation than to risk being obligated to support an unfit deadbeat, regardless of the statistical un-likelihood.

"I intone the words spoken by men 150 years ago when they argued against the Stamp Act and the Tea Act and the Writs of *habeas corpus*: a law that is no good for the people is a bad law. The Health Laws are bad laws and because of that, no good has come to Carrie Beck."

Loretta reshuffled the pages of her brief and fingered her pencil as she stared at the men in their robes. "Miss Frontenac." Loretta thought the man who addressed her was Justice Brandeis. "What standards or tests were used to determine the level of intelligence of the Becks?

"A nurse's opinion was used to determine that Vivien was backward," Loretta explained, "It was made when she was six months old. There was no test or examination by a physician, your honor. Carrie was subjected to a written test, the results of which are subject to biases and inconsistencies. Professor Goddard, the chief proponent of the Intelligence-Quotient tests in America, readily admits to their inaccuracies and has recanted all his statements made in the past that were based and dependent upon the results of these tests. Most significantly, he is at a loss to explain why 95% of the American women tested were deemed to be feebleminded; or why 47% of the army inductees for service in the Great War were deemed to be feebleminded. Who is there to condemn the flower of American motherhood as being dolts and idiots? How is it that we were able to beat the Kaiser with such a feebleminded army?"

Brandeis spoke again. "Was this information entered into evidence at the time of Carrie Beck's trial?"

"No, your honor," Loretta replied. "The surgery was performed five years ago and Professor Goddard only recently has made public this information."

"Miss Frontenac," another voice spoke and she did not recognize the justice. "Do you agree that the state maintains the right to utilize and spend their resources, their money, as they see fit. Do they not have the right to conserve their money by limiting the number of prospective and future residents at their institutions?

"The Commonwealth reasons that one confined person will eat more cheaply than two," Loretta answered. "They rejoice that one less shiftless or mindless pauper will be less of a drain on a welfare system. They have determined that it is far cheaper to eliminate a class of people than to try to improve them, heal them or grant them opportunities to improve themselves. 'Eliminate the entire class and solve a money problem' they espouse, words that come out of the mouths of elected officials living in the richest nation on the face of the earth."

The room remained quiet and still after she finished. The faces of the judges remained frozen. Loretta returned to her seat and with no fanfare Elbridge Passmore rose and walked to the podium.

"The case of Carrie Beck, a former patient at the Norwood County Home for the Mentally Infirm, was prosecuted in accordance with the laws of the Commonwealth. Her case was reviewed in its entirety. She was represented by counsel. She was assigned a guardian who could have assisted her with her appeal. As per the disposition of the court she underwent a surgical sterilization operation from which she recovered without incident. Following her operation she continued to show improvement and was discharged from the institution. Currently she is gainfully employed leading a productive life.

"Carrie Beck's family history was investigated thoroughly. At the time of her hearing it was shown that her mother, Annabelle Beck, was a faithless wife, an adulteress, had a record of prostitution and syphilis, and was a product herself of pauper elements from Green County. At the time of Carrie's hearing, when she was 46 years old, Annabelle Beck was shown to have the intelligence of a 10 year old child.

"Carrie's father remains unknown, but different from the fathers of her sister and her brother. While living with her aunt she ran away from home, became pregnant and gave birth to a child. She was deemed to be incorrigible and feebleminded and was committed to the Norwood County Home. Prior to Carrie's hearing, her child was evaluated and determined to be abnormal and mentally defective. All such testing and evaluating was performed in accordance with and under the laws of the Commonwealth.

"Expert testimony at the time of her hearing determined Carrie Beck to be feebleminded, so mentally weak that she was unable to maintain herself in the ordinary community. Expert testimony at the time of her hearing thoroughly explained the hereditary predisposition and likelihood that any additional children Carrie Beck might produce would also be feebleminded. Carrie Beck's future children would not be assets to the state. On the contrary they would be debits to the future population of the Commonwealth. A bad trait clearly is carried in her blood. To protect Carrie from future impositions, to protect the state from the future obligations to support unfit offspring and to protect society in general, the Commonwealth had no alternative other than to proceed with Carrie Beck's sterilization.

"Recall again that the Health Laws, as adopted by The Commonwealth, were done so with the full approval of the people of the Commonwealth and their elected representatives. The state Senate approved the laws 30-0. The House of Delegates approved the measure 75-2. Within the week the Governor signed the laws into existence. Hardly a law exists that was not so well accepted and wished for as the Health Laws of The Commonwealth.

"The question is raised whether the Commonwealth has the power to enact and execute the Health Laws. The answer is most affirmatively 'Yes.' As per previous rulings by this court, the state may intrude on almost all personal liberties when the public welfare is at stake. The state has the power to execute prisoners who are convicted of crimes. The state has the power to draft soldiers, raise armies and send them into battle where they may lose their lives for the benefit of the nation's safety. The state has the power over life and death. Why then should it not have power over birth? Why then should the state not have the power to limit its reproductive activities? The state most assuredly has the power to mark some people for sterilization as part of its native police power. Just as the soldier must make sacrifices on the battlefield, the unfit must make sacrifices for the betterment of society.

"Sterilization of the unfit is a public health measure. The health and welfare of the individual and common good of society are promoted and served by such an act. Compulsory vaccination, not unlike compulsory quarantine, is in place to protect the public at large from an infected person. The principle that sustains vaccination as being compulsory by the state is broad enough to cover the cutting of fallopian tubes or a vasectomy."

When Passmore finished he looked up to the judges. The old man, Justice Holmes, cleared his voice. "Miss Frontenac, a question please." Loretta nodded and stood. "Miss Frontenac, I am certain you are familiar with the ruling of *Jacobson vs. Massachusetts.*"

"Yes, your honor," Loretta replied. "The compulsory vaccination case."

"Do you not see the similarities between these two cases, as Mr. Passmore notes?" Justice Holmes asked.

Loretta rolled the pencil in her fingers and considered her possible answers. Tell them what was true or tell them what they wish to hear? *Bloody hell.* "There are similarities, your honor, but the fine to Reverend Jacobson for his refusal to undergo a *second* vaccination after having suffered complications with his first vaccination was five dollars. The cost to Carrie Beck for being committed to a State institution and adjudged feebleminded was surgical mutilation."

The marshal of the court approached the two lawyers and said, "Thank you for your appearances." He looked toward the back of the court room, at the door, and it became clear they were being asked to leave.

*　*　*

A fortnight later a special envelope arrived. Phoebe noted the printing in the upper corner as she handed the white envelope to Loretta:

Supreme Court
Washington, D.C.

With hands that trembled ever so slightly, Loretta lifted the letter opener from her desk and slit open the envelope. There were three type written pages within the envelope.

SUPREME COURT OF THE UNITED STATES

---

274 U.S. 200
Beck v. The Commonwealth
ERROR TO THE SUPREME COURT OF APPEALS OF THE COMMONWEALTH

No. 292 Argued: April 22, 1927 — Decided: May 2, 1927

Mr. JUSTICE HOLMES delivered the opinion of the Court.

This is a writ of error to review a judgment of the Supreme Court of Appeals of the Commonwealth affirming a judgment of the Circuit Court of Norwood

County by which the defendant in error, the superintendent of the Norwood County Home for the Mentally Infirm, ordered to have performed the operation of salpingectomy upon Carrie Buck, the plaintiff in error, for the purpose of making her sterile. 143 Co. 310. The case comes here upon the contention that the statute authorizing the judgment is void under the Eighth Amendment, subjecting the plaintiff in error to cruel and unusual punishment; and the Fourteenth Amendment, denying to the plaintiff in error due process of law and the equal protection of the laws.

Loretta sat down and slowly read through the judgment that in large part recapitulated the facts of the case and points contained in the two briefs that were submitted and presented. Phoebe stood by silently as Loretta's eyes moved back and forth across the pages.

The attack is upon the procedure and upon the substantive law. It seems to be contended that in no circumstances could such an order be justified. It certainly is contended that the order cannot be justified upon the existing grounds. The judgment finds the facts that have been recited, and that Carrie Buck is the probable potential parent of socially inadequate offspring, likewise afflicted, that she has been legally sexually sterilized without detriment to her general health, and that her welfare and that of society has been promoted by her sterilization, and thereupon upholds the order.

Loretta let the pages fall from her hand. "We lost."

Phoebe picked up the pages and read the opinion. As she finished the last page she mouthed softly, "Judgment affirmed. Only one dissention."

Loretta nodded and grimly said, "Yeah, without even the courtesy to generate a dissenting opinion. Eight to one with hardly a peep." She took the pages from Phoebe and re-read the opinion. Her eyes focused on the next to last paragraph.

We have seen more than once that the public welfare may call upon the best citizens for their lives. It would be strange if it could not call upon those who already sap the strength of the State for these lesser sacrifices, often not felt to be such by those concerned, in order to prevent our being swamped with incompetence. It is better for all the world if, instead of waiting to execute degenerate offspring for crime or to let them starve for their imbecility, society can prevent those who are manifestly unfit from continuing their kind. The principle that sustains compulsory vaccination is broad enough to cover cutting the Fallopian tubes.

Loretta closed her eyes, took in a deep breath and re-read the last sentence.

Three generations of imbeciles are enough.

TWENTY

The waiter poured the last of the wine from the bottle into Dorothy's glass. She placed her hand atop Simon's as it rested on the table. "Florida was a lovely escape from the cold weather, Uncle Billy, but I don't know that I could live there. It's more of a rustic getaway by my way of thinking."

"You're correct," William Cheltenham replied. "They have neither the glitz nor the glitter that we think is so important here in civilization."

"Yeah, but the fishing was great and the train ride was relaxing," Simon added.

"And you met the wizard of Menlo Park?" Uncle Billy offered.

"We did," Simon answered. "He's an amazing man. We met Thomas Edison several years ago in New York at a reception but meeting him on his home turf is all together a different and enlightening experience. He is nearly twice our age and he is the epitome of a perpetual motion machine. He scurried from one project to the next. His newest quest is to develop a rubber tree that will live and grow in North America."

"Which of course will make his neighbor a very happy man," Uncle Billy said.

"If richer and happy are meant to be the same thing," Dorothy said with a chuckle. "Yes, Henry Ford would be most happy if Edison could invent a cheap, home grown, American rubber tree."

"Ford's irascible manner and perpetual scowl are a canard," Simon said. "He was gay and all flavors of sweetness; he could not have been more cordial to us if we were potentates from Araby," Simon said.

"Bah!" Uncle Billy waved a hand. "His Model A is a rousing success and the sparkle you mistook for a smile was the gold that continues to fill his coffers."

"Rumor has it," Dorothy offered, "that not one accountant is employed by his company. He uses little dwarves with shovels to collect all his money, which he secrets away into vaults that would put Fort Knox to shame."

"Ford, like Rockefeller, is making money hand over fist." Uncle Billy sipped from his old fashion glass. "They *are* America. They produce what America wants. They produce what the whole world wants. They are carving a path to a place where America wants to go; commercial suc-cess and conspicuous ex-cess."

"That sounds like Gloomy Gus talking," Dorothy said.

"Are you familiar with the saying that 'too much of a good thing is not always good,'" he replied.

"That coming from the man who is serving in his second term as a U.S. Senator, eying up a run for his third term," countered Simon.

"Since the end of the war, we as a nation have experienced uncommon prosperity," Cheltenham offered. "Nine years of relentless prosperity."

"'Tis the price we pay for being the showcase of the world and its most successful nation." Simon spouted, raised his wine glass and tilted it at Uncle Billy for emphasis. "The world seeks the goods manufactured in America. The world prefers the machines and the trucks and the cars made in America." Twirling his glass for greater emphasis he added, "Except for the occasional bottle of wine or can of caviar, there is nothing that Europe produces that can hold a candle to what we have here in the good old U. S. of A."

"Which in part makes our economists nervous," Uncle Billy said. "They fear if America sneezes, the rest of the world will catch a cold."

"Gloomy Gus," Dorothy repeated.

"We are living in grand times," Simon offered. "The farmers are fortunate enough to sell everything they grow. The commercial gurus and the industrialists are producing goods and services that everyone clamors to buy. Most everyone who wants to work can find a job. It is only the idle philosopher who is a drain on our economy."

"One might ask whether that is good or bad," Cheltenham said.

"The business of this country is business," Simon replied. "President Coolidge has said so and my future boss has said so."

"I agree with you. There is no doubt in my mind that Mr. Hoover will carry on that same mantra," Cheltenham said. "He will merely change hats, relocate from the Commerce Department to the big house on Pennsylvania Avenue and continue to practice commerce, only on a larger scale.

"Hoover's nomination and election will be the easiest bet in town," Cheltenham said. "The democrats have no one with the mettle to unite the party or wow the nation. In all likelihood the governor from New York will land the democratic nomination."

"Al Smith?" Dorothy answered.

"And with his nomination the party will fracture," Cheltenham said. "The nation does not want a Catholic president and millions of voters won't give a tinker's damn to whatever he says because whatever he says will come out of the mouth of a Catholic." Simon nodded his approval as he drank from his wine glass.

"How well do you get along with Hoover?" Cheltenham asked.

"Herbert and I have served in the same cabinet for nearly eight years. I've never had a run in with him and I hope that he respects my work," Simon replied.

Cheltenham took in a deep breath, exhaled and asked, "Do you have any skeletons in the closet that he might not share, or that he or someone else might wish to expose?"

Simon cleared his throat and reached for a dinner napkin with his right hand. "We both were appointed by Harding and served under him. Harding's dead. We both survived Coolidge's housecleaning. We both can only hope that the ghosts of that administration have long ago vacated the Capital."

"Hoover is going to need a Vice-President," Cheltenham said. Simon eyed him cautiously. "Your political capital continues to accumulate."

"You flatter me." Simon said and then emitted a soft chuckle. "Eight years ago I went to Harding's people with my hat in my hand and lobbied to keep the job Woodrow Wilson had given me. Four years ago I had to hustle again to keep my job with Coolidge's people. I'm half suspecting that I may have to go through the same song and dance routine again to keep my job with whomever runs for office. Now you're suggesting I might be a candidate for a new job?"

"Stranger things have happened," Cheltenham answered.

"I think you are half right, Uncle Billy," Simon offered. "Hoover probably will garner the nomination. Who best to continue us along the road to prosperity than a successful businessman turned leader of the free world? But the party will have to name someone to the second seat with electoral clout. As the nation views Hoover as a business-commerce man, his running mate will have to appeal to the farmers and the agriculturalists. I, of course, have no electoral clout at the moment. I, of course, have no dirt beneath my fingernails. I, therefore, believe the people who might champion me for the Vice-Presidential nomination will be in the minority."

"So that means you will toddle back to posturing and auditioning for your old job again?" Dorothy surmised.

"I like my job, Dorothy. There are still a few things I have left to do and a few new programs I would like to implement." He turned to Uncle Billy and said, "Besides, your niece likes living in Washington with the glitz and the glitter." Dorothy smiled and placed her hand atop Simon's again.

"But I hear what you are saying, Uncle Billy. I have given thought to a new job. We spoke of it nearly fifteen years ago and Dorothy and I speak of it often."

"Would that be the position on Pennsylvania Avenue, one step up from the Vice-President's job?" Uncle Billy teased.

"The very same," Simon replied. "I've been squirreling away favors like there's no tomorrow. On a day when I really need them I'll cash them in. Not this year, but maybe in four years or maybe eight. Like I said, I still have some projects to implement and windmills to tilt at."

"The nation has taken a shine to you," Uncle Billy offered. "They agree with the policies you have introduced and they agree with how you've done them. Just continue to keep out of trouble and the opportunity will arise. I guarantee it. Remember . . ."

"I know, I know," Simon raised his hands in mock surrender. "Propriety, appearances and I promise not to get lost along my paper trail." They shared a laugh and moved on to other topics of discussion, but Simon's thoughts continued to return to the first day he was in the Oval Office with President Wilson. He remembered how powerful the room was; how mighty and forceful and full of righteousness. He had returned to the Oval Office many times in the last eight years, and each time he did he felt more determined to make that office his.

*   *   *

Loretta handed papers to her secretary. "Send this letter to the attorney general in Indianapolis and this letter to Sacramento. They won't like what I said but they'll be forced to respond."

The secretary took the letters and left Loretta's office; Loretta's new office. It occupied the former parlor on the first floor of a house that was located within sight of the Norwood County Court House. It was an older house, perhaps built in the first decade after the Civil War, and had a modest porch in the front only two steps up off the street. The previous residents died in the past year and the surviving children were scattered in several states. Although none were interested in moving back to Norwood County, they were unsure whether they wanted to sell the home where they had been born and raised. Renting was an adequate, temporizing solution.

The house's adaptable nature allowed it to survive into the second quarter of the twentieth century. Indoor plumber had been installed in the house so that it now boasted two lavatories, with a bathtub upstairs. Metal conduit tubing snaked along the baseboards and carried wiring that delivered electricity into every room. Bedrooms and drawing rooms were converted into offices and the dining room was converted into a conference room, all complete with working telephones. The carpeting throughout the house helped to ease the groans and creaks of the wooden floors, but the busy traffic of clients, lawyers and secretaries was difficult to silence completely.

A sign stood upright on the porch of the house. It read:

Loretta Frontenac & Associates
Attorneys at Law

Three lawyers now worked for Loretta, three lawyers hired in the past year. Additional lawyers and secretaries required more desks, chairs and typewriters, which resulted in the need to move into a new office. Additional lawyers were necessary because of the additional clients. The additional clients generated revenue that paid for the additional lawyers and the new office.

Beck vs. The Commonwealth thrust Loretta into the limelight of legal circles and polarized the general population like few other issues since woman's suffrage and the introduction of the federal income tax. Loretta gained greater notoriety by losing her fight with the Supreme Court than one might have presupposed. America had a penchant for cheering on the underdog. David in a dress had put up a valiant fight with the nine Goliaths on the bench. She had been eloquent and insightful. The judges had been immutable and predictable. Unlike David of biblical yore, Loretta failed. Eight judges could not be felled by the stones she slung and with Judge Oliver Wendell Holmes' final words, he gave credence and legitimacy to the cause against which she fought.

To many, perhaps to the majority of the people who took notice of the issues, she was a muckraker and a busybody and squawked for those who were best left unnoticed and ignored. But to others, she became the voice of those who had been throttled and abused and the champion of those whose rights had been abrogated and repressed. For a select few, she became their salvation and last hope to avoid a court mandated surgical procedure. Cases poured in from all corners of the Commonwealth. Initially the cases were confined to men and women scheduled for hearings which in the past led to forced sterilization. She was also hired to file the appeals for the men and women who had received verdicts that mandated sterilization. With some frequency she was winning cases. She challenged the methods used to determine her clients' feeblemindedness and mental incompetency. She challenged and defended the attacks on her clients' loose morals and the implied indications for sterilization. In many instances she challenged the medical diagnoses that had been given to her clients, citing on more than one occasion a sordid scheme concocted between the clients' families and their physician consultants to "put away" unpopular family members. She identified instances when the state's asylums ignored well established protocols and she won many sizable judgments when punitive damages were added to the awards. In three instances surgical procedures had been performed on patients and the records indicated that the determinations of the court hearings were made weeks after the surgeries were performed.

Phoebe was the first to suggest she should hire additional lawyers to handle the ever increasing number of cases. "Place a notice in the state law journal, 'Help Wanted,' and we'll have to beat them away with a stick." Loretta at first scoffed at the idea but eventually relented. Twenty-three applicants sent resumes to Loretta. Phoebe thinned the batch to five and Loretta decided upon the final three. One was a young man from the county's Assistant District Attorney's office and another was a young woman who recently completed her second year of clerking with the Commonwealth's Attorney General. The third was a friend of her father whom she had known for years. He was recently retired and discovered he hated gardening, grew frustrated with golf, easily tired of fishing and despised being useless. He was bored and offered to work for one dollar per day just so he could stop being retired.

Success begat success. The scope and breadth of her practice widened so that the firm was busy with many issues besides the court mandated sterilization cases. Routine creation of wills and reviews of real estate transactions not only increased, but were joined by clients who sought business contracts, employment agreements and the creation of trusts and endowments. The new associates took on the new load with open arms but Loretta never lost touch with the people who were the most helpless and vulnerable. She became the heart and soul of their plight and became a lightning rod for the debate that erupted concerning court mandated sterilization procedures. She was winning cases more often than the state liked and what she was saying was being heard throughout the nation.

"Currently one half of the states have enacted sterilization laws and one half has not," Chester Kirkwood said as the group gathered around a large table in the house's dining room that seconded as their conference room. Kirkwood, balding and older looking than his 37 years, was a veteran of three years with the county ADA and the bloody fighting in Belleau Wood during the Great War. "Some of those who have not yet approved the laws were waiting for the Beck decision. Alabama and North Carolina are poised to implement laws passed by their state congresses. Others, like New Jersey and Maryland, refuse to ratify and accept the laws all together.

Pennsylvania governors have vetoed health laws passed by their state's congress for the past twenty years. We are not alone in our quest."

"I have dozens of congratulatory letters from Catholic archdioceses across the country," Phoebe said, "so I guess we can have that to be thankful for."

"In many of the states," Aubrey Grant offered, "hearings are not required. Only the institutions' administrators need give authorization to force the sterilization." Although she lacked courtroom experience, her two years of clerking with the Commonwealth's legal team made her sensitive to procedural matters.

"Needless to say," Loretta offered, "a parent's signature for a patient who is a minor trumps in value a note from the institution's administrator."

"More than a dozen states will not allow two feeble minded people to marry," Kirkwood added. "A physician's examination of the two applicants is required for approval of the license application and there is a check-off box for feeblemindedness. There is a hefty fine for the physician who completes an application fraudulently."

"There is something which is vital to keep in mind," Bill Andover said as he puffed slowly on his pipe. Now that Bill was un-retired, he was generating more billable hours than either of the other two newcomers. Loretta begged to renegotiate his 'dollar-a-day' salary, but he waved a hand and said, "Consider a year-end bonus."

He had specialized in contracts and work agreements during his busy years, so he tended to focus on detail. As the blue-gray smoke rose from the pipe bowl, he pointed the pipe stem at Loretta and said, "Our battle is not with America and our battle is not with the twenty-four states that are operating on these defenseless individuals. Our efforts must be directed against the processes that result in the sterilizations. Remember, the devil is in the detail and on a regular basis, these people get sloppy and make mistakes."

"That is where you have experienced much of your success," Kirkwood said to Loretta. "By attacking the underpinning of their decisions, you are doing exactly what Bill suggests. Keep it up."

"Yeah," Phoebe added. "I like to eat."

All smiled but Loretta offered a serious note. "Then we'll proceed on both fronts. We'll continue to chip away at the cases within the Commonwealth and make as much noise as possible. We'll continue to correspond with people in other states and share our success stories with them. We already know of many who share our concerns, so we'll continue to work with them. Ultimately I want the Health Laws removed from the scrolls of justice; not only in our Commonwealth but in every state."

"That may prove to be problematic, given that you've already gotten a bloody nose at the expense of the Justice Holmes," Bill Andover said as politely as possible.

"Each time I read his opinion I can't help but to think of Maxwell Lawrence," Loretta replied as she looked to Phoebe. "He was primed and he was on his game and he would have said what needed to be said at the right time."

"Hey, we've been down this road many times before," Phoebe interjected. "You were as prepared as well as any jurist in the country could have been. You and Grandpa were of the same mind and the same spirit and he would have beamed with pride to have watched you. I know I did."

Loretta nodded as she always did when Phoebe tried to assuage her and convince her she had been playing against a stacked deck when she confronted what she called the 'stone heads' on the Supreme Court bench. "There's another image that returns to me on a regular basis when I think back."

"The Health Czar," Phoebe said with a wry smile.

"Condescending son of a bi . . ." Loretta caught herself, embarrassed at her choice of words. "His patronizing grin and know it all attitude . . . It was like he knew something I didn't and he wasn't going to share with me what he knew."

"He did know something, Loretta," Bill said. "He had an agenda, the government had an agenda and the people employed by the government were bound and obligated to execute the agenda. He knew he and his laws would prevail."

"Which will make it all the more sweet," Loretta replied with a sneer, "when I take his legs out from beneath him and wipe the Health Laws off our state's record."

TWENTY-ONE

"Good morning Mr. Secretary."

"Good morning to you, Mr. Secretary," Herbert Hoover replied. "Please have a seat," he said as he extended his arm to the two Queen Anne chairs that sat off to the side of his desk and shared a view of the Washington Monument.

"You're a tea man Simon, aren't you?" Simon nodded and Hoover looked to his secretary who smiled at her boss to acknowledge the unspoken request.

"Thanks for seeing me this early in the morning," Simon said as he sat down. "I know your schedule will start to expand exponentially after the boys return from their convention in Kansas City next week."

Hoover waved a hand at him in a friendly manner. "You and I are alike in that manner; we do our best work in the early morning hours."

A porter entered the room rolling a tray that carried a teapot and a coffee pot and several china cups and saucers. He poured from each of the pots as Simon smiled and said, "I used to skulk through the halls and pace the floors of the hospitals in the dark and early hours. I visited with my patients then, before the bustle of activity shattered the calm."

"Do you miss being a physician, being a real doctor?" Hoover asked as he scooped sugar into his coffee cup and slowly stirred as the porter left the room.

Simon tilted his head and replied, "I miss the people, and yes, I miss the surgery room. Most of all I miss the honest relationship that a physician develops with his patients."

"You mean to say there isn't a sufficient quantity of *sincerity* and *integrity* and *truthfulness* in politics to warm what remains in the cockles of your heart?" Hoover teased.

"Your wit is wasted here in Commerce, Herbert," Simon replied with a broad smile. "I believe a higher calling awaits you."

Again Hoover waved a hand at Simon. "I'm not counting my chickens just yet."

"The party has no one else better to carry on President Coolidge's policies than you," Simon said. "He was never more correct than when he said this country's business is business, and there is no one better qualified than the man who has been running this nation's business for the past seven years."

"Perhaps what you say will come to pass," Hoover answered. "Let us hope that the men at the convention don't contract a widespread case of apoplexy or senility."

"My two cents are on Senator Curtis from Kansas to be tabbed as your running mate," Simon added.

"Charles is a powerful man and would represent the heartland of this country in a fine manner."

And he would collect electoral votes from the states west of the Mississippi like a vacuum cleaner, Simon said to himself what all took for granted.

"You didn't come here to chat politics with me, Simon. What's on your mind?"

"As your platform develops and evolves, I have something to offer that is unrelated to tariffs and immigration quotas and highway expansion," Simon replied.

"Go on."

"Our nation is ready for a program that will allow for the people to have a government sponsored hospital and health coverage program." Simon waited and observed the man whom nearly everyone had penciled in as the next President of the United States.

Hoover lifted his coffee cup and stared at the floral pattern on the china. He sipped from the cup and then replaced in on the saucer. "Say again."

"The program I propose is a hospital insurance program that would be mutually beneficial to patients who require hospitalization and to the hospitals that provide the services," Simon answered. "In more instances than you can imagine, a medical condition financially devastates the families of the patients who do not have the resources to pay the bills. Likewise, hospitals frequently provide services for which they are not reimbursed."

"It's a rather noble thought," Hoover replied.

"Think about it; many of the maternity problems that persist are directly related to the fact that patients decline to seek a physician's care and deliver their babies at home. You have no idea how many people decline to seek medical care for serious conditions because they believe they can't afford the treatment. In many instances their problems could have been corrected or cured; and once cured or healed, they would be able to resume being productive members of society again. There are thousands of family members of hard working fathers who are forced to forego life-saving services. Consequently they remain ill or crippled and never get back into the flow of life. Their state of affairs is grim but we, as a nation, are in a position to correct the situation."

"How will the hospitals react to this idea?" Hoover asked.

"The hospitals will welcome the idea with open arms; who wouldn't? People forget that hospitals are major employers and have their own budgets and payrolls and hundreds of employees. They can't all depend on charity. If they can't pay their bills, the electricity gets turned off, the doors get locked, hundreds of people are thrown out of work and necessary medical treatment goes undelivered."

Hoover sipped from his coffee cup. "Since we now sit in the building that houses the Department of Commerce, may I ask a simple question? How do you propose to pay for this insurance plan?"

"A dedicated tax; a small tax on employers."

"A government tax on employers to provides services, free services, for the people?" Hoover challenged.

"Not free, Herbert, but very affordable," Simon replied.

"Such a plan smacks of socialism, Simon. I thoroughly understand you enjoy the title of Health Czar, but I would prefer not to be known to as 'Herbert the Red.'"

Simon smiled. "No, we would require a nominal contribution from each family for multiple reasons. You are correct. This country is founded on consumerism and on market economics and the taint of Bolshevism would sink any endeavor. No. The plan only works if the people agree to it, and by paying fifty cents each month, the working man's family will be eligible for hospital insurance."

"Thirty million families paying six dollars each year sounds like a great deal of money, but both you and I know that is a mere drop in the bucket." Hoover tapped slowly and gently on the arm of his chair. "The balance would come from this tax you propose?"

"Our economy is growing by leaps and bounds and companies everywhere prosper." Simon shifted to the edge of his seat and became more animated. Now that he had Hoover's complete attention his voice rose ever so slightly and he spoke more quickly. "The tax would be imposed on the employers. It wouldn't be a crippling tax, nor would it impact on their operations. You numbers guys can crunch out the proper rate. Maybe a dollar each month is the correct amount, just enough to get the program started. I would also propose a small tax on cigarettes and alcohol. Neither is great for one's health, so taxing people for their own sins is sellable to the public. The tobacco, distillery and brewery lobbyists will squawk, but we can make it up with crop subsidies. One cent here and two cents there and before you know it you're talking about a lot of money. Down the road tax riders could be added to construction proposals and public works projects that would be earmarked for this program. There is ample money out there, no question about it."

Simon stopped talking and smiled sheepishly, finally conscious that he was now rattling ideas and propositions in rapid fire fashion. He took a breath and said, "We just have to know where to mine for the money."

Hoover smiled also, for it was a well known fact that Herbert Hoover became a rich man as the owner of a mining and drilling company. Simon continued, "The country needs a program like this to cement our position as the greatest nation on earth. Right now we are number one in providing goods for the world. By implementing this national hospital coverage, we will be the first in the world to do so. It will be one more item to be copied and duplicated by other nations."

"You've been working on this plan for a while, haven't you Simon?"

Simon smiled proudly. "It is a program whose time has come. It is both progressive and practical. Republicans everywhere will love it. It will help the little man just as much as the big business moguls, so the democrats will love it also. It is by the people and for the people and everything the people need. It will improve the health standards of this nation like no other idea or invention before."

"In some respects," Hoover replied, "the platform we adopt for the November election and the next four years will be a continuation of what we've been doing for the past eight years. This health coverage program is a new horse in the stable. How much political capital will it require?"

"Come the new year you will have a republican senate and a republican house. You will be carried forward on a wave of mounting popular aggrandizement that will know no limits." Simon thought back to all the favors he had been accumulating and storing over the past years. "To smooth the road we'll form committees with favorable members. Guidelines will be created, protocols will be established. Leave all the devilish details to me." He paused and then said, "Herbert, if you give the people this program, you will be revered as one of the most forward thinking leaders of any nation in the world, for all time."

"Are you trying to turn my head, Simon?"

"I'm trying to convince you to give the American people the opportunity to live more healthy lives," Simon replied. "It's almost like giving the 'gift of life.'"

*　*　*

Fourteen piles of papers lay neatly arranged on the normally barren desk of Simon Kraft. The sheets of paper contained in the piles were covered with hand written notes, type written outlines, drawings and schematics. To the untrained eye many of the notes made no sense. Scientific terminology and medical jargon predominated among the written words. The multiple directional arrows from one page to the next would have made a seasoned mariner queasy. The papers were stacked two to three inches high and each page on the desk was coded and numbered to avoid the insanity that most certainly would ensue if the piles inadvertently were jumbled or shuffled together.

Thousands of hours of research, discussion, collation, cross referencing and recopying were evident in the rough copy of the

National Hospital Coverage Plan that rested on Simon's desk. The project was nearing completion and *The Plan* still required some editing and fine-tuning, but Simon was as pleased and proud as a first time papa. Technically, the rudiments of The Plan emerged from dozens of workshops and conferences that had taken place over the past six months. The Plan was the consensus of multiple panels of medical specialists, lawyers, actuaries, accountants and even an Episcopalian minister who had been invited to one of the meetings. Each of the panel members was encouraged to offer his thoughts and ideas specific to his own profession. Each was encouraged to challenge concepts with which he did not agree and offer alternative models and theories. Debates became heated and tempers wore thin, but all of the members of the panels were seasoned professionals, academics and veterans of verbal jousting. They understood that the goal of the project was to produce a workable plan.

In reality, the members of the panels were as neatly stacked by Simon Kraft as were the piles on his desk. He knew well the men he wanted on the panels. He hand-picked those who shared similar views and opinions, if not exactly the same views and opinions, as he did on what should be included in the plan. Routinely he sat in on panel discussions as a silent observer and rarely offered more than a 'good morning' or 'good afternoon.' He listened, he observed and during the meetings he allowed the members free rein. After each meeting his input became evident as he reviewed the transcribed products of the meeting. It was then that his red pencil went to work and redefined that which he determined to be unclear and retooled that with which he did not agree. The panel members were slow to appreciate how their work was being manipulated and only after two or three months did a few of the more inquisitive offer comment. Simon and the others who were less concerned would shrug their shoulders and move on to the next topic. Within the week the inquisitive ones were replaced.

As Simon sat at his desk he was imbued with an overwhelming sense of accomplishment, for the National Hospital Coverage Plan was the flower of his ideas, dreams, politicking and cajoling. He had envisioned how the plan would be implemented since his days working in the Commonwealth. He had scribbled out dozens of different options and scenarios during his early years as the department secretary. He had nurtured relationships, kowtowed to political hacks and orchestrated deals that added to his political clout. At last he was able to sell the idea of the plan to Herbert Hoover. When the presidential candidate incorporated the concept of the plan into his political platform, Simon was more than happy to explain it and discuss it with newspapermen across the country. He spent hours expounding upon its virtues and marketed the plan as if it were a shiny new automobile that ran on air instead of gasoline. His plan became Hoover's plan and each time Secretary Kraft spoke about the plan, he was campaigning for Candidate Hoover; a chicken in every pot, a car in every garage and hospital coverage for every working man.

To no one's surprise Herbert Hoover was elected president. There was no one factor that allowed him to win the November election in a landslide. Rather it was a combination of the uncoordinated efforts of the Democratic Party, the nation's desire to continue with good times and their belief that a prosperous economy would be guaranteed if a republican remained in office. Hoover garnered nearly 60% of the popular vote and laid claim to electoral votes from forty states. Simon was reappointed as Secretary of the Department of Health and Welfare and was busily putting his ideas onto paper when Hoover was inaugurated in March of 1929. Now serving under his fourth president, Simon harkened back to what Hoover said when he accepted his party's nomination the previous August: "We in America today are nearer to the final triumph over poverty than ever before in the history of any land." Such a statement ensured that ample money would be available to fund Simon's plan.

Simon sipped at his tea and was hesitant to allow the papers to leave his sight, fearful of what might become of them it they were removed from his guardianship. A few more times through the typing pool, a few more revisions and by the early part of next year the Plan would be ready for the public.

"That's quite a bit of paper for the parakeet cage, Dr. Kraft," Ed Preller said as he entered Simon's office.

"Why would you expect anything less than eternal damnation when speaking such blasphemy," Simon replied.

"You're like the little girl who just baked her first cupcake," Ed countered. "Proud of what she made, fearful of the knave who would reduce her masterpiece to crumbs."

"Once again I say . . ." Simon growled as he placed each stack of papers into a separate envelop. "What you see is the National Hospital Coverage Plan in it nascent form. Once it emerges from its shell, it shall be the saving grace of American health and wellness and the envy of all civilized nations across the globe."

"It certainly is quite the testimony to your hard work and political prowess, but . . ."

"But what Ted my boy?" Simon egged him on.

"I'm a numbers guy, Simon," Ed replied. "When I look at the amount of money that will be generated by the employers and the contributions of the workers, allowing every so often for a tax or a tariff to be added to the pile . . . There's not enough money to cover the cost for all the hospitalizations for calendar year 1928; by a wide margin. Now consider the increased costs that will ensue when people realize that someone else will pay the hospital bill. People will line up to enter hospitals for operations they might previously have declined because they could not afford them. How many women who delivered their babies at home will now decide to go to the hospitals to have their babies delivered? How many men will agree to surgery to repair their hernias instead of wearing an ill fitting truss? How many people who used to lie in their beds and die at home will now go to the hospitals to die? I know how many; a lot. We're not going to be able to collect enough money to pay for it."

"The solution to that conundrum is contained within the plan," Simon said as he pointed to the fourteen envelops that lay on his desk. "We will be selective in what is covered and who is covered. Remember, only people who pay into the system will be eligible for coverage; no free-loaders. There will be administrative officials at every hospital who will utilize strict criteria to approve or decline each patient's admission to the hospital, and we will hold them highly accountable for their determinations. Absent approval for coverage, the patients must make their way to the charity wards or return home. There will be age cut-offs for surgery. People over sixty-five years of age will not be approved coverage for surgery, neither emergency nor elective operations. Not all diseases will qualify for hospitalization. For people with advanced cancers and other terminal diseases, the administrators will have the authority to decline hospital coverage for their admissions. Inherited abnormalities will receive no treatment. Hospitals will be treatment centers, not dying centers. For your mothers delivering babies, only the first two deliveries will be covered in full. For the next two deliveries, we will cover only half the costs. There will be no coverage for anyone past her fourth pregnancy."

Simon drained his teacup. "There's a great deal more detail in the plan, but we think we have a handle on it. It's not perfect. It will require refinement on a regular basis, but right now the people have nothing. Following implementation of the plan, at least they'll have something. As more and more tax money becomes available, we'll add more benefits to the plan."

"What is your projection for the timeline that will be required to implement the plan," Ed asked, "from right now until Mr. Hoover signs it into law?"

"Less than two years, more than one. First a congressional committee will have to review it and chew on it. They'll babble and try to wriggle in a few changes based solely on their desire to meddle. Next it will go the Senate, the House and then to the Oval Office." Simon paused as a mischievous smile crossed his face. "If someone were to do a bit of public relations work, explaining to the good people of this country all the benefits of the plan, the timeline might shrink."

"Good luck," Ed offered. "I saw your calendar and noted you are scheduled to be out of the office later today."

"I'll be paying a visit to Professor Van Kirk," Simon replied and Ed nodded. "I like the ol' guy and he has been very successful with his Tomorrow's Children program. I'm going there today to watch him perform a few more of his procedures."

"I know he's been successful; what is the magic number of his successes?" Ed asked.

"He is not too far from one thousand I believe."

Ed whistled through his teeth. "Very impressive. So if his results are shown to be, let us say, *reproducible,*" he said with a grin, "will they be implemented in other laboratories across the country?"

"Absolutely," Simon replied, "but they will be licensed and strictly controlled by the government. Naturally I would demand that the Department of Health be the oversight and regulatory entity. Loads of restrictions and criteria would apply, but yes, my goal is for clinics like Tomorrow's Children to be established in every state. Van Kirk's program has made nearly one thousand families very happy and has given hope to thousands more. If it continues to perform as it has in the past, Tomorrow's Children offers a great deal to America."

"Sounds great," Ed replied. "By the way, how heavily are you invested into the stock market?"

"Not so much," Simon answered. "I have some money invested with the telephone company and I think Henry Ford runs a good shop. Why do you ask?"

"You really have been in a cave working on your plan. Last week wasn't very good for Wall Street and this week looks no better. Buy a newspaper on your way out to see Van Kirk."

Simon waved an indifferent hand and said, "The stock market had a hiccough. It's had them before and it will have them again. Some days up and some days are down. Rest assured, Mr. Hoover will calm the troubled waters." He scooped up the envelopes and carried them to his secretary's desk. "I'll see you when I see you."

*   *   *

After the bailiff swore in the witness he said, "Could you state your name for the court records, please?"

"Tama Rhodes," she replied.

"Thank you, ma'am."

Loretta Frontenac approached the woman who sat on a chair beside the judge in the Jefferson County courtroom. "Good morning Miss Rhodes. Could you tell the court your age; how old are you?"

"Twenty," the woman replied.

"Where do you live, Miss Rhodes?"

"I live with my mother in Marysville."

Tama Rhodes looked presentable enough sitting in the witness chair. Her hair was tied back and her light colored dress was neatly pressed. She wore no discernible make-up and sat with her hands folded on her lap. Tama's case was the first of four similar complaints filed by Loretta's law firm. Chester Kirkwood would handle the other cases, but the members of Loretta's firm decided that Tama's case was the strongest. With the greatest likelihood to prevail, they agreed that Loretta should present it. Tama was coachable, attractive and of some importance, Tama was white and not a Negro. Although it pained her to allow race to influence her thinking, Loretta was pragmatic enough to agree with her associates that in the most southern counties of the Commonwealth, a white woman would fare better with her complaint than a woman of color.

"Miss Rhodes," Loretta continued, "have you ever lived in a state institution?"

"No ma'am."

"Have you ever been committed to, or a patient in, an insane asylum?"

"No ma'am."

"Have you ever been arrested for a crime?"

"No ma'am."

Loretta paused a moment before asking the next questions of her client, allowing Tama time to embolden herself for what would be a series of harsh and probing issues that would place her in a less than holy light. It was imperative that she, Tama Rhodes' attorney, ask the questions rather than the County's defense attorney. For several hours each day during the past week, Loretta and Phoebe reviewed the questions with Tama that would be asked of her. Over and over the questions were repeated and four rules were emphasized to her. "Face the jury when answering the questions. Keep your answers as short as possible. Answer the same questions with the same answers. If you do not know the answer to a question, do not guess or make up an answer; say 'I don't know.'"

"Are you married, Miss Rhodes?" Loretta asked.

"No ma'am," she replied.

"Have you ever been married?"

"No ma'am."

"How many children do you have?"

"Three."

By entering the history into to the record, Loretta hoped to avoid much of the scathing and derisive commentary the County most assuredly would offer. Her objective was to soften the disparaging opinions the jury was certain to form and transform their scorn into sympathy as best possible.

"Are your children all little girls?"

"No ma'am. I have one boy and two girls."

"How old is your oldest?"

"Six years old."

Loretta paused again as she allowed the jury to do the arithmetic. She looked to the jury and then looked back to Tama Rhodes. "Do all your children have the same father?"

"No ma'am."

A brief gasp was heard from the jury, a gasp that Loretta predicted and expected, for most certainly more than one jury member's sensitivities had been accosted. But Tama Rhodes remained unfazed; not because of the many hours of training and practicing in Loretta's law office, but because such was the life of Tama Rhodes.

Loretta had taken three bullets out of the gun of the defense attorney. Tama wasn't married, she starting having babies when she was fourteen years old and several men had fathered her children. No further discussion was needed. Loretta would offer one objection after another if the defense attorney were to try to probe any deeper into her breeding history. 'Asked and answered,' or 'Relevancy, your honor,' would be repeated incessantly, so that the defense attorney would be ordered by the judge to 'Move on.'

"Do you work, Miss Rhodes?"

"No ma'am."

"You just look after your children and care for them?"

"Yes ma'am."

"You said that you did not work, Miss Rhodes," Loretta offered. "Where or how do you get the money to pay for the food to feed your children or buy them clothing?"

"I collect welfare," Tama replied. "Or rather, until three months ago I collected welfare."

"You collected welfare from the Commonwealth?"

"Yes ma'am."

"You no longer collect welfare from the Commonwealth?" Loretta asked.

"No ma'am. They cut me off three months ago."

Loretta paused again, walked to the railing that separated the jury members from the floor of the court room. "Are you a prostitute, Miss Rhodes?"

Loretta continued to scan the jury as Tama replied, "No ma'am." The expressions on the faces of the jury members were unrevealing. Having once been shocked by Loretta's opening the door to Tama Rhodes' sexual past, the jury was less surprised with the ensuing questions. Loretta was taking a chance that Tama had been completely honest with her and Phoebe when asked this same question in their office. The list of the defense witnesses did not include the names of any men who might possibly have been past sexual partners of Tama's, a fact born out during the course of the pre-trial depositions. Loretta continued with questions she thought safe to ask.

"Miss Rhodes, have you ever accepted money from a man in returned for having sexual relations with the man?"

"No ma'am."

"Have you ever had sexual relations with a man whom you did not know?"

"No ma'am."

"In the past, have the fathers of your children given you any money for their children's necessities; for food or clothing?" Loretta pressed on.

"The father of my oldest girl, Joanie," Tama replied, purposely declining to identify him by name at the very stern insistence of Loretta, "he gave me $100 wonst. The father of Sally gives me $20 from time to time. The other man ain't much interested."

Tama Rhodes was an attractive young woman in a country sort of way. She was a bit heavier now than before she started having babies six years ago, but she still could turn a man's eye. The home of Tama's mother's was on the outskirts of Marysville, the home where Tama was born and raised. Southern Jefferson County was tobacco country. Tama spent no more than three or four years in grammar school and like most of the other children and young adults in the region, she helped her family with the farm. When Phoebe visited Marysville to question some of the residents of the town about Tama Rhodes, the answers were similar. They knew the family, they knew her and they knew she had a 'passel of children of her own.' Responses from the young men in the town were also consistent: pretty girl, a nice girl, but a 'fast' girl. Phoebe wasn't entirely certain what was meant by a 'fast' girl in Jefferson County, but she didn't have to think too long to speculate on how much trouble a fast girl in a slow town could get herself into.

"So you are, or were, all but totally dependent upon the Commonwealth for financial support for your children?" Loretta asked and Tama replied in the affirmative.

"How long have you been collecting money from the welfare department?" Loretta asked.

"Five years."

"And you said that you no longer collect money from the Commonwealth?"

"Yes ma'am."

Loretta addressed the jury when she asked, "Could you explain to the court why your welfare payments were stopped?"

"A social worker come to the house. She tol' me that if I wanted to continue receiving welfare money, I would have to have an operation."

"What operation was that?"

"An operation so's that I wouldn't have no more children. She said the state didn't want to pay for no more babies."

"Miss Rhodes, are you telling us the state threatened to terminate your welfare money if you refused to undergo the surgery that would make you sterile?"

"Yes ma'am."

"Did you have the operation?"

"No ma'am."

Loretta walked to her table and Phoebe handed her several papers. "Exhibit A, your honor," she said as she returned to the bench and handed the judge the papers. "Documents from the welfare department mandating her sterilization procedure."

Loretta turned from the Judge to Tama and asked, "Miss Rhodes, have you ever heard of a 'Commonwealth Appendectomy?'"

"Yes ma'am. Tha's the operation that the social worker wanted me to have."

Loretta turned and faced the jury. "The judge ordered you to have a Commonwealth Appendectomy so that you would no longer be able to become pregnant and you would no longer be able to give birth to any more babies?"

"Yes, ma'am."

Still facing the jury Loretta asked, "How old are you Miss Rhodes, again please?"

"I'm twenty years old."

"Thank you, Miss Rhodes. No more questions, your honor."

Loretta returned to her table and took a seat. She knew better than most that Tama Rhodes' sexual history would be on trial every bit as much as the actions perpetrated by the Commonwealth. She was satisfied that she had done her best to soften the former while highlighting the latter. Her thoughts flashed to the other cases yet to be presented; other cases that she thought were more egregious than Tama's. Mrs. Renfro was an illiterate Negro woman who unknowingly put her 'X' on a permission form that resulted in the sterilization of her two daughters who were 12 and 13 years old. Mrs. Williams, recently arrived from Jamaica, was pregnant with her ninth child. As her delivery date was fast approaching, the only physician in the town of Ellington refused to accept her as a patient unless she agreed to undergo a sterilization procedure following the delivery. Sarah Winston was a fourteen year old colored girl who gave birth to twin boys and was refused to be accepted into the welfare program unless she underwent a sterilization operation. In order to feed her children she agreed to undergo the sterilization surgery. All were women on welfare, all were from families that were vitally dependent on money from the state for their existence, and all were victims deceived or blackmailed by the Welfare Department to undergo sterilization procedures.

TWENTY-TWO

It was Simon's third ocean voyage, and the third one was proving to be a charm. The voyage itself, in June of 1930, was one party after another for Dorothy and Simon. She enjoyed the dancing and the entertainment and reveled in the cotillion-like atmosphere that enveloped her every evening. Simon enjoyed not being transported with 900 other doughboys like his last trip across the Atlantic. He was also being treated as if he were minor royalty, for he was to be presented with the Rudolf Virchow Award by the International Society of Public Health and Social Medicine. It was a prestigious award that paid tribute to the physician who was considered to be the father of medical pathology and the grandfather of public hygiene. The award was presented annually to the physician who made the greatest impact on the improvement of health standards and living conditions throughout the world. Although the award wasn't so commonly recognized in the United States, the fact that the award carried with it an honorarium of $10,000 generated a great deal of attention and made for great headlines in the American newspapers.

Upon their arrival in Havre de Grace, France, they were whisked away to Paris to meet with various dignitaries and university professors. Simon renewed acquaintances with the U.S. Ambassador, Walter Edge. They had known each other for ten years while Edge served as the senator from New Jersey. Simon, as recipient of the Croix de Guerre, was remembered and lauded as a hero of the Great War. In the heady post war years in Paris, such an honor was no small accomplishment, but it was Dorothy who stole the show. She sparkled on the arm of Simon and wowed them at every turn. She displayed her mastery of their language and served as interpreter for Simon and their entourage. She enchanted the Parisians with her poignant observations and raised eyebrows with her pithy comments. She exuded charm and fashion and was the polar opposite to the doughty wife of President Hoover. Never in one hundred and fifty years could the State Department have invented a woman who best epitomized the zenith of American womanhood. She was beautiful, she was erudite and in the City of Light she won them over.

The American couple was welcomed to the Sorbonne and feted at Versailles. It was while they were in the great hall of mirrors that they met eleven-time elected Prime Minister Aristide Briand. Mr. Briand was the 1926 recipient of the Nobel Peace Prize for his work on the creation of the Locarno Treaty that joined together Great Britain, France and Germany, the major protagonists in the last war.

Dr. and Mrs. Kraft traveled by train to Berlin, the former home of Rudolf Virchow after whom Simon's award was named. There they were greeted by George Messersmith, the American consul general serving in Germany and by Gilbert Stockton, the U.S. Ambassador to Austria. The Dean from the University of Heidelberg presented Simon with an honorary degree. More dignitaries, more university professors, more heads of state. There was a whirlwind of activity as punctuality and professionalism replaced eloquence and savoir faire. The rust on Simon's command of the German language, learned during his undergraduate days in college, was too thick to polish away and he struggled to grasp every third or fourth word. He was, however, able to decipher enough from their speeches to know when to stand and where to go to receive the award and the honorarium that accompanied it.

Following the award dinner a very distinguished man with a full beard and a thick crop of gray hair approached Simon. He was dressed in the formal attire that was *de rigueur* for the evening. He bowed slightly at the waist, extended his right hand by way of greeting and said in moderately accented English, "Dr. Kraft, for many years I have followed your work and your successes. I am Dr. Ploetz. Alfred Ploetz."

"Thank you for your kind words, Dr. Ploetz. I must admit that your English is superior to *mein Deutsch*."

"I spent nearly five years in your country," Ploetz replied, "and while many families in America still speak our language, one needed to be conversant in English so as not to be, to be too shackled."

"Yes, I agree," Simon smiled as he replied to the grandfatherly man. "I *am* somewhat shackled here in Berlin. I am also familiar with your work, Dr. Ploetz, although I believe we look at the same vase of flowers from different vantages. I strive for the improvement of our race of Americans and you strive for the advancement of the German race."

Dr. Ploetz nodded his head at the compliment. "An intriguing balancing act, would you not agree, Dr. Kraft?"

"Ah yes," Simon replied and recited, "to balance individual hygiene with the 'hygiene of human collectivity.'"

"You flatter me, Herr Doktor," Ploetz replied.

"On the contrary, Professor, your good works give us all food for thought."

"Perhaps in the morning," Ploetz offered, "we may meet over a cup of coffee and share our thoughts. You in America have been able to implement much of what our politicians and do-gooders only talk about and debate. Although I do not agree with all of the measures that have been taken, I commend you for your efforts and your successes."

Simon nodded at what he perceived to be a compliment. "Perhaps in the morning," he offered.

"Ach so," Ploetz replied. "At your hotel, in the restaurant, at the eight o'clock hour." Simon nodded his agreement at the not so subtle command. They shook hands as they parted.

Simon was sure to be seated at a table in the hotel restaurant fifteen minutes before the agreed upon hour. He suspected that his newfound colleague revered punctuality as a state of grace. At the appointed hour Dr. Ploetz arrived, followed by a man in a brown woolen suit. The suit appeared to be a size too large for the man and the warm June weather made the choice of the heavy suit curious. When Simon stood to greet the men he noted that Ploetz' guest was reasonably short and slightly built.

"Guten Tag, Herr Doktor Ploetz," Simon said to his guest.

"Your German improves, Dr. Simon," Ploetz replied. "Perhaps you have decided, if I may borrow a phrase, 'when in Berlin, to do as the Berliners would do.'"

"I try," Simon replied.

"Allow me to introduce you to a friend of mine. Herr Adolf Hitler."

Simon nodded to the man in the rumpled brown suit and extended his right hand. Hitler used both hands as he shook Simon's right hand. He rattled off a few sentences in a thick German dialect and although he spoke with apparent warmth and earnest, Simon was able to decipher very little of it. Hitler's eyes were clear and dark and while the men were still shaking hands his gaze seemed to penetrate deep into Simon's soul. He was a strange looking man with straight, black hair that was combed oddly to the side. His mustache was also strange. It was narrow and abbreviated beneath his nose, not typical of the long flowing *schnurrbarte* so common to the men of Europe.

"Herr Hitler comes to us from the south, from Munich," Ploetz explained. "There he is the elected leader of the National Socialist Party. He is a kindred spirit when the discussion turns to the advancement of good traits and the elimination of unsavory and unwanted characteristics."

Hitler spoke again. Simon listened politely and after a few sentences Ploetz cut in. "Herr Hitler proudly admits to being of a student of yours. He has followed your work in America. He admires a government that is able to enact laws meant to limit the impact that the weak and the unfit may have on society. America is the world's leader in this respect and you have earned well such a reputation."

"*Danka,*" Simon replied to his guest. The man spoke again, for a longer period this time.

"Herr Hitler lauds you and your nation for the measures you have taken to improve the vibrancy of your population. He agrees with you, and with your nation's belief, that the weak and unfit are a severe drag on society. Sterilization currently is an outstanding solution to the predicament. Such continued propagation by the unfit would lead to the degeneracy of the population. One harkens back to the thoughts of Professor Schallmayer who suggested that the state should intercede and deny the unfit certain medical treatment. Currently we are not able to enact such a policy. As a Christian nation, we might come under unwanted criticism. On the contrary, you, in America, do not seem to be so . . . so." Ploetz paused, as he grasped for the correct phrase. "To borrow your words from last night, you and your country are not so shackled by such moral trivialities and ethical constraints."

Simon wasn't so sure he had ever made such statements and was certain that his country did not deprive the weak and the chronically infirm any medical treatment they might require. He was familiar with William Schallmayer's treatises that also encouraged euthanasia as a means for alleviation of pain and incurable medical conditions. Nowhere in the western world was such a practice commonplace. Before Simon could reply, Mr. Hitler spoke again, peppering his remarks with head nodding and finger-pointing.

"We here in Germany are currently limited by way of our financial resources," Ploetz interpreted and explained what the entire world knew. "Your country *now* struggles with serious unemployment and financial woes, but we here in Germany have had similar problems for the past ten years. The Treaty of Versailles mandated financial ruin for Germany and we have been challenged to fight it tooth and nail ever since. Repatriations for our war debt have had a crippling effect on our nation and inflation lurks around the corner of every street. As Herr Hitler has said many times, we Germans were betrayed by our own German bureaucrats. As we move forward as a nation, we cannot risk betrayal by the morally unfit; nor can we be subject to weakening by the physically unfit."

Hitler softened the tone of his comments. He spoke in a warm and controlled voice as he smiled glowingly at Simon. Simon returned a thin lipped smile when he heard the man use his name in what he thought was a complimentary fashion.

"Herr Hitler believes that our nation has learned a great deal from you and from America," Ploetz continued. "He firmly believes the salvation of our nation will be the emergence of a new race of Germans that will combine the best of physical attributes with the best of behavioral traits. He agrees with the scientists, your Professor Osborn in New York and even Mr. Darwin himself. Conscious selection must replace the blind tendencies of natural or random selection."

'Ah,' Simon thought to himself. Perhaps the thoughts and opinions of Herr Hitler were more consistent with his own than he at first had thought. He wondered whether now was the time to share with the two men the tenets of Dr. Van Kirk's Tomorrow's Children program. Certainly Dr. Ploetz would be impressed with the early results; as a man of science, as a man who sought improvement in his own race of people, as a man . . . No. It was too early and there was nothing to be gained by divulging early results before even his own nation was made aware of the successes of the program.

"I assure you, gentlemen," Simon offered, "conscious selection, as you make reference, is within our grasp. Conscious selection will be a valuable tool and a national asset to the great nations of the world.

Ploetz translated for Hitler who nodded and replied, "*Ja, ja, Lebensborn. Ein Land der Ubermensch.*"

* * *

Loretta stared at the picture on the front page of the Washington Post. "It's not enough they gave him $10,000. Next they'll want to give him a ticker tape parade like they gave to Lindbergh."

"At least you're not letting the massive adulation for Simon Kraft bother you," Phoebe chided at her. "Would you like me to fetch his voodoo doll so you may harpoon him again?"

Loretta stuck out her tongue at Phoebe, folded the newspaper and closed her eyes. "He is like a locomotive. He continues to build up steam and momentum and he is becoming an uncontrollable force. He is powerful, well liked, well respected . . ."

"And he's handsome, $10,000 richer, and by the way, he's a doctor. By Jove, Loretta, I just found your next husband," Phoebe teased.

"That sounds like a weak plot from a ten cent novel," Loretta countered. "No thank you very much Mrs. Belden."

Phoebe wagged a finger at Loretta and said, "Just don't let your seething contempt for this man cloud what we should or should not be doing."

"No. You're right," Loretta replied, "but I have this fear that Kraft will not be content to remain a cabinet member for much longer. He will not go away and disappear either. He wants to remain in the public's eye and he is filled with too much ambition to remain in the shadows for very much longer."

"If he were to leave government service he could do anything he wanted to do," Phoebe said.

"No," Loretta replied. "He's hooked on power. He's addicted to manipulating people to achieve his agendas. He gets an idea into his head, starts a project, runs at it full steam and he is determined to see it through to completion."

"I still think he could go into the private sector and make a small fortune," Phoebe said. "President of a pharmaceutical company, administrator for a hospital, go back to the Commonwealth and run for governor."

Loretta narrowed her eyes and pointed a finger at Phoebe. "That's not very far from what the truth may be. He likes to run things, but he wants to do more than just run things. He wants to govern. He wants to rule."

"As what?" Phoebe asked.

"As president."

"President of what?" Phoebe challenged her.

"What's the biggest *thing* in the United States?" Loretta asked. Phoebe shrugged her shoulders.

"The United States," Loretta whispered.

"That's a sobering thought," Phoebe replied. "That would make him even a better catch as a husband for you."

Loretta ignored her remark and said, "President Kraft is not a concept that would make me happy. We really can't let this happen."

Loretta closed her eyes and the room remained silent for ten seconds. She opened her eyes and asked in a pedantic tone, "In law, when the case is not going very well, what does one do? What would Maxwell Lawrence do?"

Phoebe replied, "Attack the facts?"

"Difficult, if not impossible," Loretta countered.

"Attack opposing counsel?" Phoebe offered.

"Not hardly. Attacking the defendant will not work either, especially if she's your client. What if we were to attack the expert witnesses?" She looked at Phoebe and added, "Bloody hell. Yes, that's what we have to do."

"Who's more of an expert than the Health Czar?" Phoebe added as she caught the drift of Loretta's notion. "No one."

With a sly smile Loretta said, "I haven't met a man yet who didn't have some chink in his armor or some blemish in his past. However small or however big, there is sure to be something rotten somewhere in his broom closet." Loretta picked up a pencil and started scratching notes on a pad. "Consider the premise: Simon Kraft and the Health Laws are synonymous. One way to attack and discredit the Health Laws is to attack and discredit the man who created them. If we can taint Simon Kraft and damage him, the laws will be damaged and become vulnerable. He's been in office ten years. He came in just about the same time as Harding and the whole world knows what a cesspool that administration was. There must be something that he's done in the last ten years that will be incriminating?"

"He's in politics, but he's a politician who never had to run for office. He didn't have to stump for votes or kiss a lot of babies to get elected," Phoebe observed.

"So how does he become so successful?" Loretta asked rhetorically. "He grants favors and makes deals. He's had a hand in getting a great deal of legislation passed and nobody can do that in Washington without making deals and granting favors."

Loretta paused, wrote more on her notepad and said, "We'll never be able to uncover what may or may not have been said in the back rooms, but there should be something we might be able to piece together from the public record."

"What do cabinet department secretaries do?" Phoebe asked.

"Initiate public works, create policies, sponsor research," Loretta rattled off effortlessly. "Each of which generates a great deal of paper and all of which includes a great deal of money. Follow the paper trail, follow the money trail."

"Kraft is a bit of a ham," Phoebe added. "How many times has his name been in the newspapers and how many times has he appeared before congress?"

"Some of this information may be in the Norwood Library, in the newspaper archives," Loretta said, "but I suspect just as much will be in the public record in the Capital."

"Sounds like a lot of work," Phoebe observed.

"Yes, I know. Get a good night sleep so you can start early tomorrow morning," Loretta said to Phoebe as she caught her off guard. "Nobody does it better than you, Phoebe Belden."

TWENTY-THREE

"Do you read the editorial page in the *Post-Dispatch* much these days?" Ed Preller asked Simon.

"On occasion," he replied.

"You seem to be getting some free publicity."

"That's a good thing, isn't it Ted my boy?" Simon teased.

"Not when it's bad publicity." Simon looked up from his desk as Ed gave the folded newspaper to him. "This is the third letter to the editor this month from your girlfriend."

Simon read the three paragraph item and returned the newspaper to Ed. "Old news, public record and she's not my girlfriend."

"The first letter was about a welfare case she won," Ed continued. "Last letter was about a woman who died from complications after sterilization surgery. The letter today is about the states that do not perform court mandated sterilizations."

"It is not as if she's divulging state secrets to the Bolshevik Army," Simon replied. "This is a lady who needs a soapbox to stand on and an audience to listen to her."

"I wonder what she is going to write about next week." Ed said with a mischievous grin that earned a scowl from Simon. "By the way, the President wants to meet with you at 11:30."

"About what?" Simon snapped a bit more curtly than he intended.

"I don't know," Ed replied as he raised his hands to ward off further attacks upon his person. "I'm not his good buddy like you are."

"The job market is pretty slim, Ted my boy," Simon needled at him. "Try hard to keep yours." *And Loretta Frontenac is not my girlfriend. She's a pain in my ass that will not go away.*

The fact was, the President had had very little to say to Simon Kraft in the past six months other than the perfunctory 'hello' and 'good morning' at the regularly scheduled cabinet meetings. Simon couldn't recall the last time Hoover asked him for an opinion or sent an aide with a question to his office that required his input. Times were not going well for the president. Times were not going well for the nation. People throughout the country were out of work and being evicted from their homes. The lines at the soup kitchens were growing longer, the President's popularity was vanishing and there were no signs the economy was improving.

"How is Mrs. Griffin this morning," Simon said to President Hoover's secretary in the waiting room outside the Oval Office as he arrived five minutes early for his meeting.

"I'm doing well, Doctor. The President will be with you shortly." *That was chilly.*

Simon had to wait no more than a few minutes before he was called in. A faint tingle rose up Simon's spine when he set foot on the thick, blue carpeting inside the office. It was a feeling that teased him every time he entered this room. The air in the room reeked with history and power and command. It was a feeling he experienced nowhere else. "Good morning, Mr. President."

"Good morning Simon. Take a seat." Hoover remained sitting behind his desk. "How's Dorothy," he asked. Simon couldn't remember the last time Hoover asked about his wife.

"She's doing fine, Mr. President, thank you for asking."

"Two items you're not going to like," he said as he moved a few pieces of paper on his desk from the right to the left side. "I wanted to tell you personally. Your budget for research grants and projects is going to be cut in half."

It certainly wasn't what Simon wanted to hear, but the topic of budget cuts was on everyone's agenda. Every department was being impacted and it was no longer a matter of 'if' but rather, 'how much?' To be cut in half was quite a blow. "You will also need to reduce your staff by 30%." Now the decisions were hitting close to home.

"Everyone will be scaling back. We in government will have to show the public we're trying to spend less of their money."

"Yes sir," was all that Simon could say in response.

"And your hospital health coverage plan," Hoover continued. "We have to scrap it for the foreseeable future."

A pain struck Simon in the mid-section and took the air out of him. "Sir?"

"We can't afford it, the people can't afford it and I can't afford to spend time or political capital on the plan. Twenty-five percent of this country is out of work and can't pay for bread. How are they going to pay for something new like hospital insurance? Employers can't afford to pay their workers. How are they going to pay for their workers' hospital insurance? If you want to pay for this new plan by introducing a few new taxes, think again. The one thing this country can't afford right now is a new tax. I don't care if it's a penny tax or a nickel tax or a million dollar tax. I can't sell it to my budget people, I can't sell it to Congress and I will not be able to sell it to the American people."

Simon was unsure what to say and how to say it. "Mr. President, are you certain . . ."

"I'm sorry. We thought that an increase in government spending last year would resolve matters but that didn't work. We passed a tariff and other countries passed higher tariffs. Exports of our goods are practically nil. Banks are closing left and right and crops are failing out west. I'm not telling you anything you don't know."

But not my health plan.

"That's all for now Simon. I'm afraid to say you will not be the last to get bad news this week."

But I don't care about anyone else's department.

Simon thought the ride back to his office would clear his jumbled mind, but when he sat at his desk he was just as downhearted as when he left the President. Ed Preller entered his office and asked, "What did the President have to say?"

"He said we are in the midst of a depression and he has no idea how to extricate the country from it."

* * *

"I received a letter from the publisher of the *Capital Post-Dispatch*," Loretta said to the people who sat around the table in their conference room.

"Hasn't it been the other way around for the past three or four months?" Amy Grant teased.

"He commented that more than a few of their readers were saying nice things about my letters to him," Loretta said. "I am unsure whether his circulation has increased, but it was nice reading what he had to say.

"Has anyone bothered to get a quote from Secretary Kraft?" Phoebe asked.

"They have spoken with his office," Loretta replied. "Their stock answer has been consistent if not boring: 'they do not make the laws, they merely offer advice and assistance relative to the various state laws.'"

"Not very enlightening," Chester Kirkwood offered.

"Nor is it worth printing," Bill Andover added as he puffed on his pipe, "which keeps Kraft and his department out of the newspapers when they are not controlling the story."

"I have a meeting scheduled with the *Post-Dispatch's* publisher," Loretta offered to the group. "He wants to give me my own column?"

Everyone at the table stopped what they were doing and looked to Loretta. "The column will appear in the Wednesday papers," she offered. At once everyone resumed talking, asking questions, offering congratulations, claiming some form of victory or triumph.

"Hey," Loretta said at last to restore order to the room. "Let's allow this newspaper thing to follow its own course and not get in the way of anything we do here. There are an endless supply of issues to write about without focusing solely of Simon Kraft.

"Hold that thought Loretta because I have something here and I need some ideas," Phoebe said. She held a packet of papers in her hand and said, "This is a collection of the public works projects to which the Department of Health has provided matching funds. There are more than fifty. The projects are scattered throughout the country."

"That's a lot of favors for a lot of politicians in their home towns and home states," Bill noted.

"Most of them were worthwhile projects like draining swamps and establishing health clinics for women and children," Phoebe explained. "Several of the projects involved multiple governmental agencies like the Corps of Engineers and the Treasury Department."

"Too big, too broad, too many layers of red tape and policy language," Loretta said with a frown. "Besides, even if there were gobs of overspending and interdepartmental back-scratching, no one is going to become upset when the projects produced good results. No, we have to focus on smaller issues that were restricted more to Simon Kraft and his department.'

"Like these," Phoebe said as she raised the second packet of papers in her other hand. "These are the institutions or research centers that were recipients of grant money from the Department of Health and Welfare. It's all public record and it is our tax money that has been going to these facilities." She sent the packet around the table and each of the lawyers picked out a few pages.

"As you can see, some of the projects are very technical," Phoebe explained.

"Has anyone heard of John Rockefeller and his foundation?" Chester Kirkwood asked rhetorically. "Doesn't he have enough of his own money? Why does he want Uncle Sam's money?"

"This place in the Guatemalan prison sounds juicy," Amy Grant offered. "Can I go, can I go."

"There are dozens of different projects scattered across the country," Bill offered.

"I think this area is where we should focus our attention," Loretta said. "Phoebe, request what information you can, either from Washington or directly from the agencies that received the funds. There's quite a bit of work but we are not in a hurry. Let's work methodically and efficiently. Our clients still require our full attention. Phoebe, do this research when all the rest of your work is complete."

"Got it." Phoebe shuffled the remaining papers she held in her hand. "Here's a place in Arlington."

"That's a little more within our budget," Loretta replied. "What's their story?"

"Some place called 'Tomorrow's Children,'" she answered. "What does anyone know about artificial insemination?"

* * *

Simon thought back to the many months he spent in France near the front line of fighting during the Great War. The winter of 1918 was cold and the early spring was wet and muddy. At the time he had no reason to believe he would ever be warm or dry again. During the lulls in the fighting, the intense boredom was punctuated by a steady flow of war department forms that required no more than his signature. Cold, wet and bored. Perversely, the best part of so many of those wretched days was when he attended to sick call to treat the steady flow of soldiers with hacking coughs, running bowels, dripping noses and dripping penises.

Simon caught himself smiling as memories of those days crossed his mind, for they were days that held far more enjoyment than what he was now forced to endure. Life for the Secretary of the Department of Health and Welfare was reduced to signing letters, completing forms and attending an inane number of meetings. Department meetings were becoming stale and tedious. Because of budgetary restrictions no new programs were being approved or funded. Most of the staff workers feared they were one meeting away from unemployment. Interdepartmental meetings were drudgery because they discussed topics which almost never concerned Simon's department. Cabinet meetings were the worst. The fact was, none of the department secretaries looked forward to the cabinet meetings either, and there were very few days when good news emerged from the sessions.

The nation was at war: at war with the economy, at war with unemployment and at war with crop failures and dust storms. The nation was at war with forces it could not control and by all accounts she was not winning any of the wars. President Hoover was at war also; personal wars with his own people and countrymen. War was declared by the War Department after he further reduced the number of men authorized to serve on active duty, denied their requests for airplanes and tanks and vetoed multiple requests for battleships and destroyers. Hoover was at war with the Department of the Treasury because they never gave him any information he could share with the general public to relieve their sorrows. He was at war with the budget committees because the debits and credits would never reconcile.

As one might suspect, the Democratic Party also declared war on Mr. Hoover. Like his nation, Herbert Hoover was winning none of his personal wars.

Simon Kraft reasoned there was a benefit to being ignored by the President. He was not at war with him. The initial cuts had been crippling and subsequent restrictions further demoralized his department, but Simon realized sooner than most that nothing could be accomplished by confronting Herbert Hoover and arguing with him. He was a bright man who understood business and commerce, but he was overwhelmed by the situation. There was a forlorn look in his eyes; a look of uncertainty, a look of despair, a look that suggested there was no hope. Simon had seen that look before in the eyes of so many of the soldiers who spent too many days in the trenches and too many nights listening to the whistling of bombs and missiles that flew overhead. Simon had very little government money to give away anymore. Although he continued to review dozens of requests for research grants, there were far fewer projects to approve or initiate. Money to be used for matching funds to benefit any of the 48 states had dried up. All of the states were waging their own battles and no one was certain how well any of them were doing.

Routinely Simon arrived early at his office, answered a few questions and busied himself rewriting policy protocols. He walked the hallways, met and spoke with his staff and hoped to buoy their flagging spirits. Many adopted the forlorn look of their president, unsure how best to cope with this crisis people now referred to as the 'depression.' As the summer of 1931 arrived, one dreary day was little different from the last. When his secretary notified him of a telephone call from someone whose name he recognized from the past, Simon's hands nearly trembled as he picked up the receiver.

"Lamar Schreyer, my friend from Lynchburg, how have you been?"

"I'm doing fine, Dr. Kraft. No doubt I'm doing better than this poor country of ours," he replied in a slow drawl, overemphasizing 'poor country' for Simon's benefit.

"Mr. Schreyer, we all struggle to find the answer and are optimistic better days are just around the corner."

"That sounds like the company line Mr. Hoover has been passing around for the past two years." Simon was wise enough not to comment. "Dr. Kraft, I'm in Washington. Could we meet later today?"

"Certainly. How about the Willard?" Simon offered.

"No. I'd rather meet somewhere off the beaten track. Are you familiar with Rene's Bistro in Georgetown?"

"Yes I am," Simon replied.

"How about four o'clock?" Schreyer asked and Simon agreed.

Simon found Lamar Schreyer sitting at a table in the back of the restaurant. Schreyer stood to greet him. "Are you here on business?" Simon asked as he ordered a drink from the waiter.

"Of a sort." Schreyer lifted his glass, tilted and rolled the glass so the ice cubes circled inside of it. "I represent many groups; not just the eugenics folks back in New York. I am closely aligned, closely affiliated with the folks who will run the Democratic National Convention in Chicago next June."

Simon took a swallow of his drink but his expression did not change as Schreyer offered, "The men in the party are concerned for our country."

"Many people in our country are concerned, Mr. Schreyer," Simon answered him.

"I do not wish to cast dispersions upon your boss, Dr. Kraft, but the consensus of the men who run the Democratic Party is they do not believe Mr. Hoover can win the election next year," Schreyer said. "The Democratic Party sits in a rather opportunistic position."

"Who might beat him?" Simon asked.

"Damn near anybody we democrats decide to trot out there," Schreyer answered matter of factly. "Hells bells, even Al Smith would have a chance at a rematch. The Republican Party is in quite a quandary and even a blind man can see there is no clear alternative to Hoover to run for president. All of us understand this is a global depression, but now Europe blames us for causing it. Now you have the American people *and* the European people blaming America for the depression. I don't want to say people are ganging up on us, but hey, even this ol' boy can read the tea leaves."

"How does any of this . . . ," Simon paused and searched for the correct phrase. Words said in Washington had a habit of returning to haunt the one who uttered them. "How does this conversation have a direct impact on me?"

"There is a faction in our party that would like to see you run for president next year," Schreyer said. Simon did not change his expression. "When I say a faction, I mean the people who run the party and people who donate heavily to the party."

"Why would your friends think, what leads your friends in this *faction* to believe that I would do a better job than Mr. Hoover?" Simon asked.

"When I see a horse go out and run through his paces," Schreyer said, "it doesn't take me too long to determine if he's the real thing, or whether he's better left hooked up to the plow. There's a natural flow and grace to how a horse moves that is clearly evident if one knows what to look for. You, Dr. Kraft, have that flow and grace. We've had all sorts of men as president. Teddy Roosevelt was a rough and tumbler and Wilson was an egghead. Harding was a crook and Hoover is a rich businessman. You are a little different but different in a good way. People like what you have to say and how you say it. You've gotten laws passed to back up what you say. You are what every man wants to be: an athlete and a war hero. You've still got your looks and the women have the vote. You've accomplished a good bit but I suspect there is a great deal more you wish to accomplish before you cash in your ticket. Most important, to me anyway, is that you are committed to America and to the race of people known as Americans."

"You do remember that I am a registered member of the Republican Party," Simon offered Schreyer.

"But you were a democrat," Schreyer coyly replied, "and worked for a democratic governor in a democratic state. You switched parties before and you could just as easily switch parties again, seeing as how you are so discouraged and despondent with how the Republican Party has failed so miserably to address our current financial situation."

"It would appear that in addition to reading tea leaves you are trying very hard to read me." Simon drained the last of his drink. He liked what Lamar Schreyer had to say but he was too politically savvy to have his head turned by someone who quite clearly was committed to his own agenda. "What do you want from me?"

"Be yourself," Schreyer answered him. "Go out and meet with the public, be with the public. Say good things, say the things they want to hear. We'll stay in touch and take the pulse of the situation periodically. Let's get through the year and then meet again. If I'm right, and I usually am, I'll bring along a friend or two and then we'll talk turkey."

Simon rose, shook hands with Lamar Schreyer and said, "It is always a pleasure talking with you, Mr. Schreyer."

"Likewise Dr. Kraft."

* * *

Loretta's first article appeared in the *Post-Dispatch* early in November.

> Abortion is the termination of a woman's pregnancy that results in the death of the fetus. No hospital in the United States allows abortions to be performed excepted when the mother's life is severely jeopardized.
>
> Abortion is a surgical procedure which, on occasional, is an alternative distraught women may choose as a means to eliminate the problem of an unplanned pregnancy.
>
> Abortion is a word frequently spoken in hushed tones and seldom by women with fragile and sensitive constitutions.
>
> Abortion currently is a crime, tantamount to murder and punishable with long term imprisonments and possible execution.
>
> Abortions have been performed my one means or another for thousands of years but are forbidden by the Hippocratic Oath taken by physicians upon their graduation from medical school.
>
> The ugly truth is that abortions continue to be performed by non-regulated, unauthorized facilities and operators, with major complications and a disproportionate number of maternal deaths.
>
> Abortion, by and large, is a distasteful topic. Why then have I decided to write about the topic? Most recently

I had the opportunity to re-read the writings of a young woman who is very much in the headlines, one Margaret Stringer. Mrs. Stringer is the editor of *The Woman Rebel*, founding principal of The American Birth Control League, and champion of the struggle for women the world over to escape from the shackles of unplanned motherhood.

In many respects Mrs. Stringer should be applauded for her efforts to educate and inform families of their options in regard to the determination of how large a family to raise. The madness, however, is in the method by which the *correct* family size is determined. It is readily acknowledged that Mrs. Stringer is firmly committed to the eugenics cause for the elimination of the *less than perfect*. She has taken the vitriol of her cause into a new sphere, as noted in her past ranting in "Woman and the New Race." In the article she has identified the greatest of society's mistakes and the cause of much of the world's miseries: the creation of large families. She has brought to light our greatest current crime: "the most immoral practice of the day is breeding too many children." As per Mrs. Stringer, families with too many children are the cause of world wars, rampant disease, uncontrolled pestilence and world financial ruin.

Mrs. Stringer, never one to be at a loss for a solution to any problem, does offer an alternative to abstinence and contraception: "The most merciful thing that the large family does to one of its infant members is to kill it."

She did not clarify which of her mad methods was better; murder of the infant while still in the womb or murder of the child when first identified as being a burden on society. One is left to believe that each is acceptable and works equally well. Abortion now and/or infanticide later.

We hope that Mrs. Stringer continues in what good works she does. We also hope that Mrs. Stringer adjusts her stance on the killing of children as a means to resolve the wickedness in the world.

What is the purpose of this diatribe? We note that Mrs. Stringer's efforts currently receive financial support from the U. S. Department of Health and Welfare. This is the same department that is lead by Dr. Simon Kraft, the Health Czar.

In as much as the Department supports Mrs. Stringer, how much longer will the Department continue to support her views on abortion? How much longer will the Health Czar support abortion? At what point in time will abortion no longer be a distasteful topic? When, perish the day, will abortion become acceptable, become legalized and become the law of the land? Not soon enough for Margaret Stringer.

The publisher of the *Capital Post-Dispatch* shared with Loretta that an extraordinary number of letters were written to its editor referencing her first column.

*　*　*

Simon Kraft became re-energized as he entered the speaking circuit just in time for the autumn banquets and Christmas party season. He spoke of new hope and better days that waited around every corner. He spoke of policies certain to make everyone's life better, regardless of whether or not he understood the rudiments of the policies, or whether such policies even existed. In short he told the people what they wanted to hear. He charged onto the winter cocktail party trail with Dorothy at his side and once again they became the darlings in the Capital. He renewed the many acquaintances and friendships he had developed over the past twelve years and worked hard to create new ones. He was reinvigorated and enthusiastic and attacked his project with a passion.

When he spoke in public he was cautious never to utter an ill word about the President. He occasionally would note that the results observed from such and such a policy were "not as good as expected," or "might have been better." When asked what might or could have been done differently, his stock answer was "there's always an answer to every question and the bright people in Washington will eventually arrive at the proper decision." At no point in time did he ever allude to the thought that the President was bright, nor did he suggest that Mr. Hoover would make the proper decision.

Simon stumped almost as hard for Dorothy as he did for himself. Regularly he involved her in his conversations with congressmen and the political power brokers. The lobbyists loved her and scrambled at every turn to gain her attention and notice. The women's vote in this past decade was proving to be a variable that not everyone understood very well. Most of the pundits believed the votes that wives cast would be rubber stamps of their husbands' votes. Simon Kraft disagreed. If Lamar Schreyer were correct when he said that Simon was everything most men wanted to be; i.e., a war hero and an athlete, Dorothy was everything women wanted to be, and men wanted their wives to be. She was beautiful, well spoken, very social and at ease in front of large crowds. Simon was doing his best to display her for what he wanted her to become: an excellent First Lady.

*   *   *

Loretta's columns continued to appear every Wednesday in the *Post-Dispatch*, commenting on a wide variety of issues. After the first of the year she returned to the person whom she most liked to dislike.

> Although neither a world traveler nor time traveler myself, I am familiar with the customs of several far off cultures and ancient civilizations as to how they deal/ dealt with the control of their populations. Consider first the clans in the arctic regions of the North Pole. In the land of the midnight sun they are limited not only in sunlight and warmth, but in food provisions and the basic necessities of life. Theirs is a fine balance between what they can gather from the seas and how well they distance themselves from hungry polar bears. There are no farms to till and no gardens to tend. They fish and hunt for their subsistence and are prone to prolonged periods when their bounties are lean. Consequently they cannot benefit from a brood of children who might otherwise work the fields

and help with the harvest. There are only so many fishing nets to haul and harpoons to throw and none may be accomplished by children. They know from the experience of past generations there are only a finite number of mouths that can be fed. Too many children place a burden on the clan.

So what becomes of the baby born when the numbers do not add up in its favor? The time honored solution, of course. The excess infant is placed on an iceberg and cast adrift.

There are tribes in the Kalahari Desert in Africa that also compete severely for their existence. Like their arctic brethren they also perform their calculations and cipher their own, unique economies. They too accept the facts that there are only so many mouths to feed and only a finite number of productive and useful hunters and herdsmen who will allow for the tribe to survive.

What becomes of those who are no longer productive, specifically the elderly: those who are infirm, arthritic and no longer able to cast the spear or draw the bow or manhandle the yoke? Once again we note these people in the distant lands of the Kalahari have their own solutions to their own problems. The elderly are left on the side of a hill beneath a shade tree to await the lions, the jackals and the hyenas to resolve the tribe's conundrum.

Consider also the Spartans from ancient Greece, the time honored warriors of a martial state. Only those fit and strong could undergo the severe training required of both their men and women. There was no room for the weak and deformed. The destinies of the unfit would lead them to the outskirts of the city where the wolves would cull what was of no use to army leaders.

Economic decisions, usefulness to society, contributors to a great nation; where have we heard of this mantra before? If I recall, such are the policies of the U. S. Department of Health and Welfare and the programs of Health Czar, Dr. Simon Kraft. Although executed in different forums and cloaked within the veil of medical expertise, individual rights continue to be broached and abrogated. Those considered unfit continue to be cast adrift on their own icebergs and those with debilitating medical ailments must await the arrival of the devouring carnivore.

Our politicians have told us such actions will make America a much stronger nation. Our business leaders have assured us such actions will produce and greater race of Americans. Our judges have guaranteed us such actions will perpetuate a greater society.

'Tis a wonder to observe how far a great nation and a grand civilization like ours has advanced.

TWENTY-FOUR

Chester and Phoebe posed as Mr. and Mrs. Kirkwood when they met with Professor Van Kirk in his office in Arlington.

"How long have you been married?" Van Kirk asked the couple.

"Four years," Chester replied.

"And you've been trying to have a child for how long?" Van Kirk asked.

"Four years," Chester repeated.

"After we finish talking I will perform a physical examination on each of you. We will perform several laboratory tests. We will reschedule another meeting in one week, discuss the results of the testing and the examination, and discuss treatment options."

"Would you explain again what you offer here at Tomorrow's Children?" Phoebe asked, expecting their physical examinations to be reasonably normal.

"We have been investigating and perfecting various techniques to improve the chances that young married couples may conceive and have children. When there is a problem with the husband's sperm, we utilize sperm from a donor and insert it directly into the wife's uterus. With some frequency we have been able to achieve conception. In the past nine years we have helped a good many couples."

"How many?" Chester asked.

"More than one thousand babies," Van Kirk said with pride, "with forty-one due this year."

"Is this really God's way of doing things?" Phoebe challenged.

"The way in which I view the matter," Van Kirk replied in a grandfatherly fashion, "God has given me the knowledge and talent to perform this service, so who is to say what is and is not God's will."

"Where does it say in the Bible that artificial insemination is right?" Phoebe persisted with a line of questioning that would raise the hackles of a good many people.

"The Bible describes healers and those who lay hands," Van Kirk answered smoothly as if Phoebe's questions weren't the first of their kind. "We take the Good Samaritan approach here at our clinic and strive to help all whom we may."

"Is your clinic sponsored by the government?" Phoebe continued.

"We have been fortunate to receive grant money from the government," Van Kirk replied.

"Who will supply the sperm donation?" Chester asked. "Will we be introduced to the man who will be the donor?"

"No," Van Kirk replied. "The names of the donors are held in strict confidentiality. I can assure you the donors are in excellent health and free from any inherited defects and diseases. We have been using the same donors for many years and never once has there been an inherited birth defect. Some difficulties occasionally arise during the birthing process, but not with any inherited defects in the infants."

"Is Tomorrow's Children regulated by the state?" Chester asked.

Van Kirk narrowed his eyes and had the faint impression he was being deposed. "I am licensed by the state but our facility does not require regulation or registration. We do not follow your pregnancy; your own physician will provide that care. No babies are delivered at our facility. You will deliver your baby either in your home or in the hospital of your choice. Our only function is to assist you in becoming pregnant."

"Are the results of your research published in any of the medical journals?" Phoebe continued.

Van Kirk picked up a pencil from his desk and rolled it in his fingers He said, "I suspect significant apprehension on your behalf, both of you."

"We're nervous," Phoebe replied quickly, "and we want to know all there is to know before we get involved in something that might generate second thoughts."

"I think I understand your anxiety," Van Kirk replied. "Perhaps now is not the best time for you to start with us here at Tomorrow's Children."

Phoebe took a different tack. "What are the chances we might have twins?"

"It happens. We have eight sets of twins among our mothers," Van Kirk replied.

"Could we possibly get the sperm from a great athlete?" Chester said with a smile on his face. "Perhaps from a great baseball player or possibly from Red Grange himself?"

"Such is a possibility but I would venture to say that Mr. Grange may be otherwise occupied," Van Kirk replied. "Perhaps we may proceed with the examinations."

* * *

In the early spring another article by Loretta generated more than a few letters to the editor of the *Post-Dispatch.*

> Consider a trip into the future. How far into the future I cannot say, but for the purposes of this discussion, let us consider a time beyond Thursday of next week. As we are whisked away on our magical flying carpet we arrive at a time when family planning will be performed in a new and modern way. New and modern. Such are terms we have come to embrace as a means to make our existence more pleasant and improve our way of living.
>
> The destination of our trip will be into the company of a newly married couple. Our newlyweds, like so many others before them, have agreed to accept something old to go along with something new (and modern). As we join them they are now sitting down to discuss their future family. It is a time honored practice, performed countless times daily over the past five or ten millennia.
>
> Those of us who have been married have shared similar conversations with our spouses. We are hopeful the boys will be strong and the girls will be beautiful. We want them to be wise and courteous and bring honor to

the family name. Prospective parents will pray to their respective Gods or Goddesses, hope for the best and be thankful for what gifts may be divined upon them.

The married couple whom we now visit is new and modern. A book is laid open on the table before them and has their full attention. They now are able to do more than hope and pray for a healthy child. They are able to pick and choose. They have the ability to choose whether they want a boy or a girl. Brown hair versus blond. Blue eyes instead of brown. Tall, short, something in between. No chance for a defect and nary a blemish.

"How can this be?" we travelers from the past ask. "What can make it so?"

"We profit by advancements in science, which include a thorough understanding and control of genetics," we are told by the receptionist who works in the waiting room of the physician's office where the baby will be delivered. "Here, take this catalogue and read it."

The book given to us is the same book that our newlywed couple is reading. We thumb through the book, something akin to what one might use to make a mail order purchase from a distant warehouse or department store, and indeed we note a myriad of choices for one's prospective offspring.

"How does it work?" we ask.

"You make your selections and place your order. Our physicians will provide you, the prospective mother, with chemicals and hormones, and your wishes will be fulfilled," we are told.

"What if we get something that we did not order?" we ask. As we look down at the catalogue we query, "Like a wrong delivery."

"We'll correct the mistake." We tilt our heads and beg for clarification. "We have solutions for all problems."

"What if the child has deformities or a serious illness," we ask.

"That will not be a problem," the receptionist assures us. "All our deliveries are guaranteed and we will accept any and all returns you may wish to make."

Solutions for all problems. We are still incredulous and question, "Where are we? How can this be?" This office looks like no other physician's office we have seen before. This hospital looks like no other we have visited before. We look overhead and note a sign:

Babies Boutique

Our magic flying carpet returns to 1932 and we note that a portion of the future is now with us. A medical facility located in the Commonwealth functions to help childless parents with the process of creating children. Although one does not encounter a grand wizard mixing potions and making animal sacrifices, one does encounter a wizened physician mixing solutions in test tubes in his quest to make women pregnant.

We note the above mentioned modern-day Baby Boutique receives funding and the support of the U.S. Department of Health and Welfare. Is this puppy mill, posing as a medical research facility, more concerned with quantity and volume than with concern for a warm and loving home?

We cannot comment on whether such techniques are condoned by the Great Creator. We are able to confirm that Dr. Simon Kraft, Secretary for the Department, has given his approval for the creation of test tube babies. Secretary Kraft has allowed all that is new and modern in science to irreparably change the lives of many Americans. Has the Health Czar also assumed the role of the Archangel Gabriel?

* * *

Washington was pink. Every spring the cherry trees bloomed and their blossoms turned the Capital pink, assuring one and all that winter has gone and summer will soon arrive. June was still nearly two months away, but June was very much on the mind of Simon Kraft. Early in June the republican delegates would gather in Chicago to choose who would carry the standard of the party and run for president of the United States. Two weeks later the democratic delegates would gather in the same city and repeat a similar exercise. June was still two months away and Simon still had so much to accomplish.

During the past year the thoughts of moving into the White House and working in the Oval Office fascinated and tantalized Simon. Over the winter he had been away from his office for extended periods of time. He delegated many of the mundane duties to Ed Preller at the Health Department and used his time to give weekly talks to women's clubs and Rotary clubs and Kiwanis clubs. He traveled across the country and attended dozens of lunches with congressmen and lobbyists and people who purported to know the right people. He enjoyed the opportunities to meet and mix with the people and he felt as if he were growing into the role of a politician: talking a great deal without saying too much. Routinely he harkened back to his talking points: the purity of the native population, the protection of society from the bad traits and bad behavior embedded in the blood of the unfit, the need to preserve and protect and improve the American race. Wherever he went and whenever he spoke, he was applauded and cheered and when he looked into the audiences he saw only nodding heads and approving smiles.

The more he spoke, the more he listened, and he liked what the people were telling him. He heard them when they said it was his destiny to make America healthier; both spiritually and medically. He heard them when they said it was his destiny to make America safer; from the dangers outside our borders and from within. He heard them when they said it was his destiny to make America better; economically, culturally and as a race of people. He was Simon Kraft, the Olympic athlete, the Medal of Honor winner in the Great War, the man who cured malaria and yellow fever in the Commonwealth and duplicated similar efforts for the rest of the country.

He was in a good frame of mind when he met with Lamar Schreyer in late April. Schreyer was accompanied by two men. "Dr. Kraft, so good to see you again. These gentlemen very much want to meet you. Dave Koenig from New Jersey and Walter Hughes from Ohio."

They shook hands and sat down at a table in the back of Rene's Bistro, where Simon had met with Lamar previously. "Your non-campaign is going well, Mr. Secretary," Koenig said. "We hear nothing but good things about the Health Czar."

Simon was familiar with both of the men. Koenig was based in Newark and nothing happened in New Jersey that didn't get his approval. Hughes was from Michigan. Simon replied, "At this point in time, my plan is to tell the people what they want to hear and not ruffle the feathers of Mr. Hoover."

"It's a good plan, Mr. Secretary," Hughes offered.

"Here's our plan," Lamar Schreyer interjected, "you keep doing what you're doing. You have become a very bright spot in the rather bleak cabinet of Mr. Hoover. Things is getting' so desperate for the republicans that Calvin Coolidge is talking about coming out of moth balls to run for president again. Good Lord, talk about taking a step backward. The delegates at the republican convention will not allow that. Although Hoover is drowning, their party has no option other than to re-nominate him to convince the nation that the Republican Party has been doing the right thing for the past four years. We can only hope that he takes down the entire Republican Party with him. There are 35 senator and 435 representative positions up for grabs. You are our best solution to foment a bloodbath.

"When the democratic convention starts," Schreyer said in a stern voice, "we'll do all the deal making and make all the promises."

At the mention of *deal making*, Simon's eyes widened and his ears must have twitched for Schreyer placed a hand on his elbow and said, "You keep your head low and don't do anything to rankle people you may not know very well. We'll be talking on a regular basis between now and then." Simon reluctantly nodded his approval despite the fact he suspected he was treading onto ground that had been traveled once before. "And by the way, do something about that lady who keeps writing the letters and articles in the *Capital Post-Dispatch*.

She ain't exactly helping your situation and she's starting to attract more flies than I'm comfortable with."

Loretta Frontenac.

"Do something to make her happy or quiet or make her go away," Lamar Schreyer ordered.

"Any suggestions?" Simon said as he tried to make light of it.

"You're a handsome guy, charm her. You're probably bigger than her, stuff a sock in her mouth." Schreyer narrowed his eyes when he said, "I'm serious. Her squawking will do no good for you or for us."

*   *   *

The ride from Georgetown back to Simon's office gave him time to think. By all reports, if Hoover were to run for re-election he most likely would lose. Simon's own time as Department Secretary would come to an end. His best chance to remain in Washington would be to run for the office of president like Schreyer and his boys explained. It would be an uphill battle, but it was a battle he was willing to chance. Lamar Schreyer was right; there would be deals to make and favors to grant and . . . All was part and parcel of politics and no stranger to Simon. But he harkened back to what Ed Preller said previously and Schreyer presently reiterated: he could expect nothing but continued trouble if he didn't do something about this woman who would not go away.

"How goes the good fight," Ed said by way of greeting to Simon when he returned to the office.

"Have a seat and close the door," Simon replied and explained to Ed the salient points of his meeting with Schreyer. He also shared with him the party's displeasure with Loretta Frontenac.

"She is not a woman who will go softly into the night," Ed observed.

"I have no reason to believe there is anything I could say to appease her," Simon said. "And I don't have enough money to pay her to go away."

"There is only one way I know to make her go away," Ed offered and Simon nodded his agreement.

Simon picked up the telephone receiver and dialed a number that he read from a piece of scratch paper. The telephone rang, voices spoke and finally Simon heard on the line, "Loretta Frontenac." He folded the scratch paper and put it in his pocket.

"Good afternoon Miss Frontenac, this is Simon Kraft."

There was a pause on the other end. "Good afternoon, Dr. Kraft. What can I do for you?"

"I wonder if we couldn't meet, just you and I, and possibly discuss a few issues that are of mutual interest to us." Again Kraft heard a pause on the other end of the telephone.

"That sounds like an excellent idea Dr. Kraft," Loretta replied.

"Would it be possible to meet at your office one evening next week?" Simon asked. "Send your folks home so it will be only the two of us. I don't need an audience nor do we need interference. I'll bring a bottle of wine as a peace offering."

"How's next Tuesday sound, Dr. Kraft? Six o'clock." Loretta asked.

"Six thirty sounds better and call me Simon."

"Next Tuesday, 6:30 it is, Dr. Kraft," Loretta said and broke the connection. Simon nodded silently to Ed Preller.

Tuesday arrived. Ed asked Simon, "Do you have plans for this evening?"

"I have a dinner scheduled with the Undersecretaries of the Interior and Labor," Simon replied.

"Some heavy hitters. Did you promise to pick up the check?"

"I did, which made it all the easier for them to accept the invitation," Simon admitted.

Ed replied, "I'll be on the road by mid afternoon to give myself enough time." Simon nodded and Ed left the room.

Simon enjoyed a pleasant morning. Schreyer and his political magicians were assuring him of nothing but good news. One way or another his time in this tiresome job would soon be coming to an end. He would be moving onward and upward and by the end of the day, his number one problem, Loretta Frontenac would be history.

Shortly before noon his secretary knocked on his door. "President Hoover would like to see you."

"When?"

"Now," she replied.

Now. It was a long time since the president had asked to see him, and never before on a *now* basis. Simon stood up from his desk and wondered what was so urgent that couldn't wait for the weekly cabinet meeting? He wondered if an emergency cabinet meeting was being convened.

"Good morning, Mrs. Griffin," Simon said to Hoover's secretary in the waiting area.

"The President will see you now."

The door opened and once again Simon stepped onto the plush blue carpeting of the Oval Office. He felt good walking into the room. He looked up at the walls and took a deep and comforting breath. The air was fresh and clean and what was it he detected? Oh yes, the sweet smell of power. Success. Accomplishment. It was all due him and he had earned it. It would be a grand reward to work in this office and he was the grand man who deserved it. He stiffened his back and stood a bit taller, now that he was standing in the greatest office in the world, in the greatest building in the world. He pursed his lips and said to himself, *After the November election it will be my office. The man who works in this office is the most powerful man in the world; the most successful and respected man in the world.* Oh how he loved, how he coveted this office. Oh how he looked forward with so much relish to the day when the office would be his.

With a contented and self congratulatory smile he offered, "Good morning, Mr. . . . , Mr. President." He stammered when he saw Professor Van Kirk sitting in a chair opposite the desk of the President. Standing by the wall was Uncle Billy.

"Please have a seat, Mr. Secretary," Hoover said matter of factly. "You remember Professor Van Kirk, and of course you know the senator." Simon sat down next to Van Kirk.

"Strangely enough my press secretary reads the newspapers," Hoover said. "You and your department have been mentioned frequently and ordinarily that should be a good thing. However, my attention was drawn to Professor Van Kirk's medical research clinic. So as not to leave any stone unturned, my press secretary visited with Professor Van Kirk. To help him understand the issues better he took along a physician and an accountant with him. Professor Van Kirk was quite helpful and forthright."

"I will not presuppose that I understand all facets of medical research, nor do I understand all the technical concerns Professor Van Kirk shared with us. He was, however, kind enough to clarify a few of the mundane and pedestrian issues with us. As I understand, Tomorrow's Children make's payments to men who contribute semen, their sperm, to facilitate impregnating women in his laboratory by means of a procedure he calls 'artificial insemination.' For privacy purposes the name, or names, of the donors remain anonymous. For our purposes the name, or names, of the donors were divulged.

"Professor Van Kirk's confidential records show that you have been on his payroll for the past nine years. You have received a weekly retainer of $1,000. In return for your *retainer,* you have been supplying Tomorrow' Children with semen specimens. As Professor Van Kirk explains further, you are the only donor of semen, of sperm, for his clinic."

Simon looked to Uncle Billy who turned his face away, unable to hold his gaze. He looked to Van Kirk whose face remained unchanged. Hoover continued, "Two problems come to light. One is the $52,000 you have been receiving annually from the government, *via professor Van Kirk,* for the past nine years. By my arithmetic, that figure approaches nearly $500,000 during these days of severe national financial hardship.

"The second issue of concern is that you have provided semen specimens for thousands of procedures performed by Professor Van Kirk. You are, in fact, the biological father of more than one thousand children.

"I am a businessman by training, not a lawyer. Consequently I am uncertain at this moment if any, or how many, laws have been broken. I am absolutely certain, however, there have been a number of violations of ethical conduct. Such matters may be determined at a later date. As we sit here, I can say without reservation that your actions are, by all appearances, *improper.* They are without a doubt inconsistent with this administration. Such actions are unfit. They are unfit for anyone who professes to hold a public office and serve the public. I repeat, your unfit actions are damning and may bring inexplicable embarrassment upon this administration.

"I am also aware you are campaigning for my job. Six days out of seven I would gladly give it to you. By cavorting and meeting with influential members of the opposing party you raise grievous concerns which render us vulnerable to indefensible criticism. Such activity, by all appearances, smacks of disloyalty and impropriety. I am concerned where this trail of questionable activity will lead."

Simon cast another embarrassed glance at Uncle Billy. *Appearances and impropriety.* How often had he heard those words spoken in the past?

"All funding for Professor Van Kirk's research center will be withdrawn. What he does from now on is his own business." President Hoover handed Simon a typewritten sheet of paper. "This is your resignation from office which you will sign immediately. For the sake of this administration and our country I would prefer to remain silent on this matter, but the Attorney General may have different thoughts and opinions. I also want your promise never to run for public office again, neither federal nor state; not even for town dog catcher. Essentially, I want you removed from the public picture. If you refuse to accept my offer, charges will be made against you within the hour and you will be prosecuted with the full might and fury of this office. Your story will be made public in every newspaper in the country. The court of popular opinion will vilify you and hound you for being a habitual, a habitual . . ." Hoover paused, searching for the proper phrase. "For being a habitual and professional masturbator. The good Lord only knows whatever else you may be or what you have done. You are unfit. You are unfit to hold public office."

*   *   *

Simon did not return to his office. He got into his car and drove. At first he wasn't certain where he would go, nor did he care. He wanted only to leave Washington. He sped along and tried with difficulty to organize his thoughts. His plans, his career, his reputation were all no more than a jumble. Before today his future was lining up so neatly, so orderly. How was it that matters were now falling down around him? Why? Who? As his mind raced one name, one person continually re-emerged; Loretta Frontenac. He was unsure what to do or what not to do, but there was one issue he did need to address, one person he would need to see.

As the day drew to a close Simon drove into the center of Norwood. How many years had it been since he moved away from Norwood? Twelve, thirteen? He drove past the Capitol building where he worked for so many years and learned the means and ways of politics. He turned left at the court house and parked down the street from a house with a sign in the front that read, 'Loretta Frontenac and Associates.' Simon walked to the car that was parked in front of his. Ed Preller was sitting in the front seat wearing denim coveralls. "Go home Ed, work's over for the day."

"Whaddya mean?" Ed asked.

"Loretta Frontenac is my problem now," Simon replied. "She's always been my problem."

"Are you sure?" Ed asked and Simon nodded.

"I'll take care of her for now; I settle everything now." Ed nodded, started the engine of his automobile and drove away. Simon walked into the old converted house. It was quiet and appeared to be empty. He found Loretta working at her desk in her office. He took off his hat and tapped his knuckles on her open door.

"Hello," he offered.

"Hello yourself," she replied.

"How's your day been?" he asked.

"Not bad. How's yours been?"

"I've had better," Simon replied. He stared at Loretta, recalling the day when she appeared in his office and had the gall to include him as a witness in a legal case against the Commonwealth. He thought back to the time when she named him as a defendant in a lawsuit and how angry he was. The columns in the newspaper that attacked him and his department; the letters to the newspaper that attacked his policies and his principles. Oh how she had tortured him over the past twelve years. After tonight the torturing would end.

"I wanted to tell you I am leaving office. No applause, thank you," he said with a wry smile.

"This is sudden," Loretta replied. She was tempted to ask, 'Was it something I said?' but thought better of it. "Why the change?"

"I've gotten a better offer," he replied with a deadpan expression that suggested no humor.

With some reservation she asked, "Will you be seeking a different position?"

Simon took in a deep breath and said, "No."

Loretta pushed her chair back, away from her desk and said, "So you really will be leaving." Hesitant to take him at his word she asked,

"Does this mean I will not have the opportunity to cross swords with President Simon Kraft in the near future."

Simon narrowed his eyes and his fingers tightened on the brim of his hat that he was holding, once more feeling the barbs of Loretta Frontenac. "For the present, I think not."

"Where will you go?" Loretta asked warily. "What will you be doing?"

"After tonight, after I leave here, I'm not sure. I haven't thought it out that far."

"Well, good luck, I think," Loretta replied.

Simon stared intently into the eyes of Loretta and offered, "Perhaps we'll get together again to debate the issues over lunch."

"I'd look forward to that," Loretta replied, unsure how much pleasure or credit she wanted to take for Kraft's announcement. "Let me ask you one question, Dr. Kraft, if I may? Why are the Health Laws so important to you?"

Simon paused for a moment as he put his hat on his head, ran his fingers along the brim and said, "The Health Laws are the best way to make America great; to keep America great. It is God's will that America become and remain the greatest nation on earth. It just so happens that on occasion God needs a little help." He turned, left Loretta's office and walked out of the house. He got into his automobile and drove away.

TWENTY-FIVE

———— ⌒⌒ ————

Simon Kraft sat in the backseat of the limousine with his wife Dorothy at his side. He stared out the window and studied the trees that lined the streets and dominated the walkways. It was early spring and one needed a keen eye to see the buds and young leaves on the trees as the limousine sped swiftly down the boulevard. The Capital of course was famous for the trees. The sky today was bright and the air was warm. He took Dorothy's hand in his and gently squeezed. "Nervous?" She smiled and looked down to where their hands were clasped together. She shifted her gaze up into his eyes and shook her head 'No.'

With his free hand he smoothed the front of his suit and tugged at his neck tie. He had given thought to wearing a tuxedo, possibly a morning suit of the kind a king might wear for his coronation, but thought better of it. He knew the good people in the audience today would enjoy their pomp and ceremony, but they would never relish or condone the ostentatious and the gaudy. The Good Lord could only guess how many might be in attendance. He envisioned the gathered throng staring up onto the platforms and the stages, craning their necks to catch a glimpse of history as it was being made. In his mind he repeated the words to his oath of office. It wasn't a long passage, only a few sentences really. Why shouldn't he know it by heart? He had stood in front of a mirror and repeated the oath almost daily for the past two months; pantomiming every so often when he would nod his head for emphasis, jutting out a firm jaw as a show of sincerity. Such gestures would play well before the huge crowds.

He was suddenly conscious that his mouth was dry. Not surprising. His mouth always became dry just before he had to speak in front of large crowds. Funny it should be that way, for when he did start to speak he was as glib and smooth as a snake oil salesman at a county fair. He had faced far more dangerous and difficult tasks than speaking in front of large crowds of people. With all the bullets and bombs that flew past him in the Great War, he never had a dry mouth. During the many hours and days spent in the operating rooms, he never had a dry mouth. Only now, while on the way to take his oath of office for the highest position he could ever imagine achieving in this nation, did he have a dry mouth.

He squeezed Dorothy's hand once again, looked to her and saw the face of the nineteen year old debutante whom he had courted so many years ago. "It's a long way from a share-cropper's shack in the back country."

Dorothy looked at him in poorly controlled amazement. She raised her free hand to her mouth to stifle a grin. In a soft, southern drawl she said, "Dr. Simon Kraft, you are indeed a scamp and a scallywag. You no more ever stepped foot inside a share-cropper's shack than did you ever walk on the moon. Your daddy was a rich banker and you went to college up north with the rest of those rich boys. After which you trotted back to the Commonwealth and stole my heart so that I might become a physician's wife." She moved her hand from her face and touched Simon on the nose. "But you did good for yourself, and for me, and I do love you for it."

Simon smiled back at her. Yes, he had accomplished a great deal, and this great position he would assume within the hour was a just reward for all the years and all the struggles. It was a new dawn for a new day in this country of his. At last, he would have the opportunity to implement and execute all the plans that had been so many years in the making. The nation was destined for greatness and it was meet and right that Simon Kraft should take command of the helm and help direct its course. He smiled and thought back to all he had done and all that had occurred. Today was a new day and it was a new beginning, and within the hour he would take the oath of office for the position of Chief Physician of Cultural Purification.

So many trees, Simon mused as the limousine sped down Unter den Linden, the most famous boulevard in Berlin, through the

Brandenburg Gate approached the statue of Frederick the Great astride his stallion. These people did love their heroes. On they sped to Museum Island where he and Dorothy exited the limousine and walked to where the stages and platforms were erected in the central square known as the Lustgarten. They were met by Dr. Ploetz.

"Guten Tag," Simon said by way of greeting.

"Come, come, he'll be here soon." Ploetz guided Dorothy and Simon to the stage where two dozen chairs were lined up in rows and a podium stood off to the side. The men on the stage were some of the brightest minds and gifted scientists the country had to offer. They would be his staff, Simon's men, dedicated and committed to the arduous task that awaited them. Thousands of people, perhaps tens of thousands of people mingled and walked about in the open area below the stage. They too were waiting.

At the appointed hour a motorcade of five touring cars arrived, each adorned by red and white flags with the black swastikas. Men in brown uniforms spilled out of the automobiles and moved toward the stage as if each had a specific task in mind. He then exited his automobile and moved quickly to the stage. The men on the stage moved to their assigned seats and Simon and Dorothy followed their lead. They remained standing as he ascended the stage. Herr Hitler was now the Reich Chancellor and the greeting he offered Simon was the nod of his head. He approached the podium and started speaking. *"Die Wissenschaft hat die Tür geöffnet, damit wir als Nation zu verbessern, als ein Volk."* Simon was now six months in the country and talking like a native. Now that he was able to understand what his fuhrer was saying he smiled a heartfelt smile, for the words were so very dear to his soul.

"Science has opened the door to allow us to improve as a nation, as one people. I present to you now one of the premier scientists in all the world: Herr Doctor Simon Kraft. Our nation is strong but there are many, many threats—and we must remain ever aware and ever vigilant. Germany, as a race and as a nation, is at risk for being polluted. The genetics of the German people, even as we speak, are being corrupted. Our bloodlines are being contaminated by the weak, the incurably infirm and by the degenerates. Our bloodlines are being adulterated and sullied by the unfit. The bloodlines of the criminally corrupt threaten to flow and mix with the sacred and true blood of the German people. The superior character of our race must remain pure. The inferior traits of the inferior races must not be allowed to co-mingle indiscriminately or degrade the best that is Germany. Dr. Kraft is here to make it so. Dr. Kraft is here to make us strong and make us great."

Dr. Kraft nodded, as these were words he had come to live by.

AFTERWARD

The eugenics movement first appeared during the latter part of the nineteenth century in Great Britain, championed by Francis Galton, a cousin of Charles Darwin. An eccentric man of independent means, Galton promoted as a moral philosophy the concept that humanity would improve through a selective breeding program. He proffered that if the "best" of any society were to breed, successive generations would improve. It was an elitist's philosophy, as "best" focused on physical, cultural and intellectual talents and accomplishments.

In the United States, Germany and the Scandinavian countries, the eugenics movement gained a foothold in a different fashion. It was their philosophy that humanity would best be served by preventing normal and decent people from breeding with the *unfit*. The unfit initially included epileptics, criminals, the mentally retarded and the feeble-minded. The definition was expanded during the first half of the twentieth century to include those convicted of sex-related crimes, the poor and selected ethnic groups.

The popularity of eugenics grew rapidly during the first few decades of the twentieth century and entered the mainstream of activity in America. Chapters dedicated to the topic appeared in most high school and college biology textbooks. The subject was taught in nearly 400 colleges and universities (including the eight schools that eventually would become members of the Ivy League). The American Eugenic Society became the central focus for activity for the movement in the 1920's. One of their stated goals was to allow for sterilization to be "applied to an ever widening circle of social discards, beginning always with the criminal, the diseased and the insane, and extending gradually to types which may be called weaklings rather than defectives, and perhaps ultimately to worthless race types" (from *The Passing of the Great Race*, by Madison Grant, co-founder American Eugenics Society).

Forced sterilizations were performed in most of the 48 states. Indiana was the first state to enact laws to address the issues in 1907. Although several states declined to legalize court mandated sterilizations, eventually 33 states did enact 'asexualization' laws. (Nearly all of the states did pass legislation restricting the approval of marriage licenses between two parties afflicted with epilepsy.) Despite gross under-reporting and sketchy record keeping, it is estimated that between 70,000 and 85,000 forced or coerced sterilizations were performed in the United States. The last reported procedure was performed in 1981.

During the pre World War II years, the United States and Germany were mutual admirers of each other's progress and advancement of their eugenics movements. Each was complimentary and encouraging. The movement leaders willingly invited their counterparts to speak at their conferences, offered them honorary university degrees and published their written works in their respective journals. The seminal event during this period was the United States Supreme Court decision in 1927 of *Buck vs. Bell*. The Court ruled 8-1 that Virginia's sterilization laws did not violate the U.S. Constitution. The state run asylum officials could, without jeopardy, proceed with the sterilization of Carrie Buck. Justice Holmes' ringing comment that "three generations of imbeciles are enough" became the battle cry to spur on other states and countries to legislate sterilization laws, similar in most details to Virginia's laws.

In January, 1933, Adolph Hitler and the Nazi party gained control of Germany. In July of that year the Law for the Prevention of Hereditary Offspring was passed, written to mimic the existing laws in the United States. The new law allowed for a sterilization program to be implemented on a grand and efficient scale. More than 1,000 courts were established. Physicians were required by law to report the deformed, mentally ill, retarded, deaf, blind, epileptics, etc. Initially the movement included German Jews among the unfit and unlike American laws, those destined for sterilization need not be institutionalized. Various ethnic and social groups (gypsies, homosexuals, political enemies) also were included among the unfit. Between 350,000 and 400,000 people were sterilized before the outbreak of war in 1939. Over the ensuing years, through the last days of World War II, they expanded the scope of their purification program. In 1939 euthanasia (the T-4 program) was introduced into Germany to "preserve racial purity, build a stronger master race and kill off defective genes." The T-4 program resulted in the death of more than 200,000 defectives.

Areas of operation were extended to include its conquered nations and two million people ultimately were sterilized. Mass murder was added to their initiative. The end result of course was the Holocaust and the annihilation of more than six million individuals. Following the end of World War II, during the war crimes trials in Nuremburg, Germany repeatedly pleaded they patterned their sterilization laws after the existing laws then in place in the United States.

During World War II, as rumors and the occasional report of Nazi perpetrated atrocities started to emerge, many associated the efforts of the eugenic movement with the Nazi activities. In turn, the eugenics leaders tried to distance themselves from their German counterparts. They created the Population Council and the International Planned Parenthood Federation to confound their critics but they retained their original goals. Following the war the movement experienced a phoenix-like resurgence in activity and popularity, due in large part to the efforts of Clarence Gamble, M.D., heir to the Proctor & Gamble fortune. A philanthropist and untiring proponent of global birth control, he also was president of the American Eugenics Research Association. He was the driving force in the resurgence of forced sterilizations in the southern states (7-8,000 in North Carolina alone) and was one of the founders of the Human Betterment League. Similar activities nationwide disproportionately targeted poor Native Americans, African Americans and Latina women (mostly of Mexican and Puerto Rican descent). Federally sponsored sterilization programs (committed to the tenets of family planning, public health and zero population growth) focused on low income women without regard to whether they resided in state operated or funded institutions. In countless instances, the threat of termination of welfare benefits was used as coercion to compel women to undergo salpingectomies/fallopian tube ligations. Failure to properly inform many of the women of the exact nature and purpose of the surgeries was commonplace.

As grounded as the eugenics movement was in "modern science," they ignored the published work of two men who simultaneously arrived at the same conclusion in 1908. Unknown to each other, G. H. Hardy of England and Wilhelm Weinberg from Germany developed a rather simple mathematical treatise that helped to explain that genetic variation in a population *would remain constant* from one generation to the next in the absence of disruptive circumstances (mutations, genetic drift and flow, non-random mating, natural selection). In what would later become known as the Hardy-Weinberg Principle, the two men incorporated the concept of simple Mendelian genetics (dominant and recessive genes) as the basis for their work. Application of their principle to human population studies demonstrated that repeated attempts to remove a recessive gene that carried an undesirable trait would be futile. The recessive gene would continue in the population unrecognized, masked by the dominant gene, for more than one hundred generations (and approximately two thousand years).*

---

* As their principle is applied to the doctrine of the eugenics philosophy, if only individuals who demonstrated the undesirable trait (in the recessive homozygous state) were sterilized, there would be a gross underutilization and underperformance of the service. For example, the uncommon hereditary metabolic disorder known as phenylketonurea (PKU) is seen in only one infant in 10,000. However, the defective gene is carried in recessive form in nearly 2% of the general population. If one were to consider the disease cystic fibrosis, exhibited in the general population once in every 2,500 individuals (.04%), we similarly note the recessive gene responsible for the disease is carried in 2-3% of the population. It has been shown that if a selective breeding program were focused on the isolation and elimination of the defective genes for cystic fibrosis, 21 generations would be necessary to reduce the incidence of cystic fibrosis by half, to .02%. In order to realize a tenfold decrease in the incidence of the disease (to 1 case in 25,000, i.e., .004%), 109 generations of selective breeding would be necessary; approximately 2,000 years.(Jankowska, et. al.)

In as much as Dr. Simon Kraft never existed, his interactions and conversations with the other characters in this story never occurred and are purely fiction. Unfortunately for the unfit, there was no Loretta Frontenac to champion their causes and successfully fend off those who assaulted them. Although Professor Van Kirk's Tomorrow's Children** program did not exist in the 1920's, the other programs discussed in the story that received Secretary Kraft's government funding did exist in some fashion. I took the liberty to reposition them from the various decades of the twentieth century into the timeframe of the story. The infamous Tuskegee Syphilis Study did not start until 1932 and the Guatemalan venereal disease study was started in 1946. In the second chapter of the book a form of treatment to eradicate venereal disease is mentioned, but penicillin was not discovered until 1928 and was not used clinically on a large scale until World War II.

The involvement of humans in medical experimentation has been common for many, many years and arguably necessary to some extent. Unfortunately advised consent of the participants in the studies did not become commonplace until the 1960's and 1970's; a full generation after the Nuremberg trials exposed the horrors of the Nazi medical experiments in the concentration camps. For many years, patients not only were unaware they were participants in a study, they were not informed that alternative measures were available, nor were they informed of the potential ill effects that might resolve from the experiments.

* * *

** *Tomorrow's Children* is the title of a 1934 movie that addressed the court mandated sterilization of a young woman because her family members were drunks, retarded and shiftless.

REFERENCES AND
SELECTED READING

Black, Edwin, <u>War Against the Weak</u>, <u>Eugenics and America's Campaign Create a Master Race.</u> New York, 2003.

Carlson, Elof Axel, <u>The Unfit, A History of a Bad Idea.</u> Cold Spring Harbor, 2001.

Jankowska, Dorota, "Application of Hardy-Weinberg Law to Biomedical Research," Studies in Logic, Grammar and Rhetoric, 25 (38), 2011.

Kuhl, Stefan, <u>The Nazi Connection, Eugenics, American Racism, and German National Socialism.</u> New York, 1994.

Lombardo, Paul A., <u>Three Generations, No Imbeciles.</u> Baltimore, 2008.

McCarthy, Laton, <u>The Teapot Dome Scandal</u>, New York, 2009.

Mee, Charles L., <u>The Ohio Gang</u>, Chicago, 1983.

"10 Eye-opening Quotes from Planned Parenthood Founder, Margaret Sanger," www.lifenews.com/2013/03/11.